TRAIL OF THREADS

TRAIL OF THREADS

A Virginia Davies Quilt Mystery
Book Two

By
David Ciambrone

Published 2022 by Progressive Rising Phoenix Press, LLC
www.progressiverisingphoenix.com

ISBN: 978-1-958640-09-8

Printed in the U.S.A.

Book and Cover design by William Speir
Visit: http://www.williamspeir.com

This title was originally published by
White Bird Publications
ISBN: 978-1-63363-143-4
LCCN: 2016931051

ACKNOWLEDGMENTS

Authors say writing is a solitary affair. This statement is mostly true. But, any author will tell you their writing depends on a host of others who have provided needed information, ideas, inspiration, critiques and just plain support when we needed it. To this end, I'd like to thank the following people and groups for their support bringing this book to life.

The Williamson County Coroners critique group for their sound critiques and support.

My publisher, Amanda M. Thrasher, at Progressive Rising Phoenix Press, LLC.

My wife Kathy for her support, and being a quilter with wonderful ideas for the story.

The members of the Chisholm Trail Quilt Guild.

The idea for the story came from a quilt my wife made for me call General's Wives, and a jade ceremonial dagger I obtained in the jungles of Mexico.

PROLOGUE

1866 Williamson County, Texas

Effie Dillan added a log and stoked the embers in the fireplace of the small house nestled among live oaks on a hundred-acre ranch. She heard the horses in the corral outside whinny. Effie turned up the oil lamp, walked to the small window flanking a heavy wooden door, and peered out. A black woman, carrying a large cloth bag, hurried through the trees toward the house, looking nervously behind her as the late afternoon sun cast strange shadows. She hopped up on the wooden porch and knocked rapidly on the door.

Effie yanked the door, pulled the woman inside, slammed, and barred the door. "Were you followed?"

"I don't think so, Miss Effie." The black woman stopped to catch her breath. "I done tried to avoid the patrols and town folk."

"Good, Charlotte. No one questioned your working on the quilt?"

"No, Miss Effie. No one noticed me. I worked on sewing for lots of white ladies. No one paid me no mind."

"Okay, let's see it." Effie stepped to the scarred wooden table as Charlotte pulled the quilt from the bag.

"Here, Miss Effie. If'n you don't mind, I'd just like to get my money and goes on home. That there quilt scares me."

"I'll take a quick look at it and get you your money." Effie unfolded the quilt and stared at it. "Charlotte, this is beautiful. I love it." She picked up a lamp, set it on the table, bent down and examined the quilt. "I see you've captured the details I told you to put in it. You added squares from your heritage as well as the ones about the generals I had. Right?

"Yes, ma'am."

"Nice."

"Them's important, Miss Effie?"

"Yes, Charlotte, they are part of a map. A map to something very important and valuable."

"I not see no map."

"That's because you don't have the key."

"Key? There no place for a key."

"A key is what makes the map clear. It's hidden in the map that you put into the quilt. The generals are the key."

"A map to what, Miss. Effie? Gold?"

"Yes, but more valuable than just gold." Effie jerked up at the sound of horses pulling up in front of the cabin. She reached into her apron pocket and pulled out some gold coins and handed them to Charlotte. "Quick, go out the back, Charlotte, and don't mention this to anyone."

"Yes'm." Charlotte took the money and slipped out back.

Effie moved to the bedroom and placed the quilt on the bed, and headed for the door as someone pounded on it.

Effie opened the door, stood with her hands in her apron pockets, and looked at the two men standing on the porch. "What do you want, Mr. Cramer?"

Cramer gave her a stern look. "There's been sightings around here, and I mean to finds out what they are."

"Sightings? You believe in ghosts, Mr. Cramer? I didn't think an ex-major in the Union Army would hold to superstitions like that. But, if you want to go around the barn, there's a small cemetery you can look at. I don't think the residents will mind."

He shifted his weight to his left leg and placed his hand on his sidearm. "Something's up around here. I've heard you've been seen out in those hills yonder at night. That can be dangerous for a woman alone. You being here with no man is not right or safe." He took a step closer. "Now, just what are you so fired up about finding, Miss Effie?"

"None of your concern." Effie straightened to her five feet four-inch height and glared at him. "Mr. Cramer, you and Hank there can just get back on your horses and get. Stop spying on me. What I do is my business. If I see your caboose around here again, I'll be sure to kill you."

"I aim to find out just what you're up to Effie Dillan, even if I have to beat it out of you." Cramer started to push Effie back into her house when a muffled shot cracked the air. Cramer's eyes widened as he stumbled backward into Hank, and collapsed on the wood deck. Blood spread out on the front of his shirt over his heart. Hank watched Cramer fall, then reached for his gun. His eyes followed Effie pull her hand, with the Derringer, out of her apron pocket and quickly aim it at his head. Another loud shot rang out. Hank fell back onto the dirt, a large hole in his forehead.

"We can't have any damn Yankees find what's rightfully mine and my kin." She glanced back into the house at the bed with the quilt on it. "As long as that's in the family, the secret's safe."

CHAPTER 1

Virginia Davies Clark sat back in her high-backed leather desk chair in her office at the San Gabriel Museum, in Georgetown, Texas, ran her fingers through her blonde hair, and sighed. She leaned forward to reread a document for the third time. Her gaze shot up when the office door flew open and banged against the wall. Her secretary skidded to a stop and took a breath.

Virginia stared, and cleared her throat. "What's wrong, Ann? Did one of our animal displays come to life?"

Ann plopped onto the leather cushioned wooden chair in front of Virginia's desk and handed her a business card. "There's one of your quilting friends out in the immature insect area who wants to talk to you."

"Did she say about what?"

"Yes."

"Ann—" Virginia rubbed her eyes. "What does she want to talk to me about?"

"A murder. She's very upset." Ann wet her lips. "I assured her you didn't do it."

"Well, you're right about that." Virginia read the business card with a small, blue quilt square and needle and thread embossed on it. The name on the card was Mary Jane Striker, quilter. Virginia looked at Ann. "Go get Mary Jane. We can't have a distraught woman in the immature insect displays, can we? Let's find out what's bugging her so bad."

Ann smiled. "Bugging her in the baby bug display? Cute, Mrs. Clark, cute." She rose. "I'll just go get her," Ann mumbled as she scurried out of the office. "Murder?"

A couple minutes later Ann led Mary Jane Striker, a fifty-something, doughy woman with graying black hair, cut straight to her shoulders, into Virginia's office. Ann closed the door as she left.

Virginia pointed to a chair in front of her desk. "Please take a seat, Mary Jane."

Mary Jane settled into the chair and adjusted her white blouse. "It's nice of you to see me unannounced and all, Virginia. I don't usually like to bother someone at work."

"No problem for a friend. Now, what's this about a murder? I trust you didn't do it."

Mary Jane fidgeted in the chair. "Heavens, no. Do you remember the body that was found in Lake Georgetown a couple weeks ago?"

Virginia wrinkled her brow thinking, then brightened. "I think so. Wasn't a man's body found among the rocks on the south shore near a campground?"

"Yes. Well, the Travis County Medical Examiner and the JP determined he was murdered. Blunt force trauma to the head. He was dumped in the lake after being killed. He was tortured, too."

"I didn't know that. But what does this have to do with you?"

"He was my great uncle on my father's side of the family. He owned a ranch in northwest Williamson County. It's been in the family since the eighteen fifties."

"I'm sorry. Death is always hard on the families involved, but something like this is truly terrible."

"Thank you."

"Okay. You didn't kill your great uncle, so what's the concern? Are the police after you for questioning, or do they think you're a person of interest?"

"No. The police are sure I didn't do it."

"So, why are you here?"

"Well, there were stories. You know, the type that are supposed to be fact, but are usually more fiction than real. Every family has a few stories. Mine has one about a treasure. Something from around the Civil War."

Mary Jane wiped her hands on her ankle-length green skirt. "When my great uncle died, I inherited the ranch. But three nights ago the main house and the barn were broken into and searched. Everything was... was thrown all over."

Virginia leaned toward the desk. "You notified the police?"

"Yes. The ranch is in the county, so I called the Sheriff's office. A couple deputies came out, then some detectives arrived along with some crime scene people. They spent quite a while out there. I haven't heard anything from them since they left. But when I went back out there, I noticed something strange."

"What?"

"My Great Aunt was a quilter, like you and me. She had a number of the quilts out there, and everyone was missing. I told the Sheriff's deputies when I discovered this. But whoever took them missed one. I have it. It's an antique quilt made in the eighteen sixties by a great-great-great-or more greats-aunt or grandmother. Her name was Effie Dillan."

"You think someone is after that one?"

"Yes, because last night, while I was at a guild meeting in Round Rock, someone broke into my place. They thoroughly searched my quilting workroom and disturbed a couple other rooms. My quilts were all over the floor. Nothing was missing. Whoever it was, knew what they were looking for. They didn't get the old quilt, though."

Virginia wet her lips. "Where is it, if you don't mind my asking?"

Mary Jane smiled. She whispered, "It's under the bedspread in my bedroom."

"Nice job. Okay, you still have the quilt. Then, why are you here?"

"I've heard the stories, read the reports of your sleuthing, and stuff. I need your help finding my great uncle's murderer and finding the lost treasure. I think the quilt has something to do with the treasure and the murder, and we're both in the same quilt guilds."

Virginia leaned back in her chair. "I'm not usually a regular detective or police officer."

"I know. But I've heard you're some sort of reserve or consulting special agent with the Smithsonian. And this has to do with the old quilt. You're a quilter like me, and you've handled cases involving quilts before. I know this quilt is the key to everything."

"Why do you think that?"

"Because of the stories. They talk about a map, Indians, cloth, slaves, and some old generals. The old quilt I have has been passed down for generations and is considered almost sacred by the family. That and a small, funny, stone statue." Mary Jane wet her lips. "Matter of fact, some of my relatives aren't happy I inherited the ranch and the quilt. They have asked if I really wanted the old quilt or if I'd sell it or give it to them. The University thought they were going to get the quilt as an endowment as well."

"Where is the small statue you mentioned? What is it?"

"On my fireplace mantel. It's a small jade jaguar."

"Interesting. But why me? Why not go over this with the Sheriff?"

"I did. They seem to think I'm just a crazy woman, a civilian, and I can't appreciate what they do. They think a quilt, especially an old one, probably has nothing to do with the murder."

Virginia sat back in her chair and looked at the diplomas on the far wall, and then back at Mary Jane. "I'm intrigued. I haven't worked on a case for some time, but my husband won't be happy. At least this time, I didn't find a dead body. That should account for something."

"You'll help me?" Mary Jane's face brightened. "I was hoping you would."

"Things have been a little slow around here, and I've just been a referee between the accountants and scientists. Lately, they're at each other a lot and settling disputes and finding funding is my main job. I'm afraid I'm going to find a stuffed accountant in a display one of these days. Yeah. It could be fun. I just need to figure out how to tell Andy."

"Is Andy your boss?"

Virginia chuckled. "No, my husband."

"Oh."

Virginia picked up a pen and moved a notepad to the center of her desk. "Who are the relatives not happy that you got the ranch and the quilt?"

Mary Jane cleared her throat. "Just two. John Pennington. He owns an auto repair shop here in Georgetown. Barbara Dorian is a teacher in Round Rock. She teaches first grade. Both are cousins."

"Anything unusual about these cousins?"

"Barbra is usually pretty nice. But she got quite upset about my getting the whole ranch and stuff. She got two-hundred thousand dollars in the will. John was even more upset, even though he got enough to pay off the mortgages on his shop and home, and a nice nest egg. He has a history of drinking and fighting. I'm sure the Sheriff has looked into him."

"That's a lot of money. Are they the only other benefactors?"

"The university, well, not really the university, a professor at the University, Dr. William Pine, thought he was going to get an endowment or grant or something bigger than he did. He also thought he'd get the quilt. He got a hundred grand in gold bars."

"You're joking, aren't you? If they got all that, why are they unhappy? What's with the ranch that makes it so valuable in their eyes? How did your great uncle accumulate all that wealth? How much is the ranch worth?"

Mary Jane stared at Virginia for a second. "Do you always ask so many questions at once?"

"Only when I get excited. Drives my husband bananas."

Mary Jane grinned and nodded. "I bet. But to answer your questions, I don't know why they are unhappy. I haven't had a chance to figure out how much the ranch is worth, or where my uncle got his money, but they all seem really interested in it and that quilt. Dr. Pine asked about the little statue, too."

"Can you tell me more about the quilt? You said you think it's a map?"

"Yes. It was made sometime around eighteen sixty-four or five. The family stories say there is some sort of treasure somewhere on the ranch, and the quilt holds the key. No one has ever found it or figured out the map that is supposed to be on the quilt. Maybe that's where my uncle got his money and gold."

"I'm getting the picture." Virginia stood, adjusted the waistband of her gray wool slacks. "Tell you what, go home, but do not uncover that quilt until I get there. I'll need to rearrange my schedule and tell my boss and my husband about this. I'll stop by on the way home from work. You still live on Main Street in Georgetown. Right?"

"Yes." Mary Jane stood and slid the strap of her purse over her shoulder. "Thank you, Virginia. I'll see you tonight." She left the office.

Virginia started to resume her work when her secretary burst in again. "Virginia! Your friend, Mary Jane… she's… the paramedics are on their way here."

Virginia jumped to her feet. "What happened? Is she sick, did she fall or something?"

"No. She left your office, stopped by the reptile exhibit, touched her thigh, and fell. An anthropologist is giving her CPR. She's as white as a sheet."

CHAPTER 2

Virginia bolted from her office to the small display area toward the right rear side of the museum. She skidded to a stop on the tile floor and knelt next to Mary Jane. The anthropologist, Sam Kappes, was giving CPR. Virginia looked up as Ann came running.

"I called the paramedics. They'll be here soon. How is she?"

Sam stopped the CPR and looked up at Ann. "She's breathing on her own now, but it's shallow, and her pulse is slow and weak."

Virginia saw Mary Jane move and, tense when her right side touched the floor. "Something isn't right."

Sam raised an eyebrow. "You just figured that out?"

"No. She exhibited signs of pain when her side touched the tiles." Virginia bent closer and looked at Mary Jane's skirt. She frowned and tugged it up to her upper thigh. "Look. A small puncture wound." She pulled the skirt down and glanced at Ann. "Call 911 again and tell the dispatcher there are signs Mary Jane was poisoned and call the police. Oh, also pull the surveillance tapes from the security system for the police, too."

"Okay." Ann swung around and jogged toward the lobby.

Mary Jane's eyes fluttered and opened slightly. In a whisper she uttered, "My lips are numb. Virginia, in my purse is another notebook. Take it, and go to my place. Get the quilt and the jaguar on the mantel. Please help me. The keys are there, too. Chest hurts." She blacked out.

Virginia looked at Sam. "Did you hear that?"

"Yeah. My suggestion would be to leave everything to the cops." He looked into Virginia's blue eyes. "Then, again, if there is something of an antiquity involved, I'm guessing you'll get what she wants you to get before the cops start looking around."

"Yeah. I promised I'd help her."

"Okay, unless anyone specifically asks, I don't know squat."

Virginia leaned forward and kissed him on the cheek. "Sam, you're a great guy. Thanks. I owe you."

"I'll remember that at budget time." He turned, rose, and stepped back with Virginia as the paramedics arrived.

The medics worked on Mary Jane. After looking at the puncture wound on her thigh, they installed an IV and were talking to the hospital on the radio when the police arrived. Officers talked to Ann, then Sam. Finally, a detective knocked on the doorframe of Virginia's office door.

Virginia sat back in her chair. "Come in, Detective. How can I help?"

He stepped into her office and handed her his card. It read, *Detective John Wilkinson, Georgetown Police Department.* "I'd like to ask you some questions."

"Sure, pull up a chair."

He sat, unbuttoned his gray sports coat, and opened his notebook. "Now, Mrs. Clark, I understand you're a friend of the lady who was reportedly attacked with poison. Is that correct?"

"Yes."

"How do you know her?"

"We are members of the same quilt guild and, of course, both quilters."

"I see." He scratched his short-cropped dark hair. "What made you suspect she was poisoned?"

"She's a healthy woman with no major health problems that I'm aware of, and there is a small, fresh puncture wound on the top of her right thigh. She collapsed in my museum. She was in good health when she came in, and she was on the verge of dying when she tried to leave."

"Are you an expert in poisons?"

"No."

An officer stuck his head in the doorway. "John, the museum pulled the security tapes and gave them to us. I'll take them to headquarters."

John Wilkinson nodded. "Okay." He turned to Virginia. "When we got here, your assistant said you had her pull the tapes for us. Thanks."

"No problem, Detective."

Wilkinson fidgeted in his chair. "Why was Mary Jane Striker here to see you?"

"She's a friend and needed some advice… of a personal nature."

"What kind of advice?"

"Has to do with her ranch. It's been in her family for well over a hundred and fifty years. It was about some historical issues. Someone trying to kill her was never mentioned."

Wilkinson flipped some pages in his notebook. "Do you know how she got here?"

Virginia wrinkled her nose. "I suppose she drove."

"According to my officers and the paramedics, her keys are missing. You were with her right after she collapsed; you know anything about that?"

"I got there after my anthropologist, Dr. Sam Kappes, started to administer CPR. Mary Jane's purse was on the opposite side of her from where he was, so he didn't take them. She could have gotten a ride I suppose." She rotated her chair back and forth. "The person who poisoned her could have taken them, if she had them on her."

"How about her house key?"

"How would I know?"

"That's your answer?"

"Yes."

"Mrs. Clark, I could take you to the station for more questions. The way you're answering me makes me think you're being evasive and holding out on me."

She leaned her elbows on her desk and glared at him. "Detective, you can take me down there, but as you well know, I can leave, unless you arrest me. And, I'll have my lawyer there about the time we arrive. I'm sure she'll advise I shut the hell up. Now I'm trying to be nice, but I can play this stupid game too."

Wilkinson sat back, closed his notebook, and stared. "Who are you? You've been through this type of thing before?"

Virginia leaned back. "Please close the door."

He slowly rose and shut the door and returned to his seat. "What is it?"

She stood and went to a closet, opened the door, and took out her red leather purse. She opened it and removed her brown leather credential holder and handed it to him. "Take a look."

He took the case, opened it, and read the card inside. Then, with widening eyes looked at her gold badge. "Smithsonian Central Security Service?"

Virginia stepped back to her desk and sat. "I'm a… well a kind of reserve federal special agent."

"You're a fed?" He looked at her. "I'm in the wrong department. What's this have to do with my case? Is it a federal matter?"

"Maybe. Mary Jane Striker came to me as a friend. But what she said may involve something the Smithsonian and the federal government might be interested in. I promised I'd help her."

"This is why you've been evasive?"

She nodded.

"You're going to look into what she talked to you about. Right?"

"Yes."

"If she was attacked over what she discussed with you, how are we going to proceed?"

"We?" Virginia smiled. "Detective Wilkinson, I think I'm going to like you. If you will be discrete, I'd like to do a joint investigation. Initially, I'd like you looking into her attacker. It may involve what I'm going to be investigating, so as I see it, we work discretely, together. We pool our information, and if and when the time comes, you make the collar."

He stared at her with his mouth open.

Virginia leaned forward. “Detective, you okay?”

“Ahh… yeah, I think so. This is the first time the feds have offered to work together like this, share information, and not take the credit. You understand I’ll need to run a check on these credentials?”

Virginia pushed her desk phone across the top toward him. “Knock yourself out.”

“I’ll use my radio if you don’t mind.”

“Okay. I’d better call my husband and tell him what’s up. He isn’t going to be happy.”

“I bet.”

An hour later, Virginia and Detective Wilkinson walked out of the museum toward his unmarked, black, police SUV.

He held the front passenger door for her then climbed into the driver’s seat. “Let’s see what the ER doc says about your friend. If you don’t mind, I’d like to see her ranch.”

“Okay. But understand, I may take some things from the ranch for my investigation.”

He looked over at her as they headed down Austin Ave. toward the hospital. “You’ll treat whatever you take as evidence. Right?”

“Yeah, whatever.” She tugged on her seatbelt. “Can we go a little faster?”

Detective Wilkinson switched on his emergency lights and sped up. A few minutes later, they pulled into the parking lot near the Georgetown Hospital emergency room entrance and parked. They entered the waiting area and went to the nurse on duty at the window.

Wilkinson displayed his badge, and Virginia followed. He added, “I’m Detective Wilkinson, Georgetown PD, and this is Special Agent Virginia Davies Clark. We are here about a Miss Mary Jane Striker. Paramedics brought her in a while ago.”

The nurse looked at the computer screen. “The possible poison case?”

Virginia nodded. “Yes. Is she still in emergency?”

“Yes. The doctor is with her now. You can wait over there, and I’ll tell the doctor you’re here.” They took seats near the door to the ER.

A half hour later a doctor entered the waiting area. “Special Agent Clark?”

Virginia shot to her feet. “Over here, Doctor. How is Mary Jane?”

He walked to her. “I’m Doctor Fuller. She was poisoned. The person or persons who tried to kill her used Aconite.”

She gave him a quizzical look. “Isn’t that Wolfbane or Monkshood?”

Doctor Fuller nodded. "Yes. Fortunately, for her, it's an alkaloid. It's not very water-soluble. The amount that was actually injected was small. Whoever did this didn't know a lot about chemistry. We've got her in intensive care and are treating her. She should make a full recovery." He started to say something else then stopped. "May I askhow you know about Wolfbane and Aconite?"

"I'm a curator at a museum and a history major in college. When it comes to early American history and Europe about the same time, witches were big, and they used Wolfbane."

Dr. Fuller nodded. "I guess that makes sense."

Detective Wilkinson took a breath. "That's good news. If the hospital doesn't mind, I'll put officers here to guard her. She'll be in protective custody."

Doctor Fuller smiled. "That's probably a good idea. Just don't get in the way of the nurses or physicians treating her."

Wilkinson pulled out a radio and stepped away as Virginia quizzed the doctor. "How long will she need to be here?"

"A couple days. We'll take it one day at a time. I don't think her heart was affected, but we're monitoring it now."

"Thank you, Doctor."

He rubbed his hands together. "May I ask a question?"

"Sure, what is it?"

"You're a federal special agent?"

"Yes."

"Is this a federal investigation, and are you with the ATF or FBI or DEA?"

"None of them. I'm with the Smithsonian Central Security Service."

"Smithsonian? Like the museum?"

"Yes."

The doctor shook his head. "Now I get it, and the museum stuff you said earlier. This is getting complicated. I think I'll go see how she's settling into the ICU."

Wilkinson returned. "Got her some armed babysitters, doc. The hospital won't have any problem with that, will they?"

"Just don't hinder our work and it'll be fine."

Virginia shifted her purse. "Good. Any ideas where one could get Wolfbane around here, doc?"

"Not really."

Wilkinson chuckled. "Virginia, a while ago you wanted to see her ranch. Now shopping for poison?"

Virginia smiled. "Who knows what evil lurks at the heart of the ranch?"

He tilted his head and frowned. "Where have I heard that before?"

"The Shadow on old time radio. It was on in the forties and fifties. I think it goes… 'What evil lurks in the hearts of men? The Shadow knows.'" She smiled. "That was before our time. I've heard it on XM radio in my car. My dad used to talk about it, too. Orson Wells played the first Shadow, and Agnes Moorehead played the first Margo Lane, the Shadow's lady friend."

"Oh. Okay. If you say so." Wilkinson shook his head. "Let's go see what evil lurks at the ranch."

CHAPTER 3

The unmarked police SUV rocked over the uneven gravel driveway of Mary Jane's ranch entrance. It pulled to a stop under a huge live oak in front of the large stone ranch house. Virginia slid out and looked around.

Detective Wilkinson walked around the SUV and stopped next to her. "Place is impressive. Your friend inherited it?"

Virginia nodded. "Yep." She glanced at the out buildings. "Looks like a barn, a tool shed, a greenhouse, and some other structure, along with the house. Shall we start with the house?"

"Sure. Place appears deserted, so might as well start there." He started for the house, then stopped, turned, and waited for her to catch up. "By the way, you do have the key, don't you?"

She gave him a sheepish grin and nodded. "Yeah. B & E isn't a good idea with a cop around." She proceeded up the two concrete steps to the covered front wooden deck. The massive, stained oak door stood as a silent guardian. Virginia slung her backpack around, rummaged through the main pouch, and withdrew a set of keys. She quickly unlocked the door and swung it open. A loud buzzing noise started. "An alarm."

"You know the code?"

"No." She stepped to the control box and punched in a number. The buzzing sound changed to an excruciating siren. "Oh boy. This is going to be fun."

The sound of a phone ringing further inside made them jump. Virginia raced toward the source of the ringing and picked up the receiver. "Hello?"

"This is Spelling Security. What is the code name for the alarm?"

She cleared her throat. "I don't know. The owner is in the hospital, and I came out here to get some things for her."

"I see. What is your name?" said the voice on the phone.

"Virginia Davies Clark. Special Agent Clark to be more precise."

"Can you tell me who the owner is?"

"Yes. Mary Jane Striker. She's in St. David's Hospital in Georgetown, Texas."

"Why is a so-called 'special agent' at her house?"

"I'm here with a Georgetown Police Officer, and you're trying to keep me on the phone long enough for the Sheriff to get here so, good-bye." Virginia hung up, glanced at Wilkinson, and grinned. "That'll upset the apple cart."

Detective Wilkinson tilted his head. "I bet that's a Sheriff's car stopping at the end of the driveway. They will hike up here with their guns out, so don't do anything stupid. Get your ID and badge out in plain sight."

"I hope they can turn off that damn siren." Virginia moved across the polished hardwood floor back outside onto the front porch and waited with Wilkinson next to her. After a couple minutes, they saw a deputy step from behind a tree aiming a shotgun at them.

He surveyed the landscape, crouched, and moved forward staying close to the tree line. "Sheriff! Keep your hands in plain sight, and don't make any sudden moves."

Wilkinson called out. "I'm Detective John Wilkinson, Georgetown Police Department, and this is Special Agent Virginia Davies Clark."

The deputy clicked his shoulder mike. "Two people on the front porch. Claim to be police."

A voice responded. "10-4. The rear is secure. I'll be right around to assist."

The deputy with the shotgun slowly approached the parked police SUV and peered inside, moved to the rear, and stood, pointing the weapon at them. "My back-up will be here soon. Then, we can get acquainted."

As the second deputy turned the corner, gun drawn, the one with the shotgun advanced toward the porch. They inspected Wilkinson's and Virginia's IDs and badges and called them into their station. A minute later, Wilkinson's and Virginia were cleared. The deputies lowered their weapons. The one carrying the shotgun pointed toward the house. "Can you shut that noise off?"

Virginia chuckled. "I was hoping you could."

"Just a second." He called his station, and in a couple minutes, his radio beeped. He answered the call. He listened, then spoke to Virginia. "It's 59482."

"Okay." She scurried inside, and in a second, the siren stopped. She walked back out to where the men stood. "That's better. I was getting a headache. Are we good here?"

"Yes, ma'am. We'll leave you to your task. Have a good day."

She gave them a smile. "Thank you, Deputy. We will. You have a good one, too."

Wilkinson shook his head. "I swear, you could have talked them into helping."

"We don't need any help, and we've wasted enough time. Let's take a look around." Virginia spun on her heel, her blond hair swishing, and charged inside. She looked over her shoulder. "You want to start in the kitchen and family room? I'll hit the living and dining rooms."

"Okay." Wilkinson followed her into the central hallway. "What are we looking for?"

"Anything out of the ordinary or really old."

"Anything out of the ordinary and old." Wilkinson shrugged. "That narrows it down."

Virginia watched him trudge to the kitchen. She made a beeline to the living room, stepped around an overstuffed armchair and across the large Navajo Indian rug spread on the old oak floor to the fireplace. On the mantle was a small jade Jaguar. Virginia picked it up and stuffed it into her backpack. Next, she hurried to the master bedroom, pulled back the large red bedspread, and found the quilt Mary Jane had told her about. She yanked it off the bed, folded it, and stuffed it under her arm. Virginia returned to the living room to find Detective Wilkinson sitting in a chair waiting for her.

He pushed himself up when she entered the room. "Find everything you wanted?"

Virginia nodded. "Yep."

"I figured you knew more than you were saying. What's with the quilt?"

"It could be a map to a treasure hereabout. This is what Mary Jane's relatives and the Professor were looking for when this place was burgled."

"Burgled? If someone broke in, the alarm would have sounded."

"Yeah. Either the alarm wasn't set, or the burglar knew the disarm code. Mary Jane didn't mention that for some reason. She knew this place was broken into, and the Sheriff responded. The so-called investigation has gone nowhere. They came and took a report, and that's it. Either the crooks didn't have time to do a thorough job because of the alarm and the Sheriff got here too quick, or they didn't know exactly what they were looking for." She shrugged. "Or they just plain missed it. Interesting, isn't it?"

Wilkinson chuckled. "You always talk that fast?"

"Sometimes. It drives my husband crazy."

"I bet."

Virginia smiled. "Shall we go?"

"Okay. Better set the alarm."

As they approached the car, Virginia noticed movement near the barn. She stopped and pointed. "Did you see that?"

"No. What was it?"

"Someone, or something, dashed behind the barn just now."

Wilkinson sighed. "You're going to investigate what could be an animal back there?"

"Or it could be a person. They'd be trespassing, you could arrest them, and we can question them."

"This is the county, and I'm a city cop who doesn't like traipsing around in the dirt chasing what could be a deer or a cow. And the Sheriff should arrest them out here, not me. Maybe animal control could make the bust."

Virginia's eyes narrowed. "You just want to get back to the city and file a report, don't you? This is important."

"I'll radio the Sheriff to send someone." He stepped to the SUV and glanced over the top. "You coming?"

"Yeah." Virginia stomped to the car and reached for the door when a voice called out from nearby trees.

"Hold it right there. Drop that quilt and step back!" A tall, slim man, with thinning black hair and a scraggly beard, emerged from behind a tree holding a revolver.

Virginia slowly lowered the quilt to the ground and stood, her left hand holding her backpack as her right hand slid inside. "Okay, take it easy. The man you're facing is a police officer, so I'd lower your weapon if I were you."

The man pointed his gun and attention on Wilkinson. "You're a cop? Drop your weapon."

Wilkinson moved away from the SUV. "I'm a police officer. Don't do anything stupid. Put your weapon down."

The man snarled. "I hate cops." He raised his gun to aim it at Wilkinson when a shot rang out. The gunman grabbed his side as he twisted around. Before he could do anything, Virginia shot again. He dropped his gun, staggered back, and then, fell.

Virginia rushed forward aiming her .380 semiautomatic at him. "Don't move." She kicked his gun away and stood over him, her gun aiming at his chest. She looked over at Wilkinson, who was sitting on the driver's side seat of the police car on the radio. "You calling for backup?"

"Yeah, I've asked for the Sheriff and paramedics." Wilkinson walked over to the man, knelt, and examined his wounds. "You got him in his side and shoulder."

Virginia put her gun back into her backpack, walked to the quilt, and picked it up. "He shouldn't have had me set this in the dirt. That pissed me off."

Wilkinson stared at her, "You were mad that he had you put that quilt in the dirt and not that he was going to shoot me?"

"You'd heal." She smiled at him and held her fingers about an inch apart. "I was just a little worried about you."

"Good to know." He squatted back down. "Okay, fella, who are you and what do you want with that quilt the lady has?"

The man moaned. "Name's James. James Cooper. I ain't tellin' you nothin' else. I want a lawyer anda doctor."

Wilkinson wet his lips. "Well, you're going to need both, Jimmy, especially the lawyer. The charges so far are assaulting a peace officer with a deadly weapon, trespassing, assault on a federal officer, attempted theft, and I'm sure we can think of more charges. Most are felonies."

Virginia placed the quilt in the back seat of the police SUV, then returned to Cooper and Wilkinson. "I have a suggestion, Detective. Why don't you go for a walk and let me...ahh... talk to him?"

Wilkinson rose. "Just how are you going to talk to him?"

"Don't ask."

Wilkinson looked at Cooper. "If I let her talk to you, it could be very painful. You really pissed her off. You sure you wouldn't like to just talk to us and make life easier for you?"

Cooper gritted his teeth. "You can't torture me. That's illegal."

Virginia chuckled. "Look who's talking about something being illegal." She bent down. "Look asshole, I'll talk nice. If I happen to stumble a few times and press on your wounds, well, it will hurt... a lot."

"I'm going to tell my lawyer about this."

Virginia straightened and looked at Wilkinson. "I have an idea."

"What?"

"We arrest him. After the docs at the hospital patch him up, assuming he hasn't lost too much blood, and dies, we announce to the press that we arrested him out here. Then, we announce that he cooperated and told us what he knows, then we cut him loose."

Wilkinson brightened. "Good idea."

Cooper coughed. "You can't do that."

Wilkinson looked at him. "Yes, we can."

Virginia and Wilkinson turned, as sirens grew closer. Cooper swallowed. "Okay. I'll tell you what I know, but I need a doctor first."

"Yeah, you do need a doctor." Virginia smiled at him. "I knew you weren't as dumb as you look."

A Sheriff's car raced up the drive and pulled into the brush on the side as a paramedic ambulance came up behind it.

Virginia and Wilkinson watched the medics work on Cooper while they talked to the deputies. After about fifteen minutes, they followed the ambulance to St. David's Hospital in Georgetown. The Sheriff's deputies arrived a few minutes behind them.

As they waited near the emergency room, Wilkinson's cell phone rang. He stopped and answered it. "Wilkinson."

"Detective. This is Landis. Got the information on James Cooper. Six arrests in Texas, and two in Arizona. Been convicted three times for armed robbery, ADW, and selling stolen goods. He's basically a thug for hire. Dropped out of school, held low-paying jobs, and now lives in a mobile home near Liberty Hill."

"Any of the felonies in Williamson County?"

"No."

"Got it. Thanks." He disconnected.

Virginia looked up from her notebook. Wilkinson walked up and took the seat next to her. "What's up?"

"Guy has six arrests and three convictions. It's a wonder he's walking around. He's mostly a low-level gun for hire type. Low man on the totem pole."

"Figures. Let's see how our Mr. Cooper is doing." She got up and stepped to the nurse's station and displayed her badge. "I'd like to check on Mr. Cooper's status."

She looked at her computer display and ran her fingers over the computer keys. "The doctor is coming to see you."

"Fine. But how is Mr. Cooper?" Before the nurse could answer, Virginia looked away from the nurse as a doctor in scrubs walked into the waiting area. "Doctor Fuller?"

Dr. Fuller turned his head and smiled. "Hello again, Agent Clark." He noted Detective Wilkinson walked toward him. "Hello to you too, Detective. You two are good for business. You've sent two people here in a short time."

Virginia stepped close. "Doctor, what's Cooper's condition?"

"He's dead."

Virginia felt her heart skip a beat. "I didn't think I wounded him that bad."

"He lost a lot of blood, but that's not what killed him."

Detective Wilkinson frowned. "If the gunshot wounds didn't kill him, what did?"

"Someone impersonating a nurse injected him with poison."

CHAPTER 4

Virginia stepped closer. "How do you know it was someone impersonating a nurse that injected the poison?"

Dr. Fuller gripped the ends of the stethoscope around his neck. "First, it was a blonde female. We don't have any blonde nurses working the ER at this time. Second, she didn't respond when I called to her. Third, when she turned her head, I didn't recognize her, and she rushed out of the ER toward the Radiology area. She wasn't wearing a radiation monitor. That, and she dropped the syringe on the floor."

"Good observations, Doc." Detective Wilkinson rubbed his forehead. "I'll call it in." He looked at the doctor, "You know the drill. Nobody goes near the body, and nothing is to be disturbed."

Doctor Fuller nodded. "That room is sealed off. A police officer from security is on his way to secure everything, and I have the attending two nurses in the staff dining room away from everyone else. Just so you know, there will be two other nurses coming to relieve them. Can't shut down the ER."

"Okay. Good. Thank you, Doctor." Wilkinson moved away and called police headquarters on his cell phone. Completing the call, he stepped back to Virginia and Doctor Fuller. "I've got detectives and uniformed officers coming."

Virginia looked at the doctor. "Did Cooper say anything before he died?"

"Not really. He had lost a lot of blood and was incoherent. He mumbled something about a jaguar and a quilt and someone being unhappy. I don't know what that was about."

"Thank, you. I think we can be going now." She glanced at Wilkinson, who was eyeing a young, dark haired nurse. "Detective… shall we go?"

"Huh? Oh, yeah." He turned toward the door as other officers entered. He stepped to them and explained the situation. Wilkinson returned to Virginia "Let's go." He led Virginia through the sliding doors to the driveway and his police car parked in the red zone.

Virginia slid into the front passenger seat and fastened her seatbelt as Wilkinson climbed in behind the wheel. She rested her backpack on her lap. "I can't wait to get this little jade jaguar and the quilt home so I can examine them."

Wilkinson's head jerked around. "You've got the jaguar? It, and the quilt? That's what the doctor said Cooper was mumbling about."

"Yeah. You knew I had the quilt. It's a little hard to hide."

"Yes, but that jaguar seems to have been mentioned a few times. But, you didn't say anything at the ranch house about it."

"Sorry."

"Where was it?"

"On the fireplace mantel. It was hidden in plain sight."

"What is the significance of it?"

She settled back in her seat as the car left the parking lot. "Not sure. Mary Jane was agitated about someone trying to steal the quilt, like I told you, and she said the jaguar was part of the puzzle but didn't know how the two tied together." She looked ahead. "Take me back to the museum, will you, please. My car is there."

"Okay. You going to examine the figure and the quilt there?"

"No. I'll do it at home. I have quilting tools there if needed. I'll call you in the morning if I find anything."

Wilkinson swung the police car into the museum parking lot and stopped next to Virginia's car. "If you find anything interesting, call me right away. Don't wait until tomorrow."

"Okay." She climbed out of the car and pulled the folded quilt from the back seat. "See ya later, Detective."

Virginia walked into the kitchen from the garage carrying the quilt, jaguar, and her backpack and set them down on the kitchen island. She stopped and listened. *Andy's car is in the garage, but I don't hear him. Maybe he's in the yard.* Leo, her black cat, scurried from the living room to her side, rubbed against her, and purred. Virginia bent over and picked him up. "How's my little man doing? Miss mommy?"

Leo meowed and, then, wiggled. "Okay, I'll give you a treat you little fatty. I hope you stayed out of my quilt room. My felted purse and trim are way too tempting for you." She retrieved a snack from the pantry and poured it into his bowl. Leo attacked it.

Virginia walked to the back patio door and went outside. A quick scan of the yard did not find Andy. She returned inside to find him in the kitchen holding the Jaguar. She smiled. "Hi. I wondered where you were."

"What's this toy? Looks old. Jade?"

"Yeah. I'm not sure about it, but it has to do with a new mystery."

Andy slowly set the figure on the granite counter top and turned. "Another mystery? Anyone dead yet?"

"Only of natural causes."

"Good."

Her hand flew to her mouth. "Oh, sorry, yeah one guy was murdered, so far."

"You forgot about that? That's not good. I suppose you can't let well enough alone and have the local boys in blue handle this?"

"Not really. A friend is involved, and she came to me for help when someone tried to kill her in my museum. That pissed me off. I told her I'd look into what she said. As to the guy who was murdered in the hospital, the cops are working that, and I'm working with a detective."

"I had to ask. You know you're really a curator and not a detective."

"That's not what the Smithsonian thinks and they have approved of me working this with the police."

Andy took a breath and slowly let it out. "Well… okay. At least you get paid for it. If I can help, let me know."

"Can you turn on the secondary alarm system tonight along with the regular one?"

He frowned. "That bad?"

"It's this quilt and statue that I'm worried about."

"Sure. No problem."

Virginia made a quizzical look and tilted her head. "I saw your car when I got home, but aren't you supposed to be at the university teaching today?"

"Normally yes. However, I'm working on a paper for a journal. I've got a graduate student teaching the class and another doing the lab later tonight."

"Good. I like you with me."

"I've got to get back to my den, you going to your girl cave?"

"You mean my quilt room, and yes. Later call for a pizza. I'll be working on this puzzle and don't feel like cooking tonight."

Andy grinned. "Great. Pizza it is." He turned and headed for his den, stopped, and set the alarm systems.

Virginia changed clothes, and spread the quilt out on the bed in their spare bedroom and looked at it. Leo joined her, sniffed, and examined the quilt. She leaned over the quilt for a minute. *It's old and could use some restoration, but what is it trying to tell me? What's it got to do with a jade jaguar?* She jerked upright as Andy spoke behind her.

"Just a question, but aren't jaguars found primarily in the new world like in Mexico, Central and South America?" He held the statue in his hands.

"Yes."

"Jade is more common in Asia. Right?" He petted Leo.

"Yes." Virginia wet her lips. "But if it's 'quetzal' jade, a bright green jadeite from Guatemala, it was treasured by Mesoamerican cultures. Various indigenous cultures such as the Olmec and Maya could obtain jade from Guatemala, and it was largely an elite good. It was usually carved in various ways, whether serving as a medium upon which hieroglyphs were inscribed, or shaped into symbolic figurines like the jaguar. It was often employed in the performance of ideological practices. It is also found in Burma and Asia like you said, and some actually comes from Canada."

"No kidding? Who made this jade jaguar?" He held it up at stared at it. "Was it made in the United States or Mexico?"

"Don't know."

Andy turned it over. "At least it doesn't say made in China."

She took the statue. "Don't you have something to do besides question me?"

"Yes, but this is more fun. When do you want the pizza?"

After eating the large pepperoni pizza, and sharing a slice with Leo, they threw away their paper plates and the pizza box. Andy leaned on the kitchen counter and looked at Virginia loading the silverware and glasses into the dishwasher. "I've got an idea."

Virginia looked up. "I'm not in the mood for sex right now."

"I wasn't talking about sex, but now that you mention it…"

She quickly straightened up. "What were you thinking?"

"If you want, I think I can find out where the jade for the cat came from."

She frowned. "How?"

"I have a colleague in the chemistry department who's a geochemist. He can usually place the area different minerals originated from their chemical structure, or impurities, or something. I'm not a chemist."

"Would he need to destroy it?"

"I don't think so. Maybe just a small piece."

"Call him and see what he needs, but this must be done on the hush-hush."

"Okay." Andy turned and hurried out of the room.

Virginia and Leo returned to studying the quilt. "Let's see, these blocks seem to have a theme," she mumbled to herself. She looked at the cat who was studying the quilt. "Leo, I need to see Mary Jane and get more background." She went to the family room closet, rummaged through a couple of plastic storage boxes, and found her digital camera. Returning to the bedroom, she took pictures of the quilt and close-ups of each quilt block. Then she carefully photographed the binding around the edge. Next, she turned it over and took more pictures. Leo supervised. The actual quilting was more visible on the back, and she took more pictures of it. She then folded it and set it on a chair. Next, she removed the bedspread, spread the quilt on the bed, and then recovered it with the bedspread. "That should hide it pretty well." She turned off the overhead light as she left the room. She strolled down the hall toward the family room, with Leo following when she spotted the light on in Andy's den.

Andy looked up from his computer as she leaned on the doorframe. "You done with the quilt tonight?"

"Yeah. I took a lot of pictures. I'll download them to my computer tomorrow and study them. I need to talk to Mary Jane again now that I have the two items she thinks are involved." She looked at his cluttered desk. "What are you going to do with the jaguar?"

Andy picked it up. "Figured I'd seal it in a plastic freezer bag, use the vacuum to suck the air out, and stick it in the freezer. Make it a real cool cat."

Leo looked up.

"Very funny. Not a bad idea, though." She stared at the figurine for a second. "Did you talk to your geochemist friend?"

"Yes. He said to bring it to his lab tomorrow, and he'll see what he can find out about it. Dr. Ambrose said to tell you he wouldn't hurt it. He's done tests like this for museums and the police before."

Virginia bit her upper lip. "Okay, but keep it hidden and in your sight at all times. Don't let anyone else see or touch it."

"Right. Keep in sight at all times. Got it." He handed her the jaguar. "Before I freeze our little friend I'd suggest you take detailed photographs of it from every angle, just to be safe."

"Great idea." She hurried out of his den. She walked into her quilt studio and set it on a large green cutting board. She looked at Leo as he scurried into the room. "Well, that won't work. Not enough contrast." She rummaged through plastic boxes of fabric, found a cream-colored matte fabric, and placed the jaguar on it on top of her worktable. "Perfect." She focused her camera and began shooting pictures, first, at a slight distance of all sides. Afterwards, she moved in for close-ups. She stopped as Andy entered the room.

"How's it going?" he asked.

"Good. Almost done." She clicked through the shots she'd taken in the view screen on the camera.

Andy pushed his glasses back up his nose. "Have you tried any filters?"

Virginia slowly shook her head. "No. What filters?"

"Yeah. You have some that came with the camera. Try putting them on the lens and retake the pictures. Sometimes things look different."

She shrugged. "Okay. Can't hurt." She stood staring at the jade figurine for a second. "You still got that old laser?"

"Yeah. It's in the garage. Why?"

"When I'm done with the filters, I want to shine the laser at it and see what happens, and maybe take more pictures."

Andy took his glasses off and looked at them. "I need to clean these. Tell ya what, I'll go get the laser and set it up while you finish shooting with the filters. Then, I'll help you with the laser shots."

"Okay. You never know what the laser may show."

CHAPTER 5

Andy finished setting up his old laser when Virginia hurried into the garage. He watched her scurry across the space carrying the small jaguar and her camera and stop at the bench he had his equipment on. She placed the jaguar on the work surface and plopped on a wooden stool. He finished tightening a screw on a black box and then, looked at the small figurine. "How'd the photo session go?"

"Okay, I guess. I've taken pictures from all angles and put a ruler next to it for size comparison. The filters didn't show much. It was worth a try, I guess."

"Where's Leo?"

"He went to bed. Must have had a busy day."

Andy waved his hand toward the workbench. "I've got this set up for us. We'll see what happens when I use the laser; it's at 404 nanometers. That's all I've got here. If you remember, I got this at a surplus sale. Anyway, we can take pictures of what happens. I'll use the yellow filter to remove any excess blue light from the laser. Okay?"

She gave him a blank stare and shrugged. "If you say so. Just don't break it."

"I'll be careful." He mounted the jaguar, aimed the laser at a tiny spot near the tip of the tail, adjusted the clamps, aimed the camera, and set the yellow filter. He pointed across the garage. "I'll use the light above the workbench for now. Will you turn off the garage lights?"

"Sure." Virginia hopped off the stool, walked to the far wall, and switched off the lights. She returned to Andy's side and watched. "Okay, now what?"

"I fire this Rube Goldberg up, and we see what happens. Put on your safety glasses there on the table." He turned the apparatus on and turned off the white light. The LED display turned from yellow to green and Andy hit the activate button. The laser fired and the camera took pictures. After a few minutes, Andy turned everything off and switched on the lights. "Let's see what the camera caught."

Virginia removed the jaguar from the holder, followed Andy inside the house, and to his den. She watched as he uploaded the digital pictures from the camera to his computer and pulled them up on the monitor. She leaned over his shoulder and peered at the screen. "It looks orange. Why orange?"

"Yeah, it does. I don't know why it's orange. Maybe it's because of something in it. The little thing is dark blue-green. Maybe my chemist friend can add something about it. I can have someone from the geology department look at it and our pictures, too."

"Not what I expected. Then again, I'm not sure what I expected." She straightened. "I hope your friends can tell us more. Here…" She handed it to him. "…put it in the double freezer bags like you suggested and stuff it in the freezer for safe keeping tonight."

"Tell you what, give me your camera and I'll put your pictures and these from the laser in a file and save it on the computer and on a flash drive."

"Good idea. She handed him her camera. "I'll go see what I can find on the Internet."

An hour later Virginia strolled into Andy's den. "You get everything uploaded and saved?"

"Yes. I've got it on the computer in a file in an engineering folder labeled Stress Analysis of Complex Structures. It's buried five levels down, and the file is encoded." He held up two flash drives, one red and white, the other black. "I've got everything on the black one including your quilt pictures and just the jaguar-related ones on the red and white one." He handed her the black drive. "You keep this one, and I'll put this one in my briefcase."

"Couldn't someone steal yours and see the data?"

"Not likely," Andy said. "It's filed like I said, but there is a passcode required to get in, and the file is encoded like the one on this computer."

"I'll go hide this one."

"Good idea. I put the jaguar on ice."

After putting the computer drives away, they sat in the kitchen drinking iced teas. Virginia leaned across the table. "I need to talk to Mary Jane again about the history of that quilt and jaguar. She didn't have a lot to offer at the museum, but there is something more to this than simply an attempted theft."

Andy sipped his tea. "I agree. You said she'd behome from the hospital tomorrow. Why not go see her then? The more background you have, the easier it will be to figure out this puzzle."

"I'm not sure what the connection is between the jaguar and the quilt.

I'll get the contact information on the others mentioned in the will who seemed slighted."

"Aren't the police doing that?"

"Maybe." Virginia sat back in her seat. "But I'm willing to bet they won't get very far. No one likes talking to the cops. The uncertainty of what might happen is always in the back of their minds, and people usually don't become forthcoming with information. If they aren't arresting you, don't hesitate to just get up and leave."

"You can just leave?"

"In the case of general questioning, yes. If they stop you, under federal appeals court rulings, as soon as they detain you, you are under arrest, and you can refuse to answer and demand a lawyer."

Andy shrugged. "Good to know."

Virginia looked at him. "Did you notice the car parked down the street from our house with two men in it?"

"No. Why?"

"I spotted them, and they made me nervous. That's why I had you set both alarms."

"Well, my alarms haven't sounded, so I guess it's just your nerves."

Virginia clenched her hands. "At least, we have the alarms and weapons here, and we can keep an eye on the quilt and jaguar."

CHAPTER 6

Virginia went to her quilt room and returned with a notebook to the living room where Andy had moved. She sat on the couch next to him. "You have a gun on you?"

"Yep. The nine-millimeter." He used the remote to switch on the TV, then looked at her. "What are you doing?"

She glanced at the TV. "You've seen that episode of NCIS. You're going to watch it again?"

"Yes."

"Okay. I'll just sit and make my list."

"List?"

"The names of the people Mary Jane Striker mentioned who think they should have the treasure or whatever it is they imagine the quilt will lead to."

"Oh. Okay." Andy settled back to watch the TV.

Virginia started to list the people involved that she knew of. After scribbling in her notebook, she turned to Andy. "Can I run these notes by you?"

"Yeah, but I don't know how much help I'll be. I don't know much about your case."

She flipped back to the first page. "Sometimes just talking brings things into perspective. Anyway, you always ask good questions."

Andy fluffed a throw pillow behind him and leaned back. "Okay. Shoot."

She looked at her notes. "First there's John Pennington. He's one of Mary Jane's cousins. He got enough money to pay off the garage he runs and the mortgage on his house."

"He got a nice inheritance."

"Yes, but he has a history of drinking and fighting. And he was upset he didn't get all or part of the ranch."

"Okay." Andy nodded. "But that doesn't make him a killer."

"No, but it doesn't let him off the hook quite yet."

"What else have you got?" Andy asked.

"Let's see, another cousin, Barbara Dorian. She's a first-grade teacher in Round Rock. She's usually pretty nice, but was upset about Mary Jane getting the whole ranch."

"How much did she get as an inheritance?"

Virginia looked at her notes. "Two-hundred thousand dollars."

"That's pretty good money for a teacher."

"I agree. But we have others."

"More?" Andy switched off the TV. "A lineup of relatives?"

"No. This one is a professor at Southwestern University. A Dr. William Pine. He thought he was going to get an endowment or grant and wanted the quilt."

"He didn't get anything?"

"No. He got a hundred grand in solid gold bars."

Andy's eyes widened. "That's a huge amount for a professor. Did it go to him or the university?"

"To him. He's also interested in the jade jaguar."

"Why does he want the jaguar and where did Mary Jane's great-uncle get the gold bars?"

"I don't know."

Andy rubbed his forehead. "Are there pictures of the gold bars? They usually have a stamp on them showing who refined them and the purity and stuff."

"I'll have to ask. I have a feeling there are more of them someplace. Like maybe, they are the so-called treasure. But there's more."

Andy sat up. "I need some sustenance if we're going to continue. Want some popcorn?"

"Sure."

Andy hurried to the kitchen. A couple minutes later Virginia could smell the popcorn. Andy returned with two bowls and handed her one. "Okay, continue."

"Then, there is Mr. James Cooper. Someone hired him to follow the police and me to the ranch where he tried to shoot us. He was wounded and taken to the hospital where someone dressed as a nurse poisoned him. He's a killer for hire, but who hired him, and who killed him?"

"Maybe the person who hired him had him killed so he wouldn't talk."

"My guess, too. But why hire someone to steal the quilt?" Virginia munched on a handful of popcorn. She turned at the sound of the small bell attached to her cat's collar coming down the hall. "Leo must have smelled the popcorn." Leo jumped up on the couch and stared at Virginia. "Okay, here yeah go." She put a handful of popcorn on the floor and watched Leo hop down and start eating.

Andy ate some more popcorn. "Probably to try and decode the quilt like you're doing, and to keep an eye on you and see where your investigation leads. If there is a treasure, the person who hired them will want to pounce as soon as you find it."

"If it really exists."

"Yeah, if it really exists. Anything else in your notes you want to discuss?"

"I have to include Mary Jane Stoker. She inherited the ranch, the quilt, and the jaguar. She's a quilter, so maybe her great-uncle left her the quilt because of that."

"That's plausible. Has she had a chance to explore her new ranch or figure out how much it's worth?"

"Not yet."

"Does she know where her great-uncle got all that money and gold?"

"No. Not yet. But someone tried to poison her with Wolfbane or Monkshood and did it in my museum."

"That's not nice." Andy finished his popcorn. "They all seem really interested in the ranch, that quilt, and jaguar. What else do you have?"

Virginia turned another page in her notebook. "Let's see, the quilt was made sometime around eighteen sixty-four or five. The family stories say there is some sort of treasure somewhere on the ranch, and the quilt holds the key. But no one has ever found it or figured out the map that is supposed to be on the quilt."

"Maybe that's where her uncle got his money and gold."

"My thoughts exactly. But how does the jaguar fit in?"

"I don't know. Maybe it's a clue as to where the treasure came from. I'll take the little guy with me to the university and see what my chemist friend can tell us."

"Good. I need all the help I can get."

Andy glanced over at Virginia's list. "Looks like a comprehensive starting list. I bet it will grow."

She chuckled. "No bet." She closed the notebook. "How can we find out what the yellow from the laser image of the jaguar means?"

"I'll take my copy of the images to the university and see what someone from the geology department can tell me. Between him and the chemist, maybe we'll get a lead."

"Be careful with the jaguar. We don't want it stolen."

Andy picked up the remote and switched on the TV. Another NCIS show was starting. "It's an NCIS marathon tonight, but I've seen that episode a hundred times. I know the dialog."

Virginia tossed the notebook aside. "I have an idea."

Andy tilted his head and grinned. "And what would that be?"

She wrinkled her nose. "I thought maybe we could examine the quilt some more."

Andy looked at his watch. "You want to look at the quilt now?"

"Yeah. You haven't really had a chance to study it, and it's safe right now, so why not? You might find something."

"How would I find anything if you've looked at it and I haven't?"

"Maybe I'm looking too hard. You're a pair of fresh eyes." She stood. "Coming?"

"Yeah," he mumbled. "I'm no quilter, why me?"

"What did you say?" she asked walking toward the spare bedroom.

"Nothing." He got up and followed her.

Virginia pulled the bedspread off the bed exposing the quilt. "Okay, have a look."

Leo scampered into the room and jumped on the quilt. He walked across it and skirted Virginia's swipes at removing him. He suddenly leaped off the bed and onto a window ledge and meowed.

Andy frowned. "What's with him?"

"I don't know. He's pretty upset all of a sudden." Virginia skin tingled. "Andy, check the alarms and switch on the outside spotlights. He's making me nervous."

"Good idea. You going to get your gun?"

She nodded. "Yes and your .38 special."

"Okay." Andy went to check the alarms as Virginia hurried to their bedroom. She took their pistols out of the bed stands and checked them. She returned to her quilt room and found Andy and Leo staring at the quilt.

He looked at her and took his revolver. "Better safe than sorry. I've got a 9mm and the .38."

"I agree." She slid her semiautomatic into her waistband. "Okay, now let's take a look."

Andy leaned closer to the quilt and studied it. After a couple minutes, he pointed. "Look at this block. It seems to depict something unusual. Looks like a Mayan symbol to me, but I'm no expert." He pointed to another. "That looks like a crude portrayal of a cave and that one looks like a… I don't know, something weird. Wait, maybe a bat or a bird. That faded one looks like a funny rendering of a Confederate flag."

Virginia followed his pointing. "I never noticed them like that. You may be right. What's it mean?"

"I don't know. You're the quilter. Maybe after you see Mary Jane tomorrow, you'll have a better idea."

As she turned, Andy pushed his glasses back up his nose and pointed again. "That binding looks like something out of a science fiction book, stars, and a tube or maybe a wormhole."

Virginia bent over and peered at it. "I don't know. They didn't know about wormholes in the mid-eighteen hundreds." She rubbed her eyes. "I'm tired. I'll put the bedspread back. You check the doors again and let's go to bed. I'll examine the quilt again tomorrow before I go to the museum. Maybe I'll take it with me. The light will be better in one of the labs there." She looked at Leo now curled up in a corner. "Coming with us or are you on guard duty tonight?"

Leo raised his head then went back to sleep.

Two men, George and Frank, watched the house through binoculars. George lowered his. "The lights are going out. Looks like they're going to bed. I wonder why they didn't turn off the outside spotlights."

"Maybe they forgot."

"Or they left them on to make it harder for anyone to sneak up."

"Maybe." Frank smiled. "Let's give them an hour, then go see what we can find."

George swung his head around. "Like hell. The boss liked our plan to wait and watch. That's what we're going to do. I'm not breaking in with them there. And, did you see those security alarm signs?"

"Yeah, but it takes the alarm company and the cops time to respond."

"Yeah, but it doesn't take long for a .45," said George.

CHAPTER 7

Virginia closed Andy's car door and leaned into the window. "You have your gun and permit. Right?"

"Yes, dear, but you know I can't take it out of the car on campus."

"It's concealed. Right? That means no one can see it. I'm a little worried. I'm sure Leo spotted someone outside last night watching the house. People want what we have, and I have a list of attempted murders and killings related to the quilt and that jaguar you've got. So, be careful."

"Okay. I'll be careful." He gave her a warm smile. "I'll call you as soon as I have any information about the jaguar. You be careful too."

"I will." Virginia kissed Andy goodbye as he left home for the University of Texas at Austin. She returned to the kitchen table and sat with her notebook and a third cup of coffee. Opening the notebook, she sipped her coffee, and read each line of her list about the quilt and the ranch to her cat, Leo, when the phone rang. The cat jumped from the chair next to Virginia to the floor and scooted away.

She rose and hurried to the phone. "Hello?"

"Virginia, this is Mary Jane Striker. I was released from the hospital, and I'm home. The police are coming later this morning. They said they have more questions. I wanted to let you know where I was in case you needed me."

"Mary Jane, I'm glad you are okay and home." Virginia hopped onto the kitchen counter next to the sink. "Please stay there and don't go out without someone with you. I'm not sure if you are safe yet."

"I'm locked in my house, but how can I help you? I'll be a lot safer when this mystery is solved."

"I agree. I do need to talk to you before I get to the others. Can I come over in about an hour?"

"Yes. See you then." She hung up.

Virginia gulped the last of her coffee and sprinted to the bathroom to get ready for the day.

Fifteen minutes later, and after making sure Leo had cat food and water, she backed her Toyota out of the garage and headed out of the development. Virginia watched the dark sedan following about a quarter of a mile behind. *Whoever they are, they are not very good at keeping a low profile.* She pulled her cell phone from a side pocket of her backpack and speed dialed Detective Wilkinson giving him her location and the description of the car following her. She continued East on Texas 29. As she crossed D.B. Woods Road, a marked Georgetown Police cruiser, displaying its emergency lights, made a U-turn and pulled the car following Virginia over.

She sped on down the road. In Georgetown, she turned right off University Avenue onto Main Street and pulled up in a driveway. She looked at the historic designated, white, three-story Victorian with the green shutters, large wraparound porch, and gingerbread. She slid out of the car, slung her backpack over her shoulder, and then pulled the quilt, in a large plastic bag from the rear seat and strolled to the front steps. As she jogged up the steps, the front door opened, and Mary Jane stood with a large grin waving Virginia inside.

Virginia walked into the large living room. It was decorated with period style furniture. After she and Mary Jane rearranged the furniture to make space, she spread the quilt out on the spacious floor. Virginia sat cross-legged on the floor next to the quilt. "Okay, let's take a serious look at this thing. It seems to be the center of attention to a number of your relatives and others."

Mary Jane pushed a few strands of her gray-black hair from her face and bent over staring at the quilt. "I've looked at it before. It doesn't tell me anything."

"Take another look. Based on recent happenings, it might appear different now. Think about its history."

"Okay." Mary Jane wet her lips and stared at the quilt. She pointed to a block in the middle. That seems to be a bad depiction of a bat, and that one could be a cave. There are a few..." she pointed again. "...that look like symbols of some type."

Virginia nodded. "What else?"

"On that one at the top right side, there's a colorful one that could depict a flag, but I'm not sure."

"Good. Anything else?"

"Yes. These here seem to be parts of something that was taken apart and the pieces used to make part of this quilt. But I don't see what it was. They don't all appear to be here, and they're not made of the same fabric the rest of the quilt is made from."

Virginia bent to look then pointed at some quilt blocks Mary Jane had pointed to. "You mean these?"

"Yes. I can't imagine what the maker took apart to make this. It's futile to think this is a map. Those over there look like they are something military, but I don't know what."

"Maybe you're right, but I don't think so. There is something here, and I'm going to figure out what it is."

Mary Jane shook her head. "I've tried without any luck. I hope you do better, but I don't see how."

Virginia bit her lip. She looked up at Mary Jane. "Okay, tell me about when this quilt was actually made."

Mary Jane sat in a nearby red wing backed chair. "It was made about the end of the Civil War by a great-aunt, Effie Dillan. Not sure how many greats are in front of her name, but a lot. The story goes, she and a servant, maybe a slave, made it. There were rumors that it had to do with a treasure, like I told you, and some generals. I don't see anything about generals, though, except the Confederate flag."

"Generals?"

"Yes. Generals."

"Confederate generals or Union generals?"

Mary Jane took a breath. "I don't know."

"Were any of your ancestors in the Civil War?"

"Yeah. Some great, great, great-uncles and my great, great, great, great grandfather served in the Texas regiments. Not really sure how many greats it actuallywas, but again, it's a lot. The war was a long time ago."

Virginia nodded. "Time changes things too. Even if this quilt is some sort of map, landscapes can change a lot over time. But, back to your old relatives. Any generals in the family?"

Mary Jane rested her head against the back of the chair. "I'm not sure. I think my grandmother mentioned someone who was a general. He was wounded and sent back home to Texas. He was in a brigade of some type that was used near our border with Mexico, and later he was in Northern Virginia."

"Northern Virginia?"

"Yeah. Who knew? A Texan leading Virginians, I think that was the story."

Virginia shrugged. "You could be right about that. I don't remember any military skirmishes in Texas near Mexico during the Civil War. What was his brigade doing there?"

"Either protecting Texas's border or getting something important from Mexico for the cause."

"Makes sense. Quilt blocks usually have names." Virginia pointed to other blocks. "This particular block style is about guerrilla warfare, that one is called Sugar Cane, this one is The Southern Cause, and this is one called Smallpox." Virginia rose and stepped to the top of the quilt. "This one you said could be a flag is a depiction of the Confederate flag, I agree but these with the unusual shapes I haven't deciphered, yet."

Mary Jane sat forward. "You know a lot about this."

"Yes. Besides being a quilter and curator, I have done some research on old quilts. It is an interesting history filled with warm stories, mystery, and intrigue." Virginia walked around the quilt. "I take it your family general was a brigadier general."

"I don't know for sure if he even was a general. Why? What makes you think that?"

"That block in the lower left corner." Virginia knelt next to the quilt. "It's a star, but not one for Texas. Besides, brigadier generals have one star and command brigades. It's starting to fit if you consider the binding?"

"The binding? What about it?"

Virginia rose, arched her back from bending, and twisted to stretch when she stopped and stared out the front window. "You expecting company or a delivery?"

"No."

"There is a car parked across the street with a man with a camera and very big lens watching your house. He wasn't there earlier. Help me fold up the quilt."

After they folded the quilt and pushed it back into the bag, Virginia glanced out the window again. "Still there." She stepped to her backpack and pulled out her pistol, checked the magazine and returned it to her backpack. "You going anywhere today?"

"Not today. The police are coming this afternoon to talk to me again. I was planning on going to the ranch tomorrow and start inventorying what's there."

"Can you hold off on that? It could be dangerous."

Mary Jane fidgeted. "I... I guess so. A few more days one way or another won't make any difference."

"Good. I need you safe. I'm going to take the quilt to the museum for further study and safe keeping for now. And, I'm going to visit the others you mentioned and see what they have to say."

"Okay. Good luck. How about the man across the street?"

Virginia pulled out her cell phone and called Detective Wilkinson. She gave him the description of the man and the car across from Mary Jane's house. Then, they watched from the window as an unmarked police car came down the street and stopped behind the suspect vehicle. Two plainclothes officers approached the car. After examining the man's credentials and other documents, they returned to their cruiser. A minute later, the suspicious car pulled away.

Virginia's cell phone rang. "Hello, Detective. What did your boys find?"

"The man you saw was a licensed P.I. He was hired to watch the house and report on who went in and out and when."

"Who hired him?"

"He wouldn't tell them."

"Couldn't they arrest him to get it or something?"

"No. This may be Texas, but we're still in the U.S. and can't get that without a warrant. But, the boys encouraged him to spy on wayward husbands and leave Ms. Mary Jane Striker alone. He protested until they told him there was a federal agent involved. They informed him this particular federal agent has a bad habit of not playing nice. He didn't say whether he would stop or not, but he got the message that he'd been seen, so he decided that leaving was his best course of action at this time. I don't think he'll give up. It'll be him or someone else."

"Thanks for the help. Oh, how about the car following me this morning, what's their story?"

"They told the officer they were just a couple of good old boys coming into Georgetown from Liberty Hill."

Virginia chuckled. "The officer believed that?"

"No. Especially not after he ran their IDs. He called for backup. It seems both men have long rap sheets and are on parole for a couple of felonies. And guess what?"

"What?"

"The officers asked their parole officer for permission to search them. He granted it. They found a camera with pictures of your house and you. They also found a notebook and cell phone. The last call was to a burner phone. The officers inquired as to what they were doing inside a gated community, like where you live, and why they had pictures of a federal agent."

"And, what did they say?"

"Nothing. They clammed up when one of the officers found a loaded 9 mm semiautomatic in the possession of the driver. That's a no-no for a convicted felon. They are both now resting in the Sheriff's Hotel. They'll be retuning to Huntsville soon on the Sheriff's shuttle. What are you up to now?"

"I'm going to the museum to lock up the quilt then to Southwestern University to see Dr. William Pine."

"Okay. I'll alert the university police that you're coming so when you stir up a hornet's nest, they'll be expecting you."

"Oh come on, I'm not that bad."

"If you say so. Try not to cause a shoot-out in the university."

"I'll work on it. Thanks for your help."

"No problem. Let me know what you find out. Oh, anything new with the quilt or green cat figurine?"

"Made a little progress with the quilt, but nothing too really to report yet. I'm waiting to hear from my husband about the jade jaguar."

"Okay. Keep me posted." He hung up.

Virginia said goodbye to Mary Jane and left. She looked at her watch. *Maybe I should go to the university first. It's closer.* She slowly drove the couple miles to Southwestern University and parked. Looking at her notebook, she pulled her iPhone out, got onto the Internet, and looked up Dr. William Pine. *Hmm, he's a professor of classics and history. He's got a Ph.D. from SMU. Widower. No children. He's a member of the American Philatelic Society. Hmm, he's a stamp collector. He also collects Civil War memorabilia, wine, and likes skiing. He's got quite a wide variety of expensive interests. He does all this on a professor's pay?* Virginia exited the car and strolled to the main office and looked around. It was an old building and looked and smelled like an old college. She entered the President's office lobby and asked the coed at a desk for the office of Dr. Pine. Obtaining directions, Virginia hurried to the history department and found his office on the second floor. She knocked.

"Come in," a man's voice called out.

Virginia entered and stepped to the scared, wooden desk, topped with books and papers. Behind it, and under a window, sat a table with a computer. The wall on her left was a floor to ceiling bookcase that stressed the limit with books, papers, and small statues. The wall on the right was covered with diplomas, certificates, and awards, mixed with various photographs. She looked at the man behind the desk. He appeared to be in his early sixties, grayish receding hair, wire-rimmed glasses, and dressed in a red polo shirt.

He looked up and frowned. "You aren't one of my students. Who are you?"

She smiled. "I'm Virginia Davies Clark."

The man frowned. "Another female with a hyphenated name. Can't let go huh? I'm busy. What do you want?"

Virginia stiffened. *Jerk.* She pulled her badge case from her backpack and flipped it open. "I'm a federal special agent with the Smithsonian Central Security Service. I need a few words with you."

He leaned forward and looked at her badge and ID. "Never heard of your so-called agency. Who put you up to this prank?"

Virginia moved to the edge of the desk and leaned on it. "Look, bozo, I'm a federal officer and have a few questions. We can do this the easy way or the hard way. Your choice."

"Don't give me any shit. I'm a professor, and I demand you leave at once."

"You really want me to take you into custody?"

"We'll see about that! "He grabbed the phone and called the campus police. "This is Dr. Pine. History Department. There is a woman in my office impersonating a police officer. I want her arrested and removed at once. She threatened me." He listened. "Yes, that's who she said she was." His eyes widened. "She's really a federal officer? That's a real agency she's with? Oh shit. No, I don't think sending an officer is going to help. Thank you." He hung up and squared his shoulders. "So you think you can just burst in here and demand to speak to me?"

Virginia glared. "Stand up."

"What?"

"I said stand up, jackass, and turn around." She felt her pulse quicken. "I'm going to cuff you and take you in for questioning."

"You can't do that."

"Want to bet? Ever hear of resisting arrest?"

"I don't have to answer your questions."

This guy watches way too much TV. "No, you don't. You can even get a lawyer. But I can hold you for about seventy-two hours without a charge. In that amount of time, I'm sure a deputy U.S. Attorney and I can find something to charge you with." *I hope this works, and I can really pull this off.* "And I'm also pretty sure your roommates at the jail won't find your lectures exhilarating."

Pine pulled out a desk drawer and reached inside.

Virginia swung her backpack around and, as it dropped to the floor, she pulled out her black .380 semiautomatic and aimed it at him. "Show me your hands, slowly!"

"Wait! I was just getting my pipe." Pine swallowed. "I'll just leave it in the drawer." He withdrew his hand and pushed the drawer closed and sat back. "Look. I think we got off on the wrong foot. Can we start over? It's been a bad few weeks and my nerves are on edge." Beads of sweat formed on his forehead. "I'm sorry for what just happened."

Virginia watched him squirm. *The little weasel is nervous. Good.* "Okay, Professor. We'll give it another try."

"Please have a seat, Agent Clark." Pine wet his lips as he motioned for her to sit in a side chair. "How can I help you?"

Virginia picked up her backpack and slid her gun into it. She sat in the offered chair. "We're going to talk about Mary Jane Striker, her ranch, your inheritance in gold bars, your interest in a certain jade figurine, and a quilt."

CHAPTER 8

Doctor Pine sat stiffly in his chair. "Okay. What do you want to know?"

Virginia pulled her notebook from her backpack. "For starters, you have some expensive hobbies. How does a professor of classics and history do these things on a professor's pay?"

He clenched and unclenched his fingers a couple times. "How I pay for my special interests isn't pertinentto your investigation, and I see no reason to answer you."

"Let's try this, then. When Mary Jane Striker's great uncle died, he left you a hundred grand in solid gold bars."

Pine's brows narrowed. "Yes."

"You thought you should have gotten more. Why?"

"Why are you asking all these questions? There was nothing illegal about the bequest."

"Because there have been a couple of attempted murders and an actual murder related to her uncle's death."

"Murders? Isn't that a police matter, not a federal one?"

"Normally, yes. But the Georgetown Police asked for help, especially since the case has some historical parts to it. The Smithsonian Central Security Service has me helping with the investigation. Now, about those gold bars."

He tensed. "Well—"

"Doctor, this is just an interview. As far as I know there is nothing wrong with you having the gold bars. It's the murders and the circumstances surrounding the ranch that I'm interested in."

Pine glared at her.

She smiled. "You do know the IRS will be informed of the inheritance, don't you?"

Pine fell back in his chair. "The IRS? How would they know? There isn't a 1099 form."

"There will be a form 1099 reported and who knows, maybe I'll tell them first. That's a lot of money on top of your pay. Lots of taxes. Now, about the gold bars."

"All right. I got a hundred thousand dollars in gold bars. I had a few assayed, and they are 99.6% gold. They are solid, 24 karat gold."

Virginia cocked her head. "That's a higher percentage of gold than I thought Mayan gold would be."

"You're right. Most of what Mayan gold has been found is nowhere near this good. But it has the markings, and it had some material on it I had dated, and it's fromthe right time, so I think it's authentic."

"That's interesting." Virginia made some notes."How big are the bars?"

"I'll show you." Pine opened a bottom desk drawer and slowly removed a gold bar about eight-inches-long and three-inches-wide and one-inch-thick, and carefully set it on the desk. "It's heavy for its size. Have a look."

Virginia rose and bent over the desk to look at the gold bar. "It seems like it was crudely formed and has what appears to be a strange figure on the top."

"You're right."

"Where are the others?"

"The rest of these are in a safe deposit box at the bank.

I keep this one around just to look at."

She looked at him. "Any idea what that symbol is or where it came from, professor?"

"It's the Mayan symbol for *Balam*. The Jaguar."

"The Jaguar?"

"Yes."

"Any idea where the gold bars came from?"

"I'd guess southern Mexico," Pine said. "How the lady's great uncle got them, I haven't a clue."

Virginia pulled out her cell phone and snapped some pictures then returned the phone to her backpack. "You knew her great-uncle had them, didn't you?"

Pine nodded. "Yes. He showed them to me."

"Where were they?"

"In a shack out on the ranch. Actually, they were in what looked like a root cellar. It was under the shack, and you entered through a hidden trap door."

Virginia made more notes. "Did you see anything else unusual on your visits with him?"

"Well, the ground in the cellar was deeply depressed and looked like there was once more of the gold there and some shelves that had things on them that were missing. I could tell they had been removed some time just before I was there from the dust patterns."

Virginia sat in the chair again. "Okay. How'd Mayan gold bars from southern Mexico, or somewhere around there, get on an old ranch in central

Texas?"

"I don't know."

"Any idea how long they'd been down in that cellar?"

"From the looks of them when I was there, I'd say well over a hundred years."

How could you tell? Gold doesn't oxidize."

"The boxes they were in, and some cloth in the box with them looked like it came from the Civil War era. There were markings on the boxes, and the cloths had the Confederate battle flag image in a corner. Another one had a flag of Guatemala and another of Mexico."

Virginia nodded and made more notes. "Given that you were bequeathed a hundred grand in gold, why areyou upset with Mary Jane Striker? What would you want with an old quilt and the jade jaguar?"

"I was a friend of the gentleman and helped him identify things he found on the property. I spent a lot of time out there in the Texas sun and figured I was due more than a few gold bars."

"Sorry, Professor, that sounds really lame. A hundred grand in solid gold sounds like a lot to me. That gold will increase in value. A man of your intelligence can do better than that. What's with the quilt and figurine ofthe jaguar?"

Pine stiffened. "Are we through with these questions?"

"Just a couple more." Virginia smiled and leaned forward. "Did you hire a detective to watch Mary Jane Striker?"

"I don't have to answer that."

"How about a couple goons to follow me?"

Pine stared at her.

"Why'd you have someone kill the hired gun at the hospital?" She watched a quick facial tick on his face.

Pine stood. "This... ahh... interview is over, Agent Clark. If you have any further questions, we'll do them with my lawyer present."

Virginia slowly rose, picked up her backpack, and grinned. "Thank you for your time, Professor. Trust me, we'll be in touch." She pivoted on her heel and ambled toward the door. Standing in the door frame, Virginia turned back. "Oh, one more thing. The poisons used on Mary Jane and the man killed in the hospital, are being traced. Thought you'd like to know. I'm sure you'll also be hearing from the IRS." As she walked out, she heard Pine collapse into his chair. *Unsettling that self-righteous ass was fun.*

She returned to her car and sat looking at her notes. *A Mayan symbol for the jaguar on the gold? What's it mean? That gold was purer than it should be, too.*

Virginia drove to the Wolf Ranch shopping centerand bought an orange chicken bowl at the Panda Express, parked her car under an oak tree in the shade, and atewhile studying her notes.

The gold bar with a jaguar figure on it was curious. I need to see where it was located when found. Pine's reaction to my questions about the detective and goons was interesting as was his reaction to my mentioning the poisons. But at the same time, not incriminating. He did get a little testy though when I asked about the quilt and jaguar, and he never answered my question. Okay, stirred that pot. Now, let's see... whom should I see next? How about Mary Jane's cousin John Pennington? He's got a garage here in Georgetown.

She looked him up on the Internet and found the address to his automotive repair center on Williams Drive. She drove out of the shopping center then drove along the frontage road of the North I35 Freeway, and swung onto Williams Drive. A few miles up the road, Virginia spotted the new building with a sign that read *Pennington Motor Car Service* on her left, just past Sun City Texas, and pulled into the parking lot.

Entering, she noticed the polished tile floor, faux leather and stainless steel chairs and tables, and fairly new magazines on the end table. There was a magazine rack hanging on a dark blue wall. Virginia saw a white-haired, stocky woman who looked up from behind the counter. "Hello. Can I help you?"

Virginia nodded. "Yes. I'd like to see Mr. John Pennington, please."

The woman looked Virginia up and down. "I can have one of our team talk to you about your vehicle."

"I need to see Mr. Pennington."

"This isn't about your car?"

"No."

"Look, honey, Mr. Pennington isn't seeing anyone today. He's busy. Leave your name and number."

Virginia bristled at being called "honey" by the woman. She pulled her badge and credential case out, displayed her gold badge, and glared. "Honey, I'm a federal officer, and I need to speak to him. I've had a bad day, and I'm short on humor. I just want to talk to Mr. Pennington. It shouldn't take more than fifteen minutes, if that."

The woman picked up the phone and punched in a number. "John, there's a lady here to see you." She listened. "John, she a federal cop, you'd better come out here." The woman hung up the phone and pointed. "Just take a seat over there. He'll be right out."

Virginia noticed the woman's left hand reach under the desk and back out. *Okay, plan on trouble. She just triggered an alarm. Why? I'd better see if Pennington does a rabbit.* "I'm stepping outside for a second. Be right back." Before the woman could respond, Virginia turned and hurried out the door. She stopped and looked at the building and the parking lot. A few late model, expensive cars were nosed into parking spaces, but there was no other obvious door other than the one she came through and the big overhead ones to the garage bays behind her.

She looked at the garage bay doors. Two men in pressed jeans and matching red Polo shirts stood leaning against the big doorframe watching, but not advancing toward her. The office door opened, and the woman stepped out. "Mr. Pennington is available to speak with you now."

A minute later, a tall, thin man, with shoulder length brown hair, dressed in tan Dockers, a green polo shirt and a pair of light-brown loafers sans socks walked out into the parking lot. He spotted Virginia leaning against the front right fender of her Toyota Camry and approached her. He offered his hand. "John Pennington. How can I help you, Special Agent? May I ask what agency you're a Special Agent of?"

"Smithsonian Central Security Service." Virginia pushed off the car and shook his hand. "I noticed a couple of your employees watching me over there. I'm more interesting than their work?"

Pennington looked at her. "Really? You are definitely more interesting than cars." John turned and motioned to his men to return to the garage.

"I think your receptionist triggered an alarm of sorts, and they showed up watching me. May I ask why?"

"The alarm she set off is used as a caution for when something is out of the normal. We service high-end automobiles and someone nosing around, even the police make us nervous. Our customers are, shall I say, well to do and interesting people, and appreciate privacy, and I try to afford them that." He motioned for her to follow him back to the building. "Shall we go to my office?"

Virginia smiled. "Yes, that would be nice." Pennington opened the glass door for Virginia. "Okay. What does a pretty federal officer want to talk to me about?"

"For openers, how about an inheritance, a quilt, attempted murder, and an actual murder?"

He stopped. His eyebrows shot up. His color paled. Pennington's voice quivered. "Murder?"

"Yep. That and a few other things you may be able to help us with."

"I don't know anything about a murder, but if there is something I can assist you with, I'll be happy to." He pointed up the short stairs. "My office is on the right at the top."

Virginia walked into the second-floor office of John Pennington. The space was big with a large ornate wooden desk and a high-backed leather chair with a large window behind it. In front of the desk were two arm-chairs on coasters with soft leather seats. On her left was a long wooden table with papers, books, and some tools on it. On the right was a couch facing the wall with what she figured was a fifty-inch flat-screen TV. Next to the door on her right was a bookshelf. She sat on a chair facing the desk.

John stepped around the desk and sat in his chair. He gave her a quick smile. "Now, how can I help you?"

Virginia pulled out her notebook and glanced at it. "I understand you got an inheritance from a deceased relative recently."

"Yes. I fail to see how that is of interest to the government. What's it got to do with the murder you mentioned?"

"There was an attempt on your cousin's life, and another man was murdered because of the ranch and some inheritances. That's why I'm here."

John stiffened. "Someone tried to kill Mary Jane?" His eyes grew wide. "Is she okay? Why didn't she call me?"

"It seems that you, and a couple of other people, are not exactly happy about how the estate was distributed."

Pennington leaned forward. "You're sure Mary Jane is okay?"

"Yes, she's fine." Virginia nodded. "Now, about the inheritance?"

He leaned back into the chair. "Right. I got a boatload of money. It was enough to pay off the loan on this building and everything else around here, my cars and to pay off my home mortgage. I have some left over I'm investing."

"Were you really unhappy about it all?"

"At first, yeah. I got the money and about…" He looked at Virginia "…you're not IRS. Right?"

"Nope. I don't even talk to them except on April fifteenth each year, like you. And, I will not be discussing anything you tell me with them, either. Taxes aren't my problem."

Pennington nodded. "Okay. I got about a five hundred Gs in small gold bars. I sold some to pay things off and plan on investing what was left. I've still got a few of the little bars remaining. I'd love to know where they came from. But, after I sat and thought about it, and what I got, well, I figured I came out okay. I don't really need a ranch that I know nothing about. I don't know farming or ranching. I'm cool with what I got. Hell, I got more gold than I probably deserve."

"Gold bars with a funny little figure on them, like this?" Virginia showed him the picture she took of Professor Pine's gold bar.

"Yeah, right. Like that. I don't know what it means."

Virginia leaned back in the chair. "So you have no idea who'd want to kill your cousin?"

"Not really." Pennington picked up a pen and clicked it a couple times. "There's another cousin, Barbara Dorian. She's a first-grade teacher in Round Rock. Haven't seen her in a while. I seriously doubt she would try to hurt anyone."

"Anyone else you can think of?"

Pennington frowned. "Just that nut-job professor at the University."

Virginia chuckled as she scribbled in her notebook. "I met him already."

"You could probably tell he's a little high-strung and a quart low. He's on edge all the time. He's a history professor, and he's been on some archaeological digs with archaeologists and fancies himself an Indiana Jones type. He's more like a spoiled brat."

"I take it you've met him and don't like him."

"Right on both counts."

Virginia made more notes and then, looked at Pennington. "Any chance of a tour of your establishment? I'd like to see what you've done with the place."

"Sure. Just a sec." Pennington picked up his phone and called the receptionist. "Linda, tell the boys to clean up, I'm bringing Special Agent Clark to tour the garage." He hung up and rose. "Shall we go take a look?"

He warned them we were coming? Why? Virginia followed Pennington down the stairs, across the lobby, and into the vehicle repair area. She smelled the faint odor of rubber and oil. The area was big with three large bays. There were three late model European cars in the service bays; a black Mercedes was up on a rack. She noticed three more vehicles outside. The garage area was unusually clean, everything polished and the floor spotless. *Do they actually do any work in here?*

Pennington motioned for her to follow him. "This is where we work on the cars." He pointed to a large space in the back with shelves. "That's where we store the parts we need, and over there behind that door is our computer center. We handle all our work electronically."

Virginia nodded. "Nice. Looks like a good place to work."

"When it gets cold, we close the doors. The bays are heated. Happy employees do good work."

"That's true." *Time to play the dumb blonde routine.* "Those look like expensive cars. All foreign. Do you just work on foreign cars?"

"You have a good eye, Agent Clark. Yes, we specialize in high-end European and a few from Japan."

She walked to the shiny light blue BMW in the first bay with its hood up and ran her hand over the fender. She noticed the small window wipers on the headlights. "I guess there is money in repairing these cars."

Pennington beamed. "You've got that right."

Virginia stepped to a workbench and picked up a tool. "This is clean and spotless like the workbench. Not what I would expect in a garage."

"I try to differentiate us by calling this a motor car service center instead of a garage. Cleanliness and clean attire are a must to impress our exclusive customers."

Virginia glanced at the two men working on vehicles. She noticed they were the men that watched her from the bay doors only now they wore clean, dark blue jumpsuits with a logo on the front. "I like the uniforms."

"I thought it was a nice touch."

"Well, thank you for your time and the tour Mr. Pennington. I'm sure we'll meet again."

"I look forward to it, Agent Clark. Next time I assure you my men will behave like gentlemen and not leer at you."

"Good. Thanks again." Virginia shook his hand and slowly walked back to her car.

She started her vehicle and drove east on Williams Dr. toward Georgetown. *Okay, Pennington appeared to really be upset that someone tried to harm Mary Jane. He's got a nice clean shop working on high-end cars. Not many in work or the queue. Place is spotless. Are they actually working on those cars? Maybe Detective Wilkinson should take a closer look. Wait... he'll have trouble without any probable cause that something is fishy. Maybe I can visit more and see what's going on. Can't say I don't fully believe him, but he did seem concerned about Mary Jane.*

The ringing of her cell phone jarred her back to the present. She pulled it out of the side pocket of her backpack on the seat next to her. She looked at the screen. Andy was calling. "Hi, tiger. Did you find out anything about the jaguar?"

"Good morning, doll. Boy, did I."

Virginia tightened her grip on the phone. "Well? What did your people find?"

"Where are you?"

"Where am I? Why?"

Andy's voice sounded excited. "It's almost lunch time. How about meeting me for lunch? BJ's in Round Rock? Okay?"

"Yeah. Can't you tell me what they found over the phone?"

"Yes, but I want you sitting down and not driving when I tell you, and I'm getting hungry."

"Aren't you teaching?"

Andy's chair squeaked. "My next class is at three. Lunch?"

"Okay, what time?"

"How about noon?"

"See you then. I can't wait to hear the results." Virginia hung up and put the phone back. *He's excited about something. He knows how I am. Now I'll go nuts until I get to BJ's.* She looked at the clock on the dash. *It's ten-thirty now. I'll just have time to drop the quilt off at my office and lock it up* and *meet Andy. Better try to avoid Dr. Doverspike because he'll want a blow-by-blow update. After I lock this up, I can head for the restaurant. What's Andy got? Why's he so excited?* She turned on Austin Ave. and headed for the museum.

Virginia sat in the lobby of the restaurant waiting and rubbing the strap of her backpack when Andy came through the rotating center door. She stood as he approached and kissed his cheek. "Hi. You've made me a wreck waiting for your results. Can you tell me now?" She glanced at the burnt orange University of Texas messenger bag hanging from his shoulder. "Is the jaguar in there?"

"Yes. Let's get a booth, and I'll tell you what the guys at the university found."

They were seated in a booth in the middle of the restaurant. After ordering, Andy pulled the jaguar out of the messenger bag. "Here, take a good look at the little guy."

Virginia placed her hand on Andy's. "Leave it in the bag. Those men who just got in the booth over there are watching our every move."

CHAPTER 9

Andy slid the jade jaguar back into his messenger bag then glanced slightly over his shoulder at the two men in the booth across the aisle. "I see them. They look like businessmen and now aren't paying us any attention. Maybe you're getting a little paranoid."

"Better paranoid than dead." Virginia looked up at the waitress who stepped to their table, and she ordered iced tea for her and Andy. "Okay, what did the chemists tell you?"

Andy leaned forward. "As I told you before, I had an analytical chemist and a geochemist look at it. The little guy is rare. The particular jade it's made out of is from a source in the Yucatan right near Belize and Guatemala."

"They know this for sure?" She rubbed her chin. "How?"

"The chemical makeup and the way light behaves when you look at it. It's very rare, and worth a fortune."

"Good. It is making a little more sense. I wish I knew where the gold came from."

"Do you have a sample? I could get the boys to do their magic again." He looked up. "Here comes the waitress with our drinks, shall we order while she's here?"

After finishing their lunch, Virginia showed Andy the picture she took of Professor Pine's gold bar and the figure on the top.

He stared at the image. "That looks pretty shiny. What's that symbol on top?"

"That's *Balam*."

Andy frowned. "Who's he?"

"Haven't a clue except it's a Mayan glyph for the jaguar. To make matters worse, the gold is too pure for when the Mayan's refined gold ores. At least that's what I've been told. But it seems to be old, and that figure looks

Mayan."

Andy sat back. "Could it be some sort of smuggling operation and they used the Mayan guy, orjaguar... *Balam*, to identify their gold?"

Virginia clicked off the image and slid her phone back into her pocket. "I was thinking the same thing. From what Professor Pine said, where it was stored on Mary Jane's ranch, it was there for a long time. About a hundred and fifty or sixty years."

"Cool. Old smuggled gold. If you can get a bar, I'll have the chemists look at it. Maybe they'll have some insight."

Virginia's phone rang. She yanked it out of her pocket and answered. "This is Virginia."

"Virginia, it's Mary Jane. I was thinking about going to the ranch and wanted to clear it with you."

"When?"

"Tomorrow morning if possible."

Virginia smiled. "Tell you what, I'll go with you. I need a favor while we're there."

"Sure. What do you need?"

"One of those gold bars to have analyzed."

"Oh. No problem. Stop by here when you get a chance. I have a couple here at my house."

"You do?" She scribbled on a napkin that Mary Jane had a bar and shoved it across the table to Andy.

"Yes. The remaining ones are in a bank vault in a safety deposit box."

"Mary Jane you are a dear. May my husband and I stop by soon?"

"Of course, dear. I'll make some fresh iced tea."

Virginia stuck the phone back in her pocket and looked at Andy. "You paid the bill yet?"

"She's coming back with the card and bill now."

Virginia took Andy's messenger bag with the jaguar, gave him directions to Mary Jane's house, and started to slowly walk toward her car. She pretended to answer her phone as she watched the restaurant's doorway. The two men who were sitting near her and Andy emerged and looked at Andy, going in the opposite direction to his car as Virginia. As she slipped into her car, she watched the men get into a black Buick, pull out, and start to follow her. *Not very subtle guys.*

Virginia drove down the I35 north frontage road and onto the freeway, making sure the Buick could follow a few cars behind. She speed-dialed Detective Wilkinson. "I've got a late model, black Buick, with two men in suits following me north on I35." She gave him the car's license number. "We just entered Georgetown City limits. Can you send a welcoming party?"

"*Hello* to you too. Got anything else you'd like me to do?"

"Just that I know where the jade jaguar came from and will hopefully have a location and a story for the gold bars soon. I can also fill you in more on my visits with Mary Jane's cousin and the good Doctor Pine. But, about the car following me… how about a little help first?"

Wilkinson said something Virginia could barely hear to someone, then spoke to her. "There is a state trooper coming up behind you shortly. Where are you going?"

"To Mary Jane's house to get a sample of a gold bar for Andy to have analyzed. After that, I'll go to my museum to inspect the quilt better and lock it up along with the jade jaguar."

"Okay. Call me when you're at the museum. I'll come by."

Virginia shifted in her seat. "I can come to the station to see you."

"Yeah, but this gives me a reason to get out and away from paperwork for a while."

"I get it. Okay, I'll call you." She looked in her rearview mirror. A state police cruiser was pulling the Buick over. "Looks like the state cops are taking care of my tail, thanks for the help… again. I owe you."

"More than one. Don't worry, I'll collect." He hung up.

Virginia pulled up in Mary Jane's driveway behind Andy's gray Honda Odyssey. He was leaning against it waiting for her.

She got out of her car, locked the door, and stepped toward him. "How'd you get here before me?"

"I went out a different exit from the parking lot ahead of you. I just got here."

Virginia touched Andy's arm. "Remember those two men in the restaurant?"

"Yeah."

"I think they tried to follow me. I had the police send a trooper to stop them so I could get away from them."

"Are you okay? Who are they? Were they really following you?"

"I'm fine. I don't know who they are yet. Wilkinson will call when he gets the information from the state troopers. Shall we go see the gold brick?"

Virginia led Andy up onto the porch and rang the doorbell. Mary Jane answered and ushered them into the living room.

She motioned for them to take seats. "Please sit. I have iced tea for you and under that cloth is a gold bar. You wanted."

Virginia and Andy sat and sipped their tea. Andy put his glass down, lifted the pale blue cloth, and looked at the gold bar. He picked it up. "Looks pretty. The figure of… what it called again?"

Virginia looked over her glass of tea. "*Balam*. It's a symbol for the jaguar."

Andy nodded. "Right, the jaguar, like the little guy I had analyzed at the university?"

"Yes, but probably the real kind."

"Okay, a raised figure like this means a mold was used." He held it close to his eyes and slowly rotated it. "From the looks of it, the mold was metal. No surprise there. It was crudely formed."

Virginia set the glass down. "How can you tell how the mold was made?"

"Because whoever did it did not have machining capability like today or even in the early nineteen hundreds. The mold was made by hand, I think. But I'll have some experts look at it and do an analysis of it."

Mary Jane wrung her hands, "Will it destroy the gold bar?"

"No. You probably won't notice where we'll take the small samples."

"Oh, good." Mary Jane swallowed. "When will you know something?"

Andy put down the gold bar and took a sip of tea. "Maybe, in a couple days. You and Virginia are going to your ranch tomorrow. Right?"

"Yes, Doctor Clark. I need to do a few things out there, and Virginia said she wants to look around."

"Okay." He rose. "If you ladies don't mind, I'll take this bar to the university now and get the ball rolling."

Virginia stood and kissed him on his cheek. "Be careful, dear. I'll see you tonight." She watched Andy leave then turned to Mary Jane. "Andy found out that the jade jaguar is from the Yucatan, Belize, and Guatemala area and is a rare form of jade specifically from that area."

"Will that help us?"

"It's just another piece of data right now, but things will start adding up shortly I hope."

Mary Jane sat up straighter. "I almost forgot to mention this. My cousin John Pennington called just before you got here. He was concerned about me and said if I need anything, please call him. He was upset that I was hurt. We've been cordial for years, but I never knew he cared about me. It's nice to know he cares."

"That's great. He is family after all." Virginia's phone rang. "Hello?"

"Wilkinson. About your buddies tailing you."

"Who are they?"

"According to the trooper, just some businessmen out for lunch."

"You believe them?"

"Don't have any reason not to. Their IDs check out, and they have no previous records. And, they aren't wanted anywhere. One of the men said he thought he recognized you from the museum, but wasn't sure. His daughter was in a summer camp there last year. Anyway, the trooper held them long enough for you to get away. We have their information and photos, so if they reappear, we can do more than say hello and keep your speed down."

"Okay. Thanks for backing me up. Probably just nerves."

"No problem."

"I'm heading to the museum shortly. Coming by?"

"You bet. See you in a while." He hung up.

At the museum, Virginia locked the jaguar in a safe in the storage area and set the folded quilt on a large worktable in a laboratory just off her office. She adjusted the lighting, pulled out a magnifier, and carefully started to examine the quilt. After working her way down the right side, she started at the top again and down the center when the phone on the desk rang. Virginia hurried to it and answered. "Hello?"

"Virginia," said the volunteer receptionist, "there's a policeman here in the lobby to see you. His card says, Detective Wilkinson, Georgetown Police."

"Send him to the fabrics and special projects lab."

"Did we do something wrong? Is there a problem from the other day when that lady was hurt?"

Virginia smiled. "No Joan, it's okay. We're helping the police."

"We are? Oh. Okay. I'll send him to the lab right away."

Virginia straightened up the tools she was using just as the door opened, and Wilkinson walked in.

He moved to the edge of the table and looked at the quilt. "So this is the big mystery. Is the quilt really a treasure map?"

"Treasure map, maybe. It does look like a map of some kind. There's definitely a story here and because of Leo, I may have found another clue."

CHAPTER 10

Wilkinson looked up at Virginia. “Who’s Leo, one of your colleagues here at the museum?”

She shook her head. “No. He’s my cat.”

“Your cat?” He gave her a wide-eyed expression. “He’s helping you… us? Did you take any drugs lately?Eat any funny mushrooms?”

“No.” Virginia gave him an indignant look. “I’m not taking any drugs and definitely no funny mushrooms. And, Leo has been very helpful in the past. Usually by accident, though.”

“I hope so. Okay, I know I’m going to be sorry I asked this. Just exactly how did your cat help out?”

Virginia pulled up a wooden lab stool with a back and sat. He pointed to another one. “Have a seat and I’ll tell you.” She watched as he removed his sport coat, hung it over the back of the stool, and sat. “Last night, I was in my quilt room just before going to bed. I was rearranging some quilt blocks for a project I’m working on when Leo came in. He picked up loose threads and small bits of fabric from the floor and deposited them on my worktable.”

“Okay, you’ve got a fastidious cat.”

“Yes, Leo is that. But, when he marched across a pattern that was on the worktable near him, he turned one edge. The folded paper had a whole new image. I decided to use the new idea for a quilt, when I finish the two quilts I’m working on.”

“And your new quilt idea helps us how? Did your fuzzy Sherlock point anything else out?”

“Take a look.” Virginia pointed to the quilt on the worktable. “I’ve been folding it in different ways and then… a new image appeared.”

Wilkinson looked at the folded quilt. “What am I looking at?”

“It may be a map. There are threads and lines in the cloth of the folded blocks that may be map features.

Wilkinson frowned. “Any idea what it means?”

“Not yet.”

"So what do we know at this juncture?"

"From what I've been able to piece together so far, Mary Jane's uncle inherited the old ranch. It's been in his family since the late eighteen-fifties. There was a vault of sorts under the floor of an old shed that contained bars of gold. The gold was supposedly brought to Texas from an area in Central America. I haven't got confirmation about that yet. But I know where the jade jaguar came from."

"Good. Where?"

"The little jaguar figurine we found is made of a form of jade that only comes from an area around the Yucatan in Mexico, Belize, and Guatemala, and it is said to have come with the gold."

"Interesting. What's the tie-in between the gold and the jade jaguar?"

"I don't know."

Wilkinson bit his lip. "And, back to the folded quilt here, what more can it tell you?"

"Maybe, exactly where all the gold and the jaguar came from. I just found the new image when you came. Maybe, the quilt will tell me more soon." She pointed. "Look. This quilt is a sort of map and story about it all. There are connections to the Civil War as well. I'm working on what this quilt is trying to tell us. As you know, related to all this we have the following; after Mary Jane's uncle died, his estate gave some money and gold bars to her two living relatives and a cranky old professor at the university. Recently, there has also been a private eye who is working for someone on this matter, a murder, a couple attempted murders, and they are all somehow related to this quilt."

"Have you talked to the teacher relative of Mary Jane's yet?"

"Barbara Dorian. No. But, she's high on my to-do list."

"Okay." Wilkinson sat staring at the quilt. "That was quite a lot. Do you know when the gold got to the ranch?"

Virginia picked up a piece of yellow legal paper and looked at the writing. "According to my intern, it may have come to the ranch during the Civil War. He's looking for more details. I'll call you with whatever he finds." She set the paper on the quilt. "The quilt here is old. I'd place it at being made in the eighteen sixties or so. It also displays some images from that time and the Civil War."

Wilkinson rose and stretched. "How old is the jade jaguar?"

Virginia shrugged her shoulders. "Don't know."

"You mentioned the gold bars, what about them?"

"Andy's got some chemists and geology professors looking at the gold now. Maybe that will give us more answers."

"How's all this going to get us closer to the killer?"

"As I see it, after Mary Jane's uncle died, the killer somehow found out about the gold, the jaguar, and the quilt. Like I said, there's been a lot of interest in this quilt. Why would there be so much interest if it weren't something in it of significant value? Whatever it is, it's worth killing over."

"Okay. So how do you want to proceed in flushing him or her out?"

"I figure the killer is looking for something valuable. So if I can figure out what it is, and where it is, we can use that to draw the killer out, and we've got him."

Wilkinson leaned against the wall. "What's next?"

Virginia looked up at him. "I'm studying the quilt the rest of today. Tomorrow I'm going to the ranch with Mary Jane to look around more. Maybe there's something else we can find. If I have time tomorrow, I'll contact Barbara Dorian. Perhaps by then, Andy will have some answers about the gold. Then, we can possibly put together a more detailed plan. For now, let's learn what we can, find whatever it is the killer wants, find the killer, and don't get killed doing it."

Wilkinson frowned. "That's the plan?"

"You got a better one?"

"I think it could use a little more detail. Right now, it sounds like we're going to wing it."

Virginia leaned forward, rested her elbows on the table, and her head on her palms. "I'm all ears, Detective."

Wilkinson wet his lips then ran his fingers through his thinning hair. "Maybe you should ask your cat."

Virginia stood and smiled. "Good idea. I'll do that tonight. In the meantime, what exactly are you and the other boys and girls in blue doing with this case?"

"Trying to assist you and help prevent you from being a murder statistic."

"*Touché*." Virginia smiled. "Want to come with Mary Jane and me to the ranch tomorrow?"

"I'd love to, but, unfortunately, I have a budget meeting. So, please don't get killed or shoot anyone, okay?"

"I'll do my best. I need to get back to this quilt. I'll call you if and when I get anything."

Wilkinson nodded. "Good. Be careful, Virginia. Someone isn't afraid to kill for whatever you're after." He picked up his jacket and left the lab.

CHAPTER 11

After Wilkinson left, Virginia returned to her inspection of the quilt. She moved the magnifying lamp and studied the fabric and threads used in the quilting. "What's this?" Using tweezers, she pulled a short piece of gold thread from the folded area of the quilt, which looked like a map of the areas of interest in Central America. She held the thread closer to her eyes. "What the hell? This is too stiff to be thread." She placed it in a small sample envelope, labeled it, and set it aside. In the next ten minutes, she removed four more threads along with some white powdery substance. "This is interesting." Next, she took photos of the new image formed by folding the quilt.

Virginia sat back on the lab stool and stretched. She folded the quilt and took everything to her office. She placed the quilt in her safe along with the jaguar. Downloading the digital pictures to her computer, she forwarded them to a scientist in another department who had done some fieldwork in Central America. She returned to her desk and called Andy.

Andy answered his office phone on the second ring. "Hi, beautiful, how's your afternoon going?"

"Good. I have a couple more little samples for your chemists to look at if you don't mind."

"Yeah, no problem. Oh, did you find out who was so interested in us at the restaurant? Bad guys?"

Virginia chuckled. "Not exactly. They were just businessmen. One has a daughter who went to a camp here at the museum and he thought he recognized me. Nothing sinister."

"That's a relief."

"You're right about that."

She heard Andy type something on his computer.

"I've got some news already about that little gold bar you gave me."

"That was fast." She settled back into her chair. "What about it?"

"The chemists stumbled on some interesting things."

Excitement filled her. "What did they find?"

"First, the gold was pretty well refined by someone. Somewhat better than expected." Andy cleared his throat. "That is, it was refined once and made into something. Sometime later it was remelted and cast into the little bars."

"They did that in Mexico?"

"Mexico or somewhere down there. Remember I said what they used for a mold was unique?"

"Yeah." She picked up a plastic bottle of water and took a sip.

"Well, the mold was supposed to look like it was made crudely by unsophisticated people. But it was fabricated with the funny angles that made the gold look like it was cast into old, crude molds. The facets were too well made to be have been forged by indigent people. Whoever made it knew what they were doing and had the tools to do it. That or the ancient people knew more about smelting than we thought."

"Why would someone do that?"

"Probably to hide their true origin or intentions would be my guess."

"I think I agree. Where did the gold come from and how old is it?"

"The gold's a few billion years old. Gold is gold my dear; it doesn't age. However, what the chemists did find were a few impurities left in the gold, and some stuff left from the mold. The gold bar originated in the same area as the jaguar."

Her chair squeaked as she straightened up. "It did?"

"Yeah."

Virginia sat for a second thinking. "How'd they come to those conclusions? I mean, how did they find the small amount of materials to give them that answer?"

"Mass spectroscopy, a little X-ray fluorescence analysis, some wavelength dispersive X-ray fluorescence spectrometry thrown in, and a scanning electron microscope. They analyzed the gold, the impurities, and some foreign matter on one side."

"If you say so. Any guess as to when all this was done?"

"The recasting was in the late eighteen-fifties to early eighteen-sixties. They found some other stuff in the jaguar shape, *Balam*, or whatever his name is, on top. That was a giveaway. The little figure was added after the bar was formed. There were still some markings on it."

"Added after the bar was formed? Why?" Virginia frowned.

"Don't know. Maybe, to identify them as from a certain person or group, or maybe from a particular place."

She drank more water. "You mentioned markings. What markings? I don't remember seeing any."

"They used some very high power microscopes and the SEM."

"SEM?"

"Scanning electron microscope."

"Oh yeah." Virginia wrote on a notepad. "Do they know what the figure was before it was the figure?"

"Yes. It was made from gold coins that were melted down and cast onto the bars."

"Gold coins? Are they sure?"

"Yes."

"From where?"

"The one on the test gold bar was from an eighteen sixty-five gold coin. One of the history guys here said it was probably a *Maximiliano Emperador bullion* coin, made from twenty-two karat gold. The little figure on top of the gold bar is twenty-two karat gold.

"I'll be damned." She made more notes.

"There's more."

"More?" She gripped the phone tighter. "They haven't had the samples that long."

"They had some grad students helping."

"Okay, what else did they find?"

She heard Andy shuffle some papers. "Cocaine. Not the purest stuff, but it does have a definite signature, especially with Infrared spectroscopy. And guess what?"

"It's from Central America."

"Bingo. And they also found it on that jade jaguar. They just informed me of that. They said the data from their earlier tests on the jade jaguar showed not just cocaine dust, but a substance they can't identify."

She took another sip of the water. "They can't ID the new substance even with all their spectroscopes or whatever they are?"

"No. They know its composition, but not what it is, exactly, or what it does. That, my dear, is a mystery. They need a bigger sample."

"Wow." She swept some blond hairs from her face. "Okay. Thank you. Thank the chemists for me, too. That's a lot to digest. I'll see you tonight at home, and I have the new samples for you. We can discuss this more. Maybe with all this we can piece something together."

"Okay. I'll bring you their report." He disconnected.

Virginia collapsed back into her leather chair and took a deep breath. Her phone rang. *Now, what?* "Virginia here."

"Hi, Virginia. This is Terry Sorenson. It's about your pictures from the quilt."

Virginia twisted in her chair. "Dr. Sorenson, You've got something already? I wasn't sure exactly what I photographed. It looked like a map to me."

"It's a map all right. It's a map of part of Central America. But, it shows some physical shapes in an area where there have never been any detected. If I read it right, there might be rivers we didn't know existed. Maybe they don't anymore. I called up some satellite images of the area, and with careful examination and, now, knowing what to look for, there may be something there. Something ancient. The satellite images also show what may have been some sort of more recent activity. And, this may have something to do with some old legends."

"Legends?" Virginia felt her heart race. "Can you come to my office?"

"You buying the coffee?"

"Yes."

"I'll gather up the maps, your pictures, and the satellite images, some literature, and be right there."

Virginia moved to her conference table and set the carafe of coffee on it. She sat on a side chair when Dr. Terry Sorenson knocked on the doorframe and entered.

Dr. Sorenson placed a stack of papers and photographs on the table and plopped onto a leather captain's chair next to Virginia. Terry tugged her auburn ponytail tighter. She quickly spread out the maps, satellite images, and photographs, and placed Virginia's quilt pictures above them. She waved her hand above the photographs and maps. "If you look at your pictures of the quilt and turn them as I have them here, you'll notice a very strong resemblance to these maps. But if you take a closer look," Sorenson pointed to an enlargement of Virginia's quilt picture, "you'll see what appears to be larger threads that may depict rivers. The threads are blue, and the surrounding areas are not. By comparing these blue threads to the maps, you'll notice that a number of them are actually rivers, but some don't show on the maps. Then, there are the gold threads. These are in just one area of the quilt picture. If you look carefully, there seem to be some buildings there that aren't on any maps. Even the satellite pictures don't directly show them." Sorenson picked up a satellite picture and pointed to an area she had circled with a Sharpie. "There may be something there. You may have found some ancient ruins never before seen. That would be a great discovery for the museum." Sorenson poured herself a cup of coffee and sipped it.

Virginia studied the maps, photographs, and satellite images. She pointed to a couple of the satellite pictures. "On these I see some things you can't see in the aerial photographs. I noticed the appearance of something shown on the quilt and not on any maps, but didn't know what it meant. Maybe you're right about some ancient ruins. We'd have to go there to find out." She pointed. "These look like roads."

Terry Sorenson brushed a strand of hair from her eyes and smiled. "You are very observant. Yes, I'd say you've stumbled onto something. May I ask what this quilt's history is and why it has this information on it?" She swallowed more coffee.

Virginia sat back. "It's owned by a friend and fellow quilter. She inherited it and a ranch. Since then, there's been a murder, some attempted murders, and a lot of interest in it. Why all the sudden interest in the mystery?"

"I may be able to stir up some more muck for you. There are some stories, more mythology or folklore if you will, about some events back in history involving this area in Texas and the locale depicted on the quilt."

Virginia poured a cup of coffee and drank some. "Okay, go ahead. Things can't get murkier than they presently are."

"There are old stories in some families around here that talk about a rancher who, during the Civil War, became mysteriously well to do. He'd disappear for a long stretch of time, then, come back and settle any debts, buy more land, or cattle. The stories vary. But, he's also been linked to funding some of the needs of the Confederate Soldiers from here, including taking care of their families while they were off doing their thing."

Virginia scribbled notes. "Anything else suspicious?"

"Yeah. Rumor has it he supposedly paid for things with gold. Gold bars."

"Was there anything unusual about the gold bars?"

"Yes, but for the life of me I can't recall what it was."

"Anything else in the stories about this rancher with the gold?"

"Well," Sorenson finished her coffee. "There were stories about some sort of strange substance being used hereabout in those days. The stories differ, but it's said the substance was a painkiller or a hallucinogenic, and it had some other uses, most of them not good. The church women said it was Diablo powder."

"Did the Diablo powder have anything to do with this mysterious rancher?"

Terry chuckled. "Maybe. Who knows for sure?"

"Who was this mysterious rancher?"

"I don't know for certain. I've heard a lot of names, but one does come up the most when these stories are told."

"Who?"

"Dillan. He owned a ranch around here someplace. Haven't heard much about him for a very long time. Died in the eighteen-sixties. Now the stories are just folklore."

Virginia started to cough. "Sorry." *Mary Jane's Great, great, grandfather?* "Any idea where he got the gold?"

"No. But one story says he found a place where there was gold in caves or lost buildings or something like that. For a while, people thought maybe he had found El Dorado, and it was around here. After the Civil War, there were a few men who actually looked for it but obviously didn't find anything. But, men were killed trying to find it. Of course, we know El Dorado's pure fiction. Anyway, there isn't any natural gold in Central Texas that I know of."

Virginia stopped writing and drained her coffee cup. She looked at Terry. "Don't bet on it."

CHAPTER 12

"What do you mean?" Terry Sorenson sat back. "Gold in Central Texas?"

Virginia rubbed the bridge of her nose. "Natural gold? There probably isn't any. Hidden gold? Maybe more than we think."

"Does this hidden Texas gold have anything to do with the quilt?"

"I think so. That and something weird in Central America."

"A quilt, gold, a map, and Central America? I don't understand."

Virginia chuckled. "You left off a special form of jade."

"Huh?" Terry gave Virginia a blank expression.

"Here's the story in a nutshell." Virginia went over what she knew about the quilt, the analysis of the gold and the jaguar Andy had provided. Sorenson listened intently as Virginia described the murder, attempted murders, and the inheritances. "Someone is all of a sudden very interested in what the quilt has to say," Virginia said.

Terry looked around. "Where are the quilt and the jaguar figurine? In the lab?"

"No. In my safe."

"Can I see them?" Sorenson fidgeted with the top button of her tan blouse. "The only mysteries I've been involved with were Nancy Drew or Sherlock Holmes."

"Sure." Virginia opened her safe and pulled out the quilt and jaguar. She put them on the conference table. "Here's the jade jaguar. He's made of a type of jade that is only found in the region where Mexico, Guatemala, and Belize come together."

Terry picked up the jaguar and examined it. "It's really nice. Well sculpted. I think it was originally used as an idol or in some Mayan ritual. There are others like this in museums. A find like this is rare and valuable. It could be a key to something as well."

"You think so?" Virginia rubbed her nose. "It isn't very big."

"No, it isn't. But it's too good for a peasant. It would be made for a high priest or big official. The jaguars were also used as guardians. This little guy could be a clue for something big."

"Since you're on a roll, here's the quilt." Virginia spread it out on the table. "Have a look."

Terry pulled on a pair of white cotton gloves from her lab coat pocket, rose, and examined the quilt. "I see where you folded it to get the map we were discussing. Have you tried folding it in other ways?"

"Yeah. Got nothing. At least I don't think I did."

"How about the back?"

Virginia shook her head. "Not much to see, really. But, let's turn it over and take a look."

With Terry's help, she turned the quilt over and stared at it. Terry spoke first. "Looks like some Confederate images and a couple of Texas ones. But..." She pointed to a block near the bottom. "That looks incomplete."

Virginia studied it. "No, the cloth that block is made from has a pattern from a feed sack on it. I think the person who made this used it because it has a symbol of the Eagle on it."

"Why's that important? I mean why would someone use the eagle, especially in Texas during the middle eighteen hundreds? Is there a snake?"

Virginia looked at the quilt. "No snake. Let's turn it over again."

After turning it and smoothing out the wrinkles, Terry and Virginia continued to look at the quilt. Virginia straightened. "My back is sore. You see anything?"

"No. Maybe we should put all this back in your safe and call it a day. We can get on with our mystery tomorrow."

Virginia tilted her head. "Our mystery?"

"Yes. You work, part time, for the Smithsonian Central Security Service. You get all the excitement; at least that's what Dr. Doverspike, our beloved director, and chronicler of the 'Virginia Adventures' says. I've read about your exploits. I want to be part of it. Plus, I'm an expert on Mesoamerican history, civilizations, and archaeology. You could use me."

"You're right." Virginia nodded. "I could use you." She returned to her leather desk chair and watched Terry sit in a chair in front of her desk. "You know this could be dangerous."

"I know. I need some danger." Terry sighed. "My life gets boring."

"How about your boyfriend? What will he say?"

"Trust me; he's not your husband. Your husband is cool. My boyfriend's a stick in the mud lately and is always trying to change me. I need something different. I'm thinking of a big change that doesn't include him." Terry leaned forward. "You could use me, and I really need this."

Virginia chuckled. "Well, I've got a cop who's involved, and my husband, but he really can't take time away from the university right now to help. So, if Dr. Doverspike says it's okay, then, I would welcome the assistance."

Terry sat up straighter and grinned. "He already has."

"He has?" Virginia gave her a quizzical look. "Really? When?"

"Before I talked to you on the phone. Dr. Doverspike said if I could get you to say yes, then, he has no objection. He said I sounded just like you."

She's spunky. I like her even more now. Virginia laughed. "He would say that. Okay. When can you start?"

"I already have. What do we do next?"

"For starters, we lock everything in the safe. I'll call Detective Wilkinson today and tell him you've joined the investigation. Then, I'll need to contact the Smithsonian as well and inform them about you. Tomorrow morning, I'll pick you up here at the museum, and we'll go to Mary Jane's ranch for a look around."

Terry grinned. "Okay. But what are we looking for at the ranch?"

"I'm not sure, but we'll start with the overall layout. Then, we'll look at where the gold was stored and see what we find. Maybe there will be something that leads us further."

Virginia stopped her car in front of the museum. She eyed Terry Sorenson as she slid her tall frame into the front passenger seat of Virginia's Toyota Camry and buckled her seatbelt. "Nice outfit. You look like you're going on a safari."

"I wanted to dress appropriately, especially since I'm meeting your detective and Miss Mary Jane Striker for the first time."

"Yeah, well I'm sure you are dressed fine for Mary Jane. With those tan shorts and that top, I'm positive Detective Wilkinson will approve of you." Virginia chuckled. "Now he may want a more hands-on approach." She looked at Terry's backpack. "I see you brought a backpack."

"Yes," Terry nodded. "It holds a lot and after all, you use them all the time." She looked out the window. "How long until we get to the ranch?"

"About an hour and a half. Here, I brought the reports from the university Andy gave me last night. You might want to read them. There may be something in there I missed."

Terry took the folder. "I assume the Smithsonian didn't have a problem with me being involved with this investigation."

"No. No problem. Your work is well known there. Wilkinson agreed too, especially after he ran you through their databases, and you're not a crook, you're good looking, and I wanted you along. He will probably find an excuse to come to the ranch and meet you instead of us going to the police station."

Terry frowned. "You've mentioned this Detective Wilkinson a few times. What's he like? A young guy who thinks every cute girl is a conquest?"

"No. He's really nice, and he's a dedicated police officer. He's fifty something, married with two kids in college. He's a good guy."

"Oh. Okay. If you like him, I'm sure I will. I guess I should get to work." Terry settled back and started to examine the reports from the university. She quickly glanced at Virginia. "Thank you for letting me do this."

"No problem. I can really use another set of eyes and hands on this. Especially someone with your expertise."

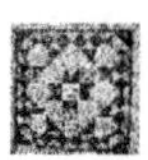

Virginia parked the car on some pea gravel in the shade under a large oak. She got out and walked toward the ranch house with Terry.

As they approached, the front door opened and Mary Jane, dressed in jeans and a red blouse, walked out onto the wraparound porch. "Hi, Virginia. Who's your friend?"

Virginia introduced them and told Mary Jane about wanting to walk around the ranch and inspect the underground area the gold was stored in. Virginia gave her a short version of the latest developments in the case.

Mary Jane nodded as Virginia talked, then smiled. "You two ladies are free to wander around all you like. Who knows, maybe you'll find something else exciting. When you're done, come on by… I'll have some iced tea in the fridge for y'all."

Virginia led Terry to the red barn. They swung open the huge doors and walked inside. It was cooler inside with beams of light streaming from window high overhead. The floor was concrete, and the main area was unstained and swept. The stalls and areas to the right had traces of hay while the part where the tractor and other machines were standing was spotless. Around the perimeter was a second floor that looked down on the central area. A staircase on the left went up. There was a large area on the second level at the back of the barn with a lift.

Virginia walked to a large, red tractor and ran her hand across the engine cover. "The farm equipment looks pretty clean."

Terry nodded. "Yeah, real clean. Does she use it?"

"I don't know if she does, or maybe someone who works the ranch for her. But whomever it is, they keep a pretty neat shop." Virginia scanned the interior. "Looks pretty normal to me, but I'm not a farm girl."

"If there is anything unusual, it'll be under the floor, or there may be a secret room. The concrete floor looks intact. I think we should do some measuring."

Virginia nodded. "You're right. Did you bring a measuring tape?"

"Yeah. I've got a laser range finder. It's standard equipment for an archaeologist. Grab that board and let's go measure the outside dimensions."

Virginia picked up a piece of plywood and followed Terry outside. Setting the board at the corners of the barn, Terry got the lengths of all the sides. Then, they went back inside and re-measured the walls. They compared the dimensions.

Terry sighed. "Okay, taking into consideration the thickness of the walls and supports, there are no hidden rooms that I can see."

"Yeah, and I looked at the floor again. The concrete doesn't show anything that looks like a door or newer concrete. I think the barn is exactly what it seems." They walked outside.

"I agree." Terry looked around. "Where is the shed with the trap door and the gold vault?"

"On the other side of the tree line just past the stable." Virginia led the way toward the shed.

Reaching the long, low, white, wooden building, Terry walked around it and examined the construction. "This building has been refurbished within the past year or so. But some of the original wood and building materials are still here."

Virginia looked at the shed. "I figured it had to be well maintained to be here for well over a hundred years. Some of the original materials are still there?"

"Yes." Terry pointed to a few beams. "These looklike old oak. They're probably as hard a steel now."

"You know a lot about building materials."

"I grew up in New York City. Some of the old buildings had used oak in the construction. It aged and became as hard as steel. Driving a nail in it was almost impossible. This looks the same."

Virginia grinned. "I didn't know you were from New York. I had an uncle who lived in Rochester."

"Where are you from? Texas?"

"No. Sothern California. Orange County to be more specific."

"Oh." Terry's eyebrow rose. "So. Cal. You a surfer?"

"No. I'm a diver, but no surfing for me."

"Shall we go in?" Terry opened the door and stepped inside. "It looks like it's had a number of uses."

"From what Mary Jane said, it's been a tool shed, a potting barn, and a storage building." Virginia walked down the center of the shed and stopped. She pointed to a hole with a trap door raised. Down there is where the gold was found." Not hearing anything, she turned around. Terry was off to one side examining something on a workbench. She hurried to Terry and looked at what she was doing."

Terry looked up and set her magnifying glass down. "This is interesting."

"What?"

"These are some ruminates of Aconitum delphiniifolum."

Virginia stooped and looked at it. “What’s Aconitum delphin… delphinioform, or what you said?”

“Aconitum delphiniifolum is also called Larkspur-leaf monkshood.”

“Wolfsbane.”

“Yes. Didn’t you say Mary Jane was hospitalized by Wolfsbane?”

“Yep.” Virginia frowned. “I didn’t think it grew in Texas.”

“Normally, Texas isn’t known for growing it, but some does grow in Southeast Texas and in hot houses. There are medical uses for it.”

“Interesting. Let’s see what else is here. Shall we take a look at the underground gold repository?’

“You bet.”

They proceeded to the open trap door and climbed down the wooden ladder to the dirt floor. On a post near them was a light switch. Virginia turned it on. A series of overhead light bulbs attached to a cord that ran the twenty-foot length of the cave came on. There were large, round, wood posts supporting massive beams holding up the plank roof. The room smelled of damp dirt and old rotting wood. Virginia knelt and examined the floor. “You can see the indentations in the dirt where the gold bricks were stacked.”

Terry knelt beside her. “I see. Why weren’t they on some kind of pallet?”

“Probably because they couldn’t get large ones down here.” They rose and stepped further into the cave. Virginia stopped. “Looks like the storage of the bars stopped about here. I wonder what the rest of this place used for?”

Terry moved down to the end looking at the floor. “Whatever it was, they used boxes to store it.”

They walked down the tunnel and stopped at a wooden wall at the end with huge beams on each side.

Terry touched the wall. “Looks like the end of the line. There’s dirt between some of the boards.”

Virginia looked around then up at the ceiling. “Maybe not. Look.” She pointed at the roof. “Those planks go beyond the end of this wall.”

“Maybe they’re cut off.”

“Maybe. Let’s look for a secret door, or latch, or something.”

“Okay.” Terry looked around. “You’ve done this kind of thing before, haven’t you?”

“Yes. And hopefully, this time it’ll turn out better.” Virginia ran her hands over each vertical board.

Terry examined the support beams. “I don’t see anything.”

Virginia moved to the left side and pushed on a table set close to the end wall on a small rectangular wood floor. Nothing happened. “Well, it was worth a try.”

Terry then set to work pulling on another table and a cord hanging from the roof on the right side of the tunnel. Nothing. She turned and looked at Virginia. "I guess this is the end."

"Probably." Virginia sat in a chair on a small raised deck and leaned back. She gazed around, then frowned. "Terry, over by that cabinet on the wall there's a funny shaped knot in the wood. Try pressing it."

"Okay." Terry pressed on the knot.

CLICK.

A section of the wood end-wall popped back into a dark area beyond. Virginia smiled. "Sometimes sitting and thinking reveals the answer." She got to her feet and stepped to the doorway. "Got a flashlight?"

"Yeah, right here." Terry switched on an LED flashlight she pulled from her backpack. She shined the light into the room. "There's another switch over here." She reached inside and turned it on. The room lit up with six old fashion light bulbs hanging from cloth insulated power lines. "These lights are really old."

Terry and Virginia entered the space. There were workbenches, iron tools, what remained of some cloth and leather aprons.

Terry pointed. "That looks like an old iron crucible. Over there in the corner is an iron ladle. There's what looks like a small pile of coal in the corner."

"That's probably coke." Virginia pointed. "That's a hearth. And," she looked at the hood above it, "that's the vent. I don't remember seeing any pipes sticking out of the ground topside."

"Me either, but I wasn't looking. The hearth, the crucible, and ladle are old. They're rusty and," Terry ran her finger across the grimy surface, "pretty dirty. Haven't been used in years."

"That and lots of cobwebs and rodent droppings." Virginia looked at the dirt floor. "There hasn't been anyone in this part of this vault before us for a long time. The dirt hasn't been disturbed, except by small animals. The only human footprints, other than ours, are back where the gold was stacked."

"I agree." Terry moved toward a small box in the far corner and knelt. She pulled open the lid and peered inside. "Oh, my. Look what I found. Mexican gold coins."

Virginia walked to her and looked over her shoulder. "You're right. And they look really old."

Terry picked one up and examined it. "Should we take a few and examine them at the lab?"

"Yeah. I'll have Andy's chemists compare their make-up to what they found in the figure *Balam* on the gold bar. I'd be willing to bet they will be the same." Virginia stood thinking. She took a deep breath. "I think we need another talk with Mary Jane about her family."

Terry pocketed a couple coins and stood. “And the Aconitum delphinii-folum. What we saw up there is not that old.”

Virginia turned and headed for the doorway. “Now I know what some of the images on the quilt meant. They were the story of this operation and the map for this tunnel. It also shows how they got the gold from Mexico to here.”

Terry followed Virginia. “We also have an idea where in Central America the gold and that cute little jaguar in your safe came from. And, according to the quilt, we know there may be some ruins of historic value hidden in the jungle. We need to go see what’s there.”

“I agree. But there are drug cartels and a couple murders to think about.”

“Details.”

“Yes, details, and the Diablo powder.”

CHAPTER 13

Virginia and Terry climbed out of the vault, closed the trap door, and walked out of the shed.

As they made their way around the barn, Virginia suddenly stopped. "Looks like we have company."

Terry squinted in the sun. "Yes, but who? That isn't a police car. Didn't you say that detective you are working with might come out here?"

"Yes, but that's not his car. I guess we'll find out soon enough. Let's go see Mary Jane and her guest."

They hurried around the corral and across the yard to the front of the house. Terry waited at the porch steps as Virginia walked to the Ford and felt the hood.

"Still hot." She returned to Terry. A board on the steps squeaked as they walked up to the screen door and knocked. "Come in, ladies, I have some iced tea for you," Mary Jane's voice called from inside.

Virginia and Terry entered and walked to the sitting room. On the couch sat Professor William Pine. Virginia scowled. "Well, if it isn't the good professor. What brings you all the way out here?"

"Nice to see you too, Special Agent Clark." Pine slowly stood. "Who's your friend, another fed?"

"No. This is Doctor Terry Sorenson. She's working with me on the case. Terry, this is Professor Pine from the University."

"Oh yeah. The Professor who got a bundle of money… no… a lot of gold, and wasn't happy."

Pine turned and looked at Mary Jane. "I think we should continue our talk when we don't have nosy government types around."

"Don't let us interrupt your meeting. Pretend we're not here." Virginia moved to the coffee table, poured a glass of tea, and handed it to Terry. Then she poured one for herself, sat on a side chair, and watched Terry lower her five-foot ten-inch frame on an overstuffed armchair. "There, isn't this nice? A bunch of friends getting together."

Pine fumed. He set his empty glass on the table and nodded to Mary

Jane. "I'll call you later."

"Yes, Professor. Do that." She waved her hand toward the door. "You know the way out."

Pine hurriedly left.

Mary Jane took a deep breath and slowly let it out. She looked at Virginia and Terry. "Thank you. Your timing was perfect. That man is abominable."

"We didn't know he was coming. Virginia and I saw the car when we left the shed," Terry said.

Mary Jane sighed. "I didn't know he was planning a visit either."

Virginia sipped some tea then leaned forward. "This really isn't any of my business, but what did he want?"

"I asked for your help, so it is your business. He thinks there is more to the gold and my inheritance than I'm telling. He thinks he's entitled to some more of whatever it is I have."

"Why didn't you just throw him out?"

"He said he has something that implicates my uncle in drug trafficking. And, if he goes to the cops they'll confiscate everything, and he'll get some of it as a reward. But he's willing to keep quiet for more gold."

Terry set her empty glass down. "That's blackmail."

"I know, but I don't know what evidence he has. If he's right, I could lose everything." Mary Jane looked at Virginia, a tear slowly sliding down her cheek. "What can I do?"

"First we have some questions for you." Virginia sat back. "They may help with getting you out of this mess."

"Okay. What do you want to know?"

"Did you know about the gold and the vault before your uncle died?"

Mary Jane shook her head. "No."

"Do you know what Aconitum delphiniifolum is?" Terry asked.

Mary Jane gave Terry a quizzical look. "No."

"How about Monkshood?"

"Yes, that's a plant that grows in parts of Texas. There is some growing on part of the ranch way in the back."

Terry wet her lips. "It's also called Wolfsbane."

Mary Jane froze. Her eyes widened. "It is? That's what the doctor in the emergency room said someone tried to poison me with. Why do you ask?"

Virginia rubbed her hands together. "We found some in your shed."

"My… my shed? I know a little of it exists on the ranch, but I didn't know it's called wolf's… what did you call it?"

"Wolfsbane."

"Yes. I know it as Monkshood and the flowers are pretty. I haven't seen or cut any in years. With the droughts we've had, there isn't a lot of anything growing."

Virginia nodded. "Who has access to the shed?"

Mary Jane shrugged. "Anyone who's out here. It wasn't locked."

"Even with the gold in the room under the floor?"

"That's been there for over a century." Mary Jane laughed. "If you close the trap door, you can't see it, and it has a hidden lock. I've been in there an untold number of times before my uncle died and didn't know it existed."

"You've been down in the vault since it was disclosed to you. Right? To get the gold to a bank vault and distribute what went to the others."

"Yes. Once I learned about it and had directions, I found the vault and opened it. I've been down inside a few times. There isn't much to see."

Terry spoke up. "Who installed the lights?"

"I guess my uncle did. The cloth insulation is ancient. They were there when I found the vault. I replaced a few light bulbs." Mary Jane put her hand to her chest. "Didyou find anything else down there?"

Virginia took a sip of tea. "Yes. A smelter of sorts."

"Oh, my. A smelter?" Mary Jane poured some more tea into her glass and sipped it.

"More like a blacksmith's shop," Virginia said.

"A blacksmith's shop? How does that help? Does it tie into what you learned from the analysis of the gold bar I gave your husband or anything from the quilt?"

"Yes. The gold was probably forged in Central America, but the little figure on top was most likely done here at the ranch."

Mary Jane sipped more tea.

Virginia continued. "Also, the quilt is a map and a story. We've translated some of it. The map indicates a location near where parts of Mexico, Belize, and Guatemala come together, where there may be some still hidden ruins of a Mayan city or temples."

"And the jade jaguar?"

"From the same place. And, both the gold bar and the jaguar had traces of cocaine and some other compound the lab couldn't identify on them."

Mary Jane shuttered. She whispered, "Cocaine and Diablo powder."

Terry sat on the edge of her chair. "What exactly is Diablo powder?"

"I don't know for sure. According to stories around here, these stories were considered more folklore than real, but there is sometimes a nugget of truth behind myths. Anyway, there were some people who had a substance that caused hallucinations, and the complete control over the individual who it. They could be made to do bad things. The stories say some people turned into animals, Zombies, but you know how things get blown out of proportion."

"I see." Virginia arched her back and stretched. "That may be actually more truth than you know."

"There is?" Mary Jane swallowed. "What do we do next?"

Terry leaned forward. "Do the stories tell of someone named Dillan? Does that name ring a bell?"

Mary Jane rose and moved to the fireplace, took down an old photograph, handed it to Terry and sat. "Dillan is my great, great, great grandfather's name. He lived here. This was his ranch? Why?"

"The name is associated with an old legend."

"About the gold during the Civil War and the Diablo powder. Right?"

"Yes."

"I've heard stories my family would tell, but each time they changed a bit, so I figured they were folklore. What do we do next?"

Virginia started to answer. "Well, we'll—"

Mary Jane glanced at the window behind Virginia then slowly rose off the couch. "Looks like your policeman friend just arrived."

Mary Jane, Terry, and Virginia stood on the porch watching Detective Wilkinson walk toward them.

When he got to the steps, Mary Jane greeted him. "Good morning, Detective. Please come inside out of the sun and have some iced tea."

"Thank you, ma'am, I think I will." He nodded at Virginia and Terry. "Hello, ladies."

After being seated in the sitting room, Detective Wilkinson looked at Terry with a warm smile. "It's nice to meet you, Dr. Sorenson. Virginia told me you'd be joining her investigation. I think your fields of expertise will be beneficial, but I now have two of you to worry about out there."

Terry grinned. "Thank you, Detective. We've made some more progress since Virginia talked to you."

"You have?" He pulled out a small notebook and opened it. "Okay, what'd you find?"

Virginia and Terry told him what they found in the vault and about the wolfsbane. Virginia informed him of the news about the gold and the jaguar that Andy reported.

Wilkinson set his now empty glass on the coffee table. "Well, you guys have been busy. But we don't know who had paid to have Miss Striker killed or who killed the man in the hospital."

"Maybe our activities will make the person do something we can catch him at," Virginia said.

Wilkinson sighed. "That's what worries me. The people behind all this won't hesitate to kill."

Terry drank the last of her tea and placed the glass on the table. "It seems to me that the people behind this may be after the source of the gold bars and the mysterious compound Dr. Clark said the chemists at the university found. The Diablo powder. I'm thinking Virginia and I should reexamine the quilt and maybe make plans to head to Central America and find the source of the gold and the powder."

Wilkinson closed his notebook. "I agree. But, the fewer people who know about your plans, the better. For now, it's just the four of us. Let's keep it this way. Better the people behind this think you are still rummaging around Texas."

Virginia shifted in her chair. "I'll have to tell Andy, and Dr. Doverspike and the Smithsonian. They have already given the green light on following up in Central America if necessary."

"Okay, but try and keep it as confidentialas possible."

Virginia nodded. "Can you arrange to have someone keep an eye on Mary Jane, so she's got some protection and maybe watch this ranch as well?"

Wilkinson smiled. "I'm ahead of you. The Sheriff is sending some plain clothed deputies here to watch the ranch and be with Miss Striker. With Miss Striker's permission, of course, one is a female deputy who will become one of your best friends and the other is a male deputy who will be your handyman here at the ranch."

Terry chuckled. "Can you keep Professor Pine on ice, too?"

"No. But we can become a pain in the ass and have the deputies keep him away from here."

Virginia gazed at Wilkinson. "I can have the Smithsonian Central Security Service ask the IRS to discuss Dr. Pine's gold inheritance and go over his past taxes. That'll keep him busy."

Wilkinson frowned. "Would the IRS do that? I mean he hasn't broken any laws that we know of."

"I'm not sure either. The IRS would just be inquiring, not arresting him." Virginia shrugged "All we can do is ask. Speaking about asking, I mentioned the traces of cocaine we found on the gold bar and the jaguar. Pine is blackmailing Mary Jane about something to do with drugs. What can we do about that?"

"You said it was trace amounts?"

"That's what Andy said. It took chemists with spectro thingies to find it. Micrograms or something like that."

"Well, most things today, even money, have traces of drugs on them. This is especially true for things from Mexico and environs south. Customs finds traces of drugs on things from Southeast Asia and the Middle East too. Trace amounts aren't going to get a lot of attention. In this case, we, the police, now already know about it and don't consider Miss. Striker a drug supplier. So, Professor Pine's so called evidence is pretty worthless. I'll advise the DEA and FBI just to make sure no one bothers her."

"Good." Virginia rose and looked at Terry. "I think we should head back to the museum and take another look at the quilt. Then, we can plan our trip to Central America."

Terry rose. “I agree. We need to do some planning.” She looked at Wilkinson. “It was nice meeting you, Detective. I hope to see more of you in the future.

Wilkinson smiled. “Nice to meet you too, Doctor.”

Virginia tilted her head and looked at Terry. “Oh, how are you with guns?”

Wilkinson shook his head. “You can’t take weapons into Mexico. It would take the Smithsonian a while, if ever, to get clearance from the Mexican authorities to allow that.”

Virginia tightened her blond ponytail. “Trust me, the Smithsonian and I have our ways. Just—”

Wilkinson sighed. “I know, don’t ask.”

CHAPTER 14

Virginia and Terry, dressed in shorts and t-shirts, stood on the deck of the 300-foot motor yacht as it docked in Cancun, Mexico. A warm breeze washed over the boat as the deck hands tied it to the pier. Music wafted towards them from the brightly painted hotels and bars near the waterfront. Bougainvilleas climbed trellises near the buildings on the dock.

Virginia clicked off some pictures. "I need to send these to Andy. He wanted to come really bad, but his teaching schedule wouldn't let him. Poor baby. I know he'd like this."

"This trip down here has been nice. And the crew… some are definite eye candy." Terry leaned on the chrome rail. "How did you pull this off? You said you don't actually know the owner of this boat."

"Someone at the Smithsonian Central Security Service secured the yacht for us. I think they have something on the owner and leaned on him to loan us this ride. The owner is a congressman or something."

"Be sure to thank them for me. I've never taken a cruise on a yacht before, especially one this big." Terry looked at the bridge of the white boat. "It even has a Jacuzzi, smoke stack, and good size crew. Most of the yachts I've seen are a heck of a lot smaller than this."

"Yeah, it's a sweet ride all right." Virginia pointed to the gangplank being lowered to the pier. "I think we should go to our cabins and gather our things. The customs and immigration officers should be along pretty soon. I'll meet you in the salon."

"Okay." Terry hurried toward the doorway as a ship's first officer walked up to Virginia.

"Mrs. Clark," the officer said, "The Mexican immigration official just called. He will be here in a half hour. He's sorry to inconvenience you."

"That's fine. Dr. Sorenson and I will wait for him in the main salon." *The official is keeping us waiting to try and establish his authority. Psycho bullshit. Probably would like to know who we really are and what we're doing here. We're spoiled, rich tourists of course.*

"Yes, ma'am. I'll have a crewman direct him there." He gave her a salute and marched toward the stern.

Terry sat on a leather couch and watched the Mexican government officer exit the salon. She glanced at Virginia. "That was hardly worth the effort. He perused our passports, asked three questions, then stamped our passports and left... with a bottle of eighty-year-old scotch. By the way, where'd you get that scotch?"

"From the liquor cabinet. It came with the yacht as a..." Virginia made air quotes. "...gift for the government gentleman from the most accommodating owner."

"What does the Smithsonian have on the owner to make him so cooperative?"

"This is one of those don't ask moments." Virginia got up and looked out the side window. "Looks like our local contact is here."

Terry rose and watched a man who appeared to be in his late fifties to early sixties with a white shirt, tan slacks, and a brown cowboy hat shuffle up the gangplank. A crewman directed him to the salon. He took off his hat exposing wavy black hair with a hint of gray at the temples as he entered the room.

"Good afternoon, ladies. I'm looking for Mrs. Clark and Dr. Sorenson?"

"Hi, I'm Virginia Davies Clark, and this is Dr. Terry Sorenson. You are?"

He quickly glanced around the yacht. "Have you been to Cozumel in the summer?"

Virginia chuckled. "No. Only Cancun in the spring."

"Good. Glad that security game is over. Welcome to Mexico." He sighed, then glanced around. "Is this room secure?"

Virginia nodded. "This is as good as it gets."

"Okay. I guess that'll work. I'm Peter York. I was told to meet you ladies and offer what services I can and also provide provisions for a... an expedition. As I understand it, this expedition is unsanctioned by the Mexican government."

Virginia pointed to a leather chair next to a table. "Have a seat, Mr. York. We have a lot to discuss. For openers," she and Terry sat across from him, "who exactly do you work for?"

"Officially, at least to the locals, I'm expat from New Jersey and own a small hotel with a restaurant and bar here in town. I also keep tabs on the local scene and a host of characters for our favorite uncle."

Terry, with wide eyes, leaned on the table. "Are you CIA?"

Peter York looked at her with a smile. "No. Sorry Doctor, not CIA. I'm with the DEA."

Virginia rubbed her hands together. "I take it you were briefed."

"Only to a point. I'm to supply you with provisions; some assorted and unusual weapons that someone thought you'd need, why exactly I'm not sure. I'm to give you some GPS units, sat phones, maps, and documents that should pass muster in the hinterland of Mexico, Honduras, Belize, and Guatemala." York leaned closer to Virginia. He quickly glanced around, then lowered his voice. "The weapons, especially the 'unusual' ones, need to be kept out of sight; the local officials don't like gringos running around armed like it's the old west."

Terry sat back. "How do we get these… things? And where do we stay tonight? Is anyone else briefing us?"

Peter looked at Virginia. "Does she always ask so many questions at once?"

"It's a habit she picked up from me."

He nodded. "Nice habit. You will be spending the next two days at my humble hotel. We will outfit you there. For some reason, Washington wants you off this boat tonight. I do have one question. Are you taking anyone else with you? To be more specific, a man?"

Virginia and Terry looked at each other then back at Peter. "We weren't planning on it. Why?"

"This part of the world is still very much a third world area, very macho and very rough. Two attractive women alone in the backcountry could, and probably will, cause some questions to be asked and invite some excessive and extremely unwanted attention. There are also some very nasty the drug guys."

Virginia tilted her head. "You looking for an invite?"

"Me?" York's hand went to his chest. "No, no. Not me. I'm too old to go traipsing around in the jungle and getting into shootouts. Too many bugs and things that go bump in the night. Anyway, I'm just not up to it anymore." He held up his left hand showing a few crooked fingers. "Arthritis. My knees and hips are not happy most of the time either. But I do have a good man who you might like to have along."

Virginia frowned. "Who?"

"He's an associate of mine. He's from Laredo, Texas. He's Hispanic, speaks Spanish, and is good in tight situations. He's a good shot too. He knows a lot of the areas it looks like you're going. He could be an asset."

"Why don't we talk to the gentleman and see how things play out?" Virginia said.

Terry nodded. "Like over dinner."

Peter rose. "Shall we say seven at my establishment? I own and run the Cancun Beach and Golf Club. I'll have one of my people come with a car to get you and your things. You will be my guests while you are here. Enjoy the beach. I'll make arrangements for the supplies we talked about and have Phil meet us for dinner."

Virginia and Terry exchanged glances. Terry spoke, "Phil?"

"Philippe Carlos Murphy. You'll like him." Peter, chuckling, headed for the door. "The car will be here in about a half an hour or so. Good day ladies." He waved as he exited and placed his cowboy hat on at an angle.

Virginia sat staring at the door. "Did he say Philippe Carlos Murphy from Texas?"

"Yeah. Phil. And he speaks Spanish. This should be interesting. Did you notice he didn't ask anything about our expedition, just commented that we're going on one, and he didn't mention the Smithsonian?"

"Yes. He probably was told we were here for something special, help us, but don't ask too many questions. He may not know about the Smithsonian either." Virginia got up. "Let's go get our other supplies from the hold so we'll be ready for our ride. I need to call Andy, too."

Terry raised an eyebrow. "What did your husband say when you told him about our trip?"

"He wasn't happy that he couldn't come. He made me promise to be careful and to come back safely. And, to call him a lot. Oh yeah, and to take a lot of pictures."

Virginia and Terry waited on the deck of the boat with their luggage, some boxes, and their backpacks as an old, faded red VW van, with blue exhaust pouring out of the tailpipe, roared up to the end of the pier. Two men in bright Hawaiian shirts, well-worn baseball caps, and brown shorts, jumped out and hurried down the dock to the yacht. They looked up at Virginia and Terry. "You are the special ladies we are to pick up, no?"

"Yes," called Virginia.

The bigger of the two men answered back. "*Señor* York sent us to get you. Do you have what you need?"

Terry eyed the men and whispered, "Do you trust them?"

"I'm not sure. Mr. York said he'd send a man for us. There are two of them here. We should be careful."

The Captain of the yacht walked up to the women and the sailor at the top of the gangplank. He nodded to Virginia and Terry then spoke to the men on the dock. "We will be bringing the ladies to the hotel. My people will follow you."

The man looked perplexed. "*Señor Capitán*, it is not necessary to put you out. We can take the *señora* and *señorita.* No problem. It is our pleasure."

"No problem for us. These ladies are in my care until they get to the hotel."

Virginia and Terry turned toward the stern where a ship's crane was lowering a huge, dark green Humvee-RV onto the pier.

The Captain glanced at the vehicle. "That's your mode of transportation on your expedition."

Terry whistled. "That's an army vehicle, Captain. It looks like an armored RV."

He leaned close to Terry and Virginia. "It's been customized and is bullet proof, at least to small arms. Your employer borrowed it from the army as well. Please try and bring it back in one piece. Just so you know, this yacht doesn't belong to a congressman. That's a cover story."

"Does Mr. York know about this?" asked Terry.

The Captain sighed. "I don't think so."

Virginia frowned. "Why didn't Mr. York know about it?"

"He didn't need to. The vehicle has some special features. If you two will accompany me, my chief engineer and I will go over the adaptations. While we do that, the crew will load your stuff onto it. You can follow these two fellows to the hotel, but we will follow, too. Just to make sure you get there in one piece."

Virginia looked confused. "This boat and the Humvee belong to the army, York said he works for the DEA, and we work for the Smithsonian Central Security Service, who do you and the crew work for, Captain, the army, too?"

He smiled. "The United States Navy."

Terry watched the Humvee being taken off the pallet. "You don't trust Peter York, do you Captain?"

"I was told Mr. York is who he says he is. His face matches the pictures we have. The fingerprints he left behind in the salon match the real Peter York of the DEA. These fellows with the VW on the dock are unknowns, therefore suspicious. We will follow you to the hotel to make sure there are no surprises along the way."

Virginia turned and leaned against the chromed railing. "Mr. York thinks we need a man along and has a candidate for us. His name is Philippe Carlos Murphy from Laredo, Texas. Can you see what you can find out about him?"

"Yes, ma'am." The captain radioed the name to the communications man then turned back to Virginia and Terry. "I'll let you know what we find. Shouldn't take long. If you need a man along, I have someone who'd be happy to accompany you and I know he would back you up if things get tight."

Terry stepped closer. "Who'd you have in mind, Captain?"

"My second officer on this yacht. He's a Navy Lieutenant in real life."

"I think I remember seeing him." Terry grinned. "Sounds good to me."

Virginia pushed off the railing. “That’s a good idea. However, we’d better meet Mr. Philippe Carlos Murphy if for no other reason than to not cause any hurt feelings with the DEA. Can the Lieutenant also join us for dinner?”

The Captain shrugged. “I’ll see.” He turned and watched the rather large armored Humvee-RV pull up to the gangplank. “Shall we go take a look at your new car?” He motioned for some of the crew to take Virginia and Terry’s belongings down to the vehicle and load them in.

Terry nudged Virginia and whispered, “The crewmen standing around the Humvee, and the ones coming for our stuff have their shirts un-tucked. Not like before. Armed?”

“Probably. I noticed the two men sent by York are similarly dressed.” Virginia watched the car roll up to the gangway. She turned to the Captain. “Why can’t we stay on the boat tonight?”

“Another agency needs her at a different location, so we need to refuel and head out tonight. Otherwise, I’d love to have you ladies remain on board. Shall we go over the modifications to your new ride.”

CHAPTER 15

Virginia sat in the driver's seat of the oversized Humvee with Terry beside her in the passenger seat. She watched the two men sent by Peter York being held back by the boat's security detail. Pointing toward the men, Virginia said, "Captain, they don't look very happy."

"I'm certain they're not. But we need to finish going over your new transportation and get you two on the road. They don't need to know how this thing operates. My men just put the magnetic Smithsonian expedition sign on the sides, too."

"This thing is big." Terry sat back on the blue cloth seat. "Okay, I've got the controls of almost everything except the driving. That Virginia has."

The Captain nodded. "Right. You have sensors for things getting near you, especially at night, and youactuate them with those controls above the window.

Terry looked around. "What if we get chased?"

"This vehicle has a lot of power, so you may be able to out run or out maneuver a pursuer and you have optional four-wheel drive." He stepped back and pointed at the front tires. "You've got special Kevlar-reinforced run-flat tires.

Virginia opened a port on the side door. "Gun ports? Like an armored car?"

The Captain nodded. "Yes, and it is. And the vehicle is armored, and the glass is six inches thick made from laminated bulletproof materials.

Terry banged on the glass. "Nice."

"The fuel tank is armor-plated and encased in special foam to protect it from rupturing in case of a collision or small-arms fire. The water tank in here is bulletproof, too."

Virginia twisted in her seat and looked in the back. "Can we safely get extra water should we need it?

"Yes. There is a filter and UV disinfection systems on the water intake line as added protection, especially from Montezuma's revenge. Small arms weapons stored on board and enough ammunition to start a small war."

Virginia looked at the dash, turned, and pointed to an instrument panel behind the passenger seat. "Go over these again."

"These are your communications devices. You have satellite phones and satellite radios. There are also GPS guidance or navigation and tracking systems."

Terry turned around in her seat and pointed to the rear. "Our stuff is stored back there?"

"Yep. Your stuff including the archaeological tools, plus a compact stove, oven, microwave, and a small fridge. You have a table back there that folds down into bunks so you can use this for camping. Oh, yes, there's a generator and a bank of large batteries for additional auxiliary power. The emergency medical equipment is under the side compartments. Over there, behind that curtain is a small toilet. Holding tanks are below."

Virginia scanned the interior. "What else does this rig have we should know about?"

"There are special night-vision cameras fore and aft and on the sides. In the arsenal, there are small rocket propelled grenade launchers or mini-RPGs. Your personal weapons are in the back, and there are two extra .38 caliber revolvers in the center console. This thing has an alarm system and self-protection using nasty gases and a couple of other special weapons." The Captain pointed. "The manuals are in that compartment under the comm. center. I think that's everything."

Virginia took a breath. "Wow. That was a lot to swallow."

"Most of it runs automatically, and the manual options are pretty simple. You should have a little time to get used to the rig before you actually get into any territory that might require the special features usage. Virginia, I've heard you've had some experience with the mini-RPGs before."

Terry's head jerked around. "You've used an RPG before?"

"Yeah. I'll explain it all later."

Virginia looked at the dash. "We both have the remote start thingies and we both have a key and our keyless ignition control we keep on us. Right? Can anyone open and drive this thing should we be compromised?"

"A little while ago, I had you both push the start button and that flat area over there on the dash. That took fingerprints of both of you. Now, only you two can use this vehicle." The Captain straightened. "I think that pretty much covers everything. Good luck. Oh, I'll have my men give you maps too."

Terry leaned across and looked at the captain. "We're getting some of the same things from Mr. York."

"Yes, but I feel better providing you with what I know is accurate. He will probably provide good information, but—"

"You trust what you gave us, and he's an unknown quantity," Virginia said.

He nodded. "Right. Now, if you need anything call me. Otherwise, have a safe trip."

Terry frowned. "How do we get this rig and us out of here when we're done?"

"Use the sat radio on the special frequency I gave you for extraction. You'll get instructions then. They will depend on where you are and what's going on when you call."

"Got it, I think. This is supposed to be a scientific expedition as well as a criminal investigation. This seems like a lot of overkill. At least, it shouldn't raise a lot of eyebrows. I'd think any bad guys would hear about it and us before we get off the pier."

The Captain chuckled. "Maybe, but, as best we can, we want to prevent you from being killed. There are a lot of unpleasant characters out there, and this will provide you with a small amount of security. So as to not spook York and company Virginia, Frank Ebner, my officer, will be at the site we talked about." He smiled. "Please try and bring everything back in one piece."

Terry frowned. "Frank who? What site?"

Virginia rubbed her forehead. "He's one of the yacht's officers who will meet us later. We could use a man along with military training, especially if we meet some really nasty characters."

"Oh. Oh! I think I remember him. Great. Won't Mr. York be pissed? He wants us to take one of his guys." She hesitated then, said, "I'd feel better with Mr. Ebner."

"Me too." Virginia looked at the vehicle and trailer. "Captain, who built this thing and who owns it?"

"I don't know who built it. I was told the Army owns it, but who actually owns it is a good question. But it's yours for now. There are papers in the glove compartment that are the vehicle's registration and insurance documents. There is also a form showing the Smithsonian has loaned it to you. This is in case any local authorities try and get you for vehicle theft."

Terry turned and looked inside. "It has a glove compartment?"

"Ya, right under the main comm. center. Good luck ladies." He closed the door and waved to his men. They turned and walked to the gangplank.

The two Mexican men motioned for Virginia to start the vehicle and follow them. Virginia pushed the red start button. The engine roared to life. "Looks like the game is starting. This should be interesting." She remotely adjusted the mirrors.

Terry fired up the sensor systems and the rear camera. "Okay, it works. System lights are all green, and there is another vehicle behind us with some of the boat crew. Looks like the Captain meant it when he said they'd follow us to the Cancun Beach and Golf Club." She adjusted the air conditioning. "Ahh, that's better. I didn't know Humvee's had air conditioning."

"They usually don't. I guess that's one of the new features for this one."

Terry sat back as Virginia slowly pulled forward behind the red VW van. She watched the monitors as they made their way through the streets. "This is some car. Why did the Smithsonian think we needed a tank? What do you think this thing weighs?"

"I have no idea to both questions. Someone is concerned about our safety. But this isn't a typical museum issue. I wonder where they got it?"

"Who cares, it's really cool." Terry pushed a button and watched the monitor screen change images. "The boat crew is still behind us."

Virginia watched the VW van in front. "I don't think we'll need much protection while we're here. I'm guessing the problems, if any, will start when we get into the interior."

"I meant to ask the Captain a question. Why did we come here to Mexico? It would have been closer to where we're going to dock in Belize City."

"Good question. When we get back, you can ask him." Virginia steered around a corner. "Looks like we're here." She pulled into the side parking lot and parked across a number of spaces in the back. "Use the cameras and IR scanner to see what may be around."

"Okay. You expecting trouble?"

"No. Might as well practice, and the guys from the ship that were following us have turned around. We're on our own. Grab your gun and slip it into the side holster and cover it with your t-shirt."

"Roger." Terry tucked her pistol under her shirt and exited the Humvee.

Virginia took a minute longer, then slid out and closed the door. She pressed the black button on the handle and the vehicle locked with a small beeping sound. "Let's follow those guys into the hotel and greet Mr. York."

Virginia and Terry followed the two men into the lobby of the Cancun Beach and Golf Club. Peter York greeted them. "Welcome, I have your rooms already prepared. I can send my men to get your bags. Will you give me your car key?"

Virginia shook her head. "We'd like to see our rooms, look around, maybe have some lunch. We'll get our bags later."

York shrugged and smiled, but looked disappointed. "Fine. I'll escort you to your rooms. I took the liberty to give you adjoining rooms with views of the ocean. They are on the third floor. Is that okay?"

Virginia nodded. "Sounds wonderful. Let's go."

They followed York to the elevator and then to their rooms. Terry opened the connecting doors and joined Virginia and York on Virginia's balcony. The smell of lemons from trees in large pots below floated in the air around them. She looked out at the white sand beach and blue-green sea. Tall palms waved in the slight breeze. "Very nice. Too bad we won't be here all that long."

York turned and leaned on the black iron railing. "You will probably be here a few days. Getting adequate transportation to the interior is not easy."

Virginia smiled. "Didn't your boys tell you? We have a Humvee and assorted equipment. I figure we'll head out in two days. We'd like to go to the beach and do some shopping while we're here."

York's eyes widened. He swallowed. "That soon? I'm not sure Phil can be ready that quick. Then, there is the question of some weapons for you for your trip. These are not easy to procure."

"We've got weapons and our Humvee, so we're good to go." Virginia leaned on the railing and looked down, surveying the surroundings. She back at York. "As for Phil, we haven't even met the man, so his going with us is still a big question."

York wet his lips. "Yes, yes, I'm sorry, I got ahead of myself. May I ask what this expedition is all about?"

Terry sat on the padded outdoor metal chair. "It's an archaeological expedition to assess a possible new Mayan find."

York gave her a blank look. "Just the two of you for such an expedition? Why all the secrecy and multiagency nervousness?"

"Haven't a clue except they might be worried about two women alone in the jungle and drug cartels. We don't know if what we're looking for even really exists. That's why there are just two of us going. Think of this as a reconnoitering trip."

York looked perplexed. "I see. Well, about dinner. We can eat here or at a place I know down the street."

Virginia pointed to a building down the beach with a seaside bar. "How about there? That looks like fun."

"I... ahh... I guess we... okay. That's the Enchanted Evening Grill. How's seven?"

"How's six?" Virginia asked.

"Six? Okay, six it is."

"We'll meet you there. Have a nice afternoon, Mr. York." Terry rose and escorted him to the door. After he'd left, Terry turned and found Virginia going around the room with an electronic device. "What are you doing?"

Virginia held up a piece of paper that read, *lookingfor bugs, keep talking, but don't say anything important.*

Terry nodded. "Nice view. I think we should change into our bathing suits and explore the beach. How about you?"

Virginia pointed under a lampshade at a small metal object. Terry followed Virginia around for a while in both rooms noting the location of the bugs. Then, Virginia turned off the device, moved away toward the TV on the stand, and turned it on loud. She whispered, "That's four listening bugs we found. Mr. York is very curious."

Terry nodded, pulled her new sat phone, and pressed a couple buttons. "It seems our vehicle's had a couple visitors who tried to gain access. Take a look." She turned her phone around so Virginia could see the screen. In the video, the men attached something to the underside of the rear bumper. "I guess Mr. York would like to know exactly where we're going. How about this guy Phil?"

Virginia motioned for them to go out on the balcony. Once seated, Virginia put her feet up on the railing. "He's way too curious for my liking. I don't care if this Philippe Carlos Murphy guy is Mr. Wonderful and one of the Chippendales, he ain't going. We don't have the room, anyway."

Terry raised an eyebrow. "Chippendales? Well, in that case, maybe he could go along." She held out her hands palms up. "Just kidding. I agree. No Phil. How do we play out tonight? York seemed kind of off balance when you switched dinner spots and the time."

"I figure he'll search the room, so we'll play that by ear when we get back. He may have someone try and drug us tonight, so we need to be careful. I don't know if he's acquainted with the owner of the restaurant we selected, or can get our drinks drugged there or not, but I'm sure he could do more here or someplace he owns."

"We said we'd meet him there. Right?"

"Yeah." Virginia looked at her. "What'd you have in mind?"

"Okay, on the way, what do you think of the idea that we stop at some random place on the beach, get our drinks to go, and meet York and Philippe Carlos Murphy at the restaurant with our drinks in hand?"

"Good idea." Virginia scanned the beach. Looks nice down there. You know after we get our bags from the car, change, and go to the beach, they'll be searched. They'll want to take another look at the Humvee, too."

"How do we avoid them getting into it?"

"They can't get into it without us and the little electronic thingamigiggies. They go with us. And, even then, only we can access anything. I used the remote control and turned on its self-defense systems, but it will alert us before doing anything."

"Okay. Sounds good. So let's play this game." Terry rose and grabbed her backpack. "Coming?"

"Yeah, coming." Virginia hurried inside, closed and locked the sliding glass door, grabbed her backpack, and followed Terry out the door.

Terry stopped in the hallway outside their rooms. "How did we get into all this? Wasn't this just figuring out who did some murders in Georgetown and figuring out the quilt?"

Virginia took a breath and slowly let it out. "Good question. My curiosity usually gets me in trouble. I guess this is no exception."

York watched Virginia and Terry walk across the parking lot to their car from his office window, and then pressed a button on the intercom. "Phil, get in here."

Philippe Carlos Murphy, tall with wavy black hair and the tan body of an athlete, entered York's office and sat in a leather chair. "This may not be as easy as you thought, boss. Right after you left the women, they turned on their TVs loud. We couldn't hear much. Just something about dinner."

"Damn it! Nothing about their plans?"

"No. Just dinner and the beach."

York slammed his hand on the desktop. "Speaking of dinner, they switched places to eat and the time. We're eating at the Enchanted Evening Grill at six. Our client wants to know what they are doing and exactly where they're going, so you need to be extremely charming tonight at dinner. I want the ladies enthralled with you and insisting you go with them."

Murphy leaned back, put his hands behind his head, and smiled. "I'm sure that can be arranged. I have a way with women. And, the room will be searched when they're at dinner."

"Good. Did the boys have any luck with that Humvee thing of theirs?"

"No. The men couldn't get in. They said when they tried to crawl under it to plant the devices, there seemed to be a solid bottom, like a tank. Even the wheels are enclosed. They fixed a tracker under the rear bumper."

"Okay, tonight you turn on the charm, and we insert you into their expedition. Have the boys try again to get into that vehicle and look around." York got up and paced. "Then, when they leave, we track their progress. Be sureto send periodic reports. Our client is paying well for this."

CHAPTER 16

On the beach, Virginia and Terry stretched out on lounge chairs near the water as waves washed the sand and applied sunscreen as admiring males watched. They settled back and enjoyed the warmth of the tropical sun.

Virginia's new iPad, given to her by the yacht's Captain, vibrated and played *Anchor's Away*. She pulled it out of her beach bag and pressed the button on the bottom. It displayed a message from the Humvee. *UNAUTHORIZED ATTEMPTS TO ENTER STOPPED. UNAUTHORIZED PERSONNEL WITHIN FIVE FEET OF VEHICLE. REQUEST USE OF NON-LETHAL DETERRENTS.* Virginia showed the display to Terry. "That car is smart. Shall we have some fun?"

Terry nodded. "Why not? Go for it. Let's see what that thing can do."

Virginia typed in the go code for the use of nonlethal deterrents. She watched the screen as another message started to type across the screen. *PEPPER SPRAY USED. UNAUTHORIZED PERSONNEL RETREATING.* "I bet that made their day." She raised her sunglasses and glanced at Terry. "Speaking of deterrents, where's your gun?"

Terry pointed to her beach bag. "How long are we going to be out here?"

"For a while. Where else would two women from America be at a place like this?" Virginia lowered her sunglasses and slipped the iPad back into her bag and reclined. "That sun feels good. When you see the bar guy around, order us something tropical." She closed her eyes.

Terry ordered two Bahamas Mamas. When the waiter arrived, Terry dripped some ice on Virginia's stomach and watched her jump.

"Damn it!" Virginia exclaimed. "That was cold!"

"I know, but it was fun. Our beverages have arrived. Think they're okay to drink? I mean do you think they're drugged?"

"No, I think they're safe. York wants information and drugging us now would be counter-productive."

Terry sipped her drink. "You know this Philippe Carlos Murphy guy is going to be dreamy, and he'll turn on the charm in order to come."

"Yeah, your point?"

"Do we go along with his pitch during dinner, then tell him no? How do you want to handle it?"

Virginia sat up and adjusted the back to the lounge chair. "Why don't you act like you're falling for the guy? Really turn on the sexual heat and the stars in your eyes approach. Act like you're falling for him and can't wait to get him in your room. He's a man; your acting should be enough to keep him happy, at least, for the evening."

Terry nodded, "Okay, but what are you going to be doing?"

"I'll play the bad guy and seem to drag the anchor. After dinner, you'll slowly stroll back with Phil, and I'll work on York. When we get back to the hotel, we'll tell him we'll let him know in the morning if he can go. You snuggle up to Phil and tell him you'll try and convince me to take him with us. Later we say good night. We are supposed to spend a couple days here, so there is no apparent rush to give them an answer tonight."

Terry eyed her. "You're not going to let him try and charm you?"

"No. I'm married, and York knows it. If I went all dreamy for Phil, they'd either suspect something or think we're a couple sluts."

Terry smiled. "I get to be sexy and hint at things to come while you play the evil one? I like this. You sure I can't..."

"No."

"Party pooper. Oh, when are we actually leaving?"

"At three tomorrow morning. That'll really throw a monkey wrench in the works. But, while York will be pissed he doesn't have a man on the inside, he'll think he's tracking us, so all's not lost."

Terry frowned. "There really is a three in the morning? A girl needs her beauty sleep."

"Yes, there really is a three in the morning." Virginia smiled.

"Are we going to leave his tracker on the car?"

"No. We'll let him track us for a while. Then, we'll slip it into the bed of a local truck or something and let him track the farmer. I don't think initially he'll risk having someone physically follow us, not with his use of technology. His losing us with his tracker should make him blow a gasket."

Terry finished her drink and looked at the glass. "You know I could get used to this life. These drinks are good." She glanced at Virginia. "What do you think he'll do when we throw him off our trail?"

"He'll get everyone in his clandestine pay to try and find us, including some crooked local cops." Virginia finished off her drink and set it on the table between them.

Terry rubbed her forehead. "Why's he doing all this?"

"He's on someone besides Uncle Sam's payroll. Padding his retirement. Washington will need to know this, too."

Terry looked at the ocean. "Care for a swim?"

"I'm not sure leaving our bags with our weapons and electronics is a good idea."

"One of us should probably stay with the stuff."

Virginia slumped. "Yeah, you're right. If you want to dip your toe in the water, go ahead. I'll wait here, and when you get back, I'll go."

"Okay." Terry jumped up, adjusted her bikini top and hurried to the water's edge. She slowly moved into the sea and swam around watching the hotel, Virginia, and people on the beach. She finally walked onto the hot sand and hurried to Virginia yelling, "Hot… hot… hot…" She plopped on the lounge chair and toweled off as Virginia moved to the water. Terry sat and watched Virginia and the people. No one was paying any undue attention to her or Virginia except a few young men who appeared to be tourists. She settled back and closed her eyes. She was suddenly aware of someone next to her near Virginia's chair. Her hand slipped into her bag and gripped her pistol. She opened her eyes and looked at the lounge chair.

Virginia sat drying herself with a large, white fluffy towel. "These things are great. Think they'd sell us a couple?"

Terry felt her heart slowing. "You scared me. I didn't hear you come back."

"You can let go of the gun now."

Terry looked down. Her hand holding the black semiautomatic was half out of the beach bag. "Yeah, especially since we're not supposed to have them here." She let the gun drop back into the bag. "How long were you out there?"

"About as long as you. Water's warm. Andy would love it here. I'll have to bring him sometime." Virginia reached into her bag and pulled out her camera. She snapped pictures of the hotel, beach, people, and some of Terry. She had Terry take a few shots of her then put the camera away. "Later I'll e-mail these shots to Andy. He'll like that." Virginia looked back at the hotel. "I think we've played the part of tourist and scientists enough to be convincing for that guy in the bar watching us."

Pedro sat at the open air bar looking at the beach and watching Virginia and Terry. He took pictures with an iPhone and e-mailed them to York. As he was setting the phone down, it rang. He answered. "*Si?*"

York's voice was abrupt. "Are the ladies still enjoying themselves on the beach?"

Pedro looked at the phone. *I just sent him the pictures, what does he think? "Si."*

"What are they doing now?"

Pedro looked at the beach. "They had some drinks, went for a swim, and are now just sunning themselves. Maybe they get ready to go to their rooms soon."

"Can you hear anything they are saying?" York cleared his throat. "Has anyone taken a special interest in them?"

"Just a few male *turista*. Some of the staff. Just looking."

"That's it?"

Pedro shifted the phone to his other ear. "*Si*."

"They have anything that looks like maps or drawings with them?

Pedro squinted as he looked at the women. "No. No drawings, no *mapas*."

"Okay. Watch them. Let me know if anyone besides one of our waiters talks to them or if they have any drawings and maps."

Pedro hung up and turned to watch Virginia and Terry. *They are bello. They're just women. Why is Señor York so nervous? Oh well, I'll watch. He's paying me to sit and drink free drinks and watch pretty ladies in bikinis, what do I care?*

Virginia looked at her sports watch. "Time to go in and start getting ready for our dinner with Mr. York and company."

Terry stretched. "Okay. Need to pick out something sexy for Phil's benefit. Want to stop in the gift shop and see about the towels?"

Virginia gathered her bag and towel. "No..." She thought about the question for a second, then responded. "Sure why not? I'll give York something else to think about."

They stopped in the gift shop off the lobby and bought two towels each. They walked to the elevators and punched three. When the elevator arrived, they and a short, stocky, gray-haired man in a rumpled suit entered. Virginia pushed the button for the third floor. The man gave them a quick smile and pushed four. The elevator gave a slight bounce, the number three lit up on the display over the door. The doors slid open on their floor. Virginia and Terry stepped out. The man followed and stopped them.

He stepped in front of them and spoke in a heavy Spanish accent. "*Señora* Clark and *Señorita* Dr. Sorenson?"

Virginia's heart skipped a beat. "Yes. I'm Virginia Davies Clark. Who may I ask are you?"

"I am Senior Inspector Rodriguez, *Policía Federal*." He displayed his badge and credentials. "I would like a word with you ladies."

Terry winced. "We haven't done anything wrong."

"Those weapons in your bags are very illegal."

"We have permits."

"*Si*. I know you do."

Virginia took a breath and stepped closer to Inspector Rodriguez.

"Then, what do you want to discuss, Inspector?"

Inspector Rodriguez gestured toward the hall. "Can we go to your rooms?"

"Mr. York, the hotel owner, has them bugged. You want our conversation listened to?"

Inspector Rodriguez sighed. "No. Why don't you two ladies change and meet me in the lobby? We can take a *paseo*… err… stroll, and talk."

Terry tilted her head. "You're not going to arrest us are you?"

Inspector Rodriguez laughed. "No. No. Just a little talk. Yes?"

Virginia nodded. "We'll meet you in the lobby in ten minutes."

"*¡Gracias. Diez minutos*, ten minutes."

Ten minutes later Virginia and Terry exited the elevator and walked into the brightly decorated lobby wearing shorts and tank tops. Inspector Rodriguez rose from his plush chair and met them next to a potted palm.

Inspector Rodriguez motioned toward the front doorway. "Shall we walk?" He looked at Virginia and Terry. "You ladies look beautiful. Welcome to Mexico."

Virginia moved to Rodriguez's left side, and Terry walked on his right. Virginia started the conversation. "Okay, Inspector, what's with the official greeting? What do you want to talk about?"

After a few steps, Rodriguez stopped and pointed at a monument. "Act like I'm showing you the sights. We're being followed."

Terry looked at the large stone edifice. "We know. Probably Mr. York's people."

"What are you doing in Mexico, exactly?" Rodriguez asked.

Virginia's hands turned sweaty, "What makes you think we're here as anything but tourists?"

"We were told of your coming by your State Department. They asked us to provide you every courtesy. My government agreed, but when we asked what you were going to be doing, they said you're on some kind of expedition into the interior and will be in my country and some of our neighbors. I know of your work and your Smithsonian Museum. You are looking for Mayan ruins, no?"

Virginia stopped and leaned on a short stone barrier between the beach and the concrete walkway. "Yes. But they may be very special. We can't go into exactly how they're different, yet."

"I see." Rodriguez shook his head. "Let me warn you, there are some very bad people between here and where you may be going. It is not safe."

Virginia smiled at him. "We'll be fine, sir. We can take care of ourselves."

"I know you think you are good at what it is you do, but trust me, this is jungle and people get lost and are never heard from again. There are dangerous animals and drug people out there as well, and they are armed."

"Yeah, I've heard. Only the military, cops, and crooks can have guns in Mexico. Right?" Virginia said.

"*Si*. Like California in your country."

Virginia nodded. "Right. California and other places in our country."

Rodriguez laughed. "*Si*. But seriously, your trip could still be dangerous. When do you expect to leave for your trip?"

"Our schedule is to leave in two days."

"I see." Rodriguez nodded. "Here is my card. If you need anything while you are on your trip, call me, especially if anyone causes you any trouble. If any Policía try to detain you, call me or have them contact me. Here is a little memento." He handed Virginia a small statue of St. Christopher.

Virginia pushed off the wall and took his card. "Thank you, Inspector. We're grateful for your help, and the saint. We'll call if we need back up."

Terry gave him a kiss on his cheek. "Would you care to have dinner with us and Mr. York from the hotel, tonight?"

"It would be nice, but I have some other duties to attend to. If I do not see you before you leave, have a safe trip."

Terry smiled. "Thank you, sir."

Virginia and Terry watched Inspector Rodriguez stroll off into the throng of people along the boardwalk. Terry turned to Virginia. "Was that a warning that the cops are watching us, too?"

"I don't know what to make of it. I liked him, and he seemed really concerned." She stuffed the statue in her backpack. "Let's head over to that bar and use the sat phone to call the Smithsonian and find out if he's the real McCoy."

Terry sat at the bar facing the boardwalk and ocean sipping her Margarita as Virginia made the call. After a few minutes, Virginia hung up and slid the phone into her backpack. "Well, Inspector Rodriguez is who he says he is, and he's our government contact if things get sticky. How he can help when we're in the interior, I don't know, but Washington says he's one of the good guys."

Terry looked at her watch. "Better get the lead out. We're going to be late for dinner."

"You just want to meet *Senior* McDreamy from Laredo."

"Yeah, there's that, too."

CHAPTER 17

After their meeting with the inspector and changing, Virginia and Terry strolled along the beach where small swells washed across the white sand. They entered the Enchanted Evening Grill restaurant wearing colorful, flowing skirts and peasant blouses, with their tropical drinks. It was six PM on the dot. They spotted Peter York and a dark-skinned, handsome man at an outside table overlooking the placid blue Gulf water. They made their way around palm trees to the two men who rose as Virginia and Terry approached.

York looked at the two women and grinned. “I see you ladies are very punctual. May I Introduce Philippe Carlos Murphy from Texas?”

Virginia and Terry shook his hand.

“Philippe, this lovely lady is Mrs. Virginia Davies Clark, and this beautiful lady is Dr. Terry Sorenson. They are also from Texas and are here representing the Smithsonian.” York stepped toward Virginia and pulled out a high-backed, wooden chair. “Please have a seat.” He watched Philippe do the same for Terry.

Philippe leaned in close to Terry. “I don’t remember doctors that looked like you when I was in college.”

She smiled. “Just because a girl is smart, it doesn’t mean she has to be plain.” She took a sip of her drink. “What do you do for Mr. York?” Terry stole a glance at Virginia, then returned her attention to Philippe to keep him occupied.

Virginia took a sip of her drink, set the glass down on the table and leaned toward York. “You have some documents for us?”

“Yes, but this is dinner, and this is Mexico. We eat and enjoy the beach and pleasant company. We do business afterwards.”

“If you don’t mind, if the documents are in that messenger bag by your chair, I’d like to get them now. In this fashion, we get business out of the way so we can enjoy the rest of the evening.”

York looked across the table at Philippe, who was doing his best to charm Terry. “It seems your friend has started the pleasure part of the evening first."

"Yes, it does." Virginia smiled. "Either I get the documents, or I put a stop to your friend Philippe going with us. Now, the documents Mr. York?"

"Oh, all right." He picked up the bag by the strap and handed it to Virginia. "Everything you should need is in there. Maps, government travel documents, weapons permits, and a couple radios. But from the look of that vehicle of yours, I'm not sure my radios are needed."

Virginia's smile widened. "All help is appreciated. Thank you." She placed the bag on the floor next to her and slung the strap over the back of her chair. "Now we can have fun." She took a sip of her drink and picked up the menu. "How's the food here?"

Strolling along the warm water on wet sand, carrying her sandals, with York, Terry, and Philippe, Virginia glanced at her watch. *10 pm. Not too late. Philippe may think it's too early to be headed back to the hotel.* She looked at Terry and Philippe. *Maybe he thinks he's going to get lucky.* When they arrived at their hotel's bar facing the ocean, Virginia stopped. "Gentlemen, it has been a nice evening; thank you for the materials in the bag. Terry and I need to go over these things tonight and finish our planning, so I'm afraid we're going to say goodnight. Philippe, we'll let you know about the trip real soon. Got to clear things with Washington. I'm sure you understand."

Philippe ran his hands through his wavy black hair, "I assure you, Washington would not have any problem with me going along. Considering the risks involved, I'm sure they would approve. And the evening is still young."

Terry took a deep breath, which Philippe readily noticed. "I think you're right about Washington, Philippe, but procedures are procedures. You as a DEA agent should know that. I bet we'll get the okay quickly." She gave him a longing look. "I look forward to being with you on the journey." She looked at Virginia. "Let's get to work." She rose up on her toes brushing her chest against his arm and kissed Philippe on his cheek. "Good night. I hope to see you tomorrow." She turned and followed Virginia toward the elevators.

In their rooms, Virginia plopped onto the edge of her bed. "That went well. We've got the stuff Mr. York promised and finally met Philippe Carlos Murphy from Texas. Now let's go through what Mr. York gave us." She watched Terry waving the electronic eavesdropping finder around the room, and pointed to the planted bugs.

Terry scribbled a note. *The new radios and phones they gave us are bugged, too.* Terry marked all the bugs with Post-It-Notes. She pulled up a chair at the small round table. "Okay, let's have a look."

At midnight, Virginia slid her chair back and stood. "Okay, I think we've gone over everything. Let's get some rest. We can run Philippe by the folks at the Smithsonian in the morning." She slid a note to Terry. *Good job charming Philippe. Have everything packed for a quick getaway?*

Terry nodded. "Yeah, let's get some rest; I'm dying to see the sights tomorrow."

Virginia nodded then picked up what looked like a small tablet computer and turned it on. She showed the images of the Humvee and data from the vehicle on the screen to Terry. Virginia switched it off and returned it to the table. She wrote a note. *Our ride looks ready and safe.*

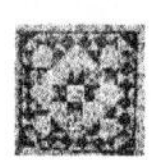

York drank his eighth cup of coffee, looked at his watch. He glanced at the couch in his office where Philippe sacked out. "Hey, wake up. They're going to bed."

Philippe sat up rubbing his eyes. "Get anything useful?"

"No. They went through what I gave them. They have no idea the radios are long-range bugs and GPS trackers. They seemed happy with the contents of that messenger bag. They're going to call Washington tomorrow about you, and going shopping. You should be prepared to accidentally bump into them and keep them company. I think you did a great job with the good doctor."

"Doctor Terry is cute, and I think she likes me. I didn't know they had Ph.D.'s that looked like her. I think that Clark broad is a little harder to impress."

"The Clark broad, as you put it, is in charge. You'd better butter her up, too. And she's probably not going to be as easy to captivate as the doctor because she's married."

"I've had my share of married ladies. They're usually not that hard to seduce. She'll come around. I'll find them in the morning and overcome their resistance. Can I go to bed now?"

At three in the morning, the dimly lit streets were nearly deserted as Virginia pulled the Humvee out the rear exit to the parking lot onto the highway. With Terry acting as navigator, they found Mexico Highway 307 and headed south.

Terry watched the sensors. "No one seems interested in us. Taking out the hotel video camera and drugging the watchmen was fun."

Virginia made a turn. "Good. Hopefully, it will be a while before anyone at the hotel figures out we're gone."

"Can we stop for breakfast?"

Virginia chuckled. "Sure. We should stop in the next village, though. It'll be too easy to spot us here. Let's find a place with off-street parking." They drove for an hour. Entering a small village, they slowed and looked for an open restaurant. Virginia pulled the Humvee behind a small restaurant and parked. "Get your gun. We're not the natives here."

"Got it." Terry exited the vehicle as Virginia slid out on the opposite side. The doors clicked locked. They headed inside.

The aroma of the freshly baked breads and the smell of cooking eggs and beef made their mouths water. They ordered, ate quickly, and, returned to their vehicle. Once inside they locked the doors and activated the scanners. Virginia pointed at a monitor. "The infrared shows two men moving slowly around those large dumpsters and crates trying either trying to stealth their way here, or they're drunk, or both."

Terry glanced at the monitor. "I don't think they have honorable intentions. Shall we leave them with something to remember us by?"

"Yes, by all means."

The men slowly approached from both sides of the Humvee hugging the trash bins and walls. Then, when close, they rushed at the car with knives drawn and reached for the Humvee's front doors.

Terry hit the button that sent a fog of pepper spray and tear gas out both sides of the vehicle. The men stopped, started to gasp and choke. They stumbled around rubbing their eyes and hitting things around them. Then, they wobbled toward a truck and fell to the ground.

Virginia started the car. "That's enough fun. Let's get rolling." After moving about six feet, she hit the brakes. "Hold the fort for a minute." Virginia jumped out of the car and hurried to the rear. Searching under the rear bumper, she found York's tracking device. She pulled the magnetically held hardware off, ran to the men's truck, and attached it to the rear bed. She dashed back to the Humvee and slid in. "Let's blow this Popsicle stand." She turned back out onto the road and disappeared into the night. "Glad we disabled the bugs you found in the radio and sat phone York gave us."

"He'll really be pissed when he finds them in our rooms." Terry settled into the front passenger's seat and looked around. "This looks like the Space Shuttle."

"Maybe. It was built by the same government contractor."

"Didn't the Captain say the registration was in the glove compartment?"

"Yeah."

"I think I'll have a look at who it's officially registered to." Terry opened the glove compartment and fished out the owner's manual and the official vehicle documents. She switched on the overhead light and read. "It's registered in Virginia to Ronald Warren Reagan. Mr. Reagan lives at 675 N.

Randolph St., Arlington, Virginia."

Virginia laughed. "Mr. Ronald W. Reagan was the fortieth President of the United States. And, that address is the address of DARPA."

Terry looked at her. "Who?"

"DARPA."

"Okay, who's DARPA?" Terry put the paperwork and manual back in the glove compartment and closed it.

"DARPA stands for Defense Advanced Research Projects Agency. They do advanced research and design new toys for the Department of Defense."

Terry's eyes narrowed, "You know this, how?"

"My husband's a professor at the University of Texas and was a professor at the University of California at Irvine. He's had grants from DARPA."

"Oh. So a DOD think tank's address was used for a vehicle on loan to us by The Smithsonian, and owned by a dead president. Cute."

York sat behind his desk fuming. He looked at the disheveled Philippe and Pedro. "Do either of you clowns know what time the women left here?"

Philippe swallowed. "Sometime between two and six this morning."

"Their room was bugged. The lobby watched. But, the parking lot's video cameras were disabled, and no one saw them leave. How the hell did that happen? Pedro, where were you?"

Pedro shifted in his chair. "I was out front watching the street."

York leaned forward. "Then, explain to me how they drove a huge, oversized Humvee out of the parking lot and down the street without you seeing them?"

"I... I don't know. I must have dozed off." Pedro rubbed his head. "I've got a splitting headache."

"You moron, they drugged you, too. They also took out the surveillance cameras and sent one of our watchmen to the hospital. He had a splitting headache as well. Andno one noticed? What do I pay you mugs for?"

Philippe rubbed the morning stubble on his face then spoke. "I thought they weren't going for two more days."

"That's what they said, and I thought you could handle them. Obviously both Mrs. Clark and Dr. Sorenson were not taken by your self-claimed charms." He glared at Pedro. "Is the tracker still working? It is still working isn't it?"

"Si."

York slammed his fist on the desk. "Then, where the hell are they now? You can track them can't you?"

"*Si.* They are heading south-west on 180D."

York frowned. "Why are they going that way?"

Pedro shrugged, "Maybe they are going to *Chichen Itza*?"

"I doubt it." He looked at Philippe. "Are the GPS devices in the radios we gave them still working? Where do they say the women are?"

"No signal this morning. Maybe they aren't turned on."

"They work even when the radio's off. Don't tell me they've outsmarted us on all fronts. You're not with them, the radio GPS's have been disabled, and I'll bet you the tracker we put under their car is now happily riding on another vehicle. We've lost them! Our customer is not going to be happy. Someone's head is going to roll, and I assure you it won't be mine."

CHAPTER 18

Virginia watched the navigation system map, switched on the radio, drove back to the highway, and turned south. "Care to check our weapons?"

"Okay." Terry unlocked and opened the panels under the seats and beds and looked at the contents. "A thirty-caliber rifle, two assault rifles, a couple MP5 submachine guns, and small RPGs hung on their holders."

"And we've got a lot of ammunition and a few smaller toys. There are some robotic thingies I saw pictures of in one of the manuals too."

"Robotic thingies? The Captain didn't say anything about these."

"We've also got a couple nine-millimeters, three .380s, a couple .357 magnums and two .38 specials, also."

Virginia switched off the headlights. "Sun's up. It's going to get warmer out there soon."

Terry got up and climbed into the systems control seat behind Virginia. "How much further until we get off this main highway?"

"A few hours."

Terry pulled out the instruction manual and thumbed a couple pages in the manual. "I think I'll try this." She turned some controls and pushed a couple buttons. An image appeared on a small screen. She bent forward and mumbled to herself. "That rectangle is us. There's the traffic in front and in the rear of us, and that eighth vehicle back is trying to gain on us. Lots of traffic for this time of day, and it's three lanes in this direction." Terry sat back. "Oh boy. We may have a problem."

Virginia spoke up. "Oh boy is not what I want to hear. What's the problem?"

Terry moved to the back and looked out the small rear window. "Yeah, it's a white panel truck of some kind with a disk on top trying to get around the cars in front of it.

Virginia glanced at the side mirror. "Any identification on it, like a sign on the doors?"

Terry squinted. "There is something, but I can't make it out. Can you put some distance between us and that truck?"

"Yeah," Virginia nodded, "but who is it? Does it belong to one of York's people, or someone else?"

"I don't think now is the time to have a dialog with them."

"I can speed up, but I don't think I can outrun them. This is a heavy Humvee, not a sports car. Try some countermeasures."

Terry leaned forward at the control panel and twisted a knob. "Virginia, floor it. I'll see if we can cause them to have other issues."

The vehicle lurched forward as Virginia hit the gas. They passed a stake-bed truck with a large Mexican family. They were riding together in the back of a truck filled with plastic picnic chairs and were laughing. After Virginia pulled ahead of the cars and trucks behind them, Terry pushed a button. There was a thump sound. "Okay, folks, let's hope we're far enough away."

Virginia yelled, "You used a little one, didn't you?"

"Yes."

"Good." Virginia kept accelerating down the road. After about a minute, she called back. "Any sign of them?" Virginia looked at the rear view display from the rear camera. "There is a huge traffic snarl back there all of a sudden and now a big accident. That truckload of people just made it; they're still moving. What did you do?" Virginia slowed the Humvee.

Terry chuckled. "It's a baby EMP device. It knocked out anything using power in a fifty-yard radius."

Virginia called back, "Any idea who they were?"

Terry looked at the monitor, leaned back in her chair, and glanced out the rear at the fading traffic accident. "Oh shit. Afraid so. It was a police van." She closed her eyes and sighed. "Great. You think they'll be after us now for causing an accident?"

Virginia shook her head. "Not unless they find that EMP device, and I don't think a local PD is going to be looking for one. I also doubt they'd know what it was if they found it."

Terry climbed back into the front passenger seat. "How are you doing?"

"Okay. Want to drive?"

"Not right now."

Virginia gave her a conspiratorial look. "I thought you'd want to give this thing a try."

"I can share. Anyway, I plan on being right here. I want to be ready to use our toys again if there is more trouble."

CHAPTER 19

Virginia was deep in thought, as they continued down Highway 307. She watched the scenery in the windows as they drove through scrub and colorful old Spanish style towns. After stopping briefly for lunch, they continued to the city of Chetumal. Virginia turned onto Highway 186 West.

Terry examined the maps again, and the pictures of the quilt blocks and, near Nicolas Bravo, she told Virginia to exit the main highway and turn south on a two-lane blacktop road with numerous potholes and weeds growing through the cracks in the asphalt. They drove into a region of increasingly dense tropical jungle.

Terry turned her head toward Virginia, "I hope that quilt is right about our heading. This isn't a very well maintained road."

Virginia cracked a smile. "You ain't seen nothing yet. We'll be in some pretty rough terrain before this job is over."

Terry fidgeted in her seat. "How long on this road?"

"We've got a-ways to go," Virginia said. "We'll find someplace to camp tonight. Might as well get use to our special, armored Humvee and its niceties. It'll be safer than stopping in a town, I hope."

Terry twisted around, her seatbelt tightening across her chest. "What do you think York is doing? He must be going crazy trying to figure out where we are."

Virginia wet her lips. "That, or he's getting reports from his spy network. That police van we stopped with the mini-EMP wasn't trying to catch us by accident. We'd better keep our guard up."

York paced his office at the Cancun Beach and Golf Club. He stepped to the large window overlooking the pool and beach beyond. Turning, he glared at Philippe Carlos Murphy sitting stiffly on the couch. "Philippe, have our sources found them yet?" York snapped.

"They were going south on Highway 307 when a police unit spotted them."

York returned to his desk and plopped in the chair. "And? Did they stop the girls, maybe follow them?"

"No. Something went wrong, and there was a big accident. Lots of traffic and all of a sudden it stopped, cold. Everything shut down. They crashed."

"Doesn't that sound a bit suspicious to you?"

Philippe shrugged. "I guess. But, how would they generate electrical failures in all the cars, a police van, and cause an accident at the same time?"

"How would I know? I'm a federal cop, not an engineer. Did the police see anything suspicious from their vehicle?"

"No. But they sped up just before the accident."

York sat back and looked at the ceiling. "Okay, they ran just before something caused the accident and tied up the police. That leads me to think the ladies caused the accident somehow. That also means they knew they were being followed."

"I think they're being careful."

"You think?" York straightened and slammed his fist on the desk. "I don't pay you to think! I paid you to charm the ladies into letting you go with them. That didn't happen. You also lost them last night. I asked that you keep tabs on them after they left. Another failure on your part." He took a sip of beer from a brown bottle. "What *do* I pay you for?" He took another swig of his beer. "Anyone seen them since the accident?"

"Well… I got a report that their vehicle was seen on Highway 186, but it's disappeared from that road, too."

"How could two women in a very oversized, funny looking, green Humvee-RV just disappear?"

Philippe's cell phone rang. He answered it and listened. Hanging up, he put it back in his shirt pocket and looked at York. "They're stopped for gas in a little town well south of 186. They're on an old road hardly anyone uses any more. Looks like they're headed for Guatemala or Belize."

York's eyes smoldered. "I knew they were headed there, just not the route or destination."

"Okay, call Clemente Ramos. Tell him they are coming near his territory."

Philippe swallowed. "Ramos? The drug lord? He'll kill them."

"Tell Clemente I would appreciate him just watching them and letting me know what they're up to. I'll let him have them when our client says they are no longer necessary."

"Okay, boss. He's going to want to kill them if they stumble on his operation."

"He can exercise some restraint. He owes me big time. So either he cooperates, or there will be some U.S. Department of Defense drones spraying his fields and destroying millions of dollars of his illicit crops. The DEA and Coast Guard will appreciate knowing their trade route to the U.S. as well. He'll cooperate… or else."

Philippe rose and headed for the door. "I'll give him a call now."

"Good." York stood and headed for the side door exiting to the pool. "I think I'll have lunch by the pool. By then, it will be *siesta* time with Aurelia."

Virginia scanned the area while Terry pumped gas into the Humvee. The petrol station looked like something out of the nineteen thirties in the U.S. dust bowl. Two red pumps, with cranks on the side to reset them, sat under a high, banged-up metal roof. A faded, ancient, Dr. Pepper sign was plastered to the wall. The gas station windows were dirty, and the single bay garage door was open. A nineteen-fifty-six, faded-blue Buick Special sat in the bay with its hood up. Rust showed around the rear window. The rear bumper was corroded. A pneumatic wrench could be heard periodically. The town was straight out of central casting back lot for a Central American village. Long whitewashed buildings covered by red clay tiles, with narrow sidewalks, lined the road. Satellite dishes sat on roofs. Power poles and wires were strung overhead. A couple of old women in black walked along the street. Kids played soccer in a small, open field next door to the gas station. A few cars and trucks rumbled through town. The whole area seemed to radiate heat. No one appeared to be paying attention to them.

Terry called out from the Humvee. "Virginia, you might want to see this."

Virginia walked back to the vehicle and climbed in. She closed the door and moved next to Terry. "What's up?"

"There is some radio chatter the computer translated. It seems someone has asked the locals to keep an eye out for us.

"Figures. I think we need to start carrying one of the pistols full time from now on."

Terry lifted her shirt. A compact .380 semiautomatic was tucked into her waistband. "I'm good. Every other bullet is a hollow point."

"Have you ever shot anyone?"

"Yes. I was on an expedition in the Middle East when some religious fanatics with guns and very large curved swords set upon us. We had to fight for our lives. I had a semiautomatic and protected a young grad student and myself. The score, when the dust settled, were four dead Arab nut jobs and the two of us still standing."

"Okay then. Good to know."

"One more thing." Terry motioned toward a monitor screen. "Looks like a couple men standing at the corner over there smoking and talking."

Virginia titled her head. "I saw them too. They don't seem dangerous."

"They've been watching us all along. Now that you climbed in, they've moved on. I don't like it."

Virginia nodded. "You may be right. Can't be too careful. You keep watch. I'll find us someplace to have lunch. After we eat, we'll keep moving until it's time for dinner. We'll drive until dusk, then camp and rest for the night."

"Okay." Terry moved to the control panel and switched the sensors back on.

Virginia started the Humvee, switched on the navigation system and pulled out of the filling station. She turned onto the main road and headed south. After making a quick stop at a cantina for lunch, she continued on the old road. An hour later, Virginia pulled onto a side road and stopped.

Terry moved forward. "What's wrong?"

"Nothing. I just want to consult the notes and the quilt block pictures."

"I'll get them for you." Terry went to the safe, unlocked it, and gave the laptop and folders to Virginia. "I need to stretch my legs. I'll be just outside."

CHAPTER 20

Virginia stole quick glances out the window at Terry milling around near the jungle. She tried concentrating on the quilt blocks, but her nerves made her keep any eye on Terry standing away from the vehicle. She scanned the pictures of the quilt blocks and examined the map folded on her lap. *Good thing these are not in order. I'm the only one who can interpret them.* She moved a couple around. *Okay, got our course for the rest of today. I wonder how long we can utilize this vehicle.*

She stuffed them back into the folder and started to move to the back when, out of the corner of her eye, she saw Terry make a dash into the jungle. A second later, she heard four distinct gunshots, two louder than the others. Virginia tossed the folder on the passenger seat. She flung opened the side door and climbed out of the Humvee, gun in hand. She ran toward the spot where Terry had entered the tropical forest. As she got to the edge of the clearing, Terry, her face flushed, her arms flailing, pushed aside vines and rushed into the open.

Terry stopped in front of Virginia and bent resting her hands on her knees catching her breath. Her pistol stuck in the back of the waistband of her shorts.

Virginia looked at her. "What happened? Is everything okay?"

Terry held up a hand then straightened. In labored breaths, she spoke. "No, everything is not okay. There was a man. He was using a hand held radio to tell someone we were here. I heard him telling someone our position and rushed in to see who he was talking to. When he saw me coming, he pulled a small silver pistol and aimed it at me."

"He shot at you?"

"I startled him, and he missed. I felt the heat of the bullet fly by my ear. I dove for the ground, pulled my gun, and fired twice. I must have hit him with the second bullet as he stumbled back and his gun fired into the air. He's on the ground back there. One bloody bullet hole. He kept twitching, then stopped."

Terry pushed her hair back from her face. "I don't do well with fresh bodies. I'm an archaeologist. My corpses are hundreds to thousands of years old, not new. Mine don't bleed. And, I still have nightmares about the last time I shot someone. I'll need a lot of counseling after this. He tried to kill me." Terry dropped to the ground, shaking.

Virginia sat next to her. "You'll be okay. You had to do something or get killed. I'll go take a look. You stay here."

Terry gave her a quick smile. "Don't worry. I ain't goin'n anywhere."

Virginia rose, held her gun with both hands in front of her and moved to the spot in the foliage that Terry had come through. She moved some vines apart and stepped into the semi-lit spaces between the trees, vines, and bushes. About fifteen feet in, lay a Mexican male. He was on his back, staring at the tree canopy above with unblinking eyes. Virginia cautiously moved closer. She spotted a small silver semiautomatic pistol a couple feet from him. Nearer to him was a satellite radio. Moved next to him. Blood had spread out from a hole in his upper chest. He wasn't breathing. She knelt next to him and checked his neck for a pulse. Nothing. She rose, stepped to the gun, and picked it up. Next, she got the radio and hustled out into the clearing. Terry sat on the ground, waiting.

Virginia walked to her and held out her hand. "Come on, we've got to move. We also need to check this radio. Maybe we can figure out who he was talking to and why he tried to shoot you."

Terry took Virginia's hand and climbed to her feet. She stole a glance at the jungle. "He was giving someone our coordinates. Whoever it was, knows where we are."

"We need to move, now. Obviously, there are some serious people after us, and we don't exactly know who. I know the heading we need to take, so let's go."

Terry swallowed and pointed at the forest. "What about the man? You're going to just leave him?"

"Yes, we leave him. Whoever he was talking to will probably be along pretty soon. Based on his trying to shoot you, I don't think we want to meet his buddies. They can take care of him. We don't really have any capability to move and store a dead body and in this heat... well... he'll get ripe in a hurry. When his friends find him, they may also get the message that we are not just a couple of helpless girls."

Terry slowly followed Virginia back to the Humvee and climbed in. Virginia started the engine and switched on the navigation system. She set in waypoints and their destination for the night. Looking over her shoulder at Terry she pointed to the control panel. "You might want to turn on the sensors and arm the security system. Things could get interesting."

"Okay." Terry moved from the bench seat at the table to the instruments and flipped switches. "All sensor monitors are green. Are we going to try and drive into the jungle?"

"Yes and no. I found a sort of trail, an old Mayan road, and it goes about where we want for today. I'd like to get some mileage between us and whoever that guy was talking to."

"Okay. I'm strapped in; let's do it." Terry looked at her hands. "I don't remember shaking and feeling sick like this the last time I shot someone."

"Take one of the pain pills in our medic kit. It will help relax you. No tranquilizers in there I'm afraid."

"I'll finish my bottle of water first and just try and relax, if that's possible."

Virginia drove ahead and found what may have passed for a dirt road a few hundred or so years ago and slowly maneuvered down the path, driving around trees, potholes, and rocks. She looked over her shoulder at Terry. She sat stiff, hands squeezing the arms of her chair, watching the two monitors on the control panel.

After two hours, Virginia checked their position. "Looks like we made a little progress, but it's getting late. I'll find a place to stop for tonight that's hopefully not too conspicuous."

Terry unbuckled and climbed into the front passenger seat. "Sounds like a plan. Do you think we're far enough so no one will find us? Like the people that guy was talking to?"

"The going's been slow, and it wouldn't take an Eagle Scout to track us. But it will be dark soon, and that should be to our advantage."

"I found the frequency he was using on his radio. It isn't a government one, but that's all I could figure out."

"That's okay. We have it... wait a minute. We'd better get rid of it. That thing may have a GPS chip that will allow someone to track it."

"If that's the case, then we're probably not too safe right now. I'll turn it off." Terry climbed into the back and grabbed the radio. "Maybe we should also drop it in that creek over there. That way everything would be shorted out."

"Good idea, but take off the back so the insides get soaked."

Terry pried off the back of the handset, slid out of the vehicle and trotted to the small creek. She threw the radio into the water. She ran back to the Humvee and climbed in. "We may have to find another spot to stop tonight."

"I'm way ahead of you. If we go another couple miles, we can use the jungle and dark to hide."

Terry strapped in. "Let's go."

They drove another half hour. Virginia stopped the vehicle and looked at the darkening forest around them. She switched on the Infrared screen in the middle of the dashboard. A few animals were visible as lighter figures than the darker background. "There were some animals over there. Maybe we can drive through that foliage and park."

"Don't hit anything big."

"I'll do my best not to." Virginia turned the Humvee and slowly advanced on some vines and bushes. The vehicle pushed through and into an area of dense underbrush. She turned on the searchlights. The jungle was packed around them. "Okay, let's lock it down and prepare for the evening."

Virginia turned off the engine and activated the generator. "Might as well use our prime source of power for a while, and then, we'll use the batteries."

Terry nodded and hit the lock switch. The doors clicked. Next, she maneuvered the controls to have four round bars extend a few feet out from the front and rear sides. She lowered the flat plate with the round tube above. Then, she lowered the plates to the ground and leveled the vehicle and activated the drills. The exterior stabilizers hummed as the drills went two feet into the earth. "Okay. We have the levelers out and the anchor rods down in the ground."

Virginia activated the window armor. "The windows will resist pretty much anything, but with the added metal armor protection we should be safer. That, and no one can see in."

Terry looked at the sensor monitors. "The panel is green, and there isn't anything bigger than a monkey on the screen."

"Good. Let's prepare dinner, and we can plan our course for tomorrow."

Virginia woke in a start. She looked around and climbed out of her bunk. Terry was sitting at the control panel staring at the monitors. "What's wrong?"

"I woke when I heard the alarm beep. There aren't any great apes around here are there?"

"You know there aren't any. Why?"

Terry pointed at a screen. "Because there are some over by the so-called road we were on. And the apes are driving something the size of a pickup truck."

"Is the truck moving?"

"Yeah, but slowly. They've got a searchlight playing across the ground and two people out in front with lights."

"That's not good. Why didn't you wake me?"

"You were exhausted, and I couldn't sleep all that well. In my sleep, I keep seeing that bullet strike that man."

"I understand. We've got the outside deterrent system activated. Right?"

"Yeah, but I've loaded the canisters of the Manchineel tree acid sap solution into the weapons in place of the pepper spray. That acid sap will burn on contact should anyone get nosey. They're on automatic."

"Let's hope it doesn't come to that."

CHAPTER 21

Virginia sat next to Terry watching the monitors. The IR image on the right screen showed up as shades of green and black. The left monitor was a live feed real time off an outside camera. They could see moving lights and shadows.

Virginia pointed at the IR monitor. "Looks like they may go by us. It would be extremely hard to track someone in the dark, even something the size of our vehicle."

Terry nodded. "I wonder who they are?"

"I don't think this is an opportune time to go and ask."

"Me either. Think they found our track because of that guy's call?"

"I don't know. Maybe they're his, or maybe Peter York's people. But whoever they are, they're persistent."

Terry sat back. "They're going in our direction. We may run into them. Do you have another route we can take?"

"You're right. They're trying to track us. They don't know our destination. And no, I don't have another route. Maybe they'll give up and go back where they came from." Virginia turned and looked at Terry. "You want to try and get some sleep? I'll stay up and keep an eye on things."

"Thanks, but I can't sleep. Even with those guys moving past us, I'm still jittery about the shooting."

Virginia put her hand on Terry's arm. "I understand." Terry leaned toward the control panel. "Look, the truck, and the men have gone, but one of the men has come back."

Virginia squinted at the monitor. "Maybe, he dropped something. Then, again, maybe he saw something and came back to investigate."

Terry went pale. "What do we do?"

"If he turns out to be a threat, we take him out." Virginia slowly rose from the chair and went to the arms locker. She pulled out a black semiautomatic, checked the magazine and safety, then picked up a sound suppressor. She screwed it on the end of the pistol. "If he gets nosey, we silence him."

"We murder him?"

"It's him or us. I consider it self-defense."

Terry wrapped her arms around herself.

Virginia returned to her seat and stared at the screen. "Where'd he go?"

Terry looked at both monitors. "I don't know. Want to use the radar?"

"No. In this jungle all we'd get is backscatter from the vegetation. Let's turn on all the outside motion detectors and monitors using the IR mode and see if he's sneaking up on us."

Terry moved some switches and dials. The right screen filled with six images and the left with another six. They displayed some sort of ground animal near the Humvee rummaging through the underbrush, a monkey sleeping overhead and the man across the road relieving himself on a bush. Terry chuckled. "Too much *cerveza.* So much for a sneak attack."

Virginia pointed to one of the small images on her monitor. "That looks like a cat. A good size one moving toward that guy. He doesn't see it."

Terry looked at the screen. "We can't warn him. If he doesn't get moving that cat may have him for a snack."

"Look, the cat just climbed that tree. Either something spooked it, or it's going to go from tree to tree. It'll probably pounce on that guy from above."

"The guy's moving away. He appears to still be looking for something."

They watched the man swing his lantern back and forth until he stopped and knelt on the ground. As he rose, the cat sprang. The man fell forward onto the ground from the impact of the animal striking his back. The cat rolled a few feet, the man's right leg held by a claw. The cat twisted, released the leg to get a better footing when a shot rang out. The round hit a tree a couple inches from the cat's head. It leaped up rotating in the air and disappeared into the jungle. Two more men ran into the area and helped the man up. They waited, surveying the area with their assault weapons, until the pickup truck reappeared. They climbed into the back. The truck drove slowly back the direction it came.

Terry let out a sigh. "I'm glad that's over. I guess we can go back to bed."

"Let's reload the canisters with pepper spray and acid sap. We'll set the system on automatic. Leave the monitors on and set the alarm, too. Then, we can go back to sleep."

Terry nodded and helped Virginia reload the weapons canisters.

Terry woke with a start. She glanced at the control station, then at Virginia, who sat with a cup of coffee. Terry moved to the two-burner stove and counter area where the coffee pot rested and poured herself a cup. She sipped it. "That's pretty good for roughing it."

Virginia chuckled. 'You call this roughing it? I thought you were a field archaeologist. Don't you camp out intents in rugged places to dig?"

"Honey, my idea of roughing it is a two-star motel or an RV with slide outs. I'm getting too old to sleep in the dirt."

Virginia took a long drink of her coffee. "Better rethink that idea. We may be sleeping in the dirt before this is over."

Terry finished her coffee. "Any chance I can get my money back from this excursion?"

"No refunds. Let's clean up and have a quick breakfast. We need to get moving before our visitors from last night reappear."

"Good idea. My stomach is still queasy from the shooting. Maybe a little breakfast will help."

An hour later, Virginia was steering the Humvee around obstacles on the old Mayan road. "Terry. Anything on the sensors?"

"Nothing unusual. Monkeys, birds, a rather large snake, some good size four-legged creatures I can't identify, and lots of vegetation."

"No trucks or vehicles?"

"Nothing yet. Let's hope they gave up."

Virginia suddenly slowed the Humvee. "What the hell?"

"What is it?" Terry climbed into the front passenger seat and looked out the front window. On two poles were human heads. One was a clean, white skull. The other was a fresh human head. "I think someone is sending a message."

"No shit. But, we need to go beyond this point whether they like it or not."

Terry scanned the area around them. "I don't see anyone. They probably put this up last night."

"I think you're right. Well, here goes nothing." Virginia drove past the poles. The trail started to get narrow and then, expanded into a wide flat area with the trees and vegetation stripped back about twenty feet from the road. She drove the Humvee on the smooth surface to the far end. There sat two makeshift buildings constructed of wood and corrugated metal. Next to one were six fifty-five gallon drums. One had a hand pump on it. "I think we just drove onto a drug cartels landing strip. We need to get out of here fast."

Terry hopped back into the rear of the vehicle and looked at the monitors. "Looks like the only animals in the area are monkeys. Want to take a look at those sheds?"

"No."

Terry looked out the front window. "I have an idea that will screw them up, and we don't have to do much."

"Like what?"

"Pour water into those fuel drums. The airplanes that use it won't get far. We'll be doing Uncle Sam a big favor."

"Okay, but let's make it quick." Virginia stopped next to the sheds and opened the door. As she started to go inside, she heard the sound of a vehicle engine rapidly approaching. She slammed the door, started the Humvee, and gunned the engine throwing Terry against the table.

Terry held on to the table as Virginia accelerated into the jungle.

A hundred yards in, she stopped and killed the engine. Virginia clambered over the seat and looked at the sensor displays. "Looks clear for now."

"What happened?"

"Someone's coming. Needed to get the hell out."

Terry climbed to her feet. "Should we go see who's coming?"

"Common sense says we haul ass. But, we can wait a few minutes to make sure they don't follow us in here. If they stop, we can go take a look. By the way, putting water in the fuel probably wouldn't have worked. The pilot would check for water in his fuel tank before he took off."

Terry tilted her head. "You know this how? You a pilot, too?"

"No. I dated a private pilot for a while when I was in college."

Terry gave her a quizzical look. "Member of the mile-high club?"

"No. He tried to initiate me into the club, but I didn't like him that much. But did you know they actually have small gold wings that say mile high club?"

"No." Terry shook her head. "I need to get out more." She opened a side window. The smell of damp earth and the heat and humidity rushed in. "I hear what sounds like a truck. I think it's stopping. There are a number of voices."

Virginia looked at the control panel. The rear sensor went red. "Someone is coming."

CHAPTER 22

Virginia quickly scanned the monitors. “The sensors indicate something good sized and maybe a number of people. We should check it out, maybe the drug guys are coming.

“Great. Just what we need. If it is them, we need to be careful.”

“Right, let’s grab some weapons and binoculars and scout around.”

“Okay, I’ll grab a couple of pistols for us.”

Virginia grinned. “It’s been my experience that the one with the biggest guns wins a gun fight. Let’s bring some insurance we hopefully won’t need. You know, just in case.”

Armed with 9mm semiautomatics, a mini-RPG launcher, and Terry’s MP-5, they left the Humvee and moved into the forest. As they got closer to the clearing, they crawled through the vegetation.

Through the vines and leaves, Virginia saw an old, battered two-and-a-half-ton stake truck with a rusted right fender, rumble across the clearing and up to the side of a shed, they had just raced past. Men dressed in faded jeans and stained t-shirts climbed out of the truck. Another large truck and a pickup roared into the clearing and drove to the far edge. Men swarmed the area, erecting a windsock and clearing off rubble. A man sat on top of the truck next to the shed with a portable radio in hand. Others unlocked the sheds and started pulled out wrapped bundles on pallets using pallet jacks from the second vehicle. One man looked quizzically at the open hasp on the door of the second shed, then shrugged, and opened it.

Virginia pointed at the pickup. “The guy standing in the bed of that truck seems to be in charge. Maybe they’re waiting for a plane to transport the stuff wrapped in that plastic.”

Terry stared. “I think you’re right. So what do we do?”

“Nothing. We’re not drug agents or Mexican police. We wait and hope they hurry up and go away without seeing us.”

“But if that’s drugs out there, shouldn’t we do something?”

Virginia moved back a little. “As tempting as that might be, there are about twenty armed men out there who have no love for do-gooders. And we are women; they'd love nothing better than to capture us and use us as playthings before they kill us. Sorry, we wait. We are two. They are over twenty."

"But–"

"If they find our tire tracks in that dirt, then, we may have to fight. Let's hope it doesn't come to that."

"We could call the U.S. and report that a drug plane may be headed their way."

Virginia sighed. "We can do that. How much it'll help I don't know. We have no idea which way it will fly."

Terry gave Virginia a dejected look and nodded. "You're right. And, if we caused them, or the plane, any harm, I'm sure the drug lord would want our sorry asses, dead or alive. I guess we wait."

They watched as the men stacked the wrapped packages on the ground. When the work was finished, the men stopped, and took a cigarette break. Others nervously swung what looked like AK-47s and old M-16s back and forth and watched the edges of the jungle. The man sitting on top of the cab of the first truck was talking to someone with the radio when the sound of an airplane engine grew louder.

Virginia took a long look through the binoculars. "How the hell is a plane going to come over those trees and drop onto that landing field?"

Terry shook her head. "I'm not a pilot, but to me it sure looks like a disaster waiting to happen. Even if he gets the plane down, how's he going to take off with the cargo on board?"

"I guess we're going to find out. Here it comes."

On the far side of the clearing, a dual engine aircraft with high wings materialized, almost brushing the tops of the forest canopy. It cut its engines and nosed down Suddenly, the engines revved, the nose rose, and the plane dropped onto the dirt strip. Dust blew out from the sides and back of the plane as it skidded down the earthen runway and stopped at the edge of the jungle. It slowly turned and rolled to where the cluster of men stood with the stacked bundles. As the engine stopped, the dust settled.

The rear door opened, and three men climbed out. They greeted the man from the pickup and handed him a satchel. The man from the pickup waved his hand and said something. The crew standing around immediately started to load the bundles into the aircraft. The truck near the shed had pulled up near the aircraft. From one of the six fifty-five gallon drums on the back, two men began refueling the plane.

Virginia watched carefully. "That didn't take long. Once they get it loaded, it'll be interesting seeing how that thing gets into the air on such a short runway."

Terry pointed. "What are those?"

"I don't know—wait, yes I do. Those are rockets. They are going to use rocket assist to take off. Cute." Virginia stared for a moment. "You know, if someone put an RPG into that truck right about now, the fuel, truck, plane, and drugs would all go puff."

"And that would give our position away," Terry replied. "They wouldn't be happy about our being here and may take action to remove us from the planet."

Virginia eyebrow raised. "Oh shit! Look over there. I didn't see that guy before. Where did he come from?"

A guard bent slightly and squinted as he spotted them. He turned and raced back toward the clearing yelling in Spanish."

"Looks like we'd better use the RPG and skedaddle." Virginia reached into the small pouch on her belt pulled out a t-shirt with Philippe Carlos Murphy's name stenciled on it around the collar and a lighter with the Cancun Beach and Golf Club insignia and name lettered on it. She held them up for Terry. "These may help us get away."

"What the hell? Where did you get those?"

Virginia smiled. "At Mr. York's hotel. We fire the mini-RPG, then drop these a-ways apart. Maybe these will temporarily give them a new target for their wrath and give us a head start out of here."

"Good idea. Got anything else in there to help with the ruse?"

"Yeah, we leave the mini-RPG launcher with Uncle Sam's name on it."

"Won't we need it later?" Terry rubbed her forehead. "The one I've got," She patted the launcher, "only shoots one rocket. It's a mini-RPG. It's a DARPA special. The other ones can shoot multiple rockets, but this one can't. We've got more of them. We need to do something to distract them while we get the hell out of here."

They quietly made their way around to a location between two sheds. Virginia hefted the launcher, aimed, and fired. She dumped the launcher and hurried as best she could through the underbrush, tearing the t-shirt and dropping it. The fuel drums, plane, and a truck along with the men around it, blew apart in a huge orange, red and black fireball with a column of billowing black smoke. She felt the heat hit her even hidden in the foliage. Startled monkeys screamed overhead as colorful birds took flight.

When the explosion erupted, Terry tossed the lighter into the tire tracks of their Humvee and stood guard with an MP-5. She watched the carnage and fire spread to the stacked bundles of drugs. The stench of burning plastic, rubber, explosives, fabrics, drugs, and fuel was almost overwhelming. Men dove for cover. Some ran screaming with their clothes on fire, others fell, wounded by flying hot pieces of metal. Several of the guards watching the jungle turned and frantically fired around the clearing and into the trees where Virginia had been. More men fell, wounded by the guard's wild shots. Terry waited nervously for what seemed like forever when Virginia came crashing through the trees.

Virginia waved toward the Humvee. "Let's get the hell out of here while we can."

They jumped into their vehicle and drove through bushes and tangles of vines. Terry, riding at the control panel pushed a button. Small contact mines dropped from the rear of the Humvee. "I hope they were the bomblets and not something important we're going to need."

Virginia chuckled, "Didn't you read the manual?"

"Are you kidding? I skimmed all three hundred pages. I didn't do an in-depth analysis. I hope that was good enough." Terry watched the monitor. "No one is pursuing us, yet. What happens when they do?"

"We pray the bomblets you dropped slow them down, and the rest we do by the seat of our pants. I'm hoping we'll get far enough that if and when they find us, they see the Smithsonian sign and think we're not suspects. With any luck, they'll be looking for York and Philippe Carlos Murphy."

"Do you have any idea where exactly we are?"

Virginia pointed at the GPS display. "We're close to Guatemala and Belize. If we can stay out of trouble for a while, we should be close to our next waypoint." She swiped a strand of blond hair from her eyes. "I'll check the quilt block pictures then."

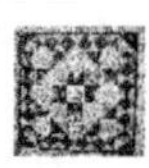

Clemente Ramos stood in shock. He gazed at the burning wreckage of the plane, drugs, and trucks. The sheds were charred embers. He slowly turned, looking at his men. Some were dead, others burned. Some were injured and bleeding from cuts and puncture wounds from flying metal. A few had gun-shot wounds from the wildly firing nutcases he used as security, and others were still dazed from the explosion. *Christ! What the hell went wrong? What had happened? Static electricity? A stray hot, cigarette butt? A rival?* He kicked the ground. Through clenched teeth he muttered, "Damn. That was a million dollars in cocaine that just went up in smoke. A million damn dollars, gone! Someone will pay for this. Someone is going to experience pain as they never knew it existed. I'm not called the butcher for nothing." He stomped toward the burning wreckage of the plane when one of his men came running up.

"*Señor Ramos! Señor Ramos! Mira lo que encontré!*" Look what I found. He slid to a stop and bowed slightly. He handed the rocket launcher to Ramos. "*Americano?*"

Ramos grabbed the launcher and rotated it. He saw the stenciling on the side. His blood pressure rose. "*Si, Americano.* That bastard, York!"

Another man with an assault rifle slung over his shoulder hurried across the dirt field and handed Ramos the torn t-shirt.

Ramos examined it. "Well, well, it seems Philippe Carlos Murphy was in a hurry to leave." He looked up at another man rushing toward him.

The man handed him the lighter. *"Señor Ramos*, I found this in the jungle about twenty meters in. Is it important?"

"*Si,* thank you, Manuel." He looked at the inscription and insignia. Ramos's fist tightened around the lighter. "Peter York, you two-timing bastard! You're going to pay for this! This is what I get for starting to look for a couple of women for you?" He looked at the man, "Where did you find this?"

The man pointed. "Over there in the jungle. Tire prints. A vehicle was there a little while ago."

Ramos motioned for his lieutenant to come to him. "Luis, Peter York seems responsible for this... this disaster. Him, and that sissy lackey of his, Philippe Carlos Murphy. I want them. Murphy may still be in the area. Have some of the men go look over there, and track that vehicle. Maybe they can pick up a trail. Whoever is in that vehicle is responsible, and I want them. I may burn them alive. Contact our friends in Cancun and have York brought to me at my house at once."

"What about the women he asked us to find?"

"Women? I want that bastard, York! They are just women. They are not important right now. We'll find them later. Right now Mr. York owes me a little over a million dollars, and I aim to collect every *centavo.*" Through clenched teeth he added, "Go, get him, and find that damn vehicle. It may have Philippe Carlos Murphy's sorry ass in it."

"Si, Señor Ramos." Luis hurried away toward a big yellow truck and got on the radio.

CHAPTER 23

Virginia skirted huge trees and rocks as she drove. Shewas thankful for the vehicle's high ground clearance as she bowled over small outcroppings of rocks and vegetation. As she plowed through tangles of vines and shrubs, she glanced over her shoulder at the control panel.

Terry sat staring at screen biting her lip. Her hands strangled the arms of her seat. "Sensors picking up anything?"

"Just some popping sounds behind us. Could be the little presents we left them blowing up. Maybe they'll give up."

Virginia nodded. "That was a drug cartel's plane and drugs we just destroyed. I think we are in some serious shit."

"Maybe the stuff we left behind will have them focusing on York and Murphy."

"Yeah. Right now, I think the drug leader will want all of us. He'll use us for entertainment before killing us. Oh, when did you start referring to Philippe Carlos Murphy as Murphy?"

"When that bastard went from potential plaything to bad guy. Can you get us out of here?"

"I'm working on it." Virginia pointed at the GPS monitor on the dash. "We're approaching what I think is the Guatemala border soon. Not sure if that buys us anything, but we're making progress."

"Oh boy." Terry glanced at the monitors. "Something is approaching, but I don't see anything."

"You can't see more than ten feet in this jungle or more than fifty feet back down this old Mayan road we just plowed through."

"Yeah, but the sensors are going from green to yellow, and one is red."

Virginia clenched the steering wheel. "There's a thinning in the trees ahead. Turn on the radar. Let's see if we can spot anything but jungle."

Terry flipped a switch. A low hum filled the vehicle. "Radar on. Okay, trees are messing it up, but something is rapidly headed our way in the air. Maybe a plane."

"Just what we need. How far out?"

"I'm an archaeologist, not a radar technician. I can't tell, especially with all the clutter from the trees. It's moving pretty fast, though."

"Look at the screen, the circles are the distance from us, how far?"

"Okay, I see them. It looked like maybe a mile and a half and closing. It's following our path."

Virginia swerved to the right and stopped under a thick canopy. "We need to buy us some time."

"How? There's still someone behind us on land, too."

"Grab that other mini-RPG and launcher and bring it to me." Before Terry could respond, Virginia hopped out of the Humvee and moved near the thinning tree cover. She could hear the faint thump-thump of rotor blades approaching. *A helicopter. I hope it's low; I'll only get one shot.* She sat and listened as Terry hurried beside her. Virginia took the launcher and inserted the mini-RPG.

Terry looked at the launcher and Virginia. "You're going to shoot it down?"

"You want to invite the men inside to dinner."

"No. Here it comes." Terry looked at the helicopter, "No markings."

They watched as the dark green chopper skimmed the treetops and slowed as it approached the thinning vegetation. Virginia raised the launcher and aimed. As the helicopter entered the open area, she fired. The projectile shot forward, the rocket ignited, and the warhead roared straight for the chopper. She watched as a man in the open side door screamed when he saw the launch and frantically pointed. The pilot jerked the helicopter to the right. The RPG hit it just aft of the cockpit. It exploded into a bright orange ball with hot shrapnel flying in all directions. Virginia and Terry dove behind the trunk of a large tree as metal slammed into the other side. The burning wreckage rotated a few seconds and then, plummeted to the ground. Burning fuel ignited the brush around them.

Virginia stood and looked at the inferno. "I think we'd better get the hell out of Dodge."

Terry sat looking at the carnage in shock. "You… you just shot down a helicopter with men on board."

"No shit. Did you happen to notice that chopper had a machine gun in the side door? Those men were carrying weapons, and they weren't for target practice. They either wanted to kill us on sight or bring us in for fun and games before they killed us. Either way, it ain't going to happen as long as I'm in charge."

Terry, her face pale, swallowed. "I know. It's just that I'm not used to this kill or be killed stuff. How do you get used to it?"

"You don't. Let's get moving, I think you said we've got someone coming behind us."

"You going to kill them, too?"

"I'd rather we got away. Now let's move." Virginia hurried to the Humvee and climbed in. She looked at Terry staring at the burning remains of the chopper. "You coming or would you rather wait for the druggies to capture you?"

Terry turned, rushed to the Humvee, and climbed in. "Let's get out of here."

Virginia started the vehicle and drove around some trees and down the old Mayan road. "I glad the drug guys still use this road. If they hadn't cleared it somewhat, we probably never would have gotten this far."

"If we hadn't blown up their plane and drugs, they wouldn't be after us either."

Virginia chuckled. "That was your idea. Remember? Anyway, that guy spotted us and gave our presence away."

"Yes, I remember. I must have been nuts to even think it, much less get involved with pissing off a drug lord on his turf." Terry sighed. "You're right; he did force our hand back there."

"Are the sensors green?"

Terry nodded. "Yeah. I wish I knew how far back our pursuers were."

Clemente Ramos sat on a large brown leather couch in the living room of his spacious hacienda, sipping a fifty-year-old scotch. He looked out on manicured grass, hedges, trimmed trees, and a high stonewall. He turned at the sound of a soft knock on the large carved wooden door. "Enter."

The door swung open, and a small, rotund man with thinning black hair scurried across the hardwood floor to Ramos. "*Señor Ramos.* We lost contact with the helicopter. No word from them in the last fifteen minutes."

Ramos set his glass down on an end table. "Where was it when it stopped responding?"

"A little over twenty-nine kilometers south of here."

Ramos slowly rose. "Did the pilot report any mechanical problems?"

"No."

"Did he say anything before it disappeared?"

"Si." The man pulled out a piece of yellow lined paper. "He screamed, *Diablo* is after us. That was the last transmission."

"The devil?" Ramos frowned. "What does that mean?"

"I have no idea, *Señor.*"

Ramos sat back down. "Anything from the men on the ground looking for whatever made those tracks?"

"Si. They hit some explosives. The little bombs crippled their vehicle and injured two of the men. The others are going ahead on foot. It is *mucho* hot, and the men didn't take a lot of water. They are going slow."

"Damn!" Ramos's jaw tightened, his eyes narrowed. "I'll give thirteen thousand pesos to whoever brings me who is driving that vehicle."

The man straightened. "I'll tell them, *Señor.* A thousand U.S. Dollars is a great incentive."

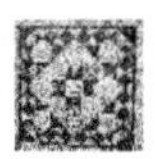

Virginia drove slower through denser brush. "I think we're at the end of the Mayan road the drug guys maintained."

Terry climbed into the front passenger seat. "What do we do when it becomes too thick?"

"We take the freeway."

"Huh?"

Virginia pointed at the GPS display. "Right now it shows us in nothing but forest. No roads. We're in the ether. But look up at the top. There's a highway. A real road. It's on the map. We'll turn onto it and try and get some mileage between us and whoever is tailing us."

"I hope he doesn't have any more aircraft."

"At the rate he's losing them, I'd be surprised if he sends any more after us. There is a village in about eighty kilometers."

"Fifty miles to a town." Terry looked at the navigation screen. She pointed. "Is that blue line in front of our icon what I think it is?"

"A river."

"I was afraid of that. How do we get across?"

"Is there anything in the manual about this thing being amphibious?"

Terry shook her head. "I don't remember anything. Wait a minute! You want to ford that river in this?"

"Just a thought. Beats swimming. There may be crocs in it."

"Crocs? I want to go home." Terry looked out the window through a clearing in the tree cover. "Isn't that smoke?"

"Too late to go home, now." Virginia squinted. "Yeah. It looks like a big campfire."

"We need to be careful; it could be the drug guys."

Virginia studied the GPS display and zoomed in on the river. "There may be a way to cross the river near where that smoke is coming from. There is a village somewhere over there. I hope it's a friendly village."

Terry frowned. "We're not going to just drive in and say 'hi,' are we?"

"No. I figure we should get close in our Humvee. Then, we go on foot and see what's there before we do anything stupid."

"Like blowing up a load of drugs, killing a drug lord's men, and reducing his aircraft to rubble?"

"Yeah," Virginia nodded, "something like that."

"Great. What could possibly go wrong?"

"Good. We agree on the plan." Virginia turned and drove through the underbrush.

Terry's eyes widened as she gave Virginia a terrified look. "You call that a plan?"

"Sometimes you need to improvise." Virginia gave Terry a quick glance. "You might want to check our supplies and see what we may need to look over the village while we go it on foot."

"Okay. Don't get too close. They might hear us coming. Driving through all this foliage isn't exactly quiet, and we are leaving a huge trail for anyone behind us to follow."

"I hope your little bomblets slowed them down."

"Me too."

CHAPTER 24

Virginia slowed the Humvee as they approached a dense stand of large trees with hanging vines. Monkeys screamed from the branches. She stopped and switched off the engine. Terry pulled out two backpacks and web belts with various items attached, including canteens and semiautomatics. "We there, yet?"

"Yes. I think this is as close as we dare drive. Let's have a look." Virginia turned and looked at the backpacks Terry had on the floor of the Humvee. "Got the bug spray?"

"Yeah," Terry smiled. "That and a few essentials every girl needs on an outing."

Virginia slid out of the Humvee and helped Terry get their supplies out the side doors. "Okay, let's gear up. We'll move carefully toward the village. Be watchful for any lookouts they may have."

"Great. Now I'm a Marine." Terry shook her head. "I don't recall my taking any military classes in grad school. You know, this may not be a good idea. This could get us killed."

"I know, but we need to know what we're facing and plan for what we're going to do."

Terry sighed. "I know, but this dangerous adventure stuff scares me. I'm not Indiana Jones."

The covered themselves with insect repellent, donned their equipment, and headed for the village. After a half hour of hiking, cutting vegetation as quietly as they could, and climbing over rocks, they crouched and hurried across a small area of tall grass. They slid behind a couple large trees and hid among low bushes between the trees. They took a drink of water from their canteens, then crawled to the edge of the clearing. From under a bush, they looked at the small village about eighty yards away.

Virginia removed her pack and took out her binoculars. She studied the encampment and the sporadic placement of huts, benches, and makeshift wooden tables. Some had bottles on them, and others had various containers. "There are some men tending the gallon jugs on those tables and others going in and out of that rectangular hut on the far side."

"I see them," responded Terry. She stared through her binoculars. "They don't look happy."

"No. There are a few men with rifles around, so we should expect there will be patrols out."

"Just what we need." Terry poked Virginia's arm, then, pointed. "Look over there. Look at the labels on those empty boxes. Batteries, drain cleaner, decongestants, and some sort of acid." She looked at Virginia. "What the hell are they doing?"

Virginia motioned toward a building. "That crate over by the hut says hypophosphorous acid."

"Is that important?"

Virginia shook her head. "I don't know. I think so, but I'm not a chemist."

"So, they took over a village to make drugs or bombs?"

"Maybe. My money is on the drugs." She took out the sat phone to call Andy at the university and ask him. "I hope he's in his office and not in class or a lab."

"Your husband? Why not the DEA or the Army or the Smithsonian?"

"I don't know anyone in the Army or the DEA. We'd get the run-a-round, and it'll take a week to get any information, assuming we got any at all. I don't have the number for the Smithsonian, and what could they do? The number for the captain of our boat that brought us is in the Humvee, and he probably couldn't do anything either. We're in a sovereign country and in an area controlled by a drug lord. We need answers now. So, I'll call my husband. He has friends who could possibly shed light on what's going on. And, I want to hear his voice."

Terry swallowed. "I see your point. Give your husband a call."

Virginia pulled out her sat phone and dialed Andy's number.

On the third ring, she heard Andy's voice. "Hello?"

Virginia said in a soft voice, "Andy. I need some help."

She could hear the strain in his voice as he replied. "Virginia! Are you okay? What's wrong? What do you need?"

"We've gotten into a little trouble with a drug lord and—"

Andy yelled into the phone. "A drug lord? Are you crazy? Get back here fast."

"I'd like to, but right now I think we need to talk to one of your organic chemist or biochemist friends."

Andy groaned. "Where are you?"

"Guatemala, near Mexico, I think."

"What are your coordinates? I will try and send help."

"I don't know. I'm not in our vehicle. This phone has a GPS chip, but I can't tell where we are from it. Andy, can you get one of your chemist friends on the line; like right now?"

"What do you need a chemist for?"

"I think we stumbled on a drug lab, but we're not sure what we're looking at."

"Shit! Can I call you back?"

"No."

"Okay, hang on. I'll try to get a conference call going." Virginia heard some clicks and the line went dead. She listened. Frustration mounted. She looked at Terry. "What's taking him so long?"

Terry shrugged. "I don't know. Just hang in there. He'll get back to you as soon as he finds someone."

After a couple minutes, she heard Andy's voice. "Virginia, you still there?"

She let out a sigh. "Yes, I'm here."

"I have Dr. Bronson on the line with me. He's an organic chemist, and he worked for a pharmaceutical company before teaching here."

"Hi, Doc. I need your help."

Dr. Bronson answered in a deep voice. "What can I do for you, Mrs. Clark?"

"We are looking at a small village in the jungle down here. They have some strange things sitting around and some funny boxes. I need to know what they could be doing."

"I'll do my best. What do you see?"

Virginia looked through the binoculars and described the situation, then, waited.

In a minute, Bronson answered with a question. "Virginia, is it hot there?"

"Hot? Yeah, it's hot. It's about 98 degrees in the shade, probably 104 or more in the sun, and the humidity feels like it's right there with it."

"Are the bottles sealed?"

"I think so. They look like it from here."

"Are they in the sun?" Bronson asked.

"Yes."

Bronson's voice rose. "Good God. Get the hell out of there. They are going to explode soon."

"Doctor, what are they doing here?"

"They're cooking meth using what is called the shake and bake method. They need to keep it cool. The hypophosphorous acid you saw is being used because they must have run out of red phosphorous. That acid is extremely volatile and *very* dangerous. It's so volatile that the slightest mistake in temperature or capping the bottles too tightly while cooking it will cause it to blow up. As for the battery boxes you saw, they're removing the center lithium strip from lithium batteries. The Decongestants– they extract the pseudoephedrine powder from them. They add it to an accelerant such as drain cleaner and the lithium strips to punch up the chemical reaction. If those bottles are sealed, and they're in the sun, they will explode. Whoever's doing it is no chemist. They're cooking meth in a very dangerous way."

"Okay, we're going to get out of here. Thanks, Doc. You too, Andy."

Andy's voice was high and strained. "Virginia, get the hell out of there and come home."

"We're working on it. Love you." She disconnected and looked at Terry. "You heard?"

"Yeah, just what we need right now, a meth lab that's going to go boom. Our drug lord is going to think we did this, too. We really don't need this right now." She looked at Virginia, "You know something? At this rate, the DEA may want to employ us. That is if we live long enough."

"Tell me about it." Virginia shoved the phone into her pack.

"While you were talking, I studied the area. If you look between those two huts, you can just make out what may be a small bridge across the river. But it looks guarded. There are some women and children in the third hut over there under guard as well." Terry stuck her binoculars back in her pack. "Are we going to plow through there and make a run for the bridge? We could destroy it behind us."

Virginia rolled over and looked at the treetops. A monkey looked down at her. Tree frogs sang; moths fluttered. "I think the drug guys took over the village and those people in the hut are there under duress."

"So? There are just two of us and over half a dozen men with guns and no sense of humor. We don't need a rehash of our last encounter with druggies."

Clemente Ramos paced the floor in his living room. He swung around as the large wooden doors opened. Two of his men, rifles slung over their shoulders, dragged a bloody and bruised Philippe Carlos Murphy into the room and tossed him on the large Oriental rug.

Murphy looked up at Ramos. "Clemente, what's this all about?"

Ramos tightened his fists. "You destroyed *mucho* cocaine and meth of mine. You cost me millions. You blew up my airplane. A dozen of my men are dead because of you. You're lucky I didn't have you skinned alive before you got here."

Murphy slowly climbed to his unsteady feet. He gritted his teeth. "I don't know what you're talking about."

"I watched as my plane was destroyed. I watched over a million U.S. dollars worth of drugs go up in smoke and I saw my men die or get injured." He picked the shirt off his desk and threw it on the floor. "I also found *your* torn shirt. He yanked the lighter out of his pocket and tossed it on the floor. "My men found this lighter from your employer, and a U.S. made rocket launcher linking *you* and York to it. Then, there is the matter of my helicopter."

Murphy rubbed his jaw. "Your helicopter? What... what about it?"

"*You* destroyed that, too! It and more of my men are dead."

Murphy held his hands in front of him. "Wait! Wait a minute. Was there a vehicle around?"

"What are you talking about?" Ramos screamed. "You want to know if we got the license number of your car? I've got the things you left behind."

"No. No." Murphy said. "Was there a vehicle around?"

"*Si.* My men tried to catch it. You should know; you were in it."

Murphy shifted his weight and let out a slow moan. "They couldn't catch it could they? Did something happen to your men chasing it, too?"

Ramos turned red. "*You* damn well know the answer to that!"

"Yes. I know the answer, but I wasn't there, and neither was York."

"How can *you* know if you were not there?" Ramos picked a dark, green jade ceremonial knife off his desk. He stepped closer to Murphy. "I would skin you alive right here, but you'd mess up my carpet." He motioned to a guard. "Take this fool outside and shoot him."

"Wait! It was the women!" Murphy screamed.

Ramos frowned. He raised his palm stopping the guard. "Women? What women?"

"The ones York asked you to find and watch for him. They have what could be described as a small tank, and they seem to have some interesting weapons. They did it. I'm sure of it."

"Two women? You expect me to believe two women, all alone, did all this? York said they work for a museum. They don't sound dangerous to me. You and York do!" Ramos waved his arms. "How could two women do all this without York's help?"

Murphy glanced at the large guard, leaned his back against a table, and slumped. "What happened when your men chased the vehicle?"

"Their jeep blew up." Ramos stood staring at the floor, then, looked at Murphy. "If what you say is true, then, these museum women must be soldiers. Their weapons, may have shot down my helicopter, destroyed my airplane, burned up my drugs, and killed some of my men. And we can't catch them. They must be Special Forces, DEA or something. I'd like to meet them before I have them killed. Maybe right after I kill you. This is what I pay York to keep from happening!"

"Look, Clemente, they aren't Special Forces or DEA. They work for a museum. And, York sent me to see how you're doing at finding them. From what you said, he may okay you killing them after we know what it is they are after."

"Museum my ass. You and York lied! They are U.S. agents." Ramos spun around. "And, I do not need York's permission to kill them, or you."

"They work for the Smithsonian. York checked."

"Museums in your country employ people like them?"

"I guess so." Murphy's face paled. "What are you going to do?"

"Find them and kill them. Then, kill you and York."

Murphy swallowed. "That may not be in your best interest."

Clemente Ramos frowned. "Why not?

"York is being paid by someone in the states to find what the women are looking for. It's supposed to be very valuable. If you follow them and find it, you're in a position to negotiate a deal with York or, if he is dead, directly with his customer. I can help you."

Ramos glared at him. "And what do *you* get out of this?"

"You pay me a… shall we say… a generous finders-fee and I go to some tropical island and forget this godforsaken part of the world. You get what the women find, and do what you like with them and York."

"This godforsaken part of the world is where I live. You attack my enterprise and insult my home and expect to live?" Ramos picked a silver revolver off his desk and pointed it at Murphy. "You and York lied. It was you who attacked me. The only thing you're going to get is a bullet."

Murphy gripped the edge of the table. "Clemente, believe me, the women did it!"

CHAPTER 25

Virginia peered through her binoculars at the small village. "I'm open to ideas about freeing the people and destroying the drug factory."

Terry looked shocked. "Again? You're going to antagonize a drug lord on his turf a second time. No, wait, if that was his chopper you shot down, that makes three attacks on this drug kingpin. Not good form. I'm sure around here we're on par in popularity with the DEA."

"Look, we need to cross that bridge if possible. A pickup truck made it across, so I'm hoping that sorry looking suspension bridge will hold us, too. That means going through there. We can just drive right down the middle of the village and let them shoot at us. Not that it'll do them any good. Then just go across the bridge, or do some damage while we drive down Main Street."

Terry looked through her field glasses at the village. "Well, the corked up meth may solve some of our problems. That building seems to be their main lab. It is either going to be an issue or will blow up too when those bottles cook off. The guards won't be a problem for us in the Humvee, but I can't say as much for the civilians out there. It also looks like the bad guys have radios. They could summon help."

Virginia continued to watch the huts. "We could drive through when the bottles go up and make a run for the bridge. But that won't help those poor people."

"I like your thinking. But, if we interfere we could get them, and us, killed and piss off the drug lord even more. You didn't learn much from our last encounters with him, did you?"

Virginia stuck her binoculars back in her pack. "I have another idea."

"I was afraid of that. What is it? Am I going to like it? Let's stick to plan A."

Virginia grinned. "Probably not. Plan A isn't that good. Here's the basic concept for plan B. When the bottles go boom, we drive into the inferno, try and take out the guards, and destroy any remaining drugs. Then we race for the bridge."

"That's it? Drive into chaos and shoot guards, burn up even more drugs and run? What if they blow the bridge? What if they blow it with us on it?"

Virginia looked back into the jungle toward the Humvee. "We find out if our mode of transportation floats."

"Wonderful. You know there are crocodiles in that river, don't you? That and it's fifty feet down to the water. Can't we just go home?"

"Crocs? I always did want a crocodile handbag." Virginia scooted backward dragging her pack. "What? You're not up for a little adventure? Coming?"

"A little adventure? This is crazy!" Terry turned her head and looked at the village. She heard Virginia start to move next to her. "Wait for me."

As they crept through the foliage toward their vehicle Virginia motioned for Terry to drop to the ground.

Terry quickly and quietly got down and moved a few feet through the damp underbrush to Virginia. "What is it?" Virginia whispered, "A couple of guards over by that tree. I think they found our tracks. Things could get messy."

"If they follow the tracks to us, then, we'll have to shoot. That'll bring their cavalry and may get us killed."

Virginia looked at the MP-5 Terry carried. "Ever shot that type weapon before? Ever shot a machine gun?"

"Ahh, no. Just handguns."

"Okay, here's what you do. If that thing is on automatic, you hold on tight, aim down toward just outside the target's right thigh, and pull the trigger. The gun's recoil should bring it up across him, I hope. If nothing else, it'll make them take cover. You could also just try firing three or four shots and then, let go of the trigger."

Terry stared at the weapon. "Why did I pick this one?"

"You've seen a lot of movies with gunfights."

"What about you?"

Virginia hefted a revolver, "I've got this .357 Magnum and a .38 Special as back up."

"Great, they've got rifles and know how to shoot. We're just a couple girls with dangerous playthings."

"They don't know that. Anyway, if you throw enough lead around, you're liable to hit something important. Machine guns are good at that."

Terry slowly moved some vines in front of her and looked into the jungle. "Looks like they're more interested in smoking weed than finding us."

"Good. Maybe most of the guards are high." Virginia peered through the hole in the vines. "They're stoned and moving away. As soon as they're gone we'll head for the Humvee."

"Okay by me."

After waiting a few minutes, they rose and scurried through the undergrowth to the camouflaged Humvee and climbed in.

Virginia pulled the instruction manual out and thumbed through it. After a couple minutes, she closed it and looked at Terry. "This thing doesn't float. It's too heavy. It can drive through water up to a point, but not float."

"That's good to know. So, plan C that involved floating down the river is out. Anyway, we'd never survive the fifty-foot fall."

"Plan C? There was a Plan C?"

"I figured plans A and B weren't all that hot, so Plan C." Terry sat on the cushioned bench seat in the back. "I had thought maybe we could attack from the river. Plan C. But with the river so darn far down, Plan C is out. We could just run for it. I don't think they'll hurt the villagers if we just plow through."

Virginia sat silent for a minute, then grinned. "Dr. Bronson said those bottles would explode soon. When they do, they'll cause a lot of confusion, fires, and general mayhem. You're right. We can then just plow right through the area, blow up the drug lab, and head for the bridge without stopping."

Terry wiped her forehead. "There is only one problem. There are unwilling villagers in that lab building."

"Right. So, we don't do any more damage than necessary to get to, and across, that bridge. Then, we blow up the bridge."

"I like it. When do we—"

A series of explosions rumbled through the forest. Virginia jumped into the driver's seat. "We go now! Hang on!" She started the Humvee and drove down what looked like a footpath running over small bushes, rocks, and trees toward the village. She steered into the main clearing and slowed to avoid a pig running across the path in front of them. The wooden tables where some of the bottles rested were now gone. Smoking pieces of wood remained. Flaming hunks of wood and other materials fell from black, billowing clouds of smoke, setting small fires. The huts closest to the site were burning. Men, with clothes on fire, ran screaming in all directions. More bottles cooked off causing more confusion, fires, and smoke. Gunfire erupted, and shots pinged off the Humvee. The building being used as a lab caught fire. Some of the guards frantically tossed buckets of water on it, to no avail, as people ran out.

Virginia gunned the engine and tore through the clearing, knocking over a set of benches with more bottles. The bottles exploded behind them. Virginia twisted the wheel and headed for the laboratory. Seeing the large vehicle swerve, the few guards, not injured or firefighting, turned toward the Humvee and opened fire with pistols and rifles. The bullets ricocheted off the vehicle. The village men inside ran out of the burning structure along with a few guards when Virginia tore through the side and down a long set of benches destroying chemicals and apparatus. She burst through the far wall and out in the open. More explosions followed from inside. Virginia turned the vehicle toward the bridge and hit the accelerator.

Terry strapped herself into the control panel seat and watched the monitors. She glanced out the front window at the bridge. "Oh shit. That thing doesn't look like it'll hold us."

Virginia swallowed. "I know. The truck made it across so I'm hoping it'll hold long enough to get across if we hit it at full speed. I remember my husband talking about something called inertia. I hope this is what he was talking about. Those three guards better get out of the way."

She kept her foot on the accelerator. The Humvee gained speed down the slight slope as they approached the old wood and rope, suspension bridge. She watched one guard aim his rifle at the oncoming Humvee. He jumped out of the way, tripped, and fell off the side of the ravine into the river fifty feet below. The second one fired a shot that hit the windshield, nicking the surface. Virginia struck him with the right fender, tossing him about five feet away, onto the dirt. The third man stood in the middle of the road at the start of the bridge and pointed a pistol at her. Virginia aimed the Humvee at him and hit him with the middle of the front end. The Humvee thumped as he rose onto the hood, struck the windshield, slid to the side, and fell off screaming into the gorge.

Virginia held her breath as the Humvee, as wide as the bridge, careened across the creaking and wobbling wood and rope supported structure fifty feet above the dark, raging river. About half way across, parts of the ropes started to unravel, some of the wood base fell, and the structure began to lean to the left. Virginia floored the accelerator keeping aim on the far side of the bridge. The moment they shot onto the dirt road on the other side of the river from the village she slammed on the brakes. The vehicle swerved in the dirt and skidded to a stop. She looked out the back. Through the swirling cloud of dust, she saw the bridge was gone. "We made it!" Virginia looked toward the control panel and noticed Terry, strapped in her seat. Blood spread out on her shirt. "Terry!"

CHAPTER 26

Virginia unbuckled her seatbelt and hurriedly climbed into the back of the Humvee. "Terry, what happened?" Terry, slumped over the control panel, didn't respond. Virginia undid Terry's seatbelt, lowered her to the floor and examined the bloody wound.

Terry started to move and shook her head. She rose up on her elbows and looked around. "What happened? Are we dead?" She cringed. "Oh. That hurts; I guess I'm not dead."

"No, you're not dead, but you managed to cut yourself and bang your head pretty good. We've got to clean up the wound in your side. Being injured in a jungle isn't good."

Terry looked down at the bloody gash. "How'd I do that? It hurts."

"How's your head?"

Terry felt her head. "I've got a headache, too."

From the floor, Virginia picked up a small jade dagger, the point, and blade covered with blood. "Were you using this before we hit the bridge?"

Terry looked at it. "No. It was lying on the back of the control panel. It's the one you brought from Texas."

Virginia examined the knife. "It's sharp. We were jostled about on the bridge. It must have moved, and you hit it when you were bounced around and bumped your head."

Terry rubbed her eyes. "Maybe. I just don't remember much after we started to charge across the bridge. We made it, huh?"

"Yeah, we made it, but the bridge didn't. Fell apart and into the river when we roared over it." Virginia rose. "I'll get the first-aid kit and see what I can do for that nasty cut and your head."

Using the large first-aid kit from under one of the seats in the back, Virginia cleaned Terry's wound, applied antibiotics, and used butterfly bandages to close it. "Looks like a clean cut, and you didn't hit anything vital."

Terry gritted her teeth. "That's good."

Virginia then looked at Terry's eyes. "Your pupils aren't dilated, and both are the same size. I guess that's good, too." Virginia held up her finger and told Terry to follow it with her eyes. Then, she moved her finger toward Terry's nose and watched her eyes. "You did good, I think, probably wasn't a severe concussion, if you even had one. She handed Terry two large white pills, two round ones, and a small bottle of water. "Take these."

Terry looked at the pills and frowned. "What are they?"

"The big ones are antibiotics and the round ones are Tylenol with codeine. I'll give you another antibiotic tonight, and you'll take two a day for a couple weeks."

"I'm not sick. Can you take a narcotic if you've had a concussion?"

"I don't know. I'm not a doctor, but I don't think your concussion, if you had one, is all that bad. You were knocked out for a short time. And, in case you missed the memo, we're in a Central American jungle. There are bad little bugs and beasties here that can make you sick really quickly and even kill you. I don't want that wound to get infected. I need you healthy. Take the damn pills."

"Okay." Terry sat up and swallowed the pills. "So, no one is chasing us?"

"I don't think so. It's pretty quiet right now, let's take a look." Virginia helped Terry up, and they looked out the side window. About forty yards away were the remains of the base posts for the old suspension bridge. Across the thirty-yard ravine stood four of the shaggy looking, armed men, staring at them. An upside down jeep rested on the side of the path. The village was burning. Men and a few women were aimlessly wandering around. "Looks like we took the fight out of them."

Terry frowned. "I wonder if they called for help."

Virginia turned. "You have the most pleasant thoughts. I hope they didn't, but we can't be sure. We ought to get moving."

Terry put her hand on Virginia's arm. "I think I saw something as we crossed the bridge."

Virginia tilted her head. "What?"

"There's a picture in that file of yours of a quilt block with a funny looking shape on it. Something like Poseidon's trident. A big fork."

"Yes. It's a little lopsided, but that's a good depiction. Mary Jane said the block was called *tridente del Diablo,* Devil's pitchfork, or devil's trident. What about it?"

"I saw it out the right window and on one of the monitors." Terry sat on a padded chair attached to the side of the vehicle. "It's a stone column of some type, and it's about a half mile, maybe a little more, downstream. If it were further inside the trees, I'd never have seen it, but it's set back a-ways from the river. I think you can see the top of it in the trees from just one angle."

"I thought we had further to go to find it. Okay, let's head in that direction."

Terry looked out the front window. "How? This so-called road doesn't go that way."

"Shit." Virginia sat on the floor. "Well, we do need to get away from here and hole up for a while. You need some time to heal and rest. Let's see how far down the road we can go before turning into the underbrush. We'll hide for the rest of the day. We'll see how you're doing tomorrow." Terry winced slightly when she moved. "I like that idea. We'd better find someplace where a plane can't see us and we can protect ourselves if those A-holes back there somehow get across the river and come looking for us. Traipsing through the jungle in this tank will definitely leave a big trail for them to follow."

Virginia rubbed her chin, then smiled. "We could drop what's left of the bomblets in case they do manage to come after us, especially after dark. That may deter them for a while."

"We still have some?

Virginia nodded. "A few, I think."

"Won't we hurt some animals if they come across them?"

"Probably. I don't know how much force is necessary to detonate them." Virginia gave her a dubious look. "And, you're worried about animals when the bad guys who want to kill us are out there?"

"Yes. I like animals and don't want to hurt any that are no danger to us." Terry crossed her arms. "So, we don't use anything deadly. How about some sensors or something that makes noise?"

"Makes noise? You mean to confuse or scare them?"

"Yeah. The noise would tell us where they are and may cause them some frustration."

"May work." Virginia looked around. "Any ideas as to what?"

"Yes." Terry cracked a smile. "In the manual, which I read and you didn't, it says there are some screamers. They make a lot of loud noises when someone comes close, and they are battery operated. We have a dozen of them. The manual says they aren't very big. And we have some remote controlled little-tracked robots with lights. They're normally used as scouts."

Virginia smiled. "We place the screamers all over the place, especially near us, but some other places to confuse them and warn us. Any animals that set them off will add to their perplexity. I like it."

"If animals set them off, they'll confuse us, too."

"There is that, but at least they'll be as bewildered as we'll be. The robots with the lights, can we radio control them?"

"Yes, but there are only three and they have a relatively short range."

Virginia wrinkled her forehead. "Define short range."

"According to the manual, they have a radio control range of about a kilometer, a little over half a mile, I think."

"Okay, we set them out in specific spots, randomly turn on the lights and move them about, then turn everything off. Repeat as needed. Could work."

"We'll need areas where they can maneuver. They won't climb trees, and I don't think they can push through much brush."

"We'll use them on the trail we blaze through the jungle, and in areas that are somewhat clear."

"Sounds good." Terry moved to the floor and laid down. "I'm tired."

"I bet you are. The drugs are kicking in. I'll get this thing moving and see how much mileage we can get between them and us, and still stay in the area of the devil's trident."

Terry yawned. "Good idea."

"Get some rest. You might as well stay where you are; the ride will be quite rough I'm sure."

"Okay."

Virginia moved to the storage locker and looked for the screamers. She found seven. *Where'd the rest of them go? Maybe they weren't here to begin with. I guess seven is better than none.* She located the three little tractor-treaded robots with halogen lights and a camera. They looked like large tracked toys, about the size of a laptop computer. The control boxes for them were in the same package. Virginia turned and looked at Terry. She was asleep. *I'll put one of the screamers out here. This could cause all sorts of confusion for them.* Virginia left the vehicle, turned on the screamer and set it off to the side of the road. Then, she climbed back into the Humvee and started to drive.

After driving a hundred yards, she found a place to the side that was mainly vines and small bushes and trees. She left a couple screamers hidden in the bushes, then turned in the general direction of the devil's trident monolith. Virginia drove the vehicle into the forest and slowly plowed through the underbrush, occasionally skirting boulders and large fallen trees and set more screamers along the way. She glanced behind her and saw the path of destruction the huge armored Humvee had left in its wake. She placed another screamer off near a big tree root and a robot to the side. She made a note of where it was. She continued for another half mile, and stopped. The trees had grown too large to bulldoze. She placed another screamer outside and the remaining two robots with the lights. *Might as well camp here for the night. It's almost dusk. It'll get dark in the jungle pretty quick.*

Clemente Ramos eyes narrowed. His hands tightened into fists as he stared across his desk at the squirming Peter York and Philippe Carlos Murphy. He yelled, "You… you sons of bitches have caused me the loss of millions of dollars and the lives of some of my men. I need to set an example with you two."

York looked at two upholstered chairs. "May we sit?"

Ramos slammed his fist on his desk. "Sit? No, you may not sit! You may not live long enough to enjoy sitting. When I'm through with you, sitting will be a luxury, if you're not dead."

York swallowed. "Look, Clemente, we're old friends. I do certain things to assist your operation, keep the DEA from spraying herbicides on your fields, and keep your *Policía Federal* away. And, in turn, you sometimes help me."

"That is the only reason you and stupid here are still alive. But, I'm reconsidering my options."

"Look, I only asked that you locate and keep an eye on the ladies, not antagonize them. They're smart and very capable of protecting themselves. You've seen what they can do, and they aren't even after you like the DEA or the *Policía Federal Ministerial* and the *Federales*."

"York!" Ramos screamed, "Yesterday I explained to your minion here, Murphy, what they had done to my enterprise. Now I just heard that my meth lab in Guatemala had a *grande* problem. The lab ran out of red phosphorous and used another chemical in its place, some kind of acid. Unfortunately, for the pseudo-chemist I had down there, everything blew up. He will pay dearly for his mistake, if he is still alive, I promise you."

York swallowed. "How is that related to the women? They didn't blow it up, did they?"

Ramos picked up a silver revolver on his desk and waved it around. "No. But they drove right through the village when the meth exploded, and then they completely ruined my lab by driving through it. They destroyed all the apparatus and chemicals in it. They also injured half dozen of my men and killed two. In addition, they destroyed a bridge. We needed that bridge to convey the meth safely out of there." Ramos glared. "Now, someone is going to pay! Those two women are doing more damage than the DEA and the… the *Federales*, combined!" Ramos plopped in his chair. He pointed the gun at York. "I will kill those women and you!"

York gulped. "You might want to reconsider that idea."

Ramos glared at him. "Why? It sounds like a good idea to me."

"They are very attractive and sexy. You might like to have them around for sexual pleasures and maybe ransom, or better yet, sell them to the slave market."

"After what they have done to me? I'll kill them slowly." Ramos took a breath. "Pretty and sexy. Huh?" He placed the gun on his desk.

"Yes."

Ramos nodded. "A little pleasure before business? I like that. If I don't make an example out of you or the women, the other cartel leaders will think I'm weak. Maybe I'll take your advice and just kill you two and enjoy the women. I can sell them on the white slave market later. Someone is going to pay!" Ramos rubbed his chin, then grinned. "If I sell them, I can recoup some of my losses."

York looked at Murphy. He was shaking. York straightened and rubbed his damp hands on his pants. "Clemente, my friend. The person I'm assisting in this matter assured me I was going to be well rewarded. I even got a retainer to cover expenses. My contact said what the ladies are after is worth millions. Millions! Maybe once they find it, we sort of take our cuts first and give the *gringo* who's paying me the rest. You can sell the women as an added bonus."

Clemente stared at York through murderous eyes. "You better damn well believe I'll take my generous cut. Now, who is this person you've agreed to help?"

"I don't know."

"You don't know?" Ramos' voice rose. "You don't know? You stupid?" Ramos shook his head. "*Estúpido.* How could you take a job and not know who's paying you? It could be the DEA, no?"

York fidgeted and shifted his weight from leg to leg. "The good faith money went into my special bank account via a wire transfer. It came through the Caymans and The Bahamas. It was there as soon as I agreed to have the ladies watched. I know the DEA. They don't work this way."

"For your sake, I hope the women find something." The phone on the desk rang. *"Hola?"* After listening for a while, he hung up. "My men have found a way across the river. They are going after the women now."

CHAPTER 27

Virginia sat watching the monitors and glancing out the windows. It was getting dark. She flipped the switches to raise the armor over the windows and sat listening to the hum of the motors. She turned on the dome light and looked around. She had placed a few weapons around the vehicle. Terry lay asleep on the floor. Virginia chewed on her lip. She thought about the devil's trident. *If that rock structure Terry saw was really the devil's trident, then, we're close to our destination. At least I think we are. I hope tonight is calm. I could use some rest, too.*

Virginia jumped at the sound of a screamer going off some distance away. The screeches of monkeys and noise of other jungle critters joined in the fracas outside. *I hope that frightened our pursuers a little.* She looked at the digital clock. *Eleven thirty. This is going to be a long night.* Virginia turned on a few lights. She sat at with the control modules and switched on the first little robot with the halogen light and looked at the camera feed on her monitor. There was movement a short distance away. Virginia held the control box on her lap and maneuvered the robot around the area and into some brush, then switched off the light. She waited a few minutes and repeated moving the small robot turning its light on and off as it moved. She drove it into some thickets and turned off the light leaving the camera on. She couldn't detect any movement, but heard more jungle animals complaining.

Again a screamer sounded, and then another. The second one was closer. Virginia frowned. Better pull out the stops. She activated the first robot and sent it up the road toward the river with its halogen light on full power. She could see on the monitor, the cliff coming up fast and spun it around on its treads and raced it back into the jungle, turned off the light, and hid it behind a fallen tree. She switched on the second robot and ran it around a small clearing, then hid it under a bush, once again leaving the camera on. She saw some figures through the foliage that were close. She turned the robot back on, activated its light, and raced in out and across the clearing. Shots rang out, and the monitor went dark. More screamers sounded off.

Shots could be heard above the noise the screamers and animals made.

Virginia turned the first robot back on and maneuvered it down the road closer to her location. She moved the light up and down as the robot moved, then she shut everything down. More shots. She used the robot again and this time a shot killed it. *One more robot before they find us. I'd better think of something fast.* Virginia cracked open the side door and retrieved the remaining bomblets. She crept down the path the Humvee had plowed and placed the explosives at the side of the trail. She then, put a few in the middle of the path and scurried back inside the Humvee. *Might as well make their night even more exciting.* She waited. Nothing. No sounds, not even the animals. *I don't think quiet is a good sign. Maybe I'll take a look around with my last robot.*

She started robot number three and drove it toward her location as fast as the little tractor treads could go. She switched on the outside cameras and waited for it to come into view. Abruptly, more shots rang out. The robot went dead. Virginia tossed the control box on the floor and leaned toward the outside monitors. Waving beams of light flashed through the underbrush. *Okay, Virginia, what are you going to do? Use this vehicle as a fort and try and hold off the Indians or drive out of here and see how many you can run over in the process?* She jumped at the sound of the bomblets going off. *That's music to my ears. I wonder how many are wounded or, better yet, dead.* She stared at the monitors. More light movement. The lights weren't getting closer. They seemed to be in the area where she had placed the explosives. The lights moved away. Virginia turned on the outside passive defenses, let out her breath, and sagged in her seat.

Virginia woke with a start. Bullets were rapidly binging off the Humvee. She tried to calm her heart as she turned to look at the monitors. On the right side, standing in front of a couple large trees, four men were firing assault rifles at the Humvee. *This has to stop. I've got things to do.* Virginia opened a drawer, pulled out a set of sound muffling earmuffs, and put them on. She picked up a short-barreled rifle with a banana clip, set the selector switch to automatic, moved to the right passenger side door, and opened the gun port. She stuck the barrel out, aimed, and fired. The clatter of spent shells hitting the ceiling, walls and equipment and the rat-tat-tat of the gun firing filled the enclosure. After she'd emptied the clip, she moved to the monitor. Three men were dead on the ground. One was hobbling down the path holding the stub of his left arm with his right hand. Blood dripped rapidly from his fingers. Virginia loaded another clip and set the weapon down. She pulled off the earmuffs and looked at Terry.

Terry sat up leaning against a cabinet holding her hands over her ears. She tentatively took her hands off her ears and looked at Virginia. "You done yet?"

Virginia nodded.

"You could have just shaken me awake."

"Yes, but this was a little more urgent."

Terry sighed. "They found us?"

"Yep. They seemed to be unhappy we're here."

"Not very neighborly. Did you take care of the situation with all that noise?"

"Yes, all that noise, and a hell of a lot of bullets. How do you feel?"

"Groggy, but okay. There's a loud ringing in my ears from your… activity." Terry rubbed her eyes. "Time for more pills?"

"Yeah. Look in the first aid kit."

Terry moved to the cabinet, removed the kit, and took two antibiotics. "How many did you get?"

"Three dead outside. One guy without an arm went limping off bleeding pretty bad. I don't think he'll get far. I had to place some of the little bombs outside last night. From the sounds of the explosions, they must have wounded or killed a few more of them."

"You didn't use the pepper spray and the electric shock for close in defense?"

"I turned them on but never had a chance to use them. They didn't get that close. And, just like stupid macho guys, they decided to stand back and shoot first."

"Oh." Terry felt her side. "Still tender. We'd better get moving before they bring help."

"My thoughts exactly. Better make sure they can't cross the river again before we start for the devil's trident."

"How are we going to do that?"

"With a mini-RPG."

"You like those things, don't you?"

Virginia grinned. "An accessory every girl should have on a camping trip to ward off muggers."

Clemente Ramos slammed the phone down. He looked at the man standing near his office door. "Get our two guests and drag their sorry asses in here now!"

"*Si.*" The large man opened the door and hurried out. A few minutes later, he returned with York and

Murphy and pushed them into the room. He closed the door behind him and stood with his beefy arms folded across his chest.

Ramos glared at them. "Well, according to a report this morning, your two ladies have managed to reduce my meth team by eight more men and wounded three. They have also destroyed the makeshift bridge my men made last night to chase them." He kicked his desk and, spun around, seething. "They did it with a rocket launcher! You sure they are not Special Forces, U.S. Marines, or SEALS?"

"No." York shook his head. "They aren't Marines or SEALS. They're just museum workers."

"You're wrong!" Ramos screamed. "They are undercover special operations people. They have to be."

"No." York hesitated. "They work for the Smithsonian."

"Well, because of your so called museum workers, I don't have enough resources out there to chase them or rebuild the meth lab. But you are going to get me what I need and rebuild the lab at your hotel."

York's eyes widened. "No! I'll get you what you need to rebuild the lab, but you can't do it at the hotel. Too many vacationers and DEA people stay there."

Clemente clenched his fists. "Where do you suggest? Your home, or are you going to build it at this cowardly minion of yours home? Take your pick."

"How about back in the jungle? Like I said, I'll get you what you need."

"I know you will. You will replace everything I've lost!" Ramos spat. "You're right. Your resort isn't the right place. But, I think someplace where it will be safer would be on your yacht."

York's eyebrows shot up. His heart pounded. "My… my yacht?"

"*Si,* your boat. If you don't want the lab on your boat, then, I'll take it and put the lab on my new boat."

York swallowed. "Your boat? I… I guess you could use it as a floating lab. The cops would never think of looking there for it. You could move it around to avoid something like this from happening again. I'll get started on the supplies as soon as I get back to my office."

"No!" Ramos yelled. "You'll do that from here. Once the supplies have been ordered, I'll send you two and some of my men, back to Cancun to set the lab up on the boat. In the meantime, you'd better pray your two museum women don't cause me any more grief."

Virginia stopped the Humvee and stared out the front window at a large tree. "Looks like the end of the line."

Terry looked over Virginia's shoulder. "Pretty much, unless this thing has a big power saw mounted on the front. I guess we go on foot from here."

Virginia turned off the engine and climbed into the back. "Yeah, so let's pack what we need and secure the vehicle for our return. Oh, don't forget the antibiotics." She eyed Terry. "You well enough for this trek?"

"Yes, mother." Terry moved to the back and started to pull things together.

An hour later, Virginia and Terry hoisted their backpacks on, locked the Humvee. All the windows and around the base were covered with metal armor. Virginia set the security system.

Terry looked back as they headed into the jungle. "You set the pepper spray?"

"Yes. I also activated the electric shock deterrent, loaded the canisters of the Manchineel tree acid sap for use with the pepper spray."

"That should do it, I hope." Terry looked around. "How far do we have to go?"

"According to my GPS, the devil's trident is about three miles from here as the crow flies."

Terry hefted her pack and web belt. "We've got enough weapons to start a war, and they are heavy. This heat doesn't help."

"I think we already have started a war." Virginia glanced at the handheld GPS display and pointed. "We go this way, and quit complaining, it's not as hot as it's going to get, yet."

Terry pulled a blue metal canister from her a pouch on the side of her backpack. "I brought the insect repellent."

CHAPTER 28

Ramos glared at York. “I’m thinking about all the carnage you and your museum ladies have caused. What’s so important that they came here with what seems like a small tank and with weapons, are traipsing around in the jungle, and tormenting me?”

York shrugged. “I don’t know. From what my customer said, it has to do with a small jade jaguar, some gold, and an old Civil War quilt from somewhere in Texas. That, and something called Diablo… Diablo something or other.”

Murphy rubbed his chin. “Yeah. The ladies had the jade jaguar knife with them and a little bar of gold with a figure of some type on it. A little jaguar I think. They said those things and the quilt were tied to something called the devil’s trident and some city.”

Ramos plopped onto his sofa and looked thoughtfully across the room at a painting of an old man in colorful early to mid-nineteenth century Spanish attire. Ramos crossed himself and muttered, “*Madre de Dios.* Can it be true? After all these years? It isn’t a legend after all?”

York looked at Murphy, then back at Ramos. “What’s wrong… now?”

Ramos rose and walked to York, his face inches from York’s. “I need to know who your customer is and who in Texas that quilt belongs to.”

“I don’t know.”

Ramos spoke through clenched teeth. “Find out and do it now! Or else!”

“But… but, how about your supplies?”

Ramos’s nostrils flared. “Find out about that damn quilt! Then you get my supplies!”

“Okay, okay, let us out of here; give me a place to use a computer, and I’ll do my best.”

“For your sake, you’d better hope your best is good enough. The pain I will cause you will make your arthritis feel like a stubbed toe.”

A breeze brushed through the leaves of towering trees. Virginia looked around at the forest as they hiked. "I wasn't sure what to expect when we came on this adventure. I had thought a jungle infers someplace dark and nasty, like what we've been through. This rainforest is neither dark nor nasty. It looks like a small percent of sunlight reaches the forest floor where we are, but you can still see clearly."

Terry shifted her web belt. "So far, it's been pretty much devoid of mosquitoes and other nasty bugs. When we were on the fringe of the forest at that meadow and pond back there, we found plenty of mosquitoes and no-see-ums. They really liked me, even with the DEET bug repellant." She looked up at the treetops, at the cough of a spider monkey

"It's funny; when we're here deep in the undisturbed jungle like this, the ground is pretty much wide open, and you can easily walk in any direction." Virginia pointed. "Back there where people have chopped trees and cleared the brush in the past is a mess of vegetation that makes passage difficult, even for our oversized Humvee."

"I'm not complaining. I thought this was going to be a rough trek. It's hot and humid, though." Terry used a handkerchief to wipe her forehead. "I'm sweating like a pig."

"You're right. The humidity is awful. It feels like a sauna." Virginia stopped and took a swig from her canteen. "Nice as it is, we still need to be watchful for jaguars and snakes."

"Snakes? I bet you're no fun at a party." Terry looked around. "I hate snakes. How much further?"

"If we don't hit brush and vines like we had to drive through, we should be there in another hour or so."

"What do we do when we get there?"

"Now you ask?"

"Better late than never." Terry froze. "I think we're being watched."

"People or animal?"

"Animal. It looked like a cat. A really big cat." Terry glanced around. "Don't see it any more. Maybe it left."

"That, or it's tracking us and deciding on which of us to eat first."

"Oh, great." Terry's eyes widened. "Do you think it will attack us?"

"Maybe. Keep an eye out and get your shotgun ready."

"Okay." Terry raised the muzzle of her shotgun and started to walk. "Tell me again why we have the shotguns in our hands and our rifles on the sides of our packs? Why not use our pistols?"

"I figured, if we came across something in the wild, like a snake or animal, and since we are not hunters, we'd probably have a tough time shooting it. So, with the shotgun, close is considered a direct hit. Especially when it comes to snakes. You want to aim at a snake's head while your hand is shaking? As for the pistol, a big animal may be hard to kill and a small one hard to hit while we're shaking."

Terry held up her shotgun and stared at it. "I get it."

Virginia pointed to a large flat rock. "Let's take a break. It's hot and sticky, and I think we need to pace ourselves. Anyway, we need to keep hydrated, and I want to look at the pictures of the quilt blocks again. Maybe we'll have an idea of what to look for, when we get to the devil's trident."

They sat on the rock and drank from their canteens. Virginia opened her backpack and pulled out the pouch with the quilt block pictures and ones of the assembled quilt. She glanced up at the light sound of wings of a flight of brightly colored parrots.

While Virginia studied the photographs, Terry took off her floppy hat and ran her fingers through her damp, dark hair. She put the hat back on and looked at a set of satellite pictures of the area. She tapped Virginia on the shoulder. "I think we may have a little tough going ahead."

Virginia's expression changed from one of serious study to one of curiosity. "What's up?"

"I was examining these pictures of the area and noticed the jungle changes color and looks different a short distance from here. I think we're about to enter a part of the jungle where our machetes will be our number one tool."

"Someone has been here before, and cut into the old rainforest?"

"As an archaeologist, I've seen aerial and satellite photos of the jungle before, and now this area." She showed Virginia a picture and pointed. "Looks like trouble. It's well grown, so I'm thinking it was cleared a long time ago and re-grown."

Virginia frowned. "I didn't want us to have to camp out here. Looks like we could be in for some slow going."

"I suggest we head out now, see how far we get, and use the Humvee as a base camp. If we can find a way to drive it into here, so much the better."

Virginia wet her lips. "It's been pretty clear in here, but really nasty back where we left the Humvee. Let's take another couple hours and see how far we get. Then, we can scout out another route from here to the Humvee, that is, if there is another way."

"Okay." Terry put the pictures away and stood. She untucked her shirt and looked at the bandage on her side. "It's started to bleed again. We may have to use more bandages."

Virginia looked at the red gauze. "Take that pack off and let's get the first aid kit out and change it now. I can add some more antibiotic as well."

Virginia went to work cleaning, disinfecting, applying more butterfly bandages, and covering the wound with gauze and tape. "I think we should bury this old bloody gauze and bandages. We don't need the smell of blood to attract any carnivores, or what you thought you saw watching us."

"That's the last thing we need." Terry unfastened an army folding shovel from the side of her pack and started to dig."

"Wait a minute. I just spent time reapplying a bandage to your side. We don't need you reopening it by digging. I'll do it." Virginia took the shovel and dug a small hole, dropped the bloody bandages in it and recovered it. "That should do it. Now, let's see what's ahead."

After replacing the shovel, they headed into the forest. About thirty minutes later, they hit increasing amounts of underbrush, vines, and dense trees.

Virginia stopped and smiled. "Well, Dr. Sorenson, it looks like you were right about the foliage changing. According to the GPS, we are about a mile, as the crow flies, from our destination. I think—"

Thunder clapped. Terry turned around. "I don't know about you, but I think this would be a good time to hurry back to the Humvee. We can strategize there, nice and dry. I don't relish camping, cooking, or sleeping in the jungle in a thunderstorm."

Virginia removed her baseball cap and shook her blond hair. "Me either."

They turned and hiked back to the Humvee. Virginia approached and punched in the code on the key fob to deactivate the external defenses. They climbed in, turned on lights, and locked the door. The cool air inside felt good compared to the jungle. Terry climbed into the back and to the control station. She reactivated the outside defense systems. The steel window shields were still in place. They set their packs on the floor, grabbed a couple bottles of cold water from the small refrigerator, and plopped onto the bench seats at the small table. They drank their water and sat recovering from the heat and their trek.

Terry pulled off her shirt. "I need a shower."

Virginia pointed to a small recess and a curtain. "Knock your socks off, but do a submarine shower."

"I know. Get wet, turn off water, soap up, and turn the shower back on to rinse off. Conserve water." Terry moved slowly to the stall and took a quick shower. Stepping out in a towel, she looked at Virginia. "Looks like you're next."

"Yep. Should feel good." Virginia took a quick shower and dressed. She grabbed another bottle of water and sat at the table. She frowned. "I just thought of something."

"What?" Terry gently touched her side, then looked back at Virginia.

"When did you see the trident?"

Terry closed her eyes and wrinkled her nose, thinking. She stared at Virginia. "I got a glance at it just about halfway or so across the bridge. It was just before I banged my head and everything went dark."

"Was it visible from the camp when we started across? I don't remember seeing it."

"I don't think so. I wasn't looking for it, but the top of it appeared out of the jungle as we were about half way or so across. I kept glancing outside and didn't notice it until then. Why?"

"Something that unusual would normally attract attention. It must have a long time ago, but not recently. I am surprised that no one from that village, or drug camp, or whatever you want to call it, had seen it."

"If my observation and memory is right—and right now, I'm not too sure of anything—you couldn't see it from the camp. You'd have to be about half way across the river and look just right to be able to see the just the tops of the trident. It's close to the edge on the ravine, at the bend in the river, but well enough back, so the jungle hides it. It's hidden by foliage, all but the tops. I'm guessing you'd have to be looking at just the right place to actually see the tops like I did. Maybe the sun has to hit it just right; I don't know. Maybe the natives know of it, but not the drug guys." Terry jumped as more thunderclaps shook them, and rain suddenly pelted the Humvee. "Looks like we made it back just in time."

Virginia climbed to her feet. "I'd better start the generator, don't want to run down the batteries. It's getting dark. You'd better take another couple antibiotics." Virginia noticed a bright flash around some edges of the steel shields. Thunder roared.

Terry took a couple tablets from the first aid kit, got a cup of water, and swallowed the pills. She looked at the cup, then at Virginia. "How are we doing on the water supply?" Virginia glanced at the water indicator. "Good. The showers didn't use all that much. When we stopped at that pond and refilled the tank, I filled it to the tip-top. The purification system is working well. The amount of chlorine that was needed for the holding tank wasn't much, so the filters, reverse osmosis, UV, and ozone sterilizing systems worked well."

Terry leaned against the side of the vehicle and tilted her head. "You know about how it works and the chemistry? How? That much detail isn't in the manual."

"I dated an inorganic chemistry grad student for a while. He lived on a boat in Dana Point, California. He and a buddy built a water treatment system similar to this one for his boat. His, also, desalinated sea water."

Terry stood straighter. "Hmm. How well did you know him? Take any cruises on that boat? How big was it?"

"You're all questions aren't you?"

"Yeah. Come on, spill it."

"I knew him pretty well. It was a good-size powerboat, maybe fifty or sixty feet. We would take the boat to Catalina and down to San Diego and a couple trips to Baja."

"Sounds like fun." Terry sighed. "I take it the boat rocked a lot while at anchor."

"Oh yeah. He was good in the sack; I'll give him that. But he was from a rich family and thought he was hot shit. Took a little while to figure him out. Then I broke up with him." Virginia looked around. "We'll be here all evening and tonight, so we can study the satellite photos, such as they are, our map, the quilt square pictures, the GPS, and see what we need to do tomorrow."

Terry moved to the chair next to the control station and looked at the monitors. "Not picking up anything and it's getting darker. Maybe the bad guys don't like to go out in the rain."

"We can only hope."

CHAPTER 29

Ramos looked up from his desk as York entered the office.

York plopped onto a leather sofa and sighed.

Ramos frowned. "From the looks of you, there wasn't much information about the women, the quilt, or your so called employer." He set his pen down. "This may not be good for you or your friend. What exactly did you find out?"

York kneaded his forehead. "I contacted the Smithsonian. They said Mrs. Clark and Dr. Sorenson are on a special assignment. They wouldn't give me anything else. I tried my contacts at the Department of Defense. No luck. The puzzling part is they were especially tight-lipped and didn't ask me why I was looking into the ladies. They just wouldn't talk about anything to do with them. DARPA was quiet. I tried DEA. Hell, I work for them. They said they knew nothing. The funny thing is, they all clammed up really fast when I mentioned the girls. There is something going on, and I'm being frozen out."

"This doesn't bode well for your continued health." Ramos glared at York. "How about your employer or customer or whatever you call him?"

"I tried reaching the contact e-mail address and the phone number I was given. No response. I tried getting my bank in the Caymans to backtrack the money transfer. They did what they could. It came through banks in Switzerland and a couple of islands known for their banking secrecy, and Monaco and some other Caribbean islands. My banker said he thought the transaction started in Monaco because it involved a sale of gold there."

Ramos frowned. "Monaco? No, the gold was just sold there. The original owner and your employer aren't in, or from, Monaco."

York's mouth gaped. "How can you know that? I can't even trace it."

"Because the owner of that quilt you mentioned is in your country. The quilt's owner, the quilt, and more of the gold are in Texas."

"Texas? Come on. How could you know that?" York gave Ramos a dismissive wave. "I asked around about such a quilt and got absolutely nowhere. No one knows anything about a quilt like that."

"The quilt is real, and the quilt is in Texas. The women are following the map hidden in it."

"A map is hidden in a quilt?" York stood and started to pace. "I don't buy it. You've seen too many spy movies."

"The Smithsonian is backing the women's expedition, *no*?"

York nodded. "Yes. I checked on that."

"The two women Smithsonian investigators, they are not from Washington, D.C. either."

York froze, his eyebrows knitted. "No. They're from... they're from Texas. How did you know that?"

Ramos pointed to the painting of the old man in colorful Mexican dress hanging on the far wall. "My great, great, great grandfather told me." He looked at York. "You have outlived your usefulness."

York started to sweat. He stared wide-eyed at Ramos. "What do you mean we have outlived our usefulness? Who's going to protect your assets from the DEA and Mexican police?"

Ramos shouted. "Go back to Cancun. Do what I pay you for, and keep your mouth shut. If you do, I may let you live a little bit longer. How long depends on my mood." He stared at York through hooded eyes. "You are going to start paying for the drugs and my airplanes those women destroyed. You will also start building my drug lab on your boat. You and Murphy will do that, or your replacements will."

York paled. "Okay. I'll go get Murphy, and we'll fly out of here in the morning. This storm is awful, and I don't want to fly in it."

"You will leave now! That plane of yours has instruments; use them!" Ramos rose and pointed at the door. "Now get out!"

"Okay, I'm gone." York hurried to the door and rushed out, heading for the rooms where he and Murphy had slept. He banged on Murphy's door. "Open up, Philippe."

Philippe Carlos Murphy answered the door. His tall frame was clad in a black, Heavy Metal t-shirt and boxer shorts. His black hair was unruly. "What? Did it go okay with Ramos?"

York pushed past him into the room. "Close the door. Being that I came up with zilch looking for that damn quilt, who the women actually are, and what they're after, Ithink we got off okay. But there is a hitch."

"No luck with the quilt, the ladies, or your customer?" Philippe raised an eyebrow. "He's not going to kill us?"

"No. Not yet." York dropped heavily into a chair "But he wants us to fly out of here tonight for Cancun."

Murphy hurried across the room and pointed out the dark window pelted with rain. "Fly in that storm. No way."

"We fly tonight, or we never fly again."

Philippe stared at York with wide eyes. "But... it's too dangerous."

"So is Ramos! We have instruments, so start packing."

"Wait." Philippe swung a chair around and straddled the seat leaning on the back. "How about what Ramos wanted to know? He's not going to just give up."

"No. But he knows where the money trail started and that the quilt's from Texas. That's where both of the women are from, too."

"How'd he know that?"

York gave a half grin. "One of his great granddaddy's told him."

"His great granddaddy? You said whatever they were after was worth millions. I'm not bugging out of here without it."

York shook his head. "You can stay and get killed, or we can fly out together. Later we'll come back, find those damn women, and whatever they're looking for, and get out of here. The hell with Ramos."

"And just how are you going to do that? We lost our tracker on that rig of theirs. This is Ramos's territory they're in, and, in case you haven't noticed, we have no idea where they went."

"We may. I used my position as a DEA operative to have satellite pictures taken of the areas they were, or are, in. I can get updates. Maybe we can follow them using space age technology. That oversized rig of theirs will leave a huge trail behind it. Once we locate them, we go directly to them and leave Ramos out of the picture."

"Right." Murphy chewed on his lip. "Let me get this straight. Somehow, we return to Ramos's territory completely unnoticed. Then, we locate and grab the women, who I might add are armed and driving a small tank. We find their treasure, or whatever it is they're after, and get the hell out without Ramos having the faintest idea we've been here. Right? You're one taco short of a meal." Murphy pointed to the window. "And, the storm is getting worse."

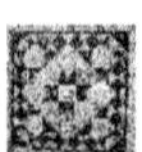

Virginia sat at the small desk, with the lamp shining on the pictures of the quilt blocks, and the photo of the whole quilt. She glanced over at the bunk where Terry rested. The pain pills and fatigue from the hike had tired her, and she had dozed off a half hour before. Virginia listened to the hum of the generator and the rhythm of the rain on the roof as she used a 50X magnifier on the blocks, looking for any detail she may have missed. She examined the block with the trident on it. *Where did that come from?* She squinted as she tried to make out the detail. *I thought that was a circle. It's a small gold cat. Without the magnifier, I would have missed it.* She moved to the pictures of the four adjacent blocks. *There is something in this block, but what? Looks like a bent tree in the background, a spiral, but it's sewn on, not part of the fabric. Important? It's in the block next to the tips of the trident.*

She jumped as an extremely bright flash was immediately followed by a loud clap of thunder. *That was close.* She rose, went to the control panel, checked the instruments, and looked at the monitor showing the jungle outside. *Sensors are green. Boy, without sun, the forest became a primordial dark jungle where we have no place. I'm glad we're in here. I'll shut the generators down and go on battery until morning. Time to hit the hay.* Again she jumped as a thunderclap rocked the Humvee. Virginia sighed. "Great, just what we need—another damn thunderstorm."

The next morning, Virginia rose early and checked the sensors. The surveillance section indicated a night vision video had been made. She hit the play button and night vision images moved across the screen. *Just some shifting shadows of nocturnal creatures, and the occasional flash of lightning. Good. Not people.* She washed up and started breakfast when Terry rolled out of the bunk.

Terry stretched and looked around. "Nuts. I dreamed I was in an ocean view suite in Cancun."

"Now that does sound nice. But, back to reality, how do you feel?"

"Pretty good. My side doesn't hurt as much." Terry pulled her shirt up and looked at the bandage. "No bleeding."

"That's great. Take your antibiotics. The coffee will be done shortly."

"Yes, mom." Terry opened the bottle with the pills and took two. "I'd like my eggs scrambled, bacon crispy, and a side of hash browns."

Virginia raised an eyebrow. "You get coffee, toast, or a choice of two kinds of cereal. And mom? You're older than me."

"I know." Terry sat at the table, poured a cup of coffee, and stuck two pieces of bread in a small, white toaster. "I take it you studied our quilt block photos last night. Get anything?"

Virginia sipped her coffee. She set her cup down and said, "I think I may have found some things. The problem is that I don't know exactly what they mean."

Terry munched on her toast. "Like what?"

Virginia told her about the spiral, the gold cat, and the inscription she found on the binding, *Ciudad de demonios oro.*

Terry thought for a minute, then straightened. "The inscription means the city of devil's gold. Your gold cat could be the jaguar, and the spiral could mean we climb up or down or there is a slide. Or it's just a twisted tree."

Virginia stared at her, took a swig of coffee, and sat back. "City of devil's gold? Like El Dorado?"

"Yeah, like that, but I'm pretty sure a city of pure gold would have been found by now. It's probably a place where they smelted the gold, or maybe a temple."

Virginia grinned. "I like my idea better."

"Yes, I'm sure you do, but we must let the data take us to whatever it is. Don't plan on the big house on the ocean or a world cruise just yet."

"I know. The thing that also concerns me is the phrase *Diablo en polvo.* Lots of Diablo stuff here. Diablo's trident, Diablo's gold, Diablo's power, Diablo's city." Virginia put some peanut butter on a slice of toast and bit it. "*Diablo en polvo. I don't like it.*"

"That means—"

Virginia swallowed. "Devil's Powder, I know. I'm getting nervous about finding whatever it is out there."

"Well, as professionals, we take the requisite care and follow protocols." Terry brushed a tendril of dark hair out of her eyes.

"The care part I get. What protocols? Archaeological protocols?"

"Anything we can think of to protect our asses from anything bad. Got any moon suits?"

"No." Virginia finished her toast.

"Respirators and big rubber gloves?" Terry finished her toast and coffee.

"Respirators, yes. Surgical gloves will have to do instead of big rubber ones. We have rubber rain gear."

"Then let's get going. I think you said you wanted to scout a way to get the Humvee closer to where we were yesterday."

"Yeah. Let's clean up, get packed up, and head out." Virginia tensed as she twisted around when a sensor sounded an alarm. "We've got company."

CHAPTER 30

Virginia peered at the monitor. "Strange. It's two women like the ones we saw in that village the drug guys were using."

Terry frowned and reached for a pistol. "What are they doing? Are they armed?"

"No weapons I can see. They are just two native women standing out there." Virginia shrugged. "I guess we should see what they want, but be careful."

"I'll switch the IR sensors to max and see if they have any people hiding." Terry looked at the monitors. "It's just the two of them."

"Okay. Turn off the defenses and I'll go out. You keep watch from in here."

"Got it."

Virginia slipped on a pair of shorts and a t-shirt and holstered a semiautomatic. She opened the side door and stepped outside into the humid air. She was treated to the scent of heavy loam, the rotted leaf sweetness of night-blooming jasmine. She approached the two women dressed in long skirts and white blouses. Their black hair tied back. "Do either of you speak English?"

"*Si.* I do," said the woman who appeared to be the youngest, more of a teenager.

"How can I help you?" Virginia asked.

The girl smiled. "You already have. The bad men who destroyed our village have left. Many of them are dead or wounded. You did much damage to them. But they are coming back to look for you."

Virginia grinned. "They made their drug wrong. They blew themselves up. We didn't really do anything."

"You used your machine to break the long building and make it blow up and burn. You also wounded or killed a lot of the bad men. They leave."

Virginia cautiously looked around. She tilted her head and gave them a questioning look. "How did you get here? We destroyed the bridge."

"There is another way. We keep it secret. No tell the bad men." The woman looked at the Humvee. "That is a big machine. It upset the bad men. They could not shoot it. I heard one of the leaders tell someone on the radio that you were the museum people from the United States. Your machine was easy to follow in the forest."

"Oh. We are looking for something and have nothing to do with the drug cartel."

The girl translated for the older lady. The older woman smiled, and nodded. She said something in rapid Spanish. The girl turned back to Virginia. "She said she knew you were not with the bad men, and you helped us. What can we do to help you? You are museum people, what are you looking for?"

Virginia rubbed her chin. "The drug men left for now. But they will be back. We didn't keep them away from your village for long. If you help us, you could be in great danger."

"They will be back looking for you. We will be gone when they come back. Our people are leaving the village. It is not our real home. It is there for the ceremonies."

"Ceremonies?" Virginia pointed to a large flat rock. "Please sit. What ceremonies?"

"We will explain later." The women moved to the rock and sat. "We want to help you so you will be able to leave before the men return."

"Okay. We're headed for a stone structure called the *tridente del Diablo,* the devil's trident, and something near it."

The women's eyes widened. They both made the sign of the cross. The girl took a long breath. "Why do you wish to go there? It is dangerous."

"We have a… well a sort of map, and there is something that the trident can help us find, we think."

The girl spoke to the older woman who responded again in rapid Spanish. The girl looked at Virginia. "If you find what you are looking for, what will you do with it?"

"I don't honestly know. I'm not actually sure what it really is. From what I've gathered from my notes, it's a temple or something with jade and gold."

"*Demonios oro.*" The older woman said.

The girl translated. "It means devil's gold. There are bad things in that area. People go there and never return."

"No one has found anything?"

"*Si.* Some have, but they either do not come back and the few that did die of the *Demonios maldición…* devil's curse*.*"

"I see. It's dangerous. Does the trident show the way?"

"*Si.* If you find this jade and gold, will you take it?"

"No. If we find it, we are supposed to let the authorities and our museum know about it and where it is."

The older woman spoke. The girl translated. "If you find it, you said you're supposed to tell others about it. Will you?"

"Why?"

"We know of the place the trident points to. It is old. Mayan, maybe, older. It is sacred to our people. It has been ours for many, many generations."

"How about this?" Virginia swallowed. "If we find it, we tell our museum we have located it, we take pictures, but do not give away its actual location."

"No one can know it actually exists. They will send others to ruin our land."

Virginia nodded. "You've got a point there. Okay, if we find it and then, if we have to tell anyone anything, we give the story that we don't remember where it is or give a false trail."

The two women conversed in Spanish accompanied with wild hand gestures. Then, the girl spoke. "The trident points the way. I can help you, but you must promise us you will not give the location away. You never found it. It is important to my people. If it is destroyed, the curse will be on you."

Virginia sat wide-eyed. "Curse? Oh boy, just what I need right now. Your friend called the gold *Demonios oro* and something about a *Demonios maldición...* devil's curse. I've also heard of a devil powder. Can you tell me about them?"

The girl sighed. "There is a curse upon the *ciudad.* People from the outside go there and die. The *Diablo de polvo* kills them."

Virginia gave her a quizzical look. "*Diablo de polvo*?"

"*Diablo de polvo* is what you call Devil's powder."

"I see. So, it's real. How do the people get exposed to it?"

"It lives there and is used by the priests."

Virginia straightened. "Priests?" *They still practice the old ways?*

"*Si.* The priests protect our sacred *ciudad.*"

Virginia frowned. "Doesn't *ciudad* mean city?"

"*Si,* we call it a *ciudad,* but it is more like *gran templo.* It is like a big temple."

"I see. You will guide us?"

"*Si. Mi madre, nuestro líder,* said you are good people and has now said I can lead you. She trusts you will keep our secret."

Virginia knitted her brow. *This seems too easy.* "Your *madre, nuestro líder*?"

The girl chuckled. "*Si.*" She pointed to the older woman. "She is my mother and our village leader. She is our elder." The girl pointed at the Humvee. "We go in that big machine?"

"Can we? I figured this was about as far as we could take it."

"*Si,* I know a way to get closer with it. Then we walk." The girls looked at the Humvee's side door as Terry stepped out.

Virginia nodded toward Terry. "This is my friend and associate. She is helping me. Her name is Terry."

The women rose and bowed slightly.

Terry stepped closer. "May I ask a question?"

The girl nodded.

"In the past, have any Americans come here and taken any gold or jade?"

The two women conversed. The girl turned and answered. "There is a story. An old story. It says, many generations ago, some local people, from a rancho, and some Americans in uniforms came. The Americans forced our people to help them, and they took a *gran cantidad de oro…* large amount of our gold. The rancho owner tried to help us stop them, but the owner of the rancho died of the *Demonios maldición* soon after. The Americans took a jade knife, too. *El jaguar sagrado cuchillo.* The sacred jaguar knife."

"Wait here a moment." Virginia hurried to the Humvee and went inside. A minute later, she returned holding the jade knife from Mary Jane Striker. She presented it to the women. "Is this the knife?"

The older woman stepped up to Virginia and took the jade knife. She slowly turned it over and examined it. She held it up to her eyes and examined the engraving on the handle. She looked at Virginia and Terry. A tear ran down her cheek. *"Nuestra hoja sagrada jaguar."*

Virginia stared at her. "What did she say?"

"This is our lost sacred jade jaguar blade. You have it?"

"Yes. It's part of what we are investigating."

The older woman, with more tears, sighed and reached out to hand the knife back to Virginia.

Virginia glanced at Terry. Terry nodded. Virginia spoke. "The knife belongs here with your people. It was yours and was taken from you by my people long ago. That was not right. Now it has returned. It is yours."

The older woman wiped her tears and smiled. "*Usted es realmente un amigo de mi pueblo.*"

The girl translated. "She said you are truly a friend of our people." The girl listened as the woman spoke again. "She said she will get word to the priests at the city to allow you to come in. She said she will have them reward you and thank you for your generosity."

Virginia felt her heart race. "Thank you."

Terry looked at Virginia. "Ask about the gold."

"Right. What is *Demonios oro?*"

The young girl took a breath and slowly let it out. "*Demonios oro,* or devil's gold, is the gold at the temple. A long time ago, our ancestors mined the gold from a special place. It was very pure. Then, they refined it more using a process our people do not know today. The gold is *mucho* pure. The stories say it involved something that caused people to get sick, and some died. Other stories said the secret is at the temple, but it is guarded by the devil's powder and the jade jaguar."

Terry brushed a strand of dark hair from her eyes. "What's with the jade jaguar?"

"The jade jaguar knife is sacred. We do not know where it came from, but the stories say it was given to our ancestors by the jade jaguar, a god, many generations ago. The jade jaguar protects our land, and us, from outsiders. The jade jaguar also protects the temple."

Terry shook her head slightly. "The jaguar didn't protect you from the drug cartel very well."

"He did." The girl pointed. "You came. Look at your machine."

Virginia and Terry turned and looked at the side of the Humvee. Near the back, low on the side was the faint image of a small jaguar. Virginia swallowed. "How did that get there?"

Terry slowly shook her head. "I haven't a clue. No one got close, or they would have ended up in a big hurt and set off the alarms. And we would have known. Gives me goose bumps."

The girl spoke to the older woman. She turned backto Virginia and Terry. "My mother said we should go now. She will get word to the temple we are coming."

Terry turned toward the Humvee. "Well, let's get going, but I'd like something to eat first."

Virginia frowned. "What? More food? You just had breakfast."

"All this makes a girl hungry."

"Good thing we aren't roughing it."

The girl raised an eyebrow, "We must go now. If you are hungry, we eat on the way, no?"

"Yes."

"Then, let us go. I do not know when the drug men will return." The girl climbed into the Humvee.

Terry held Virginia back as they reached the door. "Do you really believe all this? This is way too easy. Do you trust her?"

"I don't know. I don't see why they should help us. There is nothing in it for them. We're sure as hell going to keep an eye on her and be ready for anything. Trouble seems to find a way to follow us, and this has been way too easy."

CHAPTER 31

Ramos paced in his office. He glanced at the painting of his great, great grandfather. "You tried to protect them. If the legends are true, maybe I can do better this time. I didn't believe the stories about *El Ciudad de Oro.*" He stepped to the leather couch and plopped onto it, slumping. *What are those women looking for? El Ciudad de Oro? It has been a legend since the days of the conquistadors, but it was just stories to get funding for exploration, or was it? Could it be true? Why now?* Ramos took a bottle of aspirin from his desk, took two with a swig of water from a plastic bottle, and returned the bottle to the drawer. *Is it possible the women have just stumbled on my drug activities by accident and are really just museum people? Has El Ciudad de Oro been there in the middle of all my operations and I missed it? How? If those women are really museum workers, does that mean the stories of El Ciudad de Oro are really true? How much does York know and what is he going to do?*

He stirred at the knock at the big doors to his sanctum. "Enter."

One of his men dressed in tan pants and a white shirt entered. "*Patron,* we are ready to return to that cursed village and hunt those women down. We can leave on your order."

Ramos pushed himself off the couch and stood, his hands clasped behind his back. He moved to the painting of the old man and peered at it. He rubbed his chin, lost in thought. Then, he shook his head. "Humberto, how long have we known each other?"

"All our lives, Clemente."

"Do you remember the stories my grandfather and my father told of the Mayan temple of gold and how my great, great grandfather tried to help protect it from the *Americanos*? They said it was our sacred duty to protect *El Ciudad de Oro and its people.*"

Humberto smiled. "*Si.* They were good stories."

"*Si.* We thought they were just fables or legends told by old men." Ramos stared at the painting. "What if they were true?"

"No, no, Clemente, they are not true." Humberto shook his head. "They are just stories told to children by oldmen. They were the stuff of dreams."

Ramos knitted his brow. "I know about where the village was. But, where exactly was that village and meth lab?"

"Huh?"

"Where exactly was that drug lab?" He pointed to a map on his desk. "Show me."

Humberto crossed the room to the desk, examined the map, and pointed. "Here. In the jungle. It is many kilometers from here."

Ramos studied the map. "I see. Also, where are York and his underling?"

"Last we saw them, they were on their way back to Cancun. But, one of my men heard Mr. York say he was going to return and find the women and the gold."

"I was afraid of that. Humberto, take me to the village. Just you, me, and the pilot. And no weapons."

"Clemente, that may not be safe."

Ramos nodded. "You may be right, sidearms only."

"Why? The men are ready to go and finish off the women and rebuild the lab."

"I do not want our men back there," Clemente barked. He looked at Humberto's shocked face. "I'm sorry. You are not the problem, my friend." Ramos chuckled. "You know, we need a new chemist. The last so-called, drugged up, pseudo-chemist is dead. He at least had the courtesy to die in the explosions he caused. Saves me having to kill him." Ramos returned to his desk, opened a drawer, and pulled out a faded, handwritten notebook. "Let me know as soon as you and the plane are ready."

Virginia slowly drove the Humvee in the direction the girl, in the right front seat pointed out. Terry sat in the back at the control center watching the monitors and the navigation screen that Virginia had transferred to the control panel leaving the screen in the front blank.

The girl pointed at the black screen in the middle of the front dashboard. "What is that?"

"It's a monitor screen, like a TV. We can put maps, images from our outside cameras, and things on it." She didn't mention the night vision and IR vision capabilities. "How much further?"

"We are going the way of my ancestors. It will take a while. It is longer but easier than walking through the jungle. There are swamps and dangerous sand that way."

Virginia eyed the digital clock on the instrument panel. *She's either telling the truth or stalling. Dangerous sand? Quicksand?*

Terry watched the various screens and warning lights. All the indicators were green. The only movements she noted outside were those of monkeys, a large rodent she couldn't identify, a cougar, birds, a huge, strange bug, and a few large Iguanas. She frowned as she continued to watch the navigation system showing them going in a seemingly random direction She reached over and tapped Virginia on her shoulder and said, "We aren't going anywhere fast."

Virginia nodded. She looked at the girl. "Okay, where are you really taking us? This isn't getting us any closer to our destination." She stopped the Humvee and turned. "What are you up to?"

The girl sat, wide-eyed She quickly reached under her blouse and grabbed something stuck in her waistband. The girl froze when she felt the muzzle of a gun at the side of her head and the click of the hammer being pulled back.

Terry pushed the black semiautomatic a little harder. "You'd better not remove anything from under your blouse you can't eat." She looked at Virginia. "What's she got there?"

Virginia pulled the girl's hand away and raised the bottom of her blouse. A small pouch was tied around her waist. Virginia opened it and peered inside. "It looks like a paper in the pouch." She tugged it free and removed it. She opened the document and rested it on the steering wheel. "It looks like a map, but I can't read it. I don't think the markings are Spanish, and they definitely aren't English. It's on a skin of some kind, not made of paper or parchment." She looked at the girl. "What is this?"

"We need to go another kilometer, then stop. The map shows the way from there, but we have to go on foot."

"What language is this in?"

The girl swallowed. "It is from my ancestors."

"Is this map Mayan?"

The girl shook her head. "I don't know who made it. It is symbols only. No words."

Virginia glanced at Terry. "You're the archeologist, what do you think?" She pointed at the gun. "I think you can put that away now."

Terry pulled the pistol back, uncocked it, stuck it back in the holster on her hip, and sighed. "I don't know what to make of it from here. Let me see it."

Virginia handed the map to her.

Terry moved to the table and spread it out. She felt the skin. She bent over and examined the markings. "This is either very old Mayan or some culture that predated them. I'd say it's about fifteen hundred or so years old, plus or minus a couple hundred."

"Who were they?"

"Maybe Teotihuacán. Toltec. Early Mayan, maybe? I can't tell much more from this. Looks like they deliberately didn't actually write on this, or they had no written language. These are symbols. Whoever they were, they may not have been too friendly."

"Why do you say that?"

"I think this is made from human skin."

Virginia swung her head toward the girl and glared. "Okay, what is it, and how far are we from the trident?"

"The way from here is not far. We can ride for another kilometer or so. Then, we walk. The walk is easy. No dangerous sand and the forest is open. Mostly animals to watch for. *El tridente del Diablo* is in the forest. *Diablo* protects it and the *gran templo."*

Terry returned and handed Virginia the map. "Can you show us the way on this?"

The girl nodded and took the skin. "We are about here." She pointed at the faded sketch on the map. "Here we stop and walk. This figure is the trident. We need to be there to use the map to go further."

Virginia knitted her brow. "Huh?"

"The map… it no good to find the *Demonios oro.* We need the map and the *tridente del Diablo*."

Terry reached over the back of the seat and pointed. "What do these symbols mean?"

"They are warnings. Bad things in the jungle. *Diablo* protects the *gran templo."*

"You said the trident shows the way to the *gran templo* and the City of Gold. Is the temple in the City of Gold?

The girl looked down, slowly looked at Virginia, and then, Terry. "The City of Gold is the temple. It is sacred and cannot be desecrated by outsiders." A tear ran down her cheek. "We have kept it secret for many generations. The bad drug men do not know where it is. The church tried to destroy it once, but my people saved it. It was robbed during your Civil War, but the *Americanos* who knew of it must have died. They never came back… until now."

Virginia sat back. "We won't rob your temple or city. We will keep your secret."

The girl looked outside. "Do you hear that? It is a helicopter. The bad men must be returning to the village. They will track us. We need to go to the stop place and hide."

Virginia swung around and started the Humvee. "Buckle up, we're off." She drove further into the forest following the girl's directions. They stopped at the edge of a dense section of jungle. "I think I can drive us into that thicket. There is enough coverage to hide us from a plane and the surrounding jungle will offer some protection from anyone in a vehicle." She nosed the Humvee around a large tree, into the thick vines, shrubs and trees, then stopped.

"Okay, now what?" Terry looked around outside. "We've got a helicopter in the area. Maybe mad druggies are out looking for us. We're in the middle of a hot jungle with wild animals, snakes, bugs, and I mean *big* nasty bugs, humidity that's frizzing my hair, and we've got tohike into hell."

Virginia flipped a switch. Various jungle sounds came over the speaker. "The outside mike doesn't pick up the chopper any more. Maybe it flew away or landed somewhere."

Terry sat at the control panel and looked at the monitor. "That's funny."

Virginia looked over her shoulder. "What's funny?"

"I would swear I saw movement out there."

"Maybe an animal."

"Let's see." Terry turned on the thermal imaging cameras. "Nope. We've got the two legged type animals all around us."

"Are they armed?"

"You bet. Switching on the perimeter defenses, now." Terry activated the outside defenses. "That should deter most aggression."

The girl fidgeted with the latch on her seatbelt. It sprung loose. She turned for the door when Virginia grabbed her shoulder. "You're not going anywhere, sister. Who are these people? Drug cartel? You led us into a trap."

The girl squirmed. "No! They are my people. Not drug men. I need to talk to them. They will not hurt you if I talk to them."

Terry bent slightly and looked out the front window. "We might want to put up the steel armor. That guy has a really big gun."

CHAPTER 32

From behind a large tree, a tall, muscular man, with long black hair, in faded jeans and green shirt, approached the front of the Humvee. He held a huge revolver in his hand, aimed at the ground. He stood straight and said something the outside mike picked up. Virginia looked at the girl. "What did he say?"

The girl stared at him. "He can see me in the glass and wants to talk to me, outside."

Virginia wet her lips. "You understand we have enough firepower in this vehicle to lay waste to a small country. They won't stand a chance if they attack us. Don't try anything foolish." She glanced at Terry. "Turn off the defenses for her to get out. When she's safely away, we turn them back on."

"Copy that." Terry flipped the switches.

The girl took a breath. "I will tell them who you are. I'm sure my mother has communicated with them already." The girl opened the door and slid out. She closed the door behind her and walked to the tall man.

Virginia and Terry watched the girl approach the tall man with the large pistol. They talked. Every so often, the girl would shake her head or point toward the Humvee. Finally, the man called out and a half dozen armed men emerged from the forest carrying old rifles. They moved in front of the Humvee and squatted. The girl walked back to the Humvee as Terry turned off the defenses. The girl opened the door and slid inside, closing it behind her.

"My mother got word to them we were coming. They are nervous about this machine. I told them you are friends and helped destroy the drug lab. My mother told them the same thing. They know who you are, but are not trusting you very much. A helicopter was seen, and they are worried it is your people."

Virginia rubbed her forehead. "We don't have any planes."

"I told them that. He said they are not sure about you, but will not harm you, for now."

"For now? They'll try and kill us later?"

The girl shrugged. "My mother is the elder and has great influence. I'm sure she can protect you."

"Just great." Terry stared through the front window. "We all know what 'trust me' means. Will they be escorting us to the trident?"

"No. They will guard the trail we took to discourage anyone who may have tried to follow us. I told them this machine is dangerous and not to approach it once we leave. Bad things will happen to them if they do. They agreed."

Virginia looked at the clock, then, back at Terry. "It's after three. We've got some daylight yet, but how's the weather forecast looking?"

"Weather forecast?" Terry blinked. "What weath… oh yeah, the weather forecast. I'll check." She pushed keys on the computer keypad and got on the Internet. She called up the global weather information and radar and zoomed in on their area. "The humidity has risen, and the barometer is falling from their last check at a town about a hundred miles from here. And, the clouds didn't look good. Oh boy."

Virginia frowned. "Oh boy? That's it? What does 'oh boy' mean?"

"We've got a big storm headed our way. I mean a huge one." Terry leaned forward and examined the image on the screen. "There is a tropical storm coming from the east off the Gulf. We could possibly be marooned here for a couple days."

Virginia turned to the girl. "I think you should warn the men to go home and prepare their families and village for a big storm. One with lots of wind and rain. Tell them we are staying right here until it blows over."

The girl nodded. "*Gracious.* I will tell them." She slid out and hurried to the tall man who acted as the leader. After a number of wild hand gestures and loud voices, the man nodded and barked orders to the others. The girl returned. "I must go with them. You keep the map. I will return after the storm. We go then. The trident isn't far. There are dangerous animals and bogs around here so do not venture out without me." The girl climbed out closing the door as she walked away with the men, disappearing into the foliage.

Terry punched keys on the keypad and watched the map on the screen. "That little GPS bug you put on her, when you took the map, is working fine. We'll know right where she is." She looked at Virginia. "What are you thinking?"

Virginia sat back in the driver's seat and stared into the jungle. "I see no upside for them to help us."

Terry nodded. "I don't see why they would be eager to help us either. We are closer to the trident, I'll give her that, and we have the map." She turned and looked at the map on the table. "That is, if it's real."

Virginia climbed in the rear. "Better activate the metal shields and outside defenses. How bad is that tropical storm?"

"What tropical storm? It's just a big thunderstorm moving our way tonight. It'll probably have some good wind, rain, and impressive lightning by the looks of it, and the report on the Internet." Terry raised the shields.

Virginia plopped on the cushioned seat at the table. "Any bets they're watching us?"

"Oh, they're out there. The IR detector shows two people watching us in the foliage. Trusting bunch."

"Whoever was in that chopper a while ago may have spooked them."

"It sure didn't help any. Hell, it spooked me." Terry nodded. "I wonder who it was and where it went."

"Maybe it was the drug lord."

"Yeah. But maybe it was York and Murphy. I don't trust them, either."

"You may be right." Virginia stretched. "The way I see it, I don't trust our new friends, so we need a plan. I figure we have two options. Plan A, we can wait for tomorrow and see how things go and try to be ready for them to try something. Or there is Plan B, we sneak out tonight and look around."

"What's plan C?"

"Plan C?" Virginia frowned. "There is no plan C."

"There better be. Plan A is, at best, very risky with a high degree of probability we'll die. As you said, there is no upside for them helping us. Plan B is suicide. If the locals don't try and stop us or kill us, the storm easily could. Then, there are the local animals, large carnivores, poisonous snakes, and huge bugs, all of which might like to make us dinner or an evening snack. Also, there are the bogs or quicksand."

"Okay, we need a plan C. How about this? We wait out the thunderstorm. They're expecting a tropical storm, so I'm guessing when it gets really dark and the rain and lightning starts, our watchers will go back to the village and hunker down expecting us to do the same. Most of the nocturnal critters out there will not be hunting during a thunderstorm. That's when we head out using our thermal and IR imaging goggles to see with and wear the body armor that's in the case under this seat. That'll help protect us."

Terry shook her head. "Like I said, go out in a dangerous and strange jungle where there are large and hungry carnivores, poisonous snakes, and huge insects, in the dark. We already know there are pockets of quicksand around, and we don't know where they are. For all we know, the people could have booby traps installed on any trails, too." She crossed her arms. "And, we do this during a thunderstorm with lots of heavy rain, bad wind, and probably very impressive and powerful lightning? We're talking millions of volts. That's plan C? Looks a lot like a worse Plan B to me. Any other bright ideas?"

"You're the one with Ph.D. after her name; any other ideas come to mind?"

"No." Terry sighed and uncrossed her arms. "Not much choice is there? I'm beginning to like plan A more, only we take more weapons and use the body armor." She pursed her lips. "Oh yeah, we trust no one, especially that girl."

"Okay, we go with the modified Plan A, heavily armed and with body armor." Virginia moved toward the control panel. "Let's see where our new native girlfriend is now." She switched the monitor to the GPS tracker. "Looks like the girl's about couple kilometers from us. Not much movement." She looked up at the roof. "It's started to rain. Better start the generator." Virginia switched on the generator, turned, and looked at Terry. "Now, what's for dinner?"

The helicopter landed in a clearing twenty yards from the destroyed village. Ramos climbed out followed by Humberto. They walked to what was left of the small village and looked around.

Ramos stopped and looked down the slope at the remains of the stanchions for the old suspension bridge. "What the explosions and fire didn't destroy, the two women did. Rebuilding that bridge will take a lot of time."

Humberto nodded. "*Si,* but where did the people that lived here go? No one is around."

"Probably ran away when the trouble started. Frankly, I don't blame them. I should never have allowed this lab to be built here."

Humberto picked up what was left of a melted plastic jug, looked at it, then tossed it on the ground. "This place must have been something when it all blew up."

At the sound of footsteps behind them, Ramos and Humberto stiffened, then swung around pulling their side arms. They stopped and stared. The short, old woman stepped closer.

Ramos frowned. "Who are you?" He glanced around. "Are you alone?"

She nodded. "*Si. ¿Es usted el hombre grande de drogas?* Are you the big drug man?"

Ramos put his semiautomatic away. "*Si. Lo lamento mucho. Yo nunca se debería poner este laboratorio o perjudicado su pueblo.* I am sorry about this. I should never have put this lab here or harmed your people. Who are you?"

"*Soy el líder de mi pueblo y aldea.* I am the leader of my people and village elder." The woman gave him a quizzical look. "Who are you? Why did you do this?"

"I am Clemente Rodriguez Torres Ramos." He motioned to Humberto. "This is Humberto Alvarez. I didn't know the stories about this place were true."

The woman put her hands on her hips. "Señor Clemente Rodriguez Torres Ramos, you are a guardian. You should know. You were taught."

"We thought the stories about your people, and the City of Gold, my grandfather, and father, told us were just legends, told by old men to children. My grandfather and my father died when I was a teenager. Now we know the stories were true. But, I do not remember much."

"Your ancestors' helped protect our people and the sacred city from the world since long before the conquistadors. Señor Ramos, you have failed us. You enslaved my people. You will pay for this. The gods will make you pay."

"I am sorry. Now that I know the stories are really true, I will protect you from outsiders. I have ordered that my men do not return to this area."

"*Bueno.*"

Humberto stepped up next to Ramos and looked at the woman. "Have any other outsiders come this way?"

"*Si.* Two women in a big metal machine came. They came after the explosions and finished taking down your work. They destroyed the bridge."

"Do you know where they are now?"

"*Si.* But, because they helped drive away your men and destroy the bad medicine you make, and returned the *El jaguar sagrado cuchillo,* I gave them safe passage into our territory."

Humberto's eyes widened. "They had the missing sacred jaguar knife?"

"*Si.* The golden haired one returned it to me."

"What are they after?"

The woman moved her foot in the dirt. She tugged at a red scarf and looked at Ramos. "They seek *El Ciudad de Oro.*"

Ramos' voice rose. "We must stop them."

The woman's eyes turned cold. "My people will take care of them. They will reach *El Ciudad de Oro,* but they will never return to tell anyone." She looked up at the dark, billowing clouds. "It has started to rain. Bad storm." She pointed at a hut. "You should stay there. Not good to fly now."

CHAPTER 33

Ramos watched the old woman disappear into the foliage. He looked up at the clouds and then, at Humberto. "Think we can make it back to the ranch before this gets too bad? Or we can scout out where the two museum women went."

"I think we should follow the old woman's advice and hold up here," Humberto said. "The museum women are not going anywhere fast in a thunderstorm, and it's getting dark soon."

Ramos nodded. "Sage advice, my friend. Get the pilot and we'll stay here until this blows over."

A bolt of lightning shattered across the undersides of the black clouds, lighting the dark jungle.

With the rain pelting the Humvee and wind shaking it, Virginia sat eating her MRE of southwest-style chicken with rice and beans and drank a beer, while Terry ate her green pepper steak with rice and a can of beer.

Terry held up the bottle of beer and chuckled. "Where did you get the beer? I don't remember buying any when we left Cancun."

"After all the fun and games with York and his people, I liberated some from the kitchen fridge just before we snuck out. I bet he hasn't missed it."

"Good job." She raised her beer can in a toast. "Now, we can add thievery to our list of crimes, make that felonies, in Mexico and Guatemala. Speaking about York, I wonder how he's doing? We left a lot of incriminating stuff when we blew up that makeshift airfield, drugs, and the airplane. I'm sure the drug kingpin was happy to have someone to blame."

"Yes, but knowing York and Murphy…" Virginia sipped her beer. "…I bet they convinced him we did it."

"You're probably right. After we eat, let's go over the sat photos and the quilt map pictures and see how they match up with that skin the girl left us. It might be a good idea if we had an idea as to where we're going tomorrow. We can get our present location off the Humvee's GPS."

"I agree. Let's clean up and get to work. Sleeping in this thunderstorm isn't going to be easy."

Virginia woke to the smell of coffee and Terry humming a song. She slowly turned and looked at the digital clock on the control panel. "It's five thirty. Why are you up so early?"

Terry sat at the table sipping a cup of coffee and eating a slice of toast. "Figured we needed to get ready for when our guide arrives. We didn't set a time."

Virginia sat up and stretched. "Yeah. I'll get cleaned up and have a quick bite. We need to pack up for the trek."

Terry finished munching on the toast. "Got it covered. Our backpacks, weapons, spare ammo, sat phone, water, food, maps, backup batteries, and body armor are all ready."

"What time did you get up and how'd you do all this in the dark?" Virginia dressed in olive drab pants, hiking boots, and a khaki long-sleeved shirt. She pulled her hair back into a short ponytail. "Okay, what's for breakfast?"

Terry sat back, slipping more bread into a small white toaster. "I got up about four-thirty. I was thinking about today all night and was restless. I used the red tactical lights to see by."

Virginia poured a cup of coffee, stepped to the table, and sat. "Nice work, doctor. How are we doing on weapons?"

"Well, there are no more mini-RPGs. You used all we had." Terry put peanut butter on a slice of toast and took a bite. "We have lots of ammunition for the MP-5, the two nine-millimeters, your .357 Magnum and .38 revolvers and the .380 semiautomatic. We have about three hundred rounds of 5.56mm for the M4-CQBR and the M16. We have a hundred twelve-gauge shotgun shells.

"We'll each take one of the rifles, a pistol, and a shotgun, and split up some of the required ammo. And, when did you get so familiar with the military weapons?"

"I read the manuals while you slept. I also packed some pepper spray. It seems you put some bear strength pepper spray in our arsenal."

Virginia ate her toast and sipped her coffee. "Yeah, those bear strength sprays pack a wallop. It'll stop just about anything. Does a lot of serious damage to humans."

"Nice to know."

They finished breakfast and after cleaning up, they put on their body armor. Terry pulled the Velcro straps tight. "You know this is going to be very uncomfortable, and hot."

"Yes. But I haven't got any other ideas on how to protect us. We can always take it off later."

The red light on the control panel lit up followed by a loud buzz. "We've got company." Virginia switched on the outside cameras. "Looks like our guide and a couple friends have arrived. They're sitting on the ground in front of the vehicle. I guess it's time to go."

Virginia and Terry pulled on their backpacks with the shotguns attached to the sides and web belts with their side arms and canteens. They exited the Humvee carrying their rifles and were treated to the sun filtering between the treetops, the scent of heavy loam, and the rotted leaf sweetness of night-blooming Jasmine. The humidity was like a wet blanket. Virginia set the security system with the key fob.

Terry adjusted a strap. "It's humid and already pretty warm. It won't get much better."

They walked to the small group and stopped.

The girl, a machete strapped to her waist, rose and smiled. "I am ready to take you to the devil's trident."

Virginia pointed at the two men. "Are they coming, too?"

"No. They will remain here and guard your vehicle."

"Tell them not to get too close. It doesn't like strangers."

"I already told them. You ready to go?" A Mexican beaded lizard watched from a rock under a fern.

Virginia suddenly turned around and jogged back to the Humvee. "I'll be right back." She opened the front passenger door and after a minute, she returned, relocking and setting the security system. "Okay, let's go."

Terry leaned close and whispered as they walked into the rainforest behind the girl. "What did you do?"

"I got the little Saint Christopher statue Inspector Rodriguez of the *Policía Federal* gave us and the little gold jaguar."

"You went back for a religious statue?"

Virginia nodded. "Yeah. I'm not really all that religious, but I'll take all the help we can get."

After they had trekked through the forest, hacking their way through vines and foliage for an hour, Terry called for a rest stop. She and Virginia dropped their packs, set the rifles next to them, and sat. They drank some water and rested, watching the girl sitting on a thick tree branch lying across the ground. Near her was a large termite nest. Terry returned her canteen to its holder, leaned close to Virginia, and whispered, "It's been pretty quiet. No noise, even animal. I keep expecting trouble."

"I think they will let us get to the City of Gold. We'll have trouble there, or on the way back. I've been dropping markers on my GPS as we've walked in case we have to make it back on our own."

"Then, can we take off these damn vests? I don't know about yours, but mine is hot and uncomfortable."

The girl slid off the tree trunk. "Are you ready to go? We have just a little way to go to the trident."

Virginia hoisted her backpack and slid into it. "Yes, the sooner we get there and to the City of Gold the better."

They followed the girl over large tree roots and boulders for about twenty minutes when they stopped. The girl pointed at the huge stone edifice. "There is *El Tridente del Diablo*."

Terry walked up to the stone structure and touched it. "Funny, it's cold."

The girl looked wide-eyed at it. "*El Tridente del Diablo* is the key to the *El Ciudad de Oro.*"

Virginia walked around the structure, stopping every few feet touching it, brushing off sections that contained some figures or writing.

Terry examined the figures. "These look like the markings on the skin map. Maybe Teotihuacán. Toltec."

Virginia stepped back and looked at the trident, and then at the surrounding earth. "The trident and the figures match the quilt. I think the reason it is cold to the touch is it is acting as a heat pipe. It's drawing heat from here into a cave or something below us."

Terry looked at her. "You sound like an engineer."

"I'm married to one." Virginia pointed at a small hill. "According to the quilt blocks, the skin map, and the figures on the trident, the entrance to the City of Gold is somewhere inside that hill over there. I'm guessing the City of Gold is actually under us."

Terry looked at the ground. "Under us? By the looks of the vegetation, I think that's a stretch."

"Let's find the entrance and we'll see." Virginia motioned to the girl. "The entrance to the City of Gold should be over there, at or near that small hill. Help us find it."

She nodded, pulled out her machete, and started for the rise. She hacked through some low vegetation and vines as they moved close to the hill.

Terry held up her hand stopping them. "Okay, we're close to the base of the hill. We can't clear the entire area. What kind of entrance or markers are we looking for?"

Virginia adjusted her web belt. "According to the information we have, it will be at the base of a large stone outcropping with a figure of a jaguar on it." There are boulders over there, let's try that area first."

They spent a half hour cutting underbrush to reach the large stones. Terry and Virginia examined all the rocks. Terry sat on a flat boulder the size of a table. "Nothing here. Let's look up there. There is a large overhang and some unusual stone formations." Two large Iguanas looked down at them.

Virginia wiped the sweat from her forehead and eyes. "You want to climb up there and look?"

"Why not?"

"I can't think of any reason not to other than it's damn hot and humid, and I'm tired."

Terry swatted a mosquito. "Up there is probably too high for mosquitoes."

Virginia sighed. "Okay, let's go. We can stop and rest when we get up there without the pesky mosquitoes."

They climbed up the steep side of the hill and stopped at the outcrop. Terry pointed at it. "This is man-made. This hill is too steep and regular to be natural. It's a pyramid of some type buried under a lot of dirt and foliage."

Virginia looked around. "Where is the girl?"

Terry scanned the forest from her rock. "I don't see her. How'd she disappear so fast?"

"In this jungle it wouldn't be hard. But, her sudden departure doesn't give me a warm feeling. She slipped away as soon as we found this. Better keep our guard up." Virginia crouched down and slowly moved under the flat cover rock. She brushed off some caked dirt and plant roots from the side of the formation. "Okay, here is what may be a figure of a jaguar. This could be the entrance."

They hacked away vegetation and discovered a large rectangular stone with more markings in the formation standing in front of them. Virginia looked at it. "Can you decipher what it says?"

Terry stepped closer. "Not all of it. This seems to be a secondary way in. The main entrance is for the…" She rubbed her hands over some figures. "…the caretakers or something like that. Maybe the commoners enter there. This entrance is for the priests. Others who try and enter here will suffer the *Demonios maldición…* devil's curse. Great. Just what we need now."

Virginia touched the monolith. "Anything there telling how to open it?"

"If there is, I can't translate it." Terry frowned. "I doubt they'd put instructions here for just anyone to open it. It's the entrance for the priests. Not us. There's another entrance someplace for the people."

Virginia looked around. "Where's that?"

Terry shrugged. "Haven't a clue. Maybe on the other side of this formation, but I don't know."

"There must be something to indicate the route." Virginia slowly turned and scanned the terrain. "It would be almost impossible to find in this vegetation. Another thing that worries me is where is that girl and just how many of her friends are now here watching us, or getting ready to kill us."

CHAPTER 34

Terry shaded her eyes with her hand and glanced around the area. "Yeah. They could take us out without much trouble."

Virginia looked at the large stone edifice. She glanced back into the jungle. "Did you happen to bring any explosives?"

Terry turned and looked wide-eyed at Virginia. "What! You want to blow it up? That would be a sacrilege. This is a very old artifact. That, and it would bring down the wrath of the local people. As if they aren't already planning on killing us."

Virginia looked back at the large stone. "Did you bring any explosives?"

Terry frowned. "You aren't serious about blowing this thing up, are you?"

"No. It's because there are a number of people over there in the jungle, and I've spotted at least four who are armed. "I figured a little bobby trap, or using it as a makeshift grenade might slow down their attack."

"No, I didn't bring any explosives. We've only got a half-pound of C-4, and it's in the Humvee. And…" Terry scanned the area. "…where are they? I don't see anyone."

"Duck!" Virginia yelled as she pulled Terry down behind a boulder next to her. A dart about six inches long dug into a tree trunk a foot above their heads.

Terry looked at the dart. "Holy shit. That was close. I guess the natives are none too happy we found the entrance to their City of Gold. So much for safe passage and help the old woman told us about."

"Ya think?" Virginia unstrapped her shotgun and tied her rifle to her pack. She bolted up from behind the rock and rapidly fired her shotgun into the brush below, pumping it and re-firing until she ran out of shells. She dropped back down behind the rock and reloaded as Terry rose and fired. After firing six shots into the trees below, she dropped back down.

Terry reloaded. "Think we hit any of them?"

"I doubt it, but we may have given them something to think about."

Terry slipped her pack back on when Virginia did. "Are we going someplace?"

A shot rang out as a bullet pinged off a boulder just below their hiding place, followed by three more darts into the thick branches around them.

"Yeah, I'd like to find more cover." Virginia scooted across the moss-covered ground nearer the stone edifice as Terry fired her shotgun into the foliage below. Leaning on a stone outcropping a few feet from the large slab, Virginia removed her binoculars from her pack. She tensed when she heard a click. "Oh shit!" A puff of fine powder sprayed in her face.

Terry, next to Virginia, looked around. "What was…?" The ground under them shifted, and they tumbled down a smooth, stone tunnel.

Virginia lay on her side on the packed earth floor and looked up. The opening they fell through was closed. The area had a dim light coming from her right. Pain cascaded up her left leg. Her ankle throbbed. She groaned as she sat up and felt her ankle. More pain. Her back hurt but her ankle pounded. *Shit, that hurts—either sprained or broken. Great. Just what I need right now.* She sneezed. *Must have been that stuff I breathed just before I fell. I hope that wasn't the Diablo de polvo, Devil's powder.* Motion on the far side of the area drew her attention. Terry sat up holding her left arm. Virginia called her. "How are you doing? Anything hurt?"

"Not so good. I think I broke my arm. I landed on my shotgun. She grimaced. "It really hurts." Terry looked at Virginia. "You okay?"

"I think I sprained, or broke, my ankle."

"Right now, together we don't make one healthy person. In this predicament, it could be disastrous." Terry glanced around. "Any idea where we are and where the light is coming from?"

They ducked at the ultrasonic swoop of a funnel-tailed bat. Terry put her hand on her chest. "I don't like those things."

"Me either. My guess is we're at, or near, the city or temple of devil's gold."

"We made it to our destination, but not in one piece." Terry cradled her arm. "What do we do now?"

"I'll get the first aid kit out and see what we've got. One thing for sure, we need to get patched up and away from here pretty darn quick."

Virginia pulled the first aid kit out and rummaged through it. "I found an air splint we can use on your arm. There are some Ace Bandages we can use for my ankle. We've got some painkillers, too. I think that's the best we have to offer."

"Okay. I'll move over near you so we can put that splint on my arm. Then, I'll tend to your ankle."

In twenty minutes, they had the air splint on Terry's arm and elastic bandages around Virginia's ankle. After cutting off the top of her boot, her foot and the bandage barely fit. Virginia made a makeshift slung out of a strip of cloth she tore off the bottom of her shirt. They took a couple of pain pills each and hobbled to their feet.

Terry picked up her shotgun and examined it. "I broke more than my arm. This thing is toast."

"Empty it." Virginia handed her a small rock. "Put this rock in the barrel and ram it in on the ground. Then, dump it over in that dark corner."

After sabotaging the broken shotgun, they slipped on their packs and with Virginia using Terry for support, they moved slowly toward the light.

Virginia looked at the sides of the tunnel and ran her hand over the smooth surface. "What is this? It looks like it's natural, but man-made at the same time."

"I think it's a lava tube that's been honed out by the people who originally built all this. I've seen structures like this before. They built the pyramid on top of it." She stopped and pointed. "Look. That cave must be a hundred or more feet tall and, there's the temple of gold."

Virginia stared. "It's huge. It's a step pyramid, and it has to be fifty or sixty feet in height. The sides look steep." She took a breath. "I guess they wanted to keep it secret from the outside world or their enemies and built it down here. But the area looks too…too pristine to be abandoned. Looks like pathways and some sort of drainage system have been made on the ground." She looked up at the top of the large cavern. "Look, there's a large hole off to the side, and light is coming in. The light hits a polished mirror on top of the pyramid and is reflected to more mirrors around the cave. That's the source of the light." She jumped as an Iguana scampered around a large rock to their left.

"I think you're right. And, if you remember what that old woman said, they still use this temple. There are priests who use it and are responsible for it." Terry pointed. "Looks like a lot of footprints in the dirt."

"Then we'd better be on our toes. The group above wanted us dead, so I have to believe once we found this, we'll be higher on their, and the priest's, hit lists."

Terry looked around. "So, why aren't they already here?"

"The way we came in hasn't been used for years. Maybe they have to use another entrance. Let's move closer, but keep a sharp eye out for any movement." Virginia staggered. "My head hurts."

They hobbled down a shallow incline to the base of the temple pyramid. Terry lowered Virginia to a large gold block. "Stay here if your head hurts. I'll go look around." She walked around the immediate area examining the stones. She returned and sat next to Virginia. "Looks like they managed to make the building blocks very smooth and covered them with a thin sheet of gold. Notice the intricate seems around the ends and corners. Very advanced." She pointed toward the top. "This is a real piece of work. And, these glyphs are unusual." She pointed, "There is a figure of a jaguar. Over there are carvings of skulls and crossed bones. There are figures of what look like deities on that stone column." Terry took out her camera and snapped a few photographs of the jaguars and other figures. She slowly moved around the area snapping dozens of pictures from different angles of the structure, glyphs and wall markings. "I wonder what's on top, besides the large reflector."

Virginia twisted around and looked up. "I don'tknow. Maybe a sacrificial alter? Funny, whatever it is, it has a halo around it."

Terry looked at the big reflector. "It does? I don't see it. Maybe it will be easier to see if we go up."

"I think going up there is a bad idea."

"While we're here, we need to gather all the information we can. We need to get up there."

"How? The side is very steep. You've got a broken arm. Your side where the knife cut you is still raw. My ankle is no good. We're both on painkillers that dull our reaction time. I'm starting to have funny visions. The gold seems to shimmer. I may have gotten a small dose of the Devil's powder." Virginia rubbed her eyes. "And, to make it worse, we could get company soon who would not take kindly to our trespassing on their temple. Being on the top would not give us a good defensive position. Hell, they could just let us starve to death."

"Yes, but—" Terry suddenly ducked, dragging Virginia off the gold block. "Company's coming."

Virginia and Terry heard people coming from someplace on the right side of the giant pyramid. She and Virginia scooted along the base in the opposite direction.

Virginia stopped and listened. "There are about four people coming and one is dragging something. We should keep moving."

Terry looked around. "How do you know?"

"I can hear them. They are speaking in a languagethat isn't Spanish."

"I don't hear anything other than some faint footsteps."

"Along with the funny visions, maybe the powder enhances hearing."

"Then, let's keep moving" Terry stopped and pointed back to a dark section between a couple of large stone blocks. "Look, there seems to be some sort of opening. Let's duck in there."

Virginia looked around, then where Terry was pointing. "I didn't notice that. How'd you see it?"

"Luck. If I move a couple feet either direction, it's invisible. Optical illusion or good engineering." She moved toward the opening with Virginia leaning on her for support.

Once inside the concealed gap, Virginia turned on a flashlight and shown the beam down the tunnel. "It seems to keep going. We should probably move in further and then, find a good defensive place in case they find us."

"How's your vision and headache?"

Virginia swallowed. "Vision is not as blurred as a while ago, but my head still hurts. My throat is dry, and I'm getting jumpy, agitated. This isn't like me. I'm hoping I didn't get much of that powder in my nose when we fell into this place."

Terry helped Virginia move into the recesses of the tunnel. They stopped at a bend where there were some metal boxes and a small, decaying, wooden wagon. Terry stopped and whispered, "Don't move."

"What is it?" Virginia moved the light around and spotted the snake. "What kind of snake is that? Dangerous?"

"A Fer-de-Lance. Yes, very poisonous. They are extremely nasty and strike with very little provocation and so fast it is almost impossible to actually see the strike. The only saving grace is, its striking range is very short, about 6 to 10 inches. We're out of range right now, but it could move closer."

Virginia stared at the thick snake. "He doesn't seem to care about us right now. You seem to know a lot about them."

"Yeah. I was on an expedition once in Nicaragua, and we came across a couple of them. One of our guides had placed his hand close to a hole in a boulder. The snake in it bit him. He died fairly quick. Never forgot it. I hate snakes."

"They're really that fast?"

"I read that the mongoose, which invariably can kill a cobra, has only a 50-50 chance with the Fer-de-lance."

"Wow. Let's give this one a lot of space." As they slowly moved further, Virginia moved the beam of light to the far side of the wagon. A human skull lay among some bones and tattered cloth. "Maybe he didn't notice the snake." Virginia pulled her .357 Magnum. "Between the snake and the people looking for us, we'd better be ready for anything."

"Look at the skull. The sphenoid and temporal parts of the frontal areas are smashed."

"English, please." Virginia looked at the skull. "It's shiny, and the front side of it's caved in."

"That's what I said. That guy died of blunt force trauma to the head. The snake had nothing to do with his death." Terry felt Virginia's warm head. "Honey, the skull isn't shiny. I agree with your assessment that stuff that you breathed, when we fell in here, *was* the *Diablo de polvo*, the devil's powder. It's having an effect on you."

CHAPTER 35

Virginia and Terry slowly moved back into the narrow rocky recess around a slight turn and stopped.

Virginia switched off the light. "Let's wait here for a minute and see if anyone follows us."

"I'd feel safer if that light was on." Terry leaned against the sidewall. "We could see if that snake followed us, or if it has any friends around."

"Someone outside this tunnel might see it."

"I doubt it. We made a couple turns." Terry cocked her head. "I think someone is calling us."

Virginia listened. "There are people who are speaking some language other than Spanish. But, yeah, you're right, there's a man, he just said something in Spanish. And, he knows our names, but it isn't York or his buddy."

"Great. Just what we need, more enemies."

Virginia turned on the flashlight and shined it further up the tunnel. "Looks like there are two branches of this up ahead. Let's move down there and see what things look like. Maybe there's another way out."

"Always the optimist. Okay, let's go." Terry had Virginia lean on her as they shuffled down the tunnel. "Lots of dust, but no snakes." She ran into a big spider web across part of the tunnel and hysterically waved her arms shredding the web. "Spiders, yuck." At the fork, they examined each branch.

Virginia pointed. "That one looks like it inclines upward. The dirt is more disturbed than the other one. Maybe more people use it. I think we'd have better luck following the left one."

"That logic beats tossing a coin, I guess." Terry shrugged. "Let's go."

As Virginia waved the light across the path in front of them, they followed the beam of light up the smooth tunnel. She commented on the pretty colors in the beam. A short time later Virginia stopped. "I see a light ahead."

"Let's hope it isn't an oncoming train."

They moved toward the light. At the mouth of the opening, Virginia cautiously peered around the side. "Looks clear. I don't hear anyone."

"Your hearing's been enhanced, so I guess it's safe for now." Terry leaned out of the opening and took a sharp breath. "Oh my god!"

Virginia turned and followed Terry's gaze. "The City of Gold."

"Well, I wouldn't call it a city necessarily. But look at those gold bars and those gold-clad buildings."

Terry, with Virginia hanging on for support, moved out into the light.

Virginia pointed. "Look. There's a jaguar carved on the side of that building. It's moving." She watched it for a second. "Is it really moving?"

"No. I think you're having hallucinations. It's the devil's powder. Just stick with me and you'll do fine."

"Okay."

They moved into the enormous cave and to a stack of small gold bars. Virginia picked up and examined one. "It's got the jaguar image stamped in it. Looks like we found the source of Mary Jane's gold." She pointed. This could have been a smelter operation, and there's a set of exhaust vents. It appears like the equipment hasn't been used for years." She sat on a pile of gold bars.

Terry started to photograph the area, moving from building to building, and a few small temples. After about twenty minutes she stopped. "And we found why the Confederate army stopped getting the gold. Look." Terry pointed to another stack of gold and half dozen skeletons. Among the bones were metal buttons, swords, and muskets, remnants of gray twill uniforms, hats, and old pistols. There were also remains of arrows and darts in the uniform fabrics and what was left of what were once wooden crates. "Looks like we found what we came for." She knelt and examined some of the bones, then rose. "These men had some serious health issues that can be identified in their bones. But, I think the poison darts and the arrows are what killed them."

Virginia rose and limped to Terry and looked at the skeletons. "Yeah. Let's take some more pictures, and figure out how to get out of here." Virginia pulled out her camera and limped around, sidestepping small puddles of water, snapping pictures of the area, the smelters, a small stream running from a crevice in the rock wall, the small piles of gold nuggets and the gold bars. "I hope what I'm photographing is real. I'm still seeing funny things," she muttered to herself. Virginia took photos of the soldier's remains. She stepped to a couple broken boxes and gathered some Confederate hardware and placed them in her pack along with a couple of the small gold bars. Virginia stuffed a couple small jade figures in her pack with the gold. She gave Terry a few gold bars and a couple jade figures for her pack, then sat on a pyramid-shaped stack of gold bars.

Terry packed the gold bars and jade. "It's too bad we can't do more here. I tried to find anything about the smelting or the location of the actual gold mine in the glyphs, but found nothing."

"Okay. Now, to get out of here, alive." Virginia rubbed her eyes. "These gold bars are shimmering. There are spider webs hanging in the air."

"It's just the powder." Terry stepped to a wall and examined a map and some symbols. "Look. I didn't see this before. This is interesting. From what I can gather from these glyphs, they were moving the gold and their technology for smelting to another site far to the north, away from their enemies. But something, or someone, interfered. They settled here after moving only part oftheir gold and equipment from somewhere else."

Virginia moved closer. "Does it say where?"

Terry took a few photos, then, stared at the faded, crude map. "It's not a Thomas Guide, but, if my guess is right, it's somewhere in northern Arizona and New Mexico near Utah." She pointed. "Take some pictures of all this, too."

"Okay. I think I can focus on them. They've stopped moving." Virginia snapped half-dozen photographs. "We should think about getting out of here."

"We could go back the way we came." Terry's head jerked around toward the opening they had come through. "Maybe not. I heard something. Someone is coming. We need to vamoose. Any suggestions, or do you want to shoot it out here?"

"The other guys who tried that didn't fair too well. I think we need to find the back door."

Terry looked around. "The back door?"

"They wouldn't and couldn't have built all this in this cave with just the tunnel we came through. It's too small. There's another way in and out."

"The clock's ticking. We better find one fast."

Virginia limped toward the far end of the cavern and halted. She pointed. "There! There is a wide opening and what looks like old boxes piled up."

Terry supported Virginia as they made their way around the ancient equipment and buildings. They hobbled across the expanse of the cave and some smaller stone structures. They moved behind the rubble next to the tunnel and sat. Virginia looked up at the top of the grotto. "There are openings up there to let in air and light. That explains the pools of water around."

"Nice to know, but I think whoever's chasing us just entered the City of Gold. Time to go."

They hobbled down the cobwebbed tunnel stopping every few minutes to listen. Virginia pointed out the ruts in the floor of the tunnel as they moved. "Probably used makeshift wagons or something with runners." Water seeped from the sides in spots. After about forty minutes, they found the exit. Terry and Virginia slowly maneuvered ahead hugging the sidewall until they were a couple feet from the opening.

Virginia limped forward, gun in hand, and peered out into the jungle. “Looks clear. Let’s go.”

They hobbled out of the cave opening and limped into the foliage, ducking behind some broad-leafed bushes. They waited. No sounds other than monkeys, insects, birds, and a burbling stream close by.

Virginia bit her lip. “I think we’re good so far. These are normal jungle sounds. If more people were around, I doubt we’d hear all this. The monkeys would be making a lot more noise, too.”

“I hope you’re right. Where exactly are we, and where’s our vehicle?”

Virginia pulled out the GPS and looked at it. “It’s pretty. The colors are shifting.”

“Yeah, it’s pretty, and the colors aren’t moving. Now where the hell are we?”

“This devil’s powder stuff sucks.” Virginia took a breath and let it out. “Okay. We’re about four miles from where we found the entrance we fell down.” She pointed. “It’s that way. We need to go around this hill and, then, backtrack to our metal home.” She showed the screen to Terry and pointed. We’re here, and our Humvee is there.”

“With our injuries, your head condition, this humidity, and heat, this could be daunting.”

Virginia nodded. “I know. Take some more pain meds, and another antibiotic, just in case. I think I’ll lay off the pain drugs for now.”

Terry took the pills with water from her canteen. She pointed off to the side at a brown area, clear of most vegetation, except for a few trees. “Looks like a trail and it’s going our way. Want to follow it? Could be easier than hacking our way through all this brush and vines.”

“Normally, I’d say no. The bad guys could be there. But, in our conditions, I think that may be a good idea. Let’s go.”

They followed the winding path. After for an hour, they stopped to rest. Terry wiped the sweat from her forehead. “Where are we?”

Virginia consulted the GPS. She held it up for Terry to see. “We’re here. The hill and the temple and City of Gold are back there, and our ride is still a few miles away.” Virginia looked at Terry. “How are you feeling?”

“Hot, sore, and my arm hurts, but other than that okay, I guess. Why?”

“You look flushed.”

“No shit. It’s hot. How are you?”

“Getting more nervous.” Virginia rubbed her hands together. “Sometimes things change color on me. Things change into funny shapes, too. I hear ringing in my ears at times. My throat is dry. I feel like I’ve got brain fog. But, the pain from my ankle seems to help offset the effects, I think.”

“I don’t think you got a full dose of the powder, I hope. Let’s go.”

They shuffled for another hour and stopped above a small ravine, about fifty feet deep, with a wide creek at the bottom. Terry looked around. "Why'd we stop?" She eased Virginia to the ground.

"I heard something."

"For real or the powder playing games with your head?" Terry listened. I don't hear anything."

"No. Listen. No jungle noise like we've had along the way, and I thought I heard a chopper. My hearing seems to be more acute, or I'm going batty."

Terry looked around. "Someone else is after us?"

"Maybe the same person I heard in the tunnel near the temple."

"Then let's go." Terry started to get up, stopped, leaned toward the gorge and pointed. "That looks like a canoe. Why don't we take it?"

Virginia looked at the GPS. "That river goes the wrong way. It bends ahead and heads away from our Humvee. And, I don't see any way down and with our ailments; I don't think jumping is a good idea."

Terry sighed. "Yeah, and there's a croc over there to boot."

Virginia and Terry rose and started toward the Humvee when a shot rang out. They ducked and waited. Nothing happened.

Terry crouched behind the massive root of a tree and looked around wide-eyed. "Whoever shot didn't shoot our way. Who was it?"

"I don't know. Maybe a hunter after game. Let's get out of here." Virginia rose and started forward. The next shot hit near a tree root next to her leg. She dove for cover, landed on a couple large elephant ear shaped decaying leaves on a muddy slope. She slipped over the side, down the steep embankment on the leaves, fell into the creek below, and went under. The weight of the gold in her pack pulled her. She fought to the surface and saw Terry tumbling down the bank and slide into the water. Virginia, the adrenaline pumping, swam to Terry and helped her to the far bank where they climbed out and up the short embankment to the side of the gorge. Virginia heard more gunfire as she watched the water. Almost immediately two crocodiles weaved their way upstream toward them. *Man, they can move fast.* She pulled out her .357 Magnum, held it with both hands, and waited. The first croc roared up and lunged for them. She fired at it point blank. It thrashed around as the three rounds blew away most of its skull. The second reptile attacked the dying one and pulled it into the river. More swam to the spot, and a fight broke out among some large reptiles for the carcass. "Time to go while they're occupied. Too bad the others are here. I could use a crocodile bag and shoes."

Terry's voice cracked. "I may be a little slow. You go."

Virginia looked at Terry. Her air splint was deflated, and blood ran down her leg from a bullet hole in her left thigh. Blood oozed from the cut in her side. "I'm not leaving you. It isn't just the Marines and Special Forces that say they don't leave their comrades behind. I'll see if I can stop the bleeding, but first I need to get us some cover. Whoever shot you is probably coming to confirm a kill."

CHAPTER 36

"You have such cheery thoughts." Terry shifted her position and grimaced. She gently touched the bullet wound. "God that hurts. It burns."

Virginia helped Terry get up and, limping, moved Terry down the river near the canoe and hid her behind some small bushes near the steep side of the gully. She applied some compresses to the bullet wound. After going through a dozen sets of gauze, she got the bleeding to diminish. Next, she washed it with water from her canteen, applied some topical antibiotic, and a dressing, tying it with strips of cloth ripped from the bottom of her shirt. She washed the cut in Terry's side and applied some more topical antibiotic and a bandage. After which, she replaced the air splint and gave Terry a couple of antibiotic and codeine tablets. "Best I can do for now."

Terry lay on the ground and stared at the sky. "Go. I will just slow you down."

"Like Hell! You're coming with me. I'll see if this canoe is seaworthy, and if so, we'll use it to get out of here."

"The river goes the wrong way."

"You want to climb that bank?"

"No. Not here anyway. Is anyone coming?"

"Not sure. I'll find out when I put the boat into the water." Virginia crouched down as more gunshots echoed above. "Those shots were closer. I'll push the boat into the river." Virginia scooted to the edge of the wooden dugout canoe and shoved. It moved slightly in the mud. *It's heavier than I thought.*

She pushed again, and the boat slipped halfway into the water. As she shoved more, she noticed the water fountain through holes in the bottom. *Just what we need. This thing won't go far. Now for plan B, whatever that is.* She moved back to Terry. "Looks like the boat don't float." She jerked up and looked at the top of the ravine as a familiar voice called out to her.

"Mrs. Clark, Dr. Sorenson, are you okay?" York peered over the side. "Don't shoot. It's me, York. I'll get some rope and help you out. Can you climb?"

Virginia looked at York and yelled. "Was that you shooting?"

"Someone was shooting at you. I shot him. What's your condition?"

"Terry has a broken arm and a bullet wound to her thigh. I sprained or broke my ankle. I don't think we can climb a rope." She didn't mention the devil's powder.

"Okay. Just stay there, and I'll see if there's another way up you can manage."

"How did you find us?"

"I'll tell you when I get you up here. By the way, you have a couple more large reptiles with big teeth creeping toward your location." He pointed down river. "From there."

"Thanks a bunch. Shoot them."

York leaned on his rifle. "Did you find El Dorado?"

Virginia rose from behind a boulder. "The City of Gold?"

York nodded. "Yes."

"Yes."

York's expression brightened. "Where is it?"

"Get us out of here and I'll tell you. Now shoot the damn crocs!"

York disappeared. He returned fifty yards downstream and tossed the body of a man into the river. "That'll keep them busy for a while. I'll be back." He disappeared again.

Virginia sat next to Terry. "That was York. He just threw a man's body into the river. Who was it and why did he do it? Where'd York come from and how'd he find us?"

Terry shook her head. "Good questions. I don't know, and I don't trust him."

Virginia limped downstream and watched the river for more crocodiles. *I hope the creatures are happy with the guy York tossed to them. Who was he? How did York find us? Was he the one in the hill at the City of Gold? Who is after us, the drug guy? Why did the natives turn on us? Duh, why wouldn't they? They want to keep their secret.* She turned and hobbled back to Terry. "How are you doing?"

"My arm and leg hurt like hell. My cut stopped bleeding. I'm hungry. I'm tired. It's damn hot. It's humid as a sauna. My hair is a sight. My wardrobe's a mess. Other than that, just peachy."

"Maybe you need more drugs."

Terry gave her a small smile. "Got more of the good stuff?"

"I'll see." Virginia opened the first-aid kit, took out two codeine tablets, and gave them to Terry. She looked at her bullet wound. It didn't look good. *That bullet needs to come out. The wound's infected.* Virginia applied more topical antibiotic and redressed the wound. "You know we're not safe here. I'll scout ahead and see if there is someplace with more cover."

"Okay. I'll keep an eye out for the crocodiles and York." Terry pulled out a pistol and set it on her lap. "Don't be long. I'm tired. Remember to take second looks. The hallucinations you've had could come back."

"I know." Virginia slowly moved upstream through low brush and around rocks. She stopped at a rock outcropping. *We could hold up under here. With the boulders in front, it will provide some semblance of cover.* She started back when she heard shots. *Shit. I hope that's Terry shooting at crocodiles. Not that it is a good option.* Virginia limped back.

Terry sat with her back to the side of the ravine holding her pistol. Ten feet away a crocodile was lying on the bank, dead. She looked at Virginia. "I think we'd better relocate. Before the others come for lunch."

"I agree. Let me help you up." Virginia helped Terry up, and leaning on each other, they made their way to the outcropping Virginia had scouted. They moved under the big rock sticking out of the bank and sat.

Terry slumped to the back of the formation. "We're in a pickle. How do we get out of this?"

"We either find our own way out, or we let York help us, then, see what he's up to."

"I kind of like the first option."

Virginia turned her head. "York is calling. I'd better see what he found. I'll be right back."

Virginia moved back toward their old location. She saw York on the top of the cliff. "Over here. What did you find, York?"

He turned and looked down the embankment. "Where'd you go?"

"A place with more cover."

"Good idea." York pointed. "Head upstream about a hundred yards. There's a place where there's been a landslide. The slope is steep but doable. I'll go there and throw a rope down you can use for support."

"Okay. We'll be there shortly." Virginia turned, then stopped, and looked up at York. "Who was that you through in the river? A native who shot at us? One of the drug guys?"

"No. Murphy."

"Murphy? He was your friend."

"The slime ball sold me out to the drug lord, Clemente Ramos. He also tried to kill you and the good doctor."

"Oh. Thanks, I guess." She turned and limped back to Terry.

Terry looked at Virginia as she ducked under the rock. "Find York?"

"Yeah. He said there's a slope up ahead. He'll toss a rope down for us to use as a support. We should move, but when we get there, we need to be ready for anything. Oh, yeah, he shot Murphy for betraying him. That's who he fed to the crocodiles."

"Good God. Murphy?" Terry's body shook. "With York up there, we won't be safe until we get back to the Humvee."

"We aren't that far. We'll make it even if we have to go through York, the drug lord, and half the natives."

"I love your optimism…or is it the devil's powder?" Terry moved her leg and cringed. She looked up at Virginia. "Okay. Let's go."

Virginia helped Terry up. They hobbled and hacked their way around rocks and bushes to the landslide. They stood looking at it. "Looks doable, but there is a little problem."

Terry nodded. "We're on the wrong side of the river."

CHAPTER 37

Virginia looked around. "I don't see anything big enough for us to use as a float."

York appeared at the top of the incline with a large coil of rope. He dropped it and stared down at the women. "We've got a little problem, don't we?"

Virginia called up to him. "Yeah, I'd say that. Got a rubber raft with you?"

"No. But I can climb down with the rope and toss it to you. Then, I'll pull you two across."

Like I'd trust him to do that. "With the crocodiles around? No way. Got any other ideas?"

Terry poked Virginia. "I think I see a way across." She pointed upstream.

Virginia looked at the rocks and boulders in the river. "You want to try and climb those to get across?"

"It's an option."

"Not a good one, especially in our conditions."

Virginia turned to see York standing near the edge with his hands in the air. *Now, what?* She watched as three men appeared. Two holding assault rifles aimed at York. One man—dressed in a pressed khaki shirt with epaulets, khaki trousers with a holster on his belt, and hiking boots stepped up to York. He said something. York stepped back. The man looked down at the women and smiled, then he pulled out his pistol and shot York.

Virginia quickly moved to Terry, and they ducked behind a boulder. "Did you see what just happened?"

Terry nodded. "Yeah. This doesn't look good. Who is that guy?"

"I don't know. But I think I heard him in the temple and City of Gold when we were there."

A man's voice, in heavily accent Spanish, called down to them. "Mrs. Clark, Dr. Sorenson. We finally meet. What is your condition?"

Virginia yelled, "Who the hell are you? What do you want?"

"I am Clemente Rodriguez Torres Ramos. You have destroyed *mucho* drugs of mine, a couple of airplanes, a laboratory, and a lot of my equipment. You are also responsible for the death and injury of a number of my men."

"You want us to pay you for them?"

Ramos laughed. "Oh, you'll pay all right. But for now, I'd like to meet you and your friend. I want to find out more about your expedition and who you work for. Then I'll see about your future, if you have any. I'd also like to visit the inside of your metal war wagon. It has recently caused five of my men serious injury when we found it."

Virginia smiled. "It doesn't like strangers."

"I noticed. You have nowhere to go. The local animals down there like fresh meat. I'd recommend you and your friend come up here."

"I don't trust you. Why'd you shoot York?"

"I understand. But, under your present condition, I'd say you have to trust me, for now. Shooting York was a long time coming. He betrayed me. He was being paid by someone in your Texas to find you. York, and the person he worked for, wanted to see if you could find the *Demonios Oro.* If you did, you were to die, and that person was going to come and take it."

"We are not here to steal the gold. We're conducting a search for the lost City of Gold for a museum. Based on what some local women told us, this place has some religious significance. She wanted us to promise not to disclose its location. We planned on honoring it."

"I see. You work for the Smithsonian. No? You escaped the *Demonios maldición...* devil's curse, and the *Diablo de polvo...* Devil's powder."

"I wondered about that." *Oh, I found the devil's powder all right.*

"If you had gone inside the mountain by the ceremonial entrance, you should already be dead. Somehow, you managed to survive the *Demonios maldición*. For that, I'll grant you your life, while I figure out what to do with you."

"Why do you care if we found it or not? Why haven't you stolen it?"

"I am the latest in a long line of guardians. My father, grandfather, and his father, and so on back many generations, have protected the people and their secret, their religion, and their ways."

"You're a drug lord."

"*Si.* It is a very profitable cartel. It keeps me in a lifestyle I like. It affords me the ability to help these people when needed."

Like using them as slave labor in your drug labs. Nice guy. Virginia looked at Terry. "I think we need to take his help to get out of this pickle. Then we figure out how to either get away or kill him and his men."

Terry stared at her. "Let him help us, and then, we kill a drug lord and his merry band of murderers? We don't know exactly how many are presently up there. Do all that in their territory, and just walk out? Are you nuts? That *Diablo de polvo* had a bigger effect on you than I thought."

Virginia smiled. "We wouldn't walk; we'd drive. You got a better idea?"

Terry slowly shook her head. "Ahh... no. I haven't got any other ideas."

Virginia called to him. "Mr. Ramos. It's not that I don't think you're a man of honor, but—"

"Just drop your weapons and I'll get you across the river and up here. It's that, or the crocodiles or natives... take your pick. At the moment, neither one likes you here."

Virginia looked at Terry. "I guess its plan A after all. She dropped her weapons but kept a folding knife in her pocket. She watched Terry out of the corner of her eye as she dumped her guns, but slipped a small, Ruger .380 semiautomatic into the makeshift sling on her arm.

"Okay, we're unarmed as you can see. If you would be so kind, please send down some way for us to get across the river without the aid of the crocs, and because of our injuries, help up the hill, we'd be very grateful."

Ramos talked into a walkie-talkie, turned, and barked orders in Spanish to his men. The two men shouldered their rifles and, with Ramos, sidestepped down the slope carrying a package. They opened it and pulled a cord. A large, yellow rubber raft inflated. One got in and paddled across the river. He helped Virginia and Terry into the raft and, then, paddled back. Virginia and Terry climbed out of the boat and sat on the boat's side, in front of Ramos.

Ramos gave them a slight bow. "It is nice to finally meet the two women who have caused me much grief. For museum researchers, you have done more damage these past few days than the police and your DEA combined. You have cost me many millions of dollars. York was right. You are very pretty and dangerous ladies. His suggested I sell you on the white slave market to recover some of my losses. But, you two are very resourceful. Maybe I can talk you into joining my organization instead."

"We're injured." Virginia pointed at Terry. "You won't get much for us on the slave market in our present conditions." *Joining his organization? In his dreams.* "We can talk teamwork and potential employment later. Right now we need a hospital."

"You are right." Ramos nodded. "I will take you back to my home and get you medical attention. Then, we'll see what is in your future. But for now, we will go back to your tank, and I will see inside. It will make a nice down payment for the damage you've caused, and a nice addition to my business."

As Ramos conferred with his men, Virginia leaned close to Terry. "They watched us drop our weapons, so they didn't search us. Not very bright. Maybe it's because we're women. These Latin types can be very macho and stupid when it comes to women. We can't risk trying anything here, but I have an idea. Follow my lead."

"Okay. I just hope you won't have another hallucination."

Ramos motioned to his men. One helped Terry to her feet and had her lean on him as they walked. The second man supported Virginia. They headed for the Humvee.

Arriving at the clearing, they lowered Terry and Virginia to the ground facing the Humvee. Virginia put her hand in her pocket and fingered the Humvee key fob. She looked up at Ramos. "Now what?"

"Turn off whatever you have protecting it and open it so I can go inside."

"I need to be closer and use the keypad." She climbed to her feet and took a step when a hand grabbed her.

Ramos released his grip on her shoulder. "I'll go with you."

Virginia shrugged. "Okay." She limped up to the side door, thumbing the key fob in her pocket.

"Why didn't it stop you like it did my men?" Ramos asked.

"It knows me. It is programmed to ID Terry and me, and only us. Anyone else comes close, and it takes defensive action. Something to do with biosensors and physiological sensing. I don't understand it, but it works. She punched in a code on the keypad on the side. The small blinking red light above the door turned green. "We can go in now."

Ramos grabbed her and pushed. Virginia stumbled few steps back. "I'll look first. I don't want any tricks." He motioned to his men. "Watch them."

The men looked at the two women. They turned and stared at the Humvee leaving their rifles slung across their chests. Ramos opened the door and stepped inside.

Virginia glanced at Terry sitting on the ground. With her right hand, Terry stealthily slid her pistol from the sling out and down by her leg and thumbed the safety off. She gave a slight nod to Virginia.

Virginia punched a button on the key fob. A high-pitched wail emitted from the door as Ramos screamed inside the Humvee. Virginia swung around and smashed her fist into the throat of the confused gunman standing close behind her. He staggered back gasping for breath and clenching his throat. He started to turn blue. His eyes bulged. He fell in an unmoving heap on the ground.

She flinched as Terry shot the gunman next to her in the chest. She fired three more rounds into him, one into his forehead before he hit the ground.

Virginia punched in a code on the keypad. The noise stopped. She looked inside the Humvee. Ramos thrashed about on the floor holding his bloody ears.

Terry glanced inside and then back at Virginia. "Used the Medium Range Acoustic Device paddle, I see. Where'd you put it?"

"Before we left, I put it on the side of the control module. I aimed it at the back toward the door. Set the MRAD for full blast. I figured another line of defense couldn't hurt."

"Nice. In a confined space like that, it would be murder on his ears, if he still has any. Looks painful. Good."

Virginia held the sides of the doorway for support, stepped inside. She yanked Ramos's sidearm out of the holster and nudged him with her foot. She motioned for him to get up. He rolled back and forth, then, slowly sat upright, and shook his head. He pointed at his bloody ears. Tears ran down his cheeks. Taking a small yellow pad from the table, she wrote:

High-frequency focused sound.
I burst your eardrums.
Painful isn't it?
Sell us in the slave market my ass. Get up.

He slowly rose and staggered outside. He flinched seeing his men on the ground. He dropped to his knees when Virginia pointed at the dirt.

Terry sat smiling. "I guess your plan worked. Now what? What are we going to do with Mr. Ramos?"

"I'd like to shoot him, but he's unarmed and defenseless. That would be cold-blooded murder. He's no threat right now." As Terry covered him with her gun, Virginia retrieved a length of nylon rope and tied Ramos to a tree. "That should hold him a while."

Terry fidgeted on the ground. "We could just leave him. I'm sure more of his men would find him before long."

"Yeah. That's an option." Virginia's face brightened. "We could cut him a few times and let the local carnivores help themselves. We could also take him with us to the authorities."

"Which authorities hasn't he bought?"

"Good point." Virginia helped Terry up. "We need to get you to a hospital and probably me as well. With that bullet wound in your leg and your broken arm, getting you medical attention is the most important thing right now." She helped Terry go into the Humvee and onto the foldout cot.

CHAPTER 38

Terry looked around the Humvee. “There’s no place like home.”

Virginia sat on the edge of the cot. “Ramos said York double-crossed him. Murphy tried to swindle York. Both are dead.”

“Yeah.”

“Ramos also said, York was being paid to track us to the City of Gold by someone in Texas.”

“Right. I guess his government paycheck and his nice resort weren’t enough.” Terry frowned. “Where are you going with this?”

“Who knew we were here, and why we were coming here? Especially someone in Texas.”

“Let’s see... Dr. Doverspike, our boss, and your husband.” Terry blew a tendril of dark hair.

“Then, there’s Detective John Wilkinson with Georgetown Police Department, the Smithsonian... but the Smithsonian isn’t in Texas. Oh yeah, Mary Jane Striker. If you count the Army, Navy, DARPA and DEA that’s pretty much everyone.”

“Okay.” Virginia rubbed her nose. “Of those, I think we can eliminate Dr. Doverspike and my husband as suspects.”

“I agree. And I think Detective Wilkinson can be scratched off the suspect list, too.”

“Right. I can’t think of anyone else in Texas who has a reason to want to find the source of the gold enough to go to these lengths. The others who inherited the gold would be suspects, but they didn’t know of our trip, unless Mary Jane told them.”

Terry nodded. “She’d have no reason to tell them about our trip. Doing so wouldn’t be in her best interest.”

“So, when we get back, we need to pay Mary Jane Striker a visit.” Virginia looked at Terry. She was pale; beads of sweat broke out on her forehead. Her eyes closed. Virginia felt her brow. *She’s got a fever. I need to get her to a hospital.* Virginia glanced out the door at Ramos, tied to the tree. *What do I do with him?* She got up, closed and locked the door, and, then moved to the front of the Humvee. She took her seat and started the engine. *I need help. I could use the radio, but who would I call?* A shrill, high-pitched, sound came from a speaker on the control panel. A red light flashed. *Now, what?*

Virginia fiddled with some controls. She saw a dark green shape flash between the overhead jungle foliage. *What the hell is that? More of Ramos's friends? How many planes does this guy own?* The white light above the radio switch started to blink. A voice came from the speaker, "XFPO calling WCSS."

She hit the button and picked up the microphone. "This is WCSS. Go ahead XFPO. Who the hell are you?"

"WCSS, this is Senior Inspector Rodriguez, Policía Federal. We are above your location. We can land four clicks due south of you in a clearing. Can you get there safely?"

Virginia teared up. "Inspector Rodriguez, I'm so happy to hear your voice. My friend, Terry, needs medical attention fast. She's been shot and has a broken arm. She has a fever, and her bullet wound is infected. Can you help her?"

"*Si.* Are you safe?"

"We have the drug kingpin, Mr. Ramos, tied to a tree, and a couple of his men are dead outside our Humvee. He killed Mr. York right in front of us and was going to either kill both of us or sell us on the slave market. I don't know how many more of his people are around, and the locals aren't too friendly either, but we're safe for now inside our vehicle. But, my friend needs a doctor and soon."

Rodriguez's voice hesitated. "You have him… Ramos? You really have him?"

Virginia's voice tensed. "Yes, Inspector. Can we talk about this later?"

"Standby." She waited for a few seconds. Rodriguez responded "Another chopper is coming and will lower men to take him into custody. They will also assist you and your friend, Dr. Sorenson. I will move to the clearing. The other chopper is here now and deploying more men. When they have finished, you come to the clearing."

"Okay. Wait. How'd you find us?"

"Remember the little Saint Christopher statue I gave you?" Rodriguez chuckled.

"Yes." *The little guy is in my backpack.*

"It has a GPS tracker in it. I've been following you everywhere you went. Well, almost everywhere. You disappeared for a while a few times."

"Why did you come now?"

"We lost track of you for a while in a dangerous place, and we had intelligence that a large party of men, Ramos' Mano Oro Cartel, was headed in your direction. You and your friend are in grave danger."

"Tell me about it. Glad you made it. Wait a minute, do you have jurisdiction to arrest Ramos where we are?"

"My agency is working with the Guatemalan police. They have an agent with me to arrest him. I am authorized to take him back to Mexico."

"Oh, Okay. I'll get Ramos from the tree and head out."

"Be careful. Get him only if it is safe. I'll be waiting. XFPO, out."

Virginia sat, stunned. *Inspector Rodriguez has been tracking us all this time?* She heard a helicopter overhead. Exiting the Humvee holding a stainless steel, .357 revolver, she hobbled to a clearer area, ducked behind a Banyan tree, and watched. The chopper had moved. She heard the helicopter's blades beating the air. It seemed to be hovering a short distance away before moving off. She could hear it, but couldn't see it. She watched the jungle through the hanging root vines. Through the tangle of vines, leaves, large roots, and undergrowth, she heard noise coming from the direction where the chopper had been. From the brush, eight men in jungle fatigues, carrying assault rifles, and one with a huge backpack and a sidearm, rushed toward her position. She raised her gun and aimed at who she thought was the leader. Then, gave them a quizzical look. *He looks American.* When she heard the leader shout her name in English, she called out from behind the tree. "I have you covered. Lower your weapons. You don't look like Mexican federal police. Who the hell are you?"

The man she thought was the leader barked instructions to the other seven. They lowered their weapons. He shouted to her, "Mrs. Davies Clark, I am Major Jack Adams, United States Marines. One of my men is a Navy doctor. May we approach?"

"Yes. Keep your weapons aimed at the ground."

Major Adams stepped closer, looked at a photograph, then smiled. "Mrs. Clark. We're here to assist you. The doctor can treat Dr. Sorenson, and you, if necessary. With your permission, I'll send the doc in."

With my permission? You bet. She nodded. "Yes, sir. Please do."

He motioned to the man with the huge pack. "Doc, go. She's in that… that, Humvee... thing." Adams watched the doctor rush toward the Humvee. "As soon as he has Dr. Sorenson stabilized, and we'll take your prisoner, I'd appreciate it if you could give us a lift to the LZ and our ride out of here. The Mexican and Guatemalan police are already there."

Virginia sagged. "Major, I'd be happy to take you anywhere you want to go." She limped up to him, hugged him, and stepped back. "Sorry." She touched his uniform again. "You are real. No hallucination."

Major Adams blushed. "Yes, I'm real. What's the matter?"

"I got a dose of some strange powder that's had me seeing funny things. Hallucinating. It's a lot better now. Injured my ankle as well. It may be a sprain or broken. Hurts like hell."

"I'll have the doc look you over, too. Let's go back to your vehicle, shall we?" He took Virginia's arm and helped her walk. "Any more hostiles in the area?"

"Don't know, but I'd bet good money if they aren't here now, they will be very soon."

"Then, we'd better move fast and be ready for trouble."

Reaching the Humvee, Adams looked around. The Marines had secured the perimeter, verified the two Mexican gunmen were dead and had Ramos in handcuffs. "Looks like we wait for Doc. When he is finished, we head out. You okay to drive? We may have to wait for your exam."

Virginia smiled. "I think so. Want to get the grand tour?"

"Yes, ma'am, but let's let the doctor finish whatever he needs to do first."

"Right. Can I ask a question, Major?"

"Yes, ma'am."

"Were you assigned to help the DEA, the Mexican police, and were handy to help come and get us?"

"No, ma'am, we..."

Virginia stiffened. "Major, please stop calling me ma'am. I'm Virginia."

"Okay. No, Virginia. We're from the USS George H.W. Bush."

Virginia relaxed and titled her head. "What's that?"

"It's a supercarrier, CVN 77."

"Wow, an aircraft carrier. Does it have a hospital on board?"

"Three."

"Three? Great! I'm glad you were in the area."

"Our admiral's had us off the coast with our escort ships as long as you've been running around in these parts. Along with the Mexican police, we've been monitoring your travels. Something to do with interagency co-operation and security, I think. It's all above my pay grade. My job is to get you and Dr. Sorenson back to the ship alive, and turn over your prisoner to the police." Major Adams looked at the door of the Humvee. He saw the doctor motion it was okay for them to come inside. "Looks like the doctor has done his thing. Shall we go?"

Virginia swung around and almost fell as she stepped to the door. Major Adams grabbed her. "Maybe the doc does need to see you before we go anywhere."

"It's my ankle. I'll be okay, for now." With Adams support, she limped forward when she heard automatic gunfire. The Marines started to return fire.

"Inside, now!' Adams yelled. His men hustled Ramos inside the

Humvee behind Virginia. A few seconds later, the remaining Marines stopped shooting and climbed in. They slammed the door shut and turned the locking mechanism. Shots pinged off the side. Adams looked at a sergeant. "Sitrep."

"Sir. We were attacked by at least eleven hostiles. We returned fire and may have wounded a couple and killed one. No casualties or injuries on our team, sir."

"Good job, sergeant. It's a little crowded, but have the men sit where they can and relax a bit while our lovely hostess drives us to our LZ." Adams looked around. "Hey, this is really nice."

Virginia chuckled. "You bet it is."

More shots rang against the hull.

Virginia switched on the outside monitors. Eight men stood around the outside of the Humvee firing automatic rifles at it. Virginia gritted her teeth. "My ankle hurts, my nerves are shot, and I'm tired. Time to show these macho bastards not to mess with a woman in a bad mood. Watch."

She pressed a button. A few seconds later, they heard screams outside. Virginia chuckled and pointed at the monitor. The men had dropped their weapons and were frantically wiping at their faces, clawing at their eyes, running in circles, ripping off clothing, and shrieking. A few had fallen on the ground writhing in obvious pain. "Time to go."

Adams looked at her. "What the hell did you just do?"

"Shot out a heavy fog and spray mixture of concentrated, high strength, pepper spray that'll stop a grizzly bear, and Manchineel tree acid sap that burns and blisters skin, eyes, and any other tissue really, really bad on contact. It burns like hell. Like molten metal. It can envelop an area about twenty feet out from the sides of the vehicle."

"Holy shit."

"Told you I wasn't in a good mood. That'll stop most anything in its tracks." She looked into the back at the doctor. "How is Terry, Doctor?"

"I've removed the bullet, cleaned, treated, and closed the wound as best I can. I treated the cut on her abdomen as well. I gave her morphine, some antibiotics, and a tetanus shot. We can do more in the ship's hospital. Her arm is broken, but I splinted it. You did a good job stabilizing it and treating her wounds. You also prevented that bullet wound from bleeding her out. Probably saved her life. We'll finish treating her once we're back on the carrier."

"Thanks, Doctor." Virginia looked at his fatigue uniform closer and noticed dark the oak leaf emblem indicating a major or lieutenant colonel. "Are you a major or colonel?"

He smiled. "Lieutenant Commander Frank James, M.D., U.S. Navy Medical Corps."

"Glad to meet you, Doctor."

Major Adams reached for a knob on the dash. "What does this—" Virginia turned and slapped his hand. He jerked his hand back and frowned at his men when they chuckled. "Weapons system?"

Virginia nodded. "Yep. And we even had some mini-RPGs, bomblets, robots, and some other goodies, but we used all of them." Virginia lowered the steel outer shields and slowly backed up. She could see the bodies of the two men she and Terry had killed, a couple more near the brush. Others were still writhing on the ground or running into trees compounding their injuries. One man stepped in front of the Humvee rubbing his eyes. He squinted. With a shaking hand, he raised a pistol toward them. The Humvee bounced slightly as Virginia ran him over before he could shoot. "Obviously, he didn't get the memo."

Major Adams stared out the window. He turned and looked at Virginia. "You just ran over that man."

"I wasn't going to invite him in for tea. By any chance, did you notice his gun? Anyway, he was in the way, and I don't have a horn." She consulted the GPS map and bulldozed through some brush toward the rendezvous point.

As she drove through the underbrush, around trees, and boulders, Virginia made a turn around a large tree root and stopped. "We've got company." She pointed. Ahead of the Humvee blocking the way, sat a filthy, battered, old, green-and-rust-colored Ford F350 pickup truck, with a fifty-caliber machine gun, mounted on a pedestal in the bed. The man, standing behind the big gun and aiming it at them, had long, oily, dirty black hair. He smiled displaying nicotine-stained crooked teeth. The driver with short blond hair and square jaw looked through the glassless window frame. He yelled something in Spanish.

Major Adams stared. "I think they want Ramos."

CHAPTER 39

Virginia spoke through her teeth. "Good guess. And that ain't gonna happen." She put the Humvee in reverse. As she backed up the Humvee, the man with the machine gun fired a quick burst over their vehicle. When she slammed on the brakes, the Humvee jerked to a stop.

Adams swallowed. "I don't think this thing can take many hits from a fifty cal."

"Me either." Virginia frowned. "If my memory serves me right, a fifty-caliber round can penetrate most armor."

Adams nodded. "Unless this is an M1 Abram's tank, you're right. Got any more of your nasty surprises we can use, and fast?"

Virginia bit her lip. "Hmm. Yeah. I've got just the thing. I'll be right back." She clenched her teeth in pain as she climbed into the back. Her ankle throbbed as she sat at the control station with the Marines watching her. She punched a few buttons, and an image of the truck popped up on one of the viewscreens.

Adams called to her. "Whatever you're doing, hurry it up. They're getting antsy."

"I'm trying! I haven't done this before." On the screen, a sight rested near the bottom front of the truck. She deftly twisted a hand controller, and the sight moved up, framing the front of the truck. She inched it higher to zero in on the machine gun. "Hold on," she yelled, as she flipped a switch and pressed the red trigger on the joystick controller. The Humvee jerked as a loud staccato of heavy gunfire raked the machinegun and the truck. Virginia moved the joystick as she shredded the machine gun, the truck, trees, and pulverized the two men. The Humvee vibrated.

The Marines watched out the window and clenched their weapons as the truck, and the big gun were reduced to scrap metal. Blood and flesh splattered against the jungle vegetation. Virginia released the trigger. She flipped a switch and slowly climbed back into the driver seat. She took a labored breath and slowly let it out. "That should do it." A fire was starting in the midst of the wreckage. "I think getting out of here before the fire gets to the unspent ammo out there would be a good idea."

The Marines cheered, whistled, and applauded.

She looked over at Major Adams. He stared out the window in shock. She grinned. "They pissed me off. They were in my way. I'm tired. I have a headache, and my ankle is killing me. And, Terry needs the hospital on your carrier." She twisted around. "How's your patient, Doctor? That didn't shake her up too much did it?"

Dr. James answered. "No. She's doing okay. But she needs the ship hospital, soon."

"On it." She settled into her seat and glanced at Adams. "I told you we had neat toys. We aren't just innocent, defenseless, little girls." She looked out the window at the carnage. "Adios, assholes."

One of the Marines shouted, "Mrs. Clark, you want to join us? We'd take you anytime." Others shouted agreement with their comrade. One soldier yelled, "Major, can we make her an honorary member of the team?"

Adams nodded. "Good idea, Corporal. I'll see what we can do when we get back to the ship."

One of the Marines yelled, "We'd be honored to have you, ma'am."

"Sorry boys, I already have a job… and a husband." Virginia heard some moans from the Marines. "But being an honorary member of your team would be neat."

The Marines whistled.

Adams shook his head and pointed out the window. "What the hell was that you just used on the truck and those men?"

"A very big gun near the left headlights. Neat, huh? First time we've used it. I thought it'd be louder. Must be the insulation."

"You did pretty damn well for a beginner." Adams shifted in his seat. "Define big gun."

"I think the manual said it's a fifty-caliber Gatling gun or something like that. Maybe it was the 20mm one. I don't remember all the details. Shoots depleted uranium bullets, too, whatever they are. I understand they are pretty nasty."

"Yeah, they are. They'll kill a tank. And, like I said, beginner or not, you used it very well." Adams looked at the shot-up wreckage outside, then, tilted his head toward her. "You're dangerous. Who the hell do you work for? The Army? CIA? You're not DEA are you?"

"They didn't tell you?"

"No. My orders were to come and get you, and not ask too many questions."

Virginia shifted in her seat. "The Smithsonian."

Adams fell back in his seat. "The Smithsonian? For real?"

"Yeah. You know, the big museum in Washington, DC." There were more chuckles from the Marines in the back.

He gave her a puzzled look. “A museum? You’re kidding. Right?”

“Nope. Buckle up.” She put the Humvee in gear, pressed the accelerator, and plowed through the smoking, chewed up remains of the truck. She eyed Adams as he stared wide-eyed out the window. “Don’t you dare say anything derogatory about my driving.”

Adams held up his hands in front of him in surrender. “Don’t worry, I won’t.” He looked down at his seat. “This isn’t an ejection seat is it?”

“No. You’ve been watching too many James Bond movies.” She told him about part of their adventure in the area. She continued to push through the jungle for a while to the clearing and the two waiting helicopters, their blades slowly rotating. Marines and police were stationed around the area. As Inspector Rodriguez and the Guatemalan officer took custody of Ramos, the Marines loaded Terry and the doctor onto their Seahawk chopper.

Rodriguez and the Guatemalan officer talked to Virginia, took notes, and recorded her statement and answers to their questions. They said if more were information was needed, they would contact her at home. They conferred with Major Adams. They hurried to their chopper, with Ramos, and lifted off.

Adams walked up to Virginia, leaning on the Humvee, her ankle bandaged. “How are you doing?”

“Better. The doctor said it looks like I have a bad sprain. He bandaged it and gave me a shot for the pain. Other than that, I’m doing pretty well. They’ll x-ray my foot at the ship’s hospital just in case it’s broken. He found some residue of the powder that’s been causing me to be a head case and said they’ll check on what the powder was when I get to the ship’s infirmary. I’m glad Terry is going to the hospital now. She’s been through a lot. What’s next?”

“My orders are to stay here with you and your expensive toy with the rest of my team. We’ll provide security until a heavy lift helo arrives. It’ll take us all, including this plaything of yours, back to the carrier.” They watched the chopper with Terry on board lift off.

Virginia crossed her arms and smiled. “My plaything, as you put it, and I can take care of ourselves.”

Adams nodded. “Yeah, I noticed. But a few extra trained men with guns can’t hurt. By the way, who actually owns this thing? Can’t be the Smithsonian.”

“You won’t believe it if I tell you.”

“Try me. After watching you and this contraption in action, I’ll believe anything.”

“Okay.” She sat in the open door well of the Humvee. “It’s registered in the State of Virginia to Ronald Warren Reagan. Mr. Reagan lives at 675 N. Randolph St., Arlington, Virginia.” Virginia laughed. “Mr. Ronald W.

Reagan was the fortieth President of the United States. He's dead you know. And, 675 N. Randolph St., Arlington, Virginia is the address of DARPA."

Adams raised an eyebrow. "President Reagan?"

"Yep."

"DARPA?"

"Yep."

"If DARPA owns it, it should have a government DOD registration."

"I know. But that's what the paperwork says."

"I'll be damned."

They looked up as another, larger helicopter approached. The Marines and Virginia moved to the edge of the clearing as the MH-53E Sea Dragon settled. The side door opened as the blades wound down. A sailor on blue camo fatigues jumped down, bent slightly, then, dashed to Major Adams.

He saluted. "Sir, I'm Master Chief Joiner. We can load up your men and get cables attached to that..." He turned and looked at the expanded, armored Humvee. "That thing looks like an armored RV-Humvee on steroids."

"It does, doesn't it, Chief."

"Yes, sir. Never seen anything like it before. Anyway, sir, we're to get that thing and you all out of here." He noticed Virginia and leaned close to Adams. "Sir, I hope she's coming with us."

"She is Chief. But I'd be real nice to the lady if I were you. She's dangerous. She scares the hell out of me."

He raised an eyebrow as he looked at Adams. "Sir?"

"That's Mrs. Virginia Davies Clark. She likes to be called Virginia. She told me a little about her trip down here. Virginia and her friend captured a major drug lord, the head of the Mano Oro Cartel, who is now in need of a lot of medical attention. They killed a large number of his men and injured a whole bunch more. She and her friend also burned up multi-millions of dollars of his drugs, downed and destroyed three of his aircraft. As if that wasn't enough, they demolished and burned a meth and heroin lab. They destroyed a critical bridge he needed to move his drugs, too. When we tried to get back here, Virginia took out a truck with a fifty cal that was threatening us. Then, she plowed through the jungle to get us back here in one piece. She even ran over a man who threatened us with a gun. I'm not sure exactly what she was actually doing here in the first place. She left out that part of the story. I'm sure she and her friend had some other dangerous adventures. And, get this, Virginia said she and her friend work for a museum."

The chief looked at Virginia, then back at Adams. "Her? She did all that? A museum?"

"Yep. Her and her friend. Just the two of them. And the museum is the Smithsonian."

"Wow. She's some woman. When I get home, I'll have to pay the Smithsonian a visit."

"You got that right, Chief."

As Adams helped Virginia up, walk to the Sea Dragon, and climb inside, other sailors and Marines were attaching cables to the Humvee.

Virginia leaned out of the chopper's side door and yelled, "Hey, Chief. Make sure my vehicle is secure. After all we've been through, I'd hate to lose it now."

"I'll be very careful, Mrs. Clark. We won't even scratch it."

"You better not." She laughed. "With all the scratches and dents we put on it, I'd be hard pressed to tell if you added any. Thanks, Chief." She moved inside the chopper and sat next to Adams.

When everyone was aboard, the Sea Dragon lifted off with the Humvee suspended below.

Adams conferred with the pilots. He returned to his seat next to Virginia, and handed her a set of headphones. He spoke over the roar of the engines. "When we get to the carrier, they'll lower your vehicle onto the flight deck, unhook it, and then, they'll land us. They will secure your toy below deck. You'll go to the hospital with your friend. We'll rendezvous with a U.S. Coast Guard cutter in three days, so you and Dr. Sorenson can go home."

Virginia tightened her seat restraint. "What about my toy, as you put it?"

"It goes back to wherever it came from. Probably DARPA."

"Nuts. I was hoping I could keep it. It'd be a blast to drive on the freeway, and when someone cuts me off... well, it would be interesting."

Adams laughed. "I think that's why they're taking it back. You're dangerous."

Virginia looked at the two backpacks on the floor at her feet. "How about our… ahh… stuff?"

"You can get whatever you need out of your plaything later, on the carrier. The Navy and Coast Guard have orders to get you home and not go through normal channels, like customs and immigration. Whatever you take with you, no one is to mess with. Officially, you and your friend were never here."

Virginia gave him a quizzical look. "We were never here? Why?"

"I don't know. Those are our orders from Washington."

"So, we were never here, like in a spy movie?"

Adams chuckled. "Yeah, like a spy movie. As much as I'd like to, I can't even ask what you were really doing down here."

Virginia shrugged. "Sorry about that. A girl can't give away all her secrets."

"I understand. In my business, we get used to handling people who can't divulge stuff."

Virginia shifted in her seat. “Once we get to the states, any idea where do we go next? Washington or where?”

“I understand you’re both going back home to Texas.”

Virginia settled back. “Good. We have some unfinished business in Texas.” She leaned closer to Adams, rested her head on his shoulder, and fell asleep.

Adams smiled. *Whatever her unfinished business in Texas is, I’m glad I’m not the one she has the business with.*

CHAPTER 40

Virginia sat back on the bunk in her room on the carrier. She glanced at the back of the room at the pile of boxes, backpacks, and bags she and Terry wanted from the Humvee, and their trip. Her foot, encased in a short walking cast, was propped on a pillow at the end of the bed.

She turned at the sound of a knock on the door. “Come in.”

Major Adams slowly opened the door and stepped into the room. “Hi. How are you doing?”

She smiled. “Hi, Major. Have a seat. I’m doing pretty well. Got everything I wanted from my toy, as youreferred to our ride.”

“I see that.” He turned the desk chair around and straddled the back as he sat. “How’s your ankle?”

“The doctor said the x-rays showed cracked bones, and I screwed up some connective tissue. So, I guess I broke it. They put a cast on it so I won’t do any more damage. Will you sign it for me?”

“You bet.” He pulled out a pen, leaned forward, and signed the side of her cast. “How’s your friend doing?”

“Terry had surgery on the gunshot wound in her leg. The doctors said she’ll be fine. They treated the cut she got in her side, and put her arm in a cast. She should be okay for the transfer to the Coast Guard ship in a few days.”

“Did the doctors say anything about the powder that made you… ahh… a little crazy out there?”

Virginia chuckled. “You mean made me a nutcase and seeing things? Yeah, they did. They did what tests they could here and flew a sample back to Bethesda Naval Hospital for more study.”

He waited, then said, “Okay, don’t keep me in suspense, what was it?”

“Well, it seems the natives have plants in the area they use to make the devil powder. So far they identified…” she pulled out a scrap of paper and looked at it. “They said it had myristicin, phyllobates, claviceps purpura, strophanthin, and antiarin. I don’t know what they all are, but the doctors got the lab results back quick and said they are not very friendly compounds. Any of them by themselves will kill, but this cocktail is a real winner. You're a nutcase, you see funny things, and, then you die. It was a good thing I never got hit by a full dose, which, according to them, a full dose isn't all that much. An extremely small amount will kill very fast. I was lucky. Falling through that trap door saved me. Broke my ankle, though."

Major Adams took a breath and became very solemn. "I know what the C. purpura is. That's an ergot fungus that grows on the ears of rye. It's LSD-producing fungus. You are very lucky."

Virginia swung her legs off the bed and leaned forward. "How about you giving me a tour of this boat?"

"First, she's a ship, not a boat. And is it okay for you to walk around?"

"Hand me my cane." She pointed to the side of the pile of stuff she'd taken from the Humvee. "I've got a walking cast so I can walk, just not very fast."

"I would be honored to escort you. Have you talked to your husband yet?"

"Yeah. He was very worried about Terry and me. When I told him she had been shot, I thought he'd come through the phone. He was really upset that she and I were there in the first place. When he heard what we had been doing, I thought he'd have a heart attack. He relaxed when I told him we were rescued by the Marines and were now safe on an aircraft carrier."

"Good. But, I think you saved our butts. That truck with the machine gun was... well... you saved our bacon. I'm glad your husband isn't overly upset now."

"Uh, he's upset. I'll hear about it when I get home, trust me. Now, about that tour?"

Adams handed Virginia her cane and led her into the corridor. "I take it you've seen where your unusual vehicle is stored. It's the most modified Humvee I've ever seen."

"Yes."

"Okay, we can skip the hospitals on the tour as well. How about we start in the officer's mess for some coffee, then, go to the ops center, the bridge, flight operations, and lastly, the hanger deck. Later, if you're still okay, we'll go to the flight deck."

"Sounds like fun. Lead the way. Tell me about this boa... err... ship I'm rooming on."

Adam cleared his throat. "Well, she's one-thousand-ninety-three feet long. She's nuclear powered with two Westinghouse reactors. Counting the wings contingent, she carries over five-thousand crewmembers. The ship has numerous radars and a full complement of electronic and torpedo countermeasure equipment." He pointed at the upcoming hatchway, "Duck your head. We don't need that pretty head of yours getting into more trouble.

And, watch your step."

Virginia smiled and ducked her head. "Thanks."

Adams continued his narrative about the ship as they moved down the corridor. Sailors stood aside as they passed. "The Bush also has two Mk 29 Medium-range surface to air missile launchers, two RIM-116 Rolling Air-frame Missile launchers. They're used primarily as a weapon against anti-ship cruise missiles, and four Phalanx radar controlled, twenty millimeter Gatling guns. She carries over ninety aircraft, and one hell of a lot of missiles, bullets, and bombs."

Virginia smiled and nodded. "Okay, I'm impressed even though I have no clue about what you just said. That is except for the reactors, bombs, and the airplanes." She stopped and looked at a steep set of stares going upward. "How do I get up those with my cast and cane?"

"You don't. We can take an elevator. I got special permission for you to use it."

"Good. I like special." Virginia looked around. "Who picked the color scheme around here?"

"The Navy."

"Figures."

Two hours later, Adams returned Virginia to her room. After seeing that she was safely on her bed, he said, "I hope you enjoyed the tour."

"Yes. It was very interesting. This ship is a huge city with its own airport. I loved the planes. I'm sorry you couldn't take me to the bridge and some of the areas further up. But with no elevator and my cast, climbing those stairs and ladders would have been trouble. And thanks for taking me to see Terry. She looks a lot better now that the doctors have treated her."

"I'm glad you enjoyed it. If it's okay with you, I'll come for you at seventeen hundred hours to have dinner in the officer's mess. We can drop in on Dr. Sorenson again then."

"What's seventeen hundred hours?"

"Five pm."

"I'd like that. You don't have to be my babysitter. I'm sure you have better things to do than tend to me."

"No, actually I don't. My commanding officer and the Admiral said I was to be your best friend until we turn you and Dr. Sorenson over to the Coast Guard. By the way, that is an impressive collection of service pins the crew has given you."

She looked down at a long strip of cloth someone had given her and the various service pins, pins for the different air wings, rank insignia, and a ships pin. "Yes, it is. I'll treasure these and display them proudly." She placed her ankle on the pillow at the end of her bed. "May I inquire as to the dress code for dinner tonight?"

"In your case, casual works. The fatigues they gave you when you left the hospital should work fine. And, here is something for your collection." He pinned a set of gold oak leaves to the collars of her fatigue shirt.

Virginia looked at the oak leaves. "They're like yours."

"Yes. The colonel in charge of the Marine contingent on the ship said we're making you an honorary Marine with the rank of Major. There will be a small ceremony tonight at the mess."

Virginia blushed. "I don't know what to say. Thank you. I wish I had something better to wear. But like you said, this'll have to work, especially since I didn't pack formal wear. See you at… seventeen-hundred hours."

The manager of York's Cancun Beach and Golf Club swallowed as he listened to the garbled, loud, and angry voice on the telephone. "What do you mean you can't find York or Murphy? That is unacceptable! They were to take care of a project for me. Where the hell are they? This is important!"

"I do not know. They're not here, and, I cannot reach them by phone or radio. They went south into the jungle. They may be in Guatemala. I think they said they were going to see the two women who stayed here a while ago."

"You think? Find York or Murphy right away! I need to know exactly what those women found and where they are!"

"I don't know how to find them. Policía Federal officers were here and took all the files and the computer from Mr. York's office."

"I see. The police? Do not tell the police of my calls! Keep looking. I'll contact you again tomorrow, and I hope you have better news for me." The phone went dead.

The stocky bald manager hung up the phone and looked across his desk at Inspector Rodriguez. "Did I keep the person on the telephone long enough, Inspector?"

Rodriguez set his cell phone down on the desk. "No. My office said the trace wasn't complete, but we know it originated in the United States somewhere in Texas. When that person calls back tomorrow, maybe we'll have better luck. Thank you for your cooperation." Rodriguez stood, stretched, and left the office.

Virginia, with the aid of her cane, followed Major Adams through the ship to the officer's mess. When she entered, a Marine lieutenant called the room to attention. She stopped and looked around the room and the people in it, all in Marine and Navy officer's uniforms, standing straight.

A man with silver eagles on his collars entered behind her. "Mrs. Virginia Davies Clark, I am Colonel John Storm. Please follow me to your seat."

Virginia swallowed and looked at Major Adams.

"Go ahead and follow the colonel. I'll be right here."

"Okay." She plodded, with her cast and cane, behind the row of chairs, to a seat at the end of the table. She sat when Colonel Storm pulled the chair out for her to sit. The other officers, then, sat.

Colonel Storm moved to a place halfway up the table and stopped, picked up an official looking parchment document and read:

> *Greetings:*
>
> *For all that see these presents, be it known that:*
>
> *Whereas, for outstanding service to her country,*
>
> *Whereas, for the apprehension of a drug cartel leader and the destruction of the cartel's drugs, equipment, and supply routes, Whereas, the saving of the lives of her associate and United States Marines while injured:*
>
> *Therefore, with the consent of the Secretary of the Navy, and the Commandant of the Marines Corps, The United States Marine Corps declares Virginia Davies Clark to be an honorary United States Marine with the rank of Major.*

The officers stood and applauded.

He stepped to Virginia and handed her the declaration, then, saluted her. "Thank you for what you did for our men and our country, ma'am."

Virginia took the paper and looked at it. A tear formed and ran down her cheek. She smiled. "Thank you, sir. Your men came when my friend and I really needed help. She and I had been through a lot, and we were not in the best of shape. We owe a lot to these men. They came into a hostile situation to rescue us, especially when my friend needed medical assistance. They were there for us. Destroying that truck with the machine gun was the least I could do."

Colonel Storm nodded. "You and Dr. Sorenson single-handily demolished a huge drug cartel. Something the Mexican, Guatemalan, and U.S. law enforcement agencies haven't been able to do."

Virginia looked down at her plate. "Yeah, I guess we did at that."

For the next hour, Virginia ate dinner and talked to the Marine and Naval officers around the table. She liked watching their faces when she told them that she and Terry were on an assignment for the Smithsonian.

As she was about to leave, Colonel Storm handed Virginia a rolled parchment. "This is a similar declaration for Dr. Sorenson. She's an Honorary Marine, and a Captain."

"Thank you again, sir. Major Adams is taking me to the hospital to see Terry now. I'll give this to her. I know she'll appreciate it." She hobbled down the gray corridor behind Major Adams as he led her to the hospital.

Terry rested on her bed, the back raised so she could see the TV that was rigged at the foot of her bed. She pushed herself further up on the bed and pushed the mute button on her remote when Virginia and Major Adams entered. "Hi, Virginia. Hello, Major."

Virginia moved to the side of the bed. "How's it going? Any pain?"

Terry pointed to the two IV bottles, dripping fluid into tubes running to a white box attached to the IV stand, and, then into a tube in her arm. "They've got me on antibiotics, and if I press the button on that thingamajig, I get morphine. Nice. But yeah, I'm doing good. The docs, nurses, and corpsmen have been great. I'm feeling more like my old self." She held up her arm cast. "Now we both have casts."

"I see that. We're going to be transferred to a Coast Guard cutter in a couple days. Think you'll be up for that?"

"I know. My doctor said I should be good by then, but I have to go slow and take it easy. He's going to give me some pills to take with me, and a record of what happened, and what they did for me so I can give it to my doctor at home. How's it going with you?"

"You and I are now honorary Marines, and you are a captain."

Adams stepped to Terry's bedside and handed her the document and a set of silver captain's bars in a small box.

Terry's eyes watered. "Thank you, Major. I really don't deserve this honor. It was you and your men that saved my sorry ass."

"No. What you two did was quite spectacular. It is our honor, Captain."

Terry smiled. "Thank you, Major."

Virginia pointed to her gold oak leaves. "You do notice that I outrank you."

Terry grinned. "What's new? Oh, how much of what we recovered from the site do we still have?"

"Everything. And, we don't go through customs when we return. How about that?"

"Good. I can't wait to follow up in Texas with our… ahh."

"Yeah. I know. Get better so we can both confront her."

CHAPTER 41

Two days later, Virginia, leaning on her cane, stood on the flight deck of the carrier watching the Coast Guard Cutter come alongside. She glanced at Terry, standing next to her. "You sure you should be up here?"

"The doctor said it's okay. I'm in good enough condition for the transfer to the cutter and going home. He's provided me with a bag full of drugs, and a fist full of medical information for my doctor. How about all our stuff from our metal, mobile home?"

"Major Adams said he is overseeing our stuff getting transferred to the cutter. He said we go next. My only concern is how."

Terry leaned further over the side. "Probably a rope shuttle across. They are re-rigging that line to transfer us now."

Virginia's head whipped around. "Like a zipline?"

"Yeah, something like that."

"If that's what they have in mind, I'm not going." Virginia stepped back. "No way in hell."

Terry raised her arm in a cast. "If I can go, you can go."

Virginia huffed. "Like I said, no way in hell."

"You could swim," came a male voice from behind her.

She turned and stared at a short, stocky, Navy chief in a light-blue, denim shirt, dark-blue pants and an orange hard hat. She glared at him. "Swim?" She raised her leg slightly and pointed to the walking cast on her ankle. "This cast would act as an anchor. Got any better ideas, Chief?"

"The water's calm, Mrs. Clark. The line you will use has a bosum's chair on it for you to sit on. It'll only take a couple of minutes to get you across. We're pretty good at this kind of thing."

She frowned. "Pretty good? How many people have gone in the drink doing it?"

"Ahh… not many." He looked at Virginia and Terry. "If it's any comfort, we've never lost pretty ladies doing it."

Terry poked Virginia's arm. "See. Nothing to it. Just a quick zip ride over to the other ship. I've never had a bad experience on a zipline."

"That's nice. I took a zipline once in Costa Rica with Andy. It didn't stop when it was supposed to. I ran into a rather big, hard, tree and got hurt. Got an infection, a lot of bruises, and a whole lot of pain. Cracked a rib, too."

The Chief pointed to the cutter. "See, no trees."

"No. Just steel. Got a chopper we could borrow?"

"That, ma'am is worse than the… ahh… zipline."

"Great. Use the zipline, swim, or have a helicopter drop me in the big puddle. Okay, zipline it is. I'm not happy about this."

The Chief smiled. "Would you ladies please follow me? I'll take you to the disembarking area and get you suited up. Major Adams will be there too."

Virginia plodded along next to Terry as they followed the chief. Virginia mumbled, "I hope our life insurance is paid up."

Terry chuckled. "Now you worry about life insurance?"

The manager of York's Cancun Beach and Golf Club again listened to the garbled, angry mechanical voice on the telephone. "Have you located Mr. York yet?"

"*Si.*"

"Where is he? I need to speak with him. This is extremely important."

"I understand, but Mr. York and Mr. Murphy are both dead." The manager looked across his desk at Inspector Rodriguez. The inspector nodded and motioned for the manager to keep talking.

"Dead? How? Where? Did he locate the two women?"

"Well, I was told a drug lord killed Mr. York and Mr. Murphy in the jungle. If he found the women, you are inquiring about… well, maybe you and I can make a deal. I may have information on their… ahh… adventures."

The voice turned icy. "You little weasel! Trying to extort money from me. I want to know where exactly York and Murphy were killed."

The manager looked at Rodriguez, swallowed, then continued. "In the jungle in Guatemala. But I have information about what they found. Now if you are willing to make a deal, or come down here, I'm sure the appropriate arrangements can be made."

"Damn! York and Murphy dead. That is not what I needed. Do you know if the women are alive?"

"*Si*. They are alive."

"They are?"

"*Si.* Alive." He looked down at a note the Inspector slid across the table. It read, *just another minute*. The manager nodded. "I know where they are.

But that information seems very valuable right now. It will cost you."

The voice went silent. It returned in at a slow, deliberate pace. "How much will it cost me?"

"I think fifty thousand American U.S. dollars."

"Think again."

"I don't think that you are in a position to argue. Either I get my money, or you lose the women."

Rodriguez waved his finger across his throat indicating to the manager to cut off the call.

The voice continued, "Tell me what account to wire the money into."

"I changed my mind. They may not be alive either. Good-by." The manager hung up. "That was long enough, Inspector?"

"*Si.* Thank you for your cooperation. I'll have men watching this hotel for a while to protect you and maybe catch the person who called should they show up." Rodriguez rose and walked to the parking lot.

Now I have the location and number of the caller. It was from Georgetown, Texas, but it was from a cell phone. It is probably a burner phone. But, I'll get word to Miss Virginia anyway.

Virginia and Terry sat in the coast guard cutter's wardroom, sipping coffee. Terry took a bite out of a donut, then looked at Virginia. "What's the matter? We made it across in the basket okay, and you didn't run into any trees or steel structures. Did you call your husband, yet?"

Virginia nodded. "Yeah, I called Andy. He's happy we're headed home. That basket ride from the carrier to this ship wasn't as bad as I thought. I should have known they'd make sure we'd be okay."

"Then, why so glum?"

"This little adventure isn't over yet. We both think Mary Jane is the leading suspect in this case. She's probably the only one who knew where we were going and had a plausible reason to want what we found. But there is still some doubt. What if it is someone in Washington or someone we don't know? I can't just barge in on her and accuse her of being our nemesis."

Terry took another bite of her donut before speaking. "You know; these are pretty good. The cook on this ship really knows how to bake. You're right, though. We need to approach her with caution. You know more about the investigation back home than I do. But, maybe if we took a look at all the suspects together, we might see something that was missed."

"Good idea." Virginia started to drink more coffee when a seaman entered.

"Mrs. Davies Clark?"

Virginia raised her hand. "Right here."

"Radio message for you, ma'am. It's from the Mexican Policía Federal. It is marked urgent." He handed her an envelope and left.

Virginia tore open the envelope, unfolded the paper inside, and read the message. She looked up at Terry. "It seems whoever paid York to keep an eye on us is in Georgetown, Texas."

"Big surprise there. Do they know who it is?"

"Inspector Rodriguez said they tapped York's telephone lines. They traced a call that came to his resort demanding to know where he was, if York found us and if he knew what we did while there. The person also wanted to know if we are still alive. Rodriguez said the call originated in Georgetown, Texas. It was a cell phone. He has the number here. He thinks it's a burner phone. But, it has a GPS chip. He has forward the information to the Georgetown police."

Terry finished her donut. "So, when we get home we call that number and see who answers."

"We can try that. But I think I'll ask Detective John Wilkinson to try and track the GPS location first. He may locate it before we arrive."

"That'll work if it's on."

"Well, if it's off, no one will answer it either."

"True. But trying to track it, and then, calling is a good place to start."

Virginia rose, grabbed her cane, and started for the door. "I think I'll go to the bridge and see when and where we're docking."

"You climbing these ladders with a cast and a cane? I've got to watch this. You're getting down here was almost a major catastrophe."

"I'm not staying inside."

"Okay, okay, I'll help you. First let's call that ensign who assisted you when we boarded."

Virginia smiled. "You just want to see him again."

"He is cute and single."

"Call him. I can wait a few minutes."

Ten minutes later, Virginia, Terry, and Ensign Cramer were standing at the port railing, amidships. Virginia looked out at the water then, at Cramer. "Do you know when and where we dock?"

"Yes, ma'am. We will dock in Corpus Christi in three days. I'll get you the exact time when we're closer."

Terry gave him a warm smile. "How do we get ashore without going through customs or immigration?"

"I don't know exactly. But I do know that your being aboard is secret. The captain has a communication blackout regarding the two of you. You are officially not here. He has ordered us to not mention anything about you to anyone not part of this crew. When you leave, we are to forget you were ever here." He glanced around and lowered his voice, "Are you two spies?"

Terry leaned close and whispered, "Something like that."

"Who do you work for?"

Terry gave him a conspiratorial look. "If I tell you, I'll have to kill you."

Virginia burst out laughing. "Oh for God's sake. We work for the Smithsonian."

Ensign Cramer frowned. "The museum? Oh, I get it. The Smithsonian is a cover for you. A legend."

Terry took a deep breath and slowly let it out. "Yeah. You got it. We're on a sensitive mission, and the government doesn't want what we were doing to get out. And, we aren't finished yet."

"Wow!" Cramer beamed. "This is wonderful. I actually got to meet two real spies. I guess you can't tell me about your mission, can you?"

"No. But I do have some pictures I can show you."

Cramer's eyes widened. "You do?"

Virginia looked at Terry. "You do?"

"Yes, the ones at the pool and beach at the resort and some of the sights in Cancun."

Virginia sighed. "I forgot about that." Virginia looked at the excited Cramer. She sighed and leaned close to Terry. "He'll enjoy them." She leaned close to Terry and whispered. "What are you really up to?"

Terry whispered back. "He's mine."

"He's younger than you."

"And? You're younger than your husband."

Virginia shrugged. "Okay, have fun." She turned and hobbled toward the bow leaving Terry, and the eager Ensign, heading for Terry's compartment.

Virginia and Terry stood on the deck of the cutter as she slowly docked. They watched the lines being secured and the gangplank being run across to the dock at the Coast Guard station. Coastguardsmen took their boxes and bags ashore to a waiting black SUV. A guardsman helped Virginia down the gangway to the SUV while a very happy Ensign Cramer escorted Terry. They turned and looked at the cutter and waved at the crew lined up at the deck rail waving back. Two guardsmen finished loading their things into the back of the SUV, came around the side, and said good-by. Ensign Cramer gave Terry a quick kiss on her cheek and returned to the cutter.

Virginia eyed Terry. "I see you made quite an impression on him."

"Yeah. And, he's got my number, too."

A middle-aged man, with thinning hair, an untucked, short-sleeved sports shirt, and jeans, came around from the front of the vehicle. He opened the rear side door. "If you ladies don't mind; I think you'll enjoy the ride better in the back."

Terry climbed in. Virginia looked the man over. "Who are you and which agency are you with?"

"I'm Special Agent Van Winters, USCGIS." He displayed his badge and credentials.

"Coast Guard Investigative service?"

"Yes, ma'am. Someone very important wants you and your friend protected and slipped into the country quietly. My orders are to take you from here directly to Georgetown, Texas."

"That'll take about four hours. How about stopping on the way for dinner?"

Special Agent Van Winters nodded. "Sounds like a plan. Anywhere in particular?"

"No. As long as it isn't Mexican food or MREs, we're good. We've had enough of those."

"Okay, hop in."

Virginia climbed in the vehicle next to Terry, tossed her cane in the back, and buckled up. She watched the harbor retreat as they drove toward the freeway. *I hope we entered the country pretty much unnoticed.*

CHAPTER 42

Virginia and Terry entered the Georgetown Museum. With the help of Dr. Doverspike, their boss, and Special Agent Van Winters, they unloaded all their boxes, backpacks, and bags into Virginia's office. Dr. Doverspike was all questions, as he finished stacking the last box in a corner. Virginia thanked Special Agent Van Winters and had Terry walk him out.

Virginia plopped into her high-backed, leather desk chair. "I'll give you a full report once we've had a chance to go home, clean up, and decompress. It's been an arduous trip. And, I'll include all the grisly details of how Terry and I got injured."

Dr. Doverspike grinned. "You promise?"

"Yes."

Doverspike ambled out of the office as Terry re-entered. She dropped into a chair. "Now, it seems like we just left."

"I know," Virginia nodded. "But now that this stuff is safe, I think we need to go home, clean up, relax, then, tomorrow we can plan our next steps."

"When are you going to call the police detective?"

Virginia glanced at the clock on a bookshelf. "In the morning."

"Okay. I'll see you at eight tomorrow." Terry started to get up.

"Make it nine. I want to get just a little more sleep."

"Nine it is."

"Wait a minute."

Terry sat back down. "What?"

"You actually showed those pictures of us in our bikinis in Cancun at the resort pool and the beach to the Ensign, didn't you?

Terry grinned. "Yep. He was very impressed and liked them. I made him promise not to mention them to anyone on the ship. He liked the mystique of us being secret agents and all. He wanted to know where we hid our guns in our bathing suits."

"I bet he did. You do realize that within a half hour after he left your compartment, we were the talk of the ship. Didn't you notice how the crew was overly friendly and smiled a lot?"

Terry looked perplexed. "But he promised. He gave me his word."

"Yeah, right. First, he's a man. Second, he's a sailor. He couldn't wait to tell the others about us."

"You knew this and didn't say anything?"

"The cat was out of the bag by then. And, what were you going to do about it? They brought us here without knowing what we were doing down there, so a little excitement for them was okay." Virginia leaned forward and frowned. "You didn't give him any copies did you? Wait a minute, you didn't show him the ones of us topless by the pool or at the beach, did you?"

Terry slumped in her chair. "I... ahh... well, he sort of made a couple copies of a few from the disk and to the second part of your question, ahh... yes."

Virginia leaned back in her chair and laughed. "Sort of? You mean you did make copies. The topless ones, too?"

"Ahh, yeah. On a thumb drive. He said he'd keep them for himself."

"So, we are now United States Coast Guard topless pinup girls. The whole crew probably has copies by now. Hell, all the cutters in the Gulf probably have them by now. Maybe, the Navy, too."

"He was really nice to us and... he was... never mind." Terry climbed to her feet. "Gotta go. See you tomorrow." She bolted for the door.

Virginia cracked a smile as Terry left. She shook her head, then called Andy at the University. "Hi, honey. I'm finally at the museum, can you come and get me?"

"You bet. I've been waiting for your call. Sorry, I couldn't get down to Corpus Christi when you and Terry arrived. No one would tell me exactly when you'd dock."

"That's okay. We needed to get our stuff safely here to the museum as quickly as possible. The Coast Guard sent a special agent to drive us up here and guard us. It was faster than waiting for you to drive down and get us and drive back here. When we got here, Dr. Doverspike overreacted, as usual, and wants all the grisly details as soon as possible."

"Okay. I'll leave here right away. I'm having a grad student cover the lab this afternoon. How's your ankle?"

"It's getting better. I'll make an appointment with the doctor while I wait for you."

"Okay. See you shortly."

Virginia called her doctor, made an appointment to see him in two days. She consulted the clock on her bookshelf again. She picked up the phone and dialed Detective John Wilkinson of the Georgetown Police Department. *It's late, but maybe he's there yet.*

He answered on the second ring. "Wilkinson."

"Hello, Detective. You're still at the office, good. This is Virginia Davies Clark. I'm back from our little trip."

"Virginia! I'm glad you're back. I trust you and your partner are still in one piece."

"Kinda-sorta." She took a breath. "I broke my ankle. Terry was stabbed, broke her arm, and was shot in her leg. But she's doing fine. We have some things to discuss with you based on our trip."

"Good God! You sure you're okay? Need some rest?"

"We're good. What have you found out while we were gone?"

"I've followed up on some things. I also talked to a Mexican Federal Police Inspector."

"Inspector Rodriguez."

"Yes. Nice guy. You and I need to swap notes. The cell phone he traced the call to Cancun was probably a burner, but we'll keep trying to track it. When will you be free? The sooner, the better."

"I'm going home as soon as my husband gets here. Terry and I will be back here late morning. We need to go through what we brought back. Why don't you come right after lunch? I broke my ankle, so I'd kind of like to take it easy."

"How about I pick the two of you up, and take you to lunch?"

"Tell you what. Bring a couple pepperoni pizzas around at noon, we'll eat here so we can talk, and we can show you what we've got."

"Sounds like a plan. See you, then. Have a safe evening. Oh, are you armed?"

"I have my pistol."

"Good. Keep it handy. See you tomorrow." He hung up.

Virginia yawned, gathered up her backpack, and slung it on. She limped out of her office pushing her large, wheeled, duffle bag with her cane. Virginia locked her office door and hobbled toward the front entrance. She waved good-bye to the receptionist, went out the automatic doors, and sat on a stone bench outside waiting for Andy.

Andy pulled his grey Honda minivan up in front of the museum and opened the sliding door for Virginia. He jumped out and hurried around the car to help her into the vehicle. He grabbed her when she stood and hugged her. "God, it's great to have you home! I've been worried sick. You're not planning any more of these trips for a while are you?"

"No. It's good to be back home with you." She climbed in, placed her cane in the back, buckled her seatbelt, and sighed. Andy dumped her duffle bag in the rear of the van. Andy's voice cracked as he drove toward their home. "When you told me on the phone about your ankle, I nearly had a heart attack. You sure you're okay?"

"Yes. It's not a serious break. I made an appointment with our doctor in two days to check it out."

"How did Dr. Sorenson do on her first outing with you?"

Virginia swallowed. "Terry was great and fun. Only she ended up with a broken arm, a gunshot wound in her leg, and a stab wound."

"How'd she… is she okay now? That's terrible."

"I think so. The Navy surgeons on the carrier did a good job on her. She's to see her doctor here at home."

"That's good. So, the trip was successful? You got what you need to solve the mystery here?"

Virginia stiffened. "Yeah. We did discover a lot while we were there."

Andy eyed Virginia. "Okay, what aren't you telling me? You didn't start an international incident, did you?"

She fidgeted in her seat. "No, not really. As you know, we sort of ran into a drug cartel, a big drug lord, and his henchmen while there. And, some of the natives weren't overly friendly. There were the two DEA guys who were really crooks, too."

Andy pulled into the HEB grocery store parking lot on Texas 29 and I-35 and slipped into a parking space.

Virginia looked at the store. "You stopping to pick up something?"

"No! You seem to have left out of our phone conversations anything about a drug lord, bad DEA agents, and angry natives. Spill it."

"Here? Can't we wait until we're home?"

Andy unbuckled his seatbelt and turned. "No. Look, I love you, but your antics are dangerous, and I'm concerned about you. I like you safely at home and working at a safe museum, not running around a jungle with drug guys after you. Now, what really happened that you omitted from our earlier discussions?"

Virginia pouted. "Okay. We ran into a drug cartel and managed to destroy a few million dollars of their drugs, pot, meth, and heroin for the most part. And, we destroyed a few of the cartel's leader's airplanes, three I think, and as you know, a drug lab. Terry and I also managed to kill and wound a few dozen of his men. He wasn't very happy with us. He threatened to do some really nasty things to us, and then, sell on the white slave market."

"What? The slave market! Are you serious?"

"Yeah."

"Virginia!"

"There's more. We captured him and turned him over to the police. He had the DEA agents in Cancun, who were supposed to be helping us, on his payroll, and the DEA agents tried to get him, the drug lord, to find us and see what we were doing. The DEA agents are dead. And, before you ask, no we didn't kill them." Virginia swallowed and tried to make the trip end on a positive note. "But, the Marines, who came to get us from the carrier we were airlifted to, made us honorary Marines, and I'm an honorary major. Terry's an honorary captain. We have our commission certificates and rank insignias."

Andy's breathing slowed as he frowned. "Why would they do that?"

"Ahh... we sort of got in a tight situation and... well... I destroyed a pickup truck with cartel men and a fifty-caliber machine gun aimed at us. But they fired first. It was neat, our gun, I think it was a fifty-caliber Gatling gun, shredded the truck, the machine gun... and them, and a few trees. We didn't shoot any animals or monkeys."

Andy sat with his mouth open staring at her. He finally took a breath. "I'm happy for the animals as I'm sure the ASPCA is, too." He rubbed his forehead. "You two did all that? Did you do anything to investigate what you went there for? The Marines rescued you?"

"Yes... I mean no... well, yes. Oh hell. We found the source of the gold and jade. We also found the remains of the Civil War Confederate troops who went there to get the gold and the secret of the devil powder. We found the City of Gold, but we can't tell anyone about it. We found out what the devil powder was. I got hit with a little of that, too. But I'm okay now. And, like I said, we kind of rescued the Marines and us."

Andy had his hand over his heart. "You had quite the adventure. I'm not sure my heart will recover. But at least you're back safely. You're going to tell me the gory details when we get home." He refastened his seatbelt and started the engine. "I want *all* the details when we get home."

Virginia nodded. "Yes, dear. Terry and I have a meeting with Detective Wilkinson at lunch tomorrow. He's bringing pizza." She glanced at Andy. He was sitting stiffly in his seat and held the steering wheel in a death grip. Her lips formed a small smile. "Are you angry with me?"

"Angry? No. Furious? Yes. We'll discuss this later young lady, once I've cooled down."

"Oh boy." Virginia rubbed her forehead. "Terry and I are okay. Our trip was successful, and we're back safely. What's wrong?"

"What's wrong? What's wrong? You take off on these investigative adventures, get into trouble, nearly get killed, sometimes, or I should say usually, other people die, and you want to know why I'm upset? You can't keep..."

"But I'm home now. The rest of this case should be easy. I can't get into much more trouble."

CHAPTER 43

Virginia sat on the couch in her living room with her ankle propped up on the coffee table. Andy sat slumped in an overstuffed chair near the stone fireplace. He stared at her. Leo, her black cat, sat on the coffee table studying the walking cast on Virginia's ankle and foot.

Virginia pushed herself up a little and gave Andy a small, tentative smile. "I've now told you everything. I think I've answered all your questions, and I get it. You're worried about me. I really would have liked to have had you on the trip along with Terry."

Andy nodded. "That was quite an adventure. I was really concerned, no scared, especially when you called about that drug lab and being near drug cartels. I'm glad it's over. What are your plans now that you're back? Something sane and safe, I hope. I'm not sure with you that's possible."

"Someone from here paid York and Murphy to find out where Terry and I were, and what we found, or thought we found. That person also wanted to know where whatever we found was located, and maybe have us killed. Not many people knew we were down there. So, Terry, Detective Wilkinson, and I are going to find out who it was. We figure this will tell us who is behind the trouble, attempted murders, and murders here."

Andy leaned forward, his voice raised. "Are you kidding? This is treacherous; you have a broken ankle and were exposed to a dangerous powder made of lethal drugs or poisons. And Terry has a broken arm, gunshot wound, and was stabbed. You two are not in the best of condition to go traipsing around looking for a killer. You're up to your old ways already?"

"We'll have Detective Wilkinson with us, mostly."

"It's the mostly part that worries me." He sighed. "Can't you let the detective just do his job, and you stick with the nice, safe, museum stuff now? You and Terry need time to get well. I need time to get my blood pressure under control."

Virginia gave him a pleading look. "You know I have to finish this. The Smithsonian is also behind us. I'll have Detective Wilkinson's support and Terry will be along."

Andy crossed his arms. "That's not comforting."

"What would you do if you were me?"

"I wouldn't be in these kinds of situations. But, I have been with you on some of your capers, and I know you. So, be careful." He got up, moved to the couch. and sat next to Virginia. "I need my girl in one piece. If you think it would help, I can take a little time off, and assist you."

She caressed the side of Andy's face with her fingers. "Andy, that's sweet, but Terry, Detective Wilkinson, and I can handle it. We're here in Williamson County now, not Mexico, or Central America. Once we ID the crook, Detective Wilkinson will take over. I'll stay out of the actual apprehension. Anyway, that's when the trouble usually happens."

"Not with you, it doesn't."

Leo rubbed against Virginia's cast, hopped down, and strutted toward the kitchen.

"I'll be very careful and let the detective do his job." Virginia watched Leo. "You'd better see if his food dish is full."

"Trust me, it is. While you were gone, we've bonded more." He took her hand in his. "Promise me you'll be careful."

She smiled, "Promise."

Andy started to pick up the TV remote when she put her hand on his, and pressed it down. She leaned close and whispered, "It's been a while, why don't we find something better to do on my first night home?"

He stared at her. "But your ankle. You have a cast on it."

"Help me get these shorts off, and I'll show you how to do it with a broken ankle, cast, and all."

Virginia sat in her office, with her broken ankle propped up on a short stool, looking at the pictures, drawings, and the quilt spread across her conference table. A little jade jaguar and a small gold bar rested on the top of the quilt. She looked up when Terry entered the office. Virginia pointed at a chair. "Hi. How's your arm?"

Terry took a seat and dropped some more photographs on the table. "My arm's doing good. The doctor said it was a clean break so it will mend well. It itches under the cast, though. My gunshot is still very tender and hurts a little. My knife wound doesn't hurt and is almost healed, I'm ready for duty."

"Good. I've been looking over all our materials. Earlier I went through the stuff we brought back from the temple and the City of Gold. This is where the gold from Mary Jane Striker's ranch originated. But we figured that out already. Now to see who was keeping tabs on us."

Terry looked at the clock. "When will the detective get here?"

"About noon. Hungry already?"

"Yeah, but I have some news for both of you."

Virginia eyed her cautiously. "What news? Some of York's people aren't here too, are they?"

"No." Terry shrugged. "Well, I don't know for sure, but I seriously doubt it."

"Then, what's the news? Spill it."

"Okay. I called Ms. Striker's home this morning."

Virginia laid her pencil on the table. "You did?"

"Yep. She's been in the hospital. Now she's in a rehab center."

Virginia arched a speculative eyebrow. "What happened?"

"Heart attack and something to do with her kidneys. According to the housekeeper, she had the heart attack and was in serious pain the day we left for Mexico. She's been in the hospital or the rehab center since we've been gone."

Virginia nodded. "If she had a heart attack, I doubt she was behind York looking for us. She had problems with her kidneys too?"

"Yes. That's what the housekeeper said. You may be right about her not being the one talking to York. But a talk with her wouldn't hurt. They have phones in hospitals and rehab centers, and she could sneak a cell phone in, too."

"Right. Let's wait for Detective Wilkinson and tell him. We can use the time until he gets here with the pizzas, to make a list of the suspects and their status when we left. Maybe something will jump out."

"Good idea. Maybe the good detective has been doing some investigating while we were on our adventure."

"Maybe." Virginia reached under a pile of drawings and pulled out a yellow, legal size tablet. She made columns and listed the names of the people she talked to before the trip. "Okay, here's our list of suspects.

On the top of our list is Mary Jane Striker. Next, we have John Pennington, Mary Jane's cousin. He got enough money from the estate to pay off the auto repair garage he runs and pay off the mortgage on his house. Then, there's Barbara Dorian, another cousin. She's a first-grade teacher in Round Rock. She was upset about Mary Jane getting the whole ranch. But she got two-hundred thousand dollars. She's a teacher, so I moved her down the list of people to interview. I didn't get to talk to her before we left for Mexico. May have been a mistake. And we have Dr. William Pine. He's a professor of classics and history at Southwestern University. He's got a Ph.D. from SMU. Widower. No children. He's a member of the American Philatelic Society."

Terry chuckled. "He's a stamp collector. Who would have guessed?"

"He also collects Civil War memorabilia, collects wine, and likes skiing. He got a hundred grand in solid gold bars."

Terry nodded. "That's a huge amount of money for a professor. The Civil War interest of his is curious. Especially since the stuff we're looking into has to do with the Civil War."

"Yes. He was also interested in the jade jaguar. He thought he was going to get an endowment or grant and wanted the quilt."

"Nice list. How do we investigate them?"

"Before you got involved, I talked to them. Now we need to redo those conversations and still need to talk to Barbara Dorian. We need to talk to Detective Wilkinson and bring him up to speed on our trip."

At noon, Virginia's phone rang. She reached across the desk and answered. "Hello?"

"Mrs. Clark, there is a police detective here in the lobby carrying two pizzas, and a cooler. He said he has an appointment." The receptionist laughed. "I told him he'd have to leave the pizzas with me."

"If he leaves those pizzas with you, I'll shoot you after I shoot him and have you both mounted for display. Send the officer to the conference room… with the pizzas."

"I get dibs on leftovers."

"Okay." Virginia hung up and turned toward Terry. "Lunch is served. Let's pack this stuff up and take it all and my list to the conference room."

Terry stood and helped gather up the materials. "You going to show Detective Wilkinson our collection of stuff from Mexico and Guatemala, and tell him about the devil's powder, the temple, and City of Gold?"

"Yes. Well, maybe not about the City of Gold. But, I figure the more he knows, the better off we'll be, and the sooner we'll finish this caper."

Terry headed for the door. "What kind of pizza did the good detective bring?"

"Pepperoni."

Terry smiled. "Excellent choice."

Behind Terry, Virginia hobbled on her walking cast and cane pushing a rolling plastic container ahead of her as they entered the conference room. Detective Wilkinson was standing at the far end of the long, polished-wood table, opening two pizza boxes. Next to the boxes, he'd stacked a cooler, a pile of paper plates, napkins, and plastic knives and forks.

He looked at Virginia and Terry as they entered. "Good afternoon, ladies." He chuckled. "I bring a humble form of nutrition to our meeting."

Terry dumped the materials from Virginia's office on the table, hurried to the pizza boxes, and grinned. "Detective, I love you. You can come here anytime. You have delivered my favorite gastronomic delight."

Wilkinson beamed. "I'm glad you like my choice of pizza."

"You have no idea. When I was in college, my roommates were all on diets and ate salads…" She wrinkled her nose. "Rabbit food. Pepperoni pizza was considered a mortal sin. I, on the other hand, indulged in the finer things I could afford, like hot, thin crust, Pepperoni, and sometimes sausage pizza and beer." She glanced at Virginia. "This is something we should have taken with us on our adventure."

Virginia sank into a leather chair near the food and leaned her cane against the wall behind her. She smiled and shrugged. "I agree, but you know how the government works. You should have put in your request six weeks in advance, and, in triplicate. You would have gotten a response from Washington by Thanksgiving."

Terry laughed as she placed a couple pieces of pizza on a paper plate, grabbed a napkin and a bottle of cola sitting in a portable cooler, and sat next to the pizza, and Detective Wilkinson. She opened the plastic bottle of cola. "You bring this too, Detective?"

"Yes, Dr. Sorenson, I did."

"Doctor Sorenson? We're colleagues." She glanced at the pizza. "And now, close friends. Call me Terry." She picked up another slice of pizza and took a bite. "This is good."

Virginia took a couple slices and started to eat. "Let's just eat and enjoy the company first. Then, we can get down to business."

Wilkinson nodded and mumbled with food in his mouth.

After they devoured most of the pizzas and soft drinks, Virginia had the remainder of their lunch taken to the staff break room. She and Terry spread out the papers, and photographs they had on the table, along with some artifacts they brought back from Mexico and Guatemala. Virginia rose and hobbled to the large whiteboard on the sidewall. She put up the list of suspects and a list of questions. As she sat back down, her cell phone rang. She picked it up and looked at the screen to see who was calling.

Virginia raised an eyebrow and looked at Terry and Wilkinson. "It's Andy. He can't have the lab results on the stuff I gave him already. It's too early, but I'd better check." She touched the screen and answered the call. "Hi, honey, what's up?" She listened, then responded. "Yes, I'm still at the museum, and Terry and Detective Wilkinson are both here with me. We just finished lunch and are starting our debriefing. You said you've got something for us. What?"

"Virginia," Andy continued in an excited voice, "I'm e-mailing you the actual reports, graphs, etc. from the analysis of the samples you gave me last night. The chemists were intrigued and wanted to get this done for you as quick as possible. I had to promise them you'd tell them about your adventures as soon as you can. And, a couple of the younger, single profs, want to meet Terry."

"Andy, can you give us a synopsis over the phone? I'll get the reports when we hang up. Oh, I'll put you on speaker so the others can hear you."

"Okay. The gold you brought back is the same as the ones from your friend's ranch. The jade is too. The little gold figure on top of the bars is from the same substance as before. We, the chemists and historians, thought originally it was from Maximiliano Emperador bullion coins, made from twenty-two karat gold. The little figure on top of the gold bar is also twenty-two karat gold. There are traces of cocaine on the gold bars."

"So we found the source of the gold."

"Yes. But what we thought was made from the Emperador bullion coins probably wasn't. Well, not all of it. The gold was originally mined in California. The Emperador coins were minted from 1833 to the early Twentieth Century. The U.S. minted gold coins were mainly the ten-dollar gold piece. The little jaguar on top of the ones you just brought back was made from the California gold."

"That's strange."

"Not really. I talked to a history professor, and he said the rebels may have hijacked a gold shipment from California, a Union State, and used the gold to help finance the Confederacy. They did that whenever they could hijack a gold shipment. But, he thinks some of it was used on the Mexican or Guatemalan gold bars to ID it. The Mexican or Guatemalan gold was smuggled into Texas. It was melted down into other shapes, and used to finance the war effort, and pay to sustain their ranches and farms in Texas. No one in the Confederate Army knew exactly where the gold came from, or how much. Some of the gold bars are from south of the border while others are from California gold. The little figures on top are California gold. The professor's pretty sure they didn't keep accurate records and probably didn't want to. His guess is they skimmed off the top and kept some. Probably kept more than a little. There was no IRS back then."

"That would explain the old forge and tools in the root cellar at Mary Jane's ranch."

"Yep. Oh, one more thing. The organic chemistry guys did an analysis of the sample of that Diablo powder you brought back that you were exposed to. It's really nasty stuff. The Navy doctors on the carrier, and the Navy hospital lab, were right. It was a mixture of myristicin, phyllobates, claviceps purpura, strophanthin, and antiarin. This cocktail is a real winner, if you're into murder. You're lucky you only got a very small dose. It's meant to disorient and kill. I sent the details as attachments with the e-mail. I hope this helps. You're going to be a good girl and not do anything dangerous today. Right?"

"Yes, dear. But what fun is it to being a good girl when being a bad girl is so much more enjoyable. Good-bye dear, love ya." She disconnected and looked at Terry and Detective Wilkinson. "You heard?"

They nodded.

Virginia sat the phone down on the table and looked at Wilkinson. "Why don't you go first?"

CHAPTER 44

Detective Wilkinson opened a spiral notebook and examined his notes. He pulled folders out of the bag he had set next to the cooler and rested them on the table. He opened one. "Okay, while you two were vacationing south of the border, some of us were working."

Terry poked him in the arm. "Vacationing? You usually don't get shot on vacation."

He held his hands up in front of himself. "Okay, okay. Just kidding. I did another background check on each of the people who inherited something from Mary Jane Striker's uncle's estate. The cousins check out. I also talked to both of them. I don't see anything that would suggest they are presently unhappy with their inheritances. Cell phones, business lines, and home landline phone records don't show any unusual calls."

Virginia finished off her drink. "What about the professor?"

"Yes, the good professor. Now that's another story." Wilkinson consulted his notes. "According to associates of his, he's been researching the area of Mexico and Guatemala you two were in. He has also been visiting museums looking at records from middle eighteen hundred, especially Civil War records."

Virginia rubbed her finger in little circles on the tabletop. "That's his area interest in his teaching, and it's his hobby."

"Right. But he's been asking about gold, gold refining, and jade as well. He's also a gardener and active in the Master Gardner program hereabout."

"We didn't know about the gardening thing." Terry nodded. "Suspicious yes, but not incriminating."

Wilkinson grinned. "No, not in itself, but he's made a few phone calls south of the border and to an untraceable cell phone."

"To where?"

"Some place near the Guatemalan border with Mexico." Wilkinson pulled a map from a folder and unfolded it. He pointed to a circled area. "The actual receiver was in this area. It may have been in Mexico or Guatemala. The calls were to some place very near the border. And there were three to Cancun. He also called Ms. Striker a couple times, and to the untraceable cell somewhere near Georgetown."

Terry frowned. "How could you trace the calls that far to Mexico and not know who was on the other end or the recipient's number?"

"The phone on the other end had some sort of device or something that hid its ID and actual specific location. No address or accurate GPS. No accurate fix on the mysterious cell phone here either, other than the general area of Georgetown. Sorry."

Virginia pulled out the chair next to her and, rested the cast on it. "Okay, let's get back to Professor Pine in a minute. How about Mary Jane Striker? What's up with her while we were away?"

Wilkinson thumbed through some pages in his notebook. "Okay, the day you left, paramedics were called to her ranch. She was transported to the hospital, treated for a mild heart attack, and severe kidney malfunction. It turns out she'd been given ethylene glycol. It's radiator anti-freeze fluid. I guess it's sweet and looks like something like Gatorade™. The doctors said the body turns it into oxalic acid. That in turn does something to the calcium in her blood, and that caused problems with her heart and the acid-calcium complex. Whatever that is. It also started to plug up her kidneys.

"They said that alone is very painful, and it can be fatal, to say nothing of the effect on her heart. They mentioned electrolytes. Like I knew what they were talking about. The docs gave her something with more calcium and some type of antidotes." Wilkinson consulted his notes. "The docs said the antidotes work by blocking the enzyme responsible for metabolizing ethylene glycol and, therefore, halt the progression of poisoning. They used Hemodialysis to help remove ethylene glycol and its metabolites from the blood. They also flushed her kidneys somehow. She's now in the Chisholm Rehab Center. She's been either in the hospital or the rehab center since you left."

Virginia frowned. "How'd she get the ethylene glycol?"

"The firemen who responded with the paramedics found some in her shed. How it got from the shed to her, we don't know. I'm thinking she was poisoned. We're treating this as an attempted homicide."

"I agree." Virginia straightened. "Did she call anyone while in either place?"

"Yes. We watched calls from both places and her cell phone. It wasn't easy, and we had quite a time convincing a judge to issue a warrant."

Terry titled her head. "A Justice of the Peace, municipal, county, or district judge?"

"No. We got a federal judge to issue one."

"A federal judge, nice. How did you do with the traces?"

"There were no unusual calls from the hospital or rehab center on the institution's landlines. Just to her cousins and the housekeeper. But, there were some calls made from a cell phone in, or near, her room. One not registered to Mary Jane Striker. Also, it was rigged to conceal its location and ID from normal traces. It's the same one that called Pine."

Virginia leaned forward and adjusted her cast. "If it wasn't traceable, how'd you find it?"

"One of our boys at the department is an army reserve officer in the Intelligence Corp. He used his expertise and some strange equipment he borrowed from the Army, to do it on site."

"Where did the calls from that phone go?"

"Two places. One location was in Cancun, Mexico, and the other was to Professor Pine. There were multiple calls to Mexico and a couple to Pine. But we can't actually prove it belonged to Mary Jane Striker."

Terry choked on her soda. "Holy shit! Pine is in on it? Maybe Mary Jane too, like we thought."

"It gets more interesting. The calls on the phone to Mexico suddenly stopped while you were still down there." Virginia rubbed her leg. "Does Mary Jane or Professor Pine know we're back?"

"No. When I talked to Ms. Striker last, she thought you might have been killed. I tried to talk to the professor, but he clammed up and wouldn't communicate. Like I said, we can't pin down the owner of the encrypted cell phone."

Virginia nodded. "Okay, I get that. How many calls did Mary Jane actually make to Professor Pine that you are sure she made?"

Wilkinson looked at his notes. "One. And, before you ask, she made two calls to Barbara Dorian and two to John Pennington. She also received calls from Ms. Dorian and Mr. Pennington, but none from Pine."

Virginia stared at the opposite wall, then, looked at Wilkinson. "Did any of the others make calls to Mexico?"

"Not that we are aware of."

"Did you check the others phones as thoroughly as you did Professor Pine's or Mary Jane's?"

"No. The background check and routine phone record check didn't seem to warrant it."

"I think that might be a good idea." Virginia took a breath. "Well, it seems calls on Professor Pine and Mary Jane are in order."

Wilkinson nodded. "I can do that, and get more on any funny phone calls by the cousins. I'll see what else we can do about identifying that mysterious cell phone, too. With you two being somewhat incapacitated, it may be best to leave all this to me."

Virginia gave him a hard stare. "In your dreams, Detective."

Wilkinson looked down at his notes for a few seconds. He shook his head then glanced back at Virginia and Terry. "Yeah, leaving you two behind would probably be impossible. Okay, we'll do it together."

Wilkinson closed his notebook and sat back. “Okay, now tell me about your adventures.”

Virginia and Terry related the details of their trip, the drug dealer’s operations, including the damage they did, and what happened to the DEA agents. She gave him the gory details about York’s death, and them capturing Ramos, and about the Marines. They used the maps, pictures, quilt, and artifacts they brought back as illustrations. Terry and Virginia showed him their honorary Marine Corps commissions.

Wilkinson sat quietly for a moment, then, spoke. “That was quite a ride.” He chuckled. “I’m not sure you two should be allowed in Georgetown. Maybe not even Texas. You two are dangerous.”

Virginia gave him a conspiritual look. “We did accomplish a lot. And, now this must be kept confidential, besides discovering the gold temple we told you about, we found a City of Gold and exactly where the gold was refined.”

Wilkinson’s eyes widened. “You found El Dorado?”

“Yep. But you cannot tell anyone. Think of what would happen to the place, the natives, and their religion, if this got out.”

Wilkinson nodded. “Yeah, I get it. It would be a disaster. Okay, mums the word. I’ll get my officer who does the phone and computer stuff to start searching for that encrypted phone. I’ll ask the Texas Rangers to do a more detailed look at the good professor. Now, where do you want to start?”

“I think, while the Rangers do their thing, another visit by us to Professor Pine would be advantageous. The three of us can descend on him at once. Maybe that smug creep will be somewhat unnerved.”

“Sounds like a plan. When do you want to go?”

“How about now?”

“Okay. While you get your stuff together, I’ll make some calls. Can I use this conference room?”

“Hell yes. We’ll put this stuff away and get ready. We’ll meet you in the lobby in about forty-five minutes.”

Virginia, wearing her brown, leather backpack, plodded into the lobby on her cast and cane. She spotted Detective Wilkinson chatting with Terry and the receptionist. Terry picked up her red, leather backpack with the museum’s logo on it, and nudged Wilkinson, who was concentrating his attention on the cute receptionist.

Wilkinson looked at Terry and Virginia. “I see you’re both into backpacks.”

Terry put hers on. “Yeah. I saw what Virginia did with hers, and all the stuff she can carry, and decided to get with it and do the same. I’ve noticed others around here following suit.”

“Good idea. Maybe I should get one.”

Virginia stopped and turned toward the receptionist. “Ann, will you please run into the gift shop and get a black, museum backpack for the detective. We'll wait here. Tell the clerk in there to charge it to my department."

"Sure." Ann darted to the gift shop and returned a couple minutes later with a black backpack with a gold museum emblem on it. "Here ya go." She handed it to Wilkinson.

He held it and rotated it around as he examined the backpack. "Nice. But I can't take this."

"Sure you can. Consider it a personal gift from me to a friend."

"I don't know..."

Terry tapped her foot on the floor near the door. "When you two are done figuring all this out, can we go?" Wilkinson lowered the backpack. "Since it is from a friend, I guess it's okay." He looked at Terry and Virginia. "Considering your conditions, I'll drive. I've got an unmarked SUV. We'll all fit, even with the cane, and backpacks."

The walked to the curb and climbed into the police car. As they approached, Southwestern University, Virginia leaned forward from the rear seat. "Detective, are you going to notify the campus police we're coming?"

"And spoil the surprise we're going to give Professor Pine. Hell no."

They parked in a red zone on campus and made the short walk to the History Department. Virginia, limping with her leg cast and cane, complained about the stairs to the second floor as they went up. She knocked on the dark wood door, opened it, entered, and stepped to the scarred wooden desk topped with books and papers. Wilkinson and Terry moved up behind her.

Professor Pine looked up from his desk, ran his hands through his grayish receding hair, and pushed up his wire-rimmed glasses. The color drained from his face. He looked shocked to see them. "What the... you again! Wha...what the are you doing here? Who are they?"

Virginia pointed at Wilkinson. "This is Detective Wilkinson, Georgetown Police. The young lady is Dr. Terry Sorenson. She's an associate of mine, and she's working on this case with me. From your reaction, I think you remember me. We have some more questions."

Pine slowly nodded. "You and your friend are alive?"

"No. I'm a ghost. So is Dr. Sorenson. Why'd you expect us to be dead?" She sat on a straight-backed, wooden chair, and motioned for Terry and Wilkinson to take the remaining chairs in the small office. "We're going to be here a while."

Pine's color slowly returned. He wet his lips. "I... I don't have to answer any of your questions."

Wilkinson cleared his throat. "No, you don't. But we're investigating you for possible involvement in fraud, murder, attempted murder, murder for hire, and violation of interstate commerce."

Virginia rubbed her hands together. “That, and trafficking in stolen artifacts, tax evasion, smuggling, and bribing government officials. All in all, I’m guessing a total of well over a couple hundred years in prison, not counting the murder charges. Believe me, the federal prisoners you will be meeting will think of you as new meat. You’ll be someone’s boy toy, and get a whole new definition of anal retention. Your teaching and research days are numbered. But… if you cooperate, I’m sure a lot of these issues could disappear. The first one to talk usually gets the best deal with the DA, including ignoring some potential charges. Your choice.”

Pine stiffened. Perspiration beaded on his forehead. “You can’t prove any of that! After all, I’m a respected member of the University faculty.”

Virginia leaned closer. “In fact we can, and we will. But, in the meantime, what would the reaction of the University administration, and the academic community, be if they learned one of theirs was under investigation for all this?”

Pine glared at her. “You wouldn’t.”

Virginia sat back and grinned. “Try me.”

Pine swallowed. “Can we make a deal?”

“Help us and we’ll see what we can do.” Virginia smiled. “We can also be discrete.”

He slumped in his chair, put his head in his hands, and thought for a while. “My lawyer said not to speak to you, or the police.” He looked up at her with a pleading expression. “But, maybe a little give and take wouldn’t hurt.”

Virginia smiled. “Cooperation doesn’t hurt, Professor, especially if you’re the first one to talk.”

Wilkinson cleared his throat. “Professor Pine, who did you call in Cancun, Mexico while the women were down there, and how’d you know they were in Mexico?”

“Ms. Striker told me they had gone to Mexico and Guatemala in search of the origin of her gold and the jade. As to who I called… that’s private.”

Terry spoke in a cheery voice. “If it was DEA Special Agent York who owned a hotel down there, and we’ll know that shortly, your goose is cooked. He’s dead. Thought you might like to know.”

Pine’s eyes widened. “Dead?”

“Yep. Shot and killed by a drug lord right in front of us. He was going to double cross the drug guy and whoever was paying him to watch us. He wasn’t very nice.”

Pine shook his head. “So, he is really dead.”

Virginia whistled. “You’re the one who put him onto us?”

Pine lowered his gaze. “Yes. He’s helped me before in arranging to get certain artifacts out of Mexico and into the U.S. without the inconvenience of customs. I asked him to keep track of you and let me know what you find and where. I never told him to kill or hurt you. Last I heard from him, you two were somewhere in the jungle in a tank, or something, and a drug lord was in the process of killing you."

Wilkinson scribbled in a small, spiral notebook. "Who else knew of this?"

"I… I can't… There is someone who's been involved and calls me at weird hours for updates on your progress. A few days ago… well the person calling said you were dead, and if I tell anyone, I'd be next. That person put me up to it."

Virginia frowned. "How? Who was the caller? Male or female?"

"I don't know. The voice was… it sounded like a computer or something. I couldn't tell if the caller was male or female. But, whoever it was knew of my smuggling activities. He or she said I was to keep an eye on you or my activities could come to light." Pine opened a desk door to a mini-fridge, pulled out a small bottle of water, and opened it. He took a swig. As he set it on the desk, his face contorted, he grabbed his chest, and fell forward, his head crashing on the desk spilling the water.

Virginia jumped to her feet and leaned over the desk. She felt his neck. "No pulse." She looked at his distorted, and flushed, face. "Looks like cyanide."

Wilkinson yanked out his phone, called the police station, then looked at Virginia. "How do you know it was cyanide? What's our plan now that Pine's dead?"

Terry cleared her throat. "I don't want to be a party-pooper, but I'm getting tired, and it's getting close to dinner time. Your husband isn't happy about our adventure, and may like to see you and have dinner like his life is back to normal. It's going to be chaotic around here shortly. So, may I suggest we reconvene this tomorrow at breakfast?"

CHAPTER 45

Virginia drank her orange juice and sat back in the booth at The IHOP. "Okay, we need a plan. How about this?" She wet her lips. "We know someone forced Pine to use his contacts to keep track of us. The question is who. We have three viable suspects. Mary Jane is *Numero Uno*. John Pennington is number two, and the teacher, Barbara Dorian is number three. Pennington's garage was extremely clean, and he didn't have a lot of backlog of work sitting around like most garages. He said he specializes in high-end foreign cars. There's big bucks in that."

Wilkinson consulted his notes. "Maybe, but he's had some lean times lately. His tax returns show him bleeding until he got the inheritance. Maybe he really wants more."

Terry sipped her coffee, then set the cup down. "How about the teacher?"

Wilkinson thumbed through his notes again. "Here's something interesting. She and another teacher go to Cancun during spring break. They do it every year. Guess where they stay? The Cancun Beach and Golf Club."

Virginia cut a sausage on her plate and ate it. "Any recent calls there?"

"Not recent. But just after you went down there, she did call there on her cell. We didn't catch it before. None after that."

Terry finished her pancakes. "How is her financial condition?"

"Since this is also a murder investigation and one of possible tax fraud, we got a warrant for her and Pennington's financials. She's better off than Pennington. But she seems to like going to Louisiana to the casinos. She goes there a lot. But, she comes back with winnings. I'm not sure if she reports them to the IRS. She appears to be a perpetual winner. Now just talking about it makes her activity suspicious."

Terry frowned. "Does she stay at a resort or the hotel at the casino all the time and just gamble?"

"Don't know. However, one of her school friends who went with her a few times said she'd disappear for stretches of time, but always seemed to have good luck by the time they left."

Virginia sat back and sipped more coffee. "I have the feeling we may have a group conspiracy. Maybe Mary Jane is the leader."

Wilkinson rubbed his forehead. "Maybe, but how do we prove it?"

"Before we go there, have you had any better luck with that mysterious cell phone?"

"Just a little." Wilkinson shook his head. "Only that it seems to mainly operate in places where Mary Jane and Barbara Dorian are."

Virginia nodded. "One of them is using it."

"That or the phones are clones."

"Do any of them know we are alive, except the now dearly departed Professor Pine?"

"No."

"Good. I have an idea."

Terry sighed. "We're not going back to Mexico are we?"

"No. Detective, we get one of your officers—a Hispanic one for the accent to call Pennington and say he's from Mexico. He tells Pennington that Mr. Humberto De Alvarez is sending a shipment of drugs that must be sold quickly. He says De Alvarez thinks we found the mysterious source of the gold. He says we're alive, and De Alvarez wants him to get us to tell him about the City of Gold before we tell Mary Jane. Then, he's to kill us. De Alvarez wants Pennington to arrange all this. Pennington gets a cut of the gold for his trouble. We could add something about the drugs too."

Wilkinson and Terry sat, with their mouths open, staring at Virginia.

Terry picked up her coffee mug, took a sip, Then, slowly and carefully set it down. "What's plan B? I'm not sure I like the kill us part of that one."

Wilkinson nodded. "Yeah, what's plan B?"

Virginia pushed a piece of scrambled egg around on her plate with a fork, then looked at them. "I take it you don't approve of my wondrous plan?"

Wilkinson rubbed his forehead. "Where should I begin? First, we don't know for sure Pennington is involved with drugs. Second, we don't have any reason to believe he knew, York, Murphy, Ramos, or Humberto De Alvarez. He doesn't know you're back, and probably doesn't know what you two did down south of the border. And lastly, how would he arrange a hit on either of you? We have more suspicious activity from the teacher. Why not do the same thing to her?"

Terry fidgeted in her seat. "What if we did what Virginia suggested, but add something for Barbara, too. The officer tells Barbara that we found the City of Gold and another gangster down there wants the location. He's willing to give her a generous cut if she gets the information from us. And, maybe he tells her the thing about the drugs. Like, the new drug guy is cutting in on Ramos', now De Alvarez's territory, and wants her help or something like that. He can say, if she doesn't cooperate, he'll make sure her school district, and the police learn of her activities in Louisiana. Let's face it, her actions there strongly hint at something illegal. Leave out the killing us part."

Virginia glanced around the restaurant and leaned on the table with her arms. "I like that. We tell both of them at the same time but add that someone else is working for the other drug guy. Kind of pit them against one another and let them guess it may be Mary Jane, if they take the bait."

Wilkinson nodded. "That seems reasonable."

Terry pushed her plate away and set her cast on the table with a slight thump. "If we do both as Virginia suggested, then, we have a chance to see if either of them contact Mary Jane, too."

Wilkinson beamed. "If either or both of them take the bait, we nab them when they try and find you two and get the information." He looked at Virginia. "I just hope you tell your husband about this after we've done it."

Virginia smiled. "You got that right. What if Pennington or Barbara calls back to confirm?"

Terry's face brightened. "We have the officer tell them that De Alvarez, or the new drug guy, is already on his way here to get the information from them. The situation is urgent. The officer will tell them as soon as Alvarez, or the other guy, is here, he'll contact them with the meeting location and a first good faith payment."

Virginia rubbed her chin. "I like that. Can we do it, Detective?"

"Yes. I'll get right on it." Wilkinson slid out of the booth. "I'll get this thing in motion. I'll call you as soon as I have everything set up. Probably won't be until tomorrow. Keep your cell phones on."

Terry slid out. "I think it's time we went to work. You know Dr. Doverspike is going to tie us up all day with more questions about our adventure."

Virginia heard her cell phone ring on the bed stand next to her. She opened one eye and looked at the luminous dial on the clock radio. It indicated three o'clock. The room was dark. She sat up and picked up the phone. "Hello?"

"Virginia, Wilkinson here. I've got everything set up."

"Good morning, Detective. Why the call at this hour?"

My officer made the calls as we discussed. He did them late to insure they would be home and sound dangerous. He told both Pennington and Barbara that you will be leaving for work at seven in the morning, andTerry would be at Monument café at six for breakfast. After I talk to you, I'll call Terry."

"Detective, Terry isn't armed. She doesn't have a concealed handgun license. She can't protect herself."

"I'll have a man watching her constantly."

"Who did your officer say the other drug guy was or did he?"

"Don Diego Velázquez. From what your friend Inspector Rodriguez said, he is actually trying to move in on Ramos' old cartel, now run by Humberto Alvarez's. Any calls down there to check on things will be easily substantiated."

"Good. We'll talk more in the morning." She hung up. She looked over at Andy, who was waking up, but hazy.

He rubbed his eyes. "Who is it?"

Virginia slid back under the covers. "It's Detective Wilkinson. He needs Terry and me to assist in capturing the bad guy."

He pushed himself halfway up, his voice groggy. "Why you and Terry?"

Virginia rubbed the silk edge of the blanket. "Because."

"Oh. Okay." He slid back down, pulled the sheet higher, and fell asleep.

"That was close." Virginia blew a tendril of blond hair from her forehead. "He must be really pooped."

Virginia pulled into her parking space at the rear of the museum and slid out of her car. She slipped her backpack on and using her cane, limped toward the employee entrance. A dark-green BMW roared up the back ally and into the parking lot. It slid to a stop in front of her, and the rear door flew open.

One of the henchmen from Pennington's garage jumped out and pointed a gun at Virginia. "Get in honey. Our boss wants to talk to you."

Virginia bristled. "I bet he does." *Don't call me honey, you moron.* She slowly limped toward the man standing by the car. She noticed the vehicle had just him and the driver. He waved the gun trying to get her to hurry. When she got within a few feet of the husky man, she quickly swung the cane at his gun hand, striking it, and causing his hand to move to the side. The weapon fired. The bullet struck a wooden crate. Virginia, then swung the cane at the man's head. Instinctively, he raised his arm to ward off the blow when she swung her cast into his groin. Off balance, she tumbled to the ground. He moaned, expelled air, doubled over, and toppled to the asphalt. The driver started to open the door and climb out, when she kicked the door, slamming it against his skull. He screamed and fell back into the car. Virginia rolled slightly, pulled her backpack off, yanked out her semiautomatic, and aimed it at the driver. He pulled his legs inside, put the car in drive, and sped out. Virginia climbed to her feet and moved to the man on the ground. He was slowly trying to move toward his dropped weapon.

Virginia pointed her gun at him. "I'd think twice about that. I'd like nothing better than to shoot you."

He grunted and stopped.

Virginia called Wilkinson on her cell phone, talked for a moment, and hung up. She sat on a crate and smiled at the man. "I remember you. You work for Pennington. You are going to tell me about your boss's activities and how he's involved with the Mexican drug cartel."

The man now sat up on the asphalt, gritting his teeth. "Like hell. I know my rights."

"Look, I have nothing against you. I want your boss. And the first one to talk usually gets the best deal from the DA, or in this case, maybe a DA and a federal prosecutor."

He glared at her. A cell phone rang. He glanced around and spotted it at the edge of the asphalt.

"Yours?" asked Virginia.

He continued to glare at her.

"Have it your way." Virginia limped to the phone and picked it up. It stopped ringing. "Hmm. I bet this will get interesting at police headquarters." She looked at the entrance to the parking lot as a police car came speeding in, red and blue lights flashing. A uniformed officer hopped out and walked toward Virginia. She smiled at the officer. "Hi. I'm—"

"Special Agent Virginia Davies Clark. I remember you from the station when you were there with Detective Wilkinson." He pointed at the man on the ground. "I was told to take your prisoner and hold him pending whatever you're doing."

"He and a buddy in a dark BMW attacked me. That's his gun over there. I'll send someone down to the station with the security tapes from the camera back here. Also, this was his phone. Have it checked out."

"Yes, ma'am. I know Wilkinson is on his way. You can send the tape with him."

"This guy and his friend work for Pennington. Call Wilkinson and have him picked up."

"Okay." He got the man up, handcuffed, into the police car, and retrieved the pistol by the time Virginia reached the door to the museum.

She shook her head. "I'm slow this morning. I'm usually the fast one. I hope Terry is safe."

CHAPTER 46

Barbra Dorian dialed Pennington's number. She waited for the rings to be answered; she glanced at the clock on the bookshelf across the living room. It read 6:00 am.

Pennington answered on the fourth ring. "Hi Barbara, what's up? Why the call at this hour?"

"I got a call from a man who works for Ramos' replacement. Virginia Davies Clark and another woman did a lot of damage to the organization, and he needs help rebuilding. He needs to move some more gold and some drugs. The competition is closing in, and he needs cash. He said the Clark woman found the City of Gold and he wants the location fast. He'll compensate for the information and help. Oh yeah, York and Murphy are dead."

"I know. He called me too."

"He did? Why?"

"Probably covering all his bases. We should work together. I have a couple of the boys going and getting Virginia. I'll call you when she's at the garage."

"I'll get the other woman, some scientist who works for her. A Doctor Terry Sorenson. She has breakfast at Monument Café in the morning. I'm leaving as soon as we finish talking to get her. I'll take her to your garage as well."

"Okay. I've got to go; someone's at the door. I'll see you there shortly." He hung up.

Barbara drove to the Monument Café in Georgetown and parked. She studied the photograph of Terry she'd downloaded from the museum website. She spotted Terry walking through the parking lot toward the restaurant and jumped out of her car. She approached Terry at the edge of the lot and pointed a revolver at her. "Hello, Doctor. You'll come with me. We have some questions for you."

Terry frowned. "Who are you?"

"That isn't important. I just need the location of the City of Gold you and your friend found."

"What City of Gold?"

"Don't bullshit me. Come with me, or I'll shoot."

"Here? There are people around that will see you."

Barbara tensed. "Move it, sister. Let's go to your car." She swung her head around at the sound of her name. "Oh, shit. Police." She glared at Terry. "I'll deal with you later." She sprinted across the parking lot and into bushes in a neighborhood.

Terry waited as the plain-clothes officer, holding his 9mm automatic, ran up to her. "Are you okay, Doctor?"

"Yes." Terry pointed. "She went that way."

"I saw her. I've called for more officers. We'll find her."

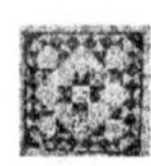

Mary Jane Striker sat on the porch of her inherited ranch. She looked across the small table on the front porch and stared out at the trees. *I hope Virginia and Doctor Terry found the City of Gold. This so far has turned to shit.* A cell phone vibrated on the table next to her. She picked it up, pressed the speaker button, and answered. "Hello?"

"Mary Jane. We've got problems," Barbara said in an agitated voice. "The plan turned to crap. I tried to get that doctor, but the police interfered. I'm hiding out, but there are cops all over the place."

Mary Jane tightened her grip on the phone. "Virginia! She's behind this!"

"Maybe. But that doesn't help me. You need to warn Pennington."

Mary Jane took short, shallow breaths. "Where exactly are you, and will they capture you?"

"I'm in a building that's under construction. They're everywhere I look. I need help."

"Let them capture you. Pretend you've been set up. You're doing what you did under duress. They'll believe you, a teacher. I'm sure they'll sympathize with a first-grade teacher."

"What about Pennington?"

"I haven't heard from him since the calls you and he got this morning. He was having Virginia grabbed."

"If they were on to me, then, he's toast. If he's got Virginia… well, he is done for. She's a federal cop. He could talk and implicate you and me to save his hide."

"He won't talk. At least, not right away. I have friends who know prisoners in the county jail. They can handle Pennington. By then, you and I can escape, with the gold we have, to a country with no extradition and live quite comfortably. The government will have to be happy with Pennington, even dead."

"I think I should get out of here somehow and make my own way to the ranch on my own. I don't want to visit with the cops."

Mary Jane sighed. "Do what you think is best, dear." She terminated the call. She took a breath, looked out at the ranch, She sat back and spoke to herself. "Barbara and Pennington tried to kill me to get the location of the City of Gold, and the rest of my treasure. Now, they need my help. Virginia probably found the City of Gold and won't divulge it's whereabouts, and she's getting too close to the truth to be comfortable. Professor Pine needed to go. He was also just too inquisitive, greedy, and weak. He wouldn't settle for the percentage I offered. Looks like Virginia, the Doctor, Pennington, and Barbara will need to be eliminated like Pine."

A man sitting on a tree limb with a camera fitted with a telescopic lens snapped pictures. He looked at the man near the fence below. "Did you get all the conversation?" The second man rested his parabolic dish on the ground and turned off the recorder. He looked up with a smile. "Yes, everything."

Virginia, Terry, and Detective Wilkinson drove through the gate and up the gravel driveway to the house on Mary Jane's ranch. Two Sheriff's cars and an unmarked, black, Suburban SUV followed. They stopped in front of the house, and everyone climbed out. The Sheriff's deputies headed for the barn, and behind the house. Virginia and Wilkinson walked up to the front door and knocked. Terry, holding the quilt, leaned on the SUV with two men, in suits, one with a white cowboy hat, and watched.

Mary Jane answered the door. "Virginia, Detective, nice to see you."

Detective Wilkinson made a slight nod. "We are here to take you into custody."

"Huh? For what?"

"Mary Jane Striker, you are under arrest." Detective Wilkinson read Mary Jane her rights and told her the multiple state and federal charges.

Wilkinson handcuffed Mary Jane and turned waving the man standing next to Terry over. "Mrs. Striker, this is U.S. Deputy Marshal Farnsworth and this gentleman is a Texas Ranger. Since we've arrested you on both federal and state charges, including murder, the Marshal and Ranger will take you to join John Pennington and Barbara Dorian in jail."

The color drained from Mary Jane's face. "You have them both?"

"Yes. And they turned state's evidence to save their hides and gave you up. You know, the first one, or ones, to talk usually get the best deal. We have the phone call Ms. Dorian made to you before she was caught, on tape.

We also searched your ranch more thoroughly and found even more evidence."

"There is nothing to find. You have no right to—"

Virginia pointed to Terry, who now was holding up the quilt. "We had a federal search warrant. And, on the back of the quilt is another map, of sorts. We found the underground facility you've been using and the rest of the gold you didn't declare, Diablo powder, cyanide, syringes, some other poisons, Monkshood, illicit drugs from Mexico, and a number of burner phones. You should have destroyed them. The drugs have traces of material that link you to Ramos' drug smuggling operations."

May Jane looked baffled.

Virginia continued. "Barbara had called Murphy and York about us and gave you their names and numbers. You were the mysterious person who paid York to have us followed to see if we could find the source of the gold. Murphy heard Ramos talk to York about the City of Gold. He got greedy and tried to cut himself in, and cut York out. Everything turned to shit for them then. York and Murphy are dead. Ramos is in a Mexican prison.

"Barbara said she told you about Humberto Alvarez and the problem she and Pennington were going to help him with. Barbara called Pennington and left a message telling him you were going to betray him to save yourself. He was already arrested by then. She shouldn't have used the burner phone in such a hurry. We found it and her. She figured, that if you'd do that to him, then, you'd do her in, too. She and Pennington also knew how you killed Professor Pine. They told us about the cyanide, how you prepared the water bottles and exchanged them in the professor's mini-frig, and where you got the cyanide. The chemical supply company identified you and Mr. Pennington."

Virginia continued, "When you were supposedly poisoned, you didn't take enough poison to kill you. You took just enough to make you sick and eliminate you as a suspect. All for show. Also, the attempts on your life earlier, like at my museum and the hospital, were the work of Barbara and a hired thug. She and Pennington wanted it all. You figured that out and used them, thinking, when the time came, you'd eliminate them, too." Virginia watched Mary Jane's eyes blaze with hate. "All the key players are either dead, or in, or going to prison. Even Humberto Alvarez, who took over the cartel after Ramos, is now in jail, and his drug organization is smashed. His competitor, Don Diego Velázquez, will eventually take over, but you will never get to meet him." Virginia looked at Wilkinson. "I guess that's that. Take her away."

As they drove back toward Georgetown, Wilkinson glanced at Virginia. "You going to the museum?"

"If you don't mind, will you drop me off at my house? I'd like to be there before Andy gets home. I've got a lot more explaining to do."

ABOUT THE AUTHOR

Dr. David Ciambrone is a retired aerospace and defense company executive, scientist, professor of engineering, and a business and environmental consultant and is now a best-selling, award-winning author living in Georgetown, Texas with his wife Kathy. He has published twenty-five (25) books: four (4) non-fiction, two (2) textbooks for a California university, and nineteen (19) mysteries and has two (2) new mysteries in work. He is the author of the Virginia Davies Quilt Mysteries.

Dave has been a speaker at writer's groups, schools, colleges, libraries, quilt guilds, writer's conferences, and business/scientific conferences internationally.

Dr. Ciambrone also wrote three newspaper columns and wrote a column for a business journal.

Dave is a member of Sisters in Crime, the San Gabriel Writer's League, the Writer's League of Texas, Mystery Writers of America, the International Thriller Writers Association, The Beacon Society, and DFW Sherlock Homes Society.

Dave was appointed a U.S. Treasury Commissioner and to the management board of the Resolution Trust Corporation (RTC) by President Clinton.

He is a Fellow of the International Oceanographic Foundation.

Visit David at

Author's Website:davidciambrone.com

Facebook:facebook.com/david.ciambrone?fref=ts

Twitter:twitter.com/mysterywriter5

LinkedIn:linkedin.com/pub/david-ciambrone-sc-d-fiof/11/ab5/bb3

Amazon:amazon.com/author/davidciambrone